GOOD THINGS

An Urban Fantasy Anthology

A. Star, Angela B. Chrysler, J. Kim McLean
Dariel Raye, K. B. Thorne, Abigail Owen
Crystal G. Smith, Kat Jameson, Christi Rigby
Viola Dawn

Edited by Mia Darien

TABLE OF CONTENTS

FOREWORD

Dear Readers,

This is the fifth anthology that I have organized and edited for charity, following *Here, Kitty Kitty* in 2013, *Reaching Out* in 2014, *Bellator* in 2014, and *Amor Vincit Omnia* in 2015. I have worked with many fantastic authors, sometimes for just one anthology and some have been willing to deal with me again and again. They benefit some great charities. This anthology, however, I think is the one I'm most excited about.

It's not at all that the past anthologies weren't awesome, they were, but this is the first time that I've been able to speak directly to the charity ahead of time. While before, we just donated the profits and said as much, this one is being done as an approved fundraiser by the charity we're giving the money to. It's not official merchandise, but we are approved to use their logo and talk about them a whole lot. This is exciting.

What's the charity, you ask? Well, that will take a little back story.

As always, I was late to the party. I didn't start watching the television show *Supernatural* until it was already airing its eleventh season. Since then, I've gone through the previous ten seasons on Netflix and am working my way through to the end of this latest season before the next begins. (Yes, they have been given the green light for season twelve, which makes it the longest running primetime genre show in history.)

And for good reason. It's amazing. This isn't the place for me to fangirl however, so I'll move on.

There's always that fear when you like a show or movie that you'll learn more about the actors and realize they're jerks. Well, that didn't happen here. Not only have I found that the actors of the show—headliners as well as return characters—love their work and their fans, but they seem like genuinely nice people and they pretty much all adore each other. They hang out together during hiatus!

They also believe in giving back, and are involved with/have created charities.

That brings me to Random Acts. This charity was co-founded by *Supernatural* star Misha Collins. I'll talk more about it at length at the end of the anthology, but basically, its goal is to promote kindness throughout the world. In a time when many of us feel like the world may, in fact, be slowly ending, when we see hatred and violence everywhere we turn, the idea of being kind resonates so strongly.

When you want to be a force against the hatred, be kind. That's what this charity promotes, and what we want to promote.

In the spirit of the show itself, I present to you an anthology of ten urban fantasy stories all involving an act or acts of kindness in some way. Since I don't like to self-congratulate, I'll only say that I know for sure nine of them are awesome! Stories from authors you've read in previous anthologies and new, stories that re-visit some of these authors' wonderful own worlds and others that go to new places, I'm sure you'll enjoy this journey.

One hundred percent of what we (the authors) receive from the sales of this anthology will go straight to Random Acts to continue their mission. We hope that you enjoy these stories, and maybe feel inspired to go out and spread some kindness in the world yourself.

Happy Reading,
Mia Darien, August 2016

ALPHA ASCENSION
(A WESLEY WEREWOLVES STORY)

A. Star

"Xavier Wesley! You are called to testify!"

I entered the lecture hall on Wesley College's campus that had been turned into a makeshift courtroom for the purposes of holding a trial that could cost my dumb ass cousin his life.

He'd broken a century-old treaty between our wolf pack and another, and now he had to answer for it. Other members of our pack were in attendance, but I was the only one who'd been summoned to testify.

I started down the narrow row of stairs on the left side of the room. Remy, Darien, my cousins, and Foster, my younger brother, looked solemn as they sat together in the middle of the lecture hall. At the front of the hall, sitting behind a long table and wearing all-black tailored suits, were the three American chiefs of the King's Congress: Stefan, Marcus, and Jackson. Much like the chiefs of Wolfland, they advised the lycan king, enforced his laws, and held court for any violators. In this land, they were the judges and the jury, and your testimony only held as much weight as they said it did.

As I approached the professors' podium, I tried to play it cool, but then I spotted Nwabueze, the king of the werewolves himself, and I almost couldn't keep it together. He was conspicuously seated in the shadows on the right side of the room in a throne-like chair that had been brought in just for him. He also wore a black suit that made me look like nothing more than a door-to-door salesman in my collared shirt and tie. I had assumed all of the wolves in suits on campus were just for the chiefs, but now that I knew the king was also here, the overly-intrusive pat down they'd subjected me to before letting me in the room made more sense.

Standing before Nwabueze and the congress, I couldn't help but think that I should have helped Kane go lone wolf–or on the lam–like he'd suggested the day before. With the king there, the chiefs would be far less likely to cut Kane some slack. In fact, if Nwabueze wanted them to, they would sentence my cousin to death without even hearing his side of the story.

Nwabueze Diallo–'Nez' to those he cared about–was descended from the purest of lycan bloodlines. Most of us shifters, my own family included, were of African descent mixed with a bunch of other stuff. But not the Diallos. They were "untainted" and Nez carried himself with all the dignity of someone who knew how important he was. He was the last male in the Diallo pack and it was mating season. He was finally going to take a female, make her his queen, and produce an heir. But apparently, not before he made Kane pay for breaking the treaty.

My cousin sat in the first row of chairs some feet behind the podium, looking smug and defiant. His younger brother, Eli, sat next to him, clearly terrified. Eli was a careful wolf who liked to avoid fights and conflict in general. I could imagine he was freaking out on the inside, as he should be. His brother was in a shitload of trouble, not that Kane seemed to care much.

I gripped the sides of the podium and bowed my head to the king. "Eze."

He didn't reply, but I saw a half-smile curve his lips. When Nez and I were pups, a smile like that had always meant he'd cooked up some trouble for us to get into. But now he was the king and I was just a subordinate. I didn't know what to make of his smile anymore. All I knew was that it couldn't mean anything good for my cousin.

"My lords," I said to the chiefs. They, like the king, had nothing to say in return, but I didn't expect them to. They were a bunch of hard-asses that showed very little mercy to those brought before them for crimes against the lycan throne. And as far as they were concerned, every crime committed by a wolf was a crime against the lycan throne.

"Xavier Wesley, son of William Wesley," Stefan said. "Are you ready to take the oath of integrity?"

"Yes," I replied. I wasn't, but I couldn't say that. The only thing that mattered now was that once I took the oath, every word that came out of my mouth had better be the truth. Lying to the congress was punishable by death, and I didn't have time to die. There were still too many females left to date in the world, and I planned on starting with the incoming freshmen at Wesley College, which was my family's private university in Mirage, Georgia.

But that was only if I survived this trial.

"Xavier, do you swear before this congress that your testimony will be honest and true, and do you understand that any false declarations are punishable by exile or death?"

"I do."

The chiefs exchanged glances and then looked at the king. Nez nodded and the questions began.

"Do you understand that your kin, Kane Wesley, has been accused of violating the sacred treaty between the Wesley and Gray packs?" Stefan asked.

"Yes," I replied. "I know."

"What exactly is your understanding of the treaty?"

"In general?"

He shrugged. "Sure."

I blew out a breath. "We, the Wesley pack, are not to venture into the Gray pack territory under any circumstances. The same applies to them. Even the call to mate must be ignored if it means violating the treaty."

The chiefs nodded their approval. "And do you know why this treaty was put in place almost a century ago?" Jackson asked.

I swallowed hard. "I do."

"Then even you must agree that Kane's actions cannot be taken lightly?"

I dipped my head. "I know that they can't."

I glanced back at Kane for a brief moment, wondering if for once I might find him in an actual state of panic. But of course, Kane was cool as ever. He almost looked as if he didn't care about anything that was happening at the moment, like he didn't even notice the king had taken time away from his court and the search for a mate just to attend his trial. I almost forgot where I was for a second and laid into Kane. This fool really thought the chiefs were just going to give him a slap on the wrist and send him on his way. But the hammer was about to come down on him, I could feel it, and he wasn't even going to see it coming.

"So on the night of December eighteenth at around eleven that night, did you witness Kane leave the Wesley territory as he claims?" Marcus asked.

"Yes," I replied. "But he wouldn't tell me where he was going. I offered to go with him anyway, but he told me no. He said he wanted to go alone and I didn't argue. It wasn't my place."

"Did you feel a certain obedience to him as your future alpha?" he asked.

"I won't lie and say that wasn't a part of it. But Kane is also my friend and I trust him."

"Did it ever occur to you that Kane had found his bloodmate and was leaving to be with her?" Stefan asked.

"No. I mean, finding a bloodmate is everything to a wolf. I guess I just didn't think that he would keep something like that from me. Even if she was a member of the Gray pack."

"Does it bother you that he didn't tell you about his mate?"

"Of course it does. We're not just pack members, we're family. The last thing I'd ever expect from any of my family is to be betrayed by them."

Stefan and Marcus shared a look. "Kane has admitted to claiming the Gray female for the first time in September," Marcus said.

"What?" That was almost four months ago! I glared over my shoulder at Kane. He didn't dare look back at me. "How did Clarence not pick up on her scent before now? Aspen is his daughter after all." Clarence Gray was the alpha of the Gray pack, and yup, Kane had screwed his daughter.

"You may not be aware of Aspen's skill as a healer. She is well trained in the art of covering up the mating scent."

I hadn't even known that was possible. Females and their tricks. "Has she been exiled yet?"

Jackson shook his head. "No, but her father has threatened to do so if there is any further contact between her and Kane."

I growled. Keeping Kane away from this female, especially since she was the one he'd blood-mated, was going to be virtually impossible.

"What are the three virtues of an alpha?" Stefan asked, catching me off guard with the change of subject.

"Uh, courage, loyalty and respect," I replied. Any wolf, alpha or not, that didn't know the three virtues wasn't worth their fur and fangs.

"Do you believe Kane embodies these virtues?"

Damn. I hadn't expected that question. "In his own way, yeah."

"What does that mean, in his own way?"

Damn. Damn. Damn. "I've known Kane my entire life and he's always been the bravest wolf I know. As pups, he was always the first to try some crazy stunt or explore some new part of our territory. I've never known him to be afraid of anything. As for loyalty, he always had my back growing up and we always respected each other."

"And now?"

"Now? I still feel the same way. I just wish he'd confided in me about his mate. Can't help thinking that maybe he wouldn't be on trial right now if he had."

"We agree," Marcus said. "As your fellow pack members in attendance have attested, you are the one the younger pack members most trust and confide in."

So I'd been wrong. The others had been called to testify. "I just try to do what I can for my pack. Sometimes that means just lending an ear."

"We're aware. The king also has good things to say about you. He's told us that your friendship is the one relationship he values more than anything."

I fought back a smile. "I value our king's friendship, too. But that's just until I find my bloodmate. Then I plan on acting like I don't even know him."

Nez burst out laughing, which gave the chiefs permission to laugh too. I allowed myself to smile and felt some of the tension ease from my shoulders.

"After hearing what each of you has had to say, a judgment has been reached," Jackson said once their laughter had died down. The smile fell from my face and I held my breath as I waited for what came next.

"Stand up, Kane Wesley."

My cousin did as he was told. He still looked stupid and smug and I couldn't help but want to strangle him.

"Is there anything else you'd like to say before we deliver our judgment, Kane?" Stefan asked.

"No, my lord," he replied. "I've told you everything there is to tell. I love Aspen and I don't regret a thing."

"We know," Stefan replied with a smile. "That is why we hereby proclaim Xavier to be the new ascending alpha of the Wesley pack."

My head jerked toward Nez. "What?" I had to make sure I'd heard right. The king nodded once and my stomach dropped to the damn floor. This was unprecedented. Throughout our family's entire history, I'd never heard of an alpha being stripped of their inheritance. Never.

"You can't do this!" Kane shouted. Finally the fool was realizing the severity of the situation. He strained against Eli, who was holding him back from doing something stupid, like going ape on the chiefs. "I'm the Wesley heir! How you just gonna up and take that from me?"

I saw Nez's eyes turn icy blue. He was about to snap and Kane's ass was finished if he did. A Wesley alpha didn't have shit on a Diallo royal. My cousin really needed to shut his damn mouth.

"You have violated a sacred treaty!" Stefan shouted at Kane. "The punishment must fit the crime!"

"But why me?" I asked to intercept any response from Kane. "Eli is Uncle Bart's son, too. Why not him?"

"You are the most senior Wesley within the pack," Jackson said. "Because of your father, you understand the politics surrounding high-ranking lycans. We see a great leader in you and know that you won't let the king down."

I stared at Nez, my childhood best friend, like he was a stranger. How could he do this to me? I didn't want to be the alpha. I wasn't the heir and I had been glad about it. Being alpha was a responsibility I wasn't sure I was boss enough to handle. However, it was clear I didn't have a choice. Uncle Bart was dead. Kane could never be alpha now and Eli was too young to take his place. I was the next eldest, so the burden fell on me. My father would have been so disappointed in me if I turned my back on the pack and went lone wolf. That's what I would have to do to escape this and I wasn't willing to do that. I loved my pack. I could never abandon them or dishonor my father like that.

Never.

"Okay," I said. "I'll do it."

"Man, that's messed up, X!" Kane exploded behind me. "We're supposed to be family!"

My fangs extended without me even forcing them to. "Nah, what you did was messed up!" I snarled. "You screwed yourself over. You knew what was going to happen if you messed with that female and you still did it! You put the entire pack in danger, so don't come at me with that family stuff, cuz. You weren't thinking about the family while you were out there getting some. I'd like to think that she was worth it, but knowing your history with females, she isn't."

Kane looked at me like I'd just throat-punched him. I'd never spoken to him like that because I'd always respected him as my alpha, even before Uncle Bart died. But it was just hard for me to believe that Kane loved Aspen, even though he'd stated that he did. Even though he'd claimed she was his bloodmate. Just because Kane embodied the three virtues didn't mean he wasn't selfish. He'd only been thinking about himself when he'd crossed into Gray territory knowing it was forbidden. Love had nothing to do with him betraying his pack. So hell no, I wasn't going to let him blame me for his idiotic mistake. He'd made the choice and these were the consequences.

Still didn't mean I wanted to be the alpha though.

Nez rose from his seat and everybody rose with him. I retracted my fangs, because best friend or not, baring my fangs to the king was a bad idea. Though him and I were both tall and built like the predators we were, Nez's pure lycan ancestry put him out of reach. With black dreadlocks that hung to the middle of his back, he was built less like a wolf and more like a lion, with dark skin that proved his bloodline was the purest of all. He was not to be tried in any way, and I knew that better than anybody.

Nez made his way over and stopped right beside me. He laid a hand on my shoulder and I looked at it before meeting his dark gaze.

"Soon, Xavier," he said to me. That was all. Then he stalked up the stairs and out of the hall in silence, not bothering to look back at a single one of us. I couldn't be sure, but I swore I heard the others breathe a sigh of relief once the door shut behind him.

"Can I request a favor, my lords?" I asked, realizing that the chiefs hadn't left with Nez. This trial wasn't over quite yet.

Marcus tilted his head in my direction. "Go ahead."

"Look, I know Kane messed up, but I'm asking you, please don't exile him."

The chiefs exchanged amused looks. "Convince us why we shouldn't," Jackson said.

I grimaced, realizing they had indeed been about to kick Kane's ass out of the fold.

"We're family," I said again, as if they hadn't heard me the first few times. "Family doesn't turn their backs on one another, especially during the hard times. Family loves. Family forgives. What kind of pack would we be if we kicked a member out every time they let us down?"

"That wasn't a problem for Bartholomew," Jackson replied, clearly referring to what had happened with Darien's father.

"I'm not Uncle Bart. I think we can work this out with the Gray pack. We can move past this."

"Oh no," Marcus said. "You're not working anything out with the Gray pack. Clarence would literally eat you alive. Leave the negotiations to us. Oh, and if my tone failed to clarify, that was an order."

I nodded, though I really wanted to argue them down some more. "I understand."

"Good. However, let me warn you. Kane is still your responsibility. We expect you to keep control of him and he is not, under any circumstances, to see the

Gray female until we have reached terms with Clarence."

"You can't do this!" Kane shouted. "She's my bloodmate! How can you keep a wolf from his bloodmate? That's torture!"

"No, that's life!" Stefan growled. "And sometimes life's lessons are torture. Our order stands. Stay away from the Gray female, Kane Wesley, or the next time we summon you, the Huntsman will be with us."

I wasn't scared of much, but just the word "huntsman" made me want to climb under my bed and hide. The Huntsman was an infamous lone wolf mercenary raised in the jungles of Wolfland. His first loyalty was to himself. His second was to Nwabueze. He hunted down anyone and anything the king wanted him to. And if Nez needed an executioner? The Huntsman was happy to lend his services. It was said he was immortal and couldn't be killed, but that was only because no one had ever tried to. He was no ordinary shifter, and if Kane wasn't willing to accept anything else, he had better accept this. If he did anything to go against the chiefs' order, the Huntsman's face would be the last one he ever saw.

"I give you my word, my lords," I said. "Kane won't see Aspen or go anywhere near Gray territory."

I could feel Kane seething with rage behind me, but this time he stayed quiet. Good deal, because I was already over his arrogant ass. If I was going to do this alpha thing, then I was going to start now. That meant putting Kane in his place if need be, and keeping him there.

"That's good to hear," Stefan said. "A tough journey lies ahead of you, Xavier. It's not easy being alpha. Seek the counsel of only those you truly trust. Seek wisdom. Stay close to the gods, and only blessings will come to you."

"Daalu," I said. Thank you. Nez had always been serious about his faith in the Alusi, so it only made sense that he would choose chiefs who were too. I wasn't crazy religious, but I was a believer and I appreciated the chiefs' advice.

Marcus' cell phone rang and he answered it without saying hello. He listened for a moment then hung up. Stefan and Jackson seemed to understand what had just happened without Marcus saying a word.

"You must excuse us now," Stefan said. He stood and the other two rose with him. "Our king will be expecting us to arrive at his estate soon after him. We cannot keep him waiting."

"Of course," I replied.

"Court is adjourned then," he said. "You're free to go."

"Go with grace," Jackson said. With that, the chiefs filed out of the lecture hall and I was left alone with my family.

I turned to face them, hating how awkward it now felt to be around them. I'd walked into that room a cousin and fellow subordinate and now I was leaving it as their alpha. How in the hell had this even happened?

Kane flopped back into his chair and stared blankly at the wall behind me. Clearly, shock had set in. He'd just been impeached as alpha and then told he couldn't see his female anymore. He would get over not being the alpha, but losing Aspen? Never. I just hoped that once the shock wore off, he wouldn't start obsessing over her or get himself killed trespassing onto Gray territory again. I wasn't above assigning him a babysitter, not when I knew how strong the bond was between a wolf and his mate.

The rest of my family hadn't yet moved from where they'd been seated during the trial. Remy, who we sometimes called "Bulldozer," crouched low to gather his momentum then pushed off, leaping over nine rows of seats to land beside me. None of us had hops like Remy, that was why Darien and Foster, who barely had any hops at all, took the stairs like normal people.

"I wonder," Remy said, "if the chiefs were high when they decided that you should be alpha."

I punched him, but Remy was a solid wall of muscle and I was pretty sure he didn't even feel it. "Honestly, I think they were," I replied. "I haven't even processed that I'm actually the ascending alpha yet."

"Well, better you than this asshole." He gestured at Kane, but our cousin was so out of it, he didn't even hear the insult.

"I told him this was gonna happen," Eli said. He looked almost as distraught as his brother. "I told him it was either exile or they were going to keep him from seeing Aspen. But the alpha thing? I didn't see that coming at all." He glanced at me, then looked away.

"I didn't ask for this," I said. "I was perfectly okay with Kane being alpha."

"I know, cuz," he replied. "I'm just worried about him. This was what he always wanted and now it's gone."

"Yeah, by the dummy's own doing," Remy said. "Breaking the treaty was literally the worst thing he could have ever done. He's lucky they only threatened to sic the Huntsman on his ass."

"But it was his bloodmate," Eli said. "We all know what that means and I bet there's not one of us here that wouldn't have been tempted to do the same thing."

"Breaking the treaty or not breaking the treaty is the same as choosing to do heroin or not choosing to do heroin," Remy replied. "It's black and white for me. A true alpha would have resisted for the sake of his pack. Kane gave in without a second thought." Eli couldn't argue with that so he just shut up all together.

Foster sat down beside him. "I'll study lycan law and see if I can find some loophole that allows Kane to see his mate. I already looked over the treaty and it seems ironclad, but I'm nothing if not resourceful." Eli gave Foster a half-smile and nodded his appreciation.

"That's cool of you, Foster," I said, feeling the need to show mine as well. "Thanks."

"No problem. I'd do anything for you guys, you know that."

This was true and Foster wasn't even our blood. He was a Wesley, but he hadn't been born one. My mother had saved him from sure death when he was just a few days old. Foster had been born a sickly runt so his mother had abandoned him in the woods at the edge of our territory. We didn't know what pack she was from, but whatever. Her loss, our gain. Not only was Foster a great brother, he was very smart and was studying pre-law at Wesley College. He could have gone to any school he wanted, but Foster wasn't one to venture too far outside of Mirage. I'd told him he would have to in order to go to law school. Just the idea of it had scared the shit out of him, so I'd let the subject drop and hadn't brought it back up since. Besides, he was only a first year. He had plenty of time to get used to the idea.

"I'm more interested in who you're going to choose as your beta," Darien said. He was the son of my father's younger brother who'd been exiled when Darien was nine years old. We all knew the story, but none of us ever brought it up. It wasn't just a touchy subject for Darien. It was a touchy subject for all of us.

"I don't even wanna think about it," I said. "None of you fools are qualified."

"Man, whatever," Remy said. "Just don't pick Kane."

"I don't want to be alpha." Kane blinked like he was finally returning to consciousness. "Or beta. Or anything. I just want Aspen."

Remy groaned. "Aw, man. If this is what love does to a wolf, I'm going monk."

"Fool, you wouldn't last a week," Darien said.

"Yeah, you're probably right," Remy laughed.

"This isn't funny," Foster said, pushing up his glasses with a finger. "He's really in pain."

"The price of betrayal usually is pain," I said. At that remark, Kane finally made eye contact with me.

"I didn't mean to betray the pack," he said, actually sounding remorseful.

"But I swear to you, I couldn't stop myself from going to her. The need...it's like nothing I've ever felt before."

"Said every asshole who's ever free-based," Remy commented, his expression flat and uninspired.

Kane glared at him. "Screw you, bitch. I can't wait to see how you handle having a mate."

"As long as she's not a Gray female, I'll handle her just fine, homeboy."

"All right, chill," I said. "You heard the chiefs, Kane. They're going to work it out with Clarence so you might be able to see Aspen. Foster's got your back, too. But if you do anything to mess this up, I'm not going to bat for you again. So get control of yourself, and don't make me regret not letting them exile your ass."

Kane nodded half-heartedly. "I got you. Imma be cool."

"You better. Now let's go. I don't know about ya'll, but my stomach is touching my back."

"Food sounds good," Foster said, standing.

"Food always sounds good to you," I said.

"This is true." To be such a runt, Foster could pack it away like nobody else I knew.

My family and I exited the hall and I let all the others, except Remy, walk ahead of me. My cousin stared at me like I'd lost my mind when I stepped in front of him and blocked his way.

"Should I be worried that you're trying to get me alone?" he cracked.

"Yo, shut up," I said to him. "I want you to lay off Kane. He's going through enough without you adding your bullshit to it."

Remy frowned. "Is that an order?"

"Pretty much."

His eyebrows shot up. "Damn, okay. I'll back off the whiny little bitch."

I shook my head. "See, this is why the rest of the pack can't stand your ass." I walked off, but Remy refused to let my comment go and followed me through the building and outside into the student commons. It was pretty cold out, especially for Georgia, but shifters didn't really feel the effects of weather change. Our bodies were built to instantly adapt.

"What do you mean the rest of the pack can't stand me?" Remy pushed.

"Are you really that dumb or do you just look like that all the time?"

"I'm serious, X. The others don't like me?"

"You care?"

"Yeah, I care!"

I stopped walking. "Remy, you're an asshole. I thought you were aware of it, but apparently not. You ride everybody, but then when they turn it back on you, the fangs come out and you're ready to rip their throats out."

He looked surprised. "Damn, I'm that bad?"

"Hell yeah. Nobody minds the jokes really, but you gotta learn to take that shit if you want to dish it out."

Remy was quiet a moment, but then he nodded. "I feel you, cuzzo."

"Good." I walked off, and he followed me again.

"So now that we've got that out the way, are you gonna make me beta or not?" I growled at him and he fell back. "I'll take that as a yes!" he shouted after me.

I didn't stop to acknowledge his arrogant ass. Remy was the obvious choice for beta, but I hadn't even come to terms with being the alpha yet. I had a lot of thinking to do first, mostly about my ascension and pending metamorphosis.

To be alpha, I couldn't stay the way I was. I was no bitch, but alphas had to be the strongest wolves in their packs or risk being dethroned by some ambitious ass subordinate and his homies. An alpha's metamorphosis was initiated during a ceremony presided over by the king himself. That's what Nez had meant by 'soon.' A letter would arrive in a few days stating the date and time of the ascension ceremony and Nez's return. I really didn't have that long to wait, especially since we didn't have an alpha at all. If Uncle Bart was still alive and had only decided to step down as alpha, the ceremony could have been delayed for weeks, months even. But with no alpha, I had two weeks tops to accept my new role and prepare my mind for the change.

Physically, a metamorphosis was brutal. I'd be out of it for days while my body transformed. Problem was, I'd feel every bit of it and would continue to suffer in silence until the process was done. For me, pain was just a part of life, but metamorphosis went beyond pain. It was physical devastation and I just wasn't ready for it.

But ready or not, this was happening.

I was the new Wesley alpha and it was time to ascend.

❧

The new winter school semester was about a week away so my days were still my own. I woke up just before sunrise the next morning and decided to go for a run. Normally, I would have dragged Remy out of bed and made him go with me, but this morning, I wanted to go alone. I'd barely slept all night because my mind was so busy running the possible scenarios of how my metamorphosis would end up. Was I freaked out? Hell yeah. It was times like this where I wished my dad was still alive to talk to. Six years had passed since he'd died and there wasn't a day that went by where I didn't wish I could take just one more run with him. If he'd been around, he would have helped me chill out and not be so anxious about the whole thing.

I stepped out into the cold, morning air and immediately shifted into my wolf form—a dark silver beast with patches of white on my paws and underbelly. Running as a human was lame and I got a much better workout as a wolf. I took off into the woods behind my den at full speed, and I didn't slow down for anything, not trees or other forest animals. I was pretty sure I ran over a few squirrels, but I didn't care. Nothing was better than this. Sprinting through the forest at a speed I could never reach as a human was exhilarating no matter how many times I did it. Twigs snapped beneath my paws as I dug in and pushed myself as hard as I could go.

Two hours later, I laid across my bed, exhausted but feeling pretty good. I showered, dressed, and then headed into town. Wesley College sat directly in the middle of Mirage surrounded by woods and not much else. The only semblance of civilization was downtown Mirage, if it could even be called that. I stopped to grab breakfast at one of the only food joints in town, Mama Patty's Good Stuff. It was owned by one of the elders in our pack, Mama Patty, and everyone ate there every chance they got. The food was great and Mama Patty was hilarious. There were times where I'd sat there shooting the shit with her for hours just because. She was that amazing.

But that morning, I couldn't stay and chat. I grabbed a couple of fried chicken biscuits to go, then headed to Genesis House, the retirement home in Mirage. I had been taught to always honor my elders and value their wisdom, so volunteering at the senior living home was a no-brainer for me. Besides, I found the elders at Genesis House entertaining. They wanted peace and quiet, but never even attempted to live up to their own expectations. They complained and argued with each other, and gave their caretakers one hell of a hard time. Elsie, my favorite, was the main shit-starter, and that morning, I found her in full rant mode as her nurse gathered up the dirty dishes from breakfast.

"They're trying to kill me, Xavier!" she shouted the second I walked into the room.

"What happened this time, Elsie?" I asked, tossing my jacket over the back of the chair across from her.

"They want me gone early. Can't wait for the cancer to take me!"

I smiled at Veronica, Elsie's cute nurse. "What is this crazy woman talking about?"

Veronica held up the tray of dishes. "She thinks we're trying to poison her."

"They are! This slop they serve can't possibly be considered healthy for anybody!"

"Yet I see you ate every bit of it," I laughed.

"Well, what am I supposed to do? Starve?" She eyed the small paper bag I was carrying. "But if I had known you were going to bring me one of Patty's chicken biscuits, I would have pretended to be asleep when Veronica came knocking."

"I didn't bring you a chicken biscuit," I said with a wink. "These are both for me." Elsie grinned.

"The food here is not that bad," Veronica said. "I eat it."

"And look at ya," Elsie said. "Nothing but skin and bones! That's because there's not a drop of nourishment in this mess."

"Veronica looks good to me," I said with a grin. "Very good."

She rolled her eyes. "Elsie, be nicer to X than you were to me. We need our companions and there are not a lot of good guys like him around Mirage."

"Ha!" Elsie laughed. "You'd be surprised how many guys like him are around." Elsie wasn't a shifter. She was just...perceptive. She knew exactly what I was and that Mirage was full of people just like me.

With an unknowing smile, Veronica shook her head. "I'll be back in an hour to take you to your treatment, Elsie." She winked at me and then left. As soon as the door closed, I gave Elsie the chicken biscuit and looked through her old record collection while she gobbled it down.

"So," she said once she was done. Her hazel eyes studied me. "What's the news, mutt?"

"Nothing much," I replied. "Kane has a mate now." I didn't want to dive into the details with her just yet.

"That's a big thing for ya'll, right?"

"A wolf's bloodmate is everything, yeah."

"Then tell him I said congrats. When's the wedding?"

"Hopefully never," I muttered.

"What was that?"

"Nothing." I returned Elsie's records to their crate and sat down. "So am I reading to you today?"

"You'd better," Elsie said, leaning closer to me. "But first, do that thing with your eyes again."

I grinned and then closed my eyes. When I opened them, I saw Elsie's face light up. I'd shown her my wolf eyes, which were bright yellow with round black irises. In all the time I'd been visiting her, it's the only part of my wolf side that I'd ever let her see.

"Hot dog!" she exclaimed. "I can't believe I still get a kick outta that!"

I laughed. "Me neither. I would think the wolf thing would be old news to you by now."

"How could such a thing ever be old news, boy?"

"I don't know. Maybe because it's just old news to me. I don't even think twice about it."

"I would think none of you would. But to us humans, you're like alien creatures to us."

"Aliens!?"

"Or something like it. You're just cuter."

I laughed but then a moment later, I got serious. "So how are the treatments going?"

"Oh, about as expected." Elsie rubbed her bald head which was wrapped in a colorful scarf. "They're eating me alive."

I shook my head. "I hate that you have to go through that."

"Me too. That's why I'm giving them up. This is my last week."

"Good." This announcement should have really hit me hard, but all I felt was relief. Chemotherapy was about as bad as the cancer itself, if not worse. Elsie had always hated the treatments and if this would help make the days she had left a happier time, then I was all for it.

"Xavier."

"Yeah, Elsie?"

"You know you're my favorite mutt, right?"

I grinned. "Yeah, Elsie. I know."

"You gotta promise me something, boy."

"Anything."

"You gotta promise that when this cancer takes me, you'll take care of Cynthia." Cynthia was Elsie's parakeet. I thought she was nothing but a winged noise box, but Elsie thought she was a feathered angel. Couldn't tell her nothing about her bird.

"Of course I'll take care of Cynthia for you," I said with a cheesy smile, eyeing the cage where the bird was napping.

Elsie's eyes narrowed. "You'd better not eat my bird!"

I burst out laughing. "I promise I won't eat Cynthia. At least, not without frying her up first."

"You ain't shit, boy!" Elsie laughed and I laughed some more with her.

"Now," I said. "Do you want me to read to you or not?"

"I certainly do. I've picked out a new one for you too. It's over there on my dresser."

I rose to retrieve the book. Once I saw the cover, I shot Elsie a look. "The Three Little Pigs is not new." I'd read it to Elsie at least fifty times. Any books with wolves, full-length novels or picture books, were her favorites.

"So I lied," she said. "Sue me. All I know is that you'd better do the voices. Growls, barks, woofs, oinks, all of it."

I sighed. "Would I ever read the book any other way?" Elsie smiled and settled back to listen. Halfway through, I stopped reading because my heart just wasn't in it. My mind was still on the trial, but even more so, the verdict and my pending metamorphosis.

"Elsie. There's something I've got to tell you."

Elsie peeked at me through one eye. "Juicy gossip?" She sounded hopeful.

"Real men don't gossip. But I have an interesting story to tell you."

She grunted as she sat up straighter. "So you did have news. Spill it."

"It's about Kane," I said. "He broke our treaty with the Gray pack."

Elsie was quiet while she processed this. I could tell she was working out the details. Cancer had incapacitated her body, not her mind. She was as sharp as ever. "His mate is a Gray girl."

I nodded. "The trial was yesterday. Nwabueze was there."

"The king?"

"Yup." I explained what had happened during the trial.

"So who's gonna be alpha if not Kane?"

I lifted my eyebrows in answer.

"You? Well, hot dog! That's great news!"

"No, it's not. I'm not ready to be alpha. I don't deserve it."

"Boy, hush your mouth. You'll make a great alpha."

"You think so?"

"A good boy like you? I have no doubt. You're smart and you have a good heart. From what Darien tells me when he visits, you're not just a cousin but a best friend as well. I think he and the others would follow you to the ends of the Earth."

I thought about that for a minute and realized she was probably right. "Thanks, Elsie." She nodded with a smile.

"So when will all of this be official?"

"Soon," I said. "There's going to be an ascension ceremony where I'll have to go through a...metamorphosis." I paused. "I won't be able to come see you for a few weeks after."

Elsie looked at me. "It's going to be that bad, baby?"

"Yeah. It is. I won't...I won't look the same."

"I picked up on that. That is what metamorphosis means, ain't it?"

I smiled. "Yeah. But what if they don't let me in to see you because they don't recognize me?"

"Hmm, good point. Guess you better come back with a good cover story to explain the changes."

"Great," I huffed. I couldn't imagine any excuse being convincing enough to explain how I had changed so drastically in only a couple of weeks. Even plastic surgery as an excuse wouldn't hold up once they really thought about it. But I was going to think of something. Being alpha wasn't going to get in the way of my being a companion at Genesis House. I refused to let it.

I read two more books to Elsie, then I headed home. I would have stopped by to visit my mother, but she'd gone out of town with her mate, Nathaniel, for the weekend. So I headed back to the Wesley campus and spent the day in the library to continue mapping out the trip around the world I planned to take in a few years.

Late that night, I was woken up by someone banging at my den door. Cursing, I got up and answered it, ready to beat down whoever was on the other side.

It was Remy.

"Why are you banging on my damn door like that?" I asked him. "What's going on?"

"It's Kane," Remy said. "He's woken everybody up looking for a fight. With you."

I dragged my hands over my face. "Damn, I haven't even been the alpha for a day yet, and I already have fools trying to challenge me!"

"I know, but Kane has realized this is the only way he'll ever be alpha. He thinks that if he goes through metamorphosis, he can take on Clarence."

"Is he out of his damn mind!?" I shouted. "Clarence Gray has twenty years on him! He'll break him in half!"

"I know this, but Kane doesn't seem to care. All he can think about is Aspen."

I growled. "This mating shit is really starting to piss me off."

"What are you gonna do?"

"Answer the damn challenge, what do you think?" As ascending alpha, I had no choice, metamorphosis or not. If a subordinate issued a challenge, lycan politics dictated that the alpha had to step up or step down. If they bitched out, their pack had the right to vote them out as alpha. I wasn't going to let this happen my first day on the job, not that my pack would ever vote me out. But if I didn't fight Kane tonight, I could look forward to being challenged on the regular in the future.

"Damn!" I pushed past Remy and stormed outside into the darkness.

All of the pack members who lived on campus, males and females, were gathered in the clearing behind the student cabins belonging to the college's benefactors, which we called "the dell." Most benefactor's kids attended other universities so the cabins remained empty for the most part. The pack usually came together here for wolf games, which ranged from wrestling as wolves to bare-knuckle boxing as humans. But tonight, the dell was going to be a battleground and I planned on establishing my authority using Kane's face.

My cousin paced the dell, huffing and growling like he was hopped up on something. Remy went to stand with Darien and Foster and I stepped up to confront Kane. The entire pack fell silent.

"Heard you're looking for a fight," I said.

Kane glared at me. "This isn't what I want, X. But I have to do it. I can't let the congress keep me from my mate."

I couldn't believe we were having to go through this again. "Do you hear yourself?" I asked. I looked around at the other pack members. "Do ya'll hear this guy? Once again, he's putting his own wants before the good of the pack!"

"She's my mate!" Kane yelled.

"She's a Gray!" I yelled back. "That's the problem! You violated a hundred-year-old treaty for her! You put us all in danger for her! And now that I'm gonna be the alpha, you'll be lucky if you ever see her again!"

That did it. Kane lunged at me, but I had expected him to.

Pivoting to the right, I wrapped my arm around his neck and flipped him over my back. He slammed to the ground and I punched him in the stomach to keep him down there. Air whooshed out of his lungs, but he was only out of it for a second.

He rolled back and drew his legs up, planting his boots in my chest. He kicked out and I went flying backwards. I hit the ground hard, popping my shoulder out of place. With a quick snap, I set it right and back-flipped onto my feet, ready to get back at it.

With a roar, I took my wolf form, shredding my clothes in the process. Kane realized I was about to go for blood so he followed suit, morphing into his brown wolf.

We circled each other, and some of the other pack members growled and snarled in an attempt to aggravate one of us to attack first. I took the initiative and went straight for Kane's throat. He tried to jump out of the way, but I had always been stealthier so he didn't get far.

My fangs clamped down on his shoulder, having just missed his throat, but that worked for me. Kane yelped in pain, twisted and batted me in the face with a paw. His claws ripped through the flesh on my muzzle, forcing me to let him go.

He came at me again, using his full strength to tackle me. We rolled toward the pack in a furious ball of fangs and claws, stopping just short of taking several of them down.

I dug my claws deep into Kane's side and slashed. He howled and reared back up onto his hind legs, batting me yet again with his paw.

The head shot dazed me for a minute and Kane knew it. He took the opportunity to try and clamp down on my throat. I dodged the attempt and when he stumbled, a blow to the back of the head took him the rest of the way down.

We don't have to keep doing this, I said, using wolfspeak to communicate with Kane.

Yes, we do, he replied, back on his feet. I have to be with Aspen. So that means I have to take on Clarence.

He'll kill you.

Probably. But for her, I'd die with a smile on my face.

You're an idiot.

I'm sure you're not the only one who thinks so. But then again, you don't have a mate yet. When you do, then you'll know. Then you'll be the idiot.

Maybe so. But I won't betray the pack I'm supposed to lead. Not for my mate. Not for anyone.

Yeah. We'll see about that.

The two of us lunged at each other at the same time. We collided and rolled, clawing at each other as we both fought to get the upper hand.

I clamped down on the scruff of his neck and rolled, flipping Kane onto his back.

I jumped on him and took a few shots at his face and ribs. My claws came back covered in blood and fur, and I knew I'd gotten in some good hits.

But Kane wasn't out yet. He knew where my weakness was and he exploited it. He swatted me so hard in the face this time, my nose broke. It hurt like hell and the pain should have put me out of the game. But it didn't. It just pissed me off.

I went kind of crazy at that point.

I bit and tore at any part of Kane I could get at. He tried to defend himself, but there was just nothing he could do. I was relentless. I was merciless. I went for blood and I got it. I went so hard, I almost passed out. Exhausted, I collapsed on the ground, choking as I tried to pull air into my lungs. After I was able to catch my breath, I used my last bit of energy and changed back into my human form, leaving Kane a bloody mess on the ground.

The pack was dead quiet as they waited for what I was going to do next. After a quick three-count, I reached up and snapped my nose back into place. The pain pissed me off all over again, so I balled up my fist and slammed it into Kane's face. He yelped as his jaw shattered and I knew the fight was officially over. He wasn't starting anything back up after that.

My cousin, back in his human form, lay curled on the ground holding his face together. I circled him like he was my prey, but I only did it to make a point to my pack. This could have been any one of them and I needed them to understand that.

"Hope ya'll were paying attention," I said to them. Then I yelled, "Were you paying attention!? This is what will happen to anyone who challenges me! I am the Wesley alpha and you are my subordinates! I make the rules, you follow them. You challenge me, I put your ass down!"

I circled the entire group, making eye contact with as many of them as possible. "In a couple of weeks, I'll go through metamorphosis and every one of you knows what that means. You're all still welcome to challenge me after that, of course, but I wouldn't suggest it." I stopped where Kane was folded up on the ground.

"Get up," I said. He peeked up at me through swollen eyes and I smiled. "You heard me. Don't make me ask again."

With grunts and groans of pain, Kane slowly climbed to his feet. One hand held his jaw and he used the other to cover himself. Eli rushed forward to bring him some clothes and I let him. Nudity wasn't something shifters thought twice about, but I knew Eli really just wanted to check up on his brother because that's what he did.

"Take him home," I said. "I'll tell Elliott to come check on him after his shift in the morning." My mother was the pack's healer, but since she was out of town, her assistant and fellow nurse at the Mirage hospital, was filling in for her.

"Thanks, X," Eli said. "Yo, Darien. Give me a hand with him." My cousin rushed forward to help. They propped a groaning Kane up between them and the pack parted to let them through.

"Good show, X," Darien muttered as he passed. A minute or so later, the three of them disappeared into the darkness, headed in the direction of Kane's cabin.

"The rest of you should turn in as well," I said to the pack. "I don't expect to be back here anytime soon. But like I said, the choice is yours. Challenge me, I'm going for blood, and you can be sure that I won't take it as easy on you as I did on Kane. Happy nightmares, bitches."

I didn't have to push through the horde of pack members to leave. They moved out of my way and practically killed one another doing it. I strolled out of the dell cool as the wind and started toward my den. I put up a good front, but Kane wasn't some punk omega who'd only learned to fight yesterday. Even though I was the victor, my cousin had been a worthy opponent and I was feeling the results of that in every part of my body. I would need at least a day to recover.

Someone followed me out of the dell. From his scent, I knew it was Remy. "You sounded real tough back there," he said. "Kind of reminded me of Uncle Bart."

I ignored him and kept moving. After a minute, I heard him stop.

"I'm just saying!'" he shouted after me. "Maybe you were always meant to be alpha!"

I stopped too and turned back to face him. I smiled. "You know what, Walker? I actually think I was."

❧

Three weeks later…

"It's time."

I nodded at my mother, who smiled at me and opened her arms for a hug. Rolling my eyes, I did what she wanted because I always did whatever my mama wanted.

"Are you ready, baby?" she asked.

"As ready as I can be to endure never-ending, mind-numbing pain for days on end."

My mom's brown eyes filled with tears. "I'm worried about you."

"Don't be. I've never heard of an alpha coming out of metamorphosis any worse than when he went in."

"I don't care about any of that. I just can't stand the thought of you going through all that pain. I'm not just a nurse. I'm your mama, and mamas can't stand to see their babies in pain."

"I'm not a baby though."

"You will always be my baby," she said with a smile. "Always."

I grinned and hugged her tight. "I'll be fine. I'm a Wesley, remember? We're as tough as they come."

My mother pinched my cheek. "Speaking of, the entire pack is here. Even Granny Marcella and Papa Mike refused to miss it. They and the other elders think this is the last ascension they'll ever be a witness to."

"I hope not," I replied, though I knew it was probably true. My grandparents were already pretty old and shifters weren't immortal. We aged just like humans.

The only difference was we had superhuman abilities and we healed fast. Other than that, we lived and died as humans did.

"Has the king arrived yet?"

"Yes," Mom replied. "And it's probably not a good idea to keep him waiting, even if he is your best friend."

"Yeah, you're right. It's never a good idea to piss off a guy you're forbidden to punch in the face."

My mother laughed and pushed me out of my room and toward the front door of my cabin. Remy and Darien were outside waiting for me.

"Hey, Aunt Cecelia," they greeted my mom.

"Hey, boys," she replied. "Why do ya'll look so sad? Like Xavier just told me, he's only been sentenced to metamorphosis, not death."

"Sorry, Aunt Cecelia," they said.

"Don't apologize," she laughed. "Just smile. Xavier needs all the support he can get tonight." She kissed my cheek and then headed into the woods toward the Alpha's Den where the ceremony would take place. School was back in session, so we couldn't very well have the ceremony on campus. There was a clearing near the cabin where all of our alphas had lived once upon a time that offered the privacy and discretion we needed.

I looked at my cousins. "Are you two about to cry?"

Remy gave me the finger. "Are you? You look scared as hell, boy."

"I'm good. Just gotta get ready to take this pain is all."

"I'm kind of hype," Darien said. "Not to see you in pain, but for you to be alpha. You're the best of us, X. The king made the right decision."

"Thanks, D," I said. "Even though you sound soft as shit right now, that means a lot."

He snorted. "Yeah, you're welcome, bitch."

I laughed. "Now I've stalled long enough. Let's go and get this ascension over with, yeah?"

We walked to the Alpha's Den in silence. It was cold out but I didn't care, even without a shirt on. I hadn't seen the point in wearing one since I was sure I would just end up ripping it off when the metamorphosis started.

The clearing around the Alpha's Den, which had been filled with voices and laughter, became dead silent the second I appeared. Nez stood in the center of the clearing with the chiefs, who all wore long, black leather jackets and leather gloves.

Like me, Nez was shirtless, exposing his seventeen tribal tattoos representing all of the wolf packs in his kingdom. This was the largest the lycan kingdom had been in over two hundred years, and that was a good thing for Nez. If he could keep the packs strong and thriving, then he could possibly be named the greatest lycan king ever.

Remy and Darien joined Kane, Eli, Foster, and the other younger members, and I entered the fire circle that Nez and the chiefs stood in. I saw my mom with Nathaniel and their two little pups, Asa and Kennedy. My little brother and sister waved enthusiastically at me, and I wanted to wave back but I had to stay focused and keep control of my emotions. I saw my grandparents sitting with the other elders, as well as the rest of my extended family that lived in Mirage. Not everyone in my pack was a Wesley, so there were several other families there as well.

The sun had pretty much set so the fire circle was our main source of light. I walked to the center of the circle and knelt in front of the king while drummers from the king's court played udu and ekwe drums. I'd never attended an ascension ceremony but I'd been schooled on it by my Uncle Bart's beta, Junior, over the last two weeks since receiving the letter from the king. The most important thing Uncle Junior had told me to do was front tough and not speak unless the king spoke to me first.

Nez circled me and I kept my eyes facing forward, focused on nothing in particular. "Xavier Wesley," he said in his booming voice. "You have been called upon to serve this kingdom as one of its treasured leaders and strongest warriors. Many eyes are upon you this day, not only of those who are present, but of those who have come before you." He lowered his voice. "I know your father would be very proud of you right now." I nodded because I didn't want to speak. I was feeling a little emotional and if I cried in front of my pack, then I was going to have to insist that they skipped the metamorphosis and killed me right there.

Nez started chanting in Igbo while the drums played. I didn't have a clue what he was saying, but then again, there weren't many of us who did. Some of the elders spoke a little Igbo, but for the most part we were an English-speaking pack. I couldn't help but think that maybe it was time to change that.

Stefan handed Nez a wooden dagger because silver was definitely our enemy and we avoided all other metal alloys just to be safe. Stretching his arm out over the bowl Marcus held, Nez slit his wrist and continued to chant as blood poured from the gash. When he was satisfied with the amount in the bowl, he licked the wound, instantly sealing it. Jackson held up a glass chalice and Marcus poured a generous amount of Nez's blood into it. The king accepted the chalice from Jackson and then turned back to face me.

This right here was why dozens of bodyguards flooded the campus every time the king came to visit. He had to be protected at all costs because the blood of a Diallo male was like a rare diamond to wolf shifters. It was laced with pure adrenaline and regenerative properties unlike any other shifter bloodline in history. Drinking it would launch my metamorphosis and change me in ways I could never imagine. I'd seen the results of Uncle Bart's transformation, but Diallo blood didn't affect every wolf the same. There was just no way to predict what Nez's blood was actually going to do to me.

The king approached and gestured for me to stand. "Are you ready?" he asked. The drums were still playing and he spoke so low, I was sure I was the only one who could hear him.

"Hell no. But I'm your servant, right? This is what you wanted."

"This is not what I wanted, X. But I needed you to be the alpha. I need someone I can trust."

I frowned. "What do you mean?"

His expression became dead serious. "Supernaturals everywhere," he whispered, "here and in the Motherland, are in great dang–"

"Eze," Stefan interrupted. "Please. Another time."

I couldn't believe how acute Stefan's hearing was to be able to hear whispering over the drums, but somehow he had. Nez and I stared at each other for another few seconds before he looked to the ground.

When he looked back up, he smiled as if everything was okay. "When I was only a pup, my father often recited a certain proverb to me. He said, if we stand tall, it is because we stand on the backs of those that came before us."

"I know that proverb," I said, having heard Uncle Bart recite it before. "I won't let our ancestors down, Eze."

The king smiled and offered me the cup. "Drink now, Xavier, so that your life may begin."

"Don't you mean my new life?"

"No," he said. "That's not what I meant at all." He forced the chalice into my hand then slowly backed away from me.

The drums played louder as a signal that the time had come. But all of a sudden, I felt very uneasy about this entire ceremony. I couldn't put what the king had said out of my mind. The supernatural realm was in danger? What did that even mean, and why did Stefan insist Nez wait to tell me?

I looked around at all the wolves gathered in the forest. They all stared at me, waiting on me. It was time to ascend. As much as I hated it, the danger to our kingdom would have to wait.

I lifted the glass in thanks to the king for his sacred offering. Then I drank it.

It went down as easy as a cup full of blood could, but it wasn't long before I was on fire.

Nez's blood burned through my body like acid. It torched my veins and turned every thought in my head to mush. All of my senses were wiped out and I couldn't see or hear anything. The pain was unlike anything I could have ever imagined. I felt my body hit the ground and if anybody tried to help me, I didn't know it. It didn't matter anyway. The metamorphosis had begun and there was no way to stop it. I was going to suffer for days. My body was being torn apart so that it could be rebuilt again. Bones were breaking, muscle was tearing, organs were dissolving and my brain was being reprogrammed to think that it wasn't as traumatic as my body was telling my brain it was.

My vision returned, blurry but there. I reached out for someone, anyone who could help me find relief. No one came because they couldn't. The pain of an alpha's metamorphosis wasn't meant to be alleviated. Metamorphosis was a test of a wolf's strength to survive the worst pain they would ever know.

I felt my ribs snap and I bellowed in agony. Claws ripped through the tips of my fingers, sharp as the blades of knives. My fangs shredded my gums as they burst from my mouth. Then all of my teeth started to fall out, one by one. I heard my mother scream and memories of my father flooded my mind.

Dad, I'm going to make you so proud.

That was my last coherent thought. Then everything went black.

❧

Eight days later...

I couldn't believe I was alive.

For days, I'd suffered pain like nothing else in this world. I was so glad it was over, shocked as hell that I'd survived it.

My eyes burned as they adjusted to the light shining in my window. I could tell it was late afternoon by the position of the sun, but if I hadn't been near a window, I wouldn't have known what time it was. I felt like I'd been out of it for months, a year even. My body was that thrown off.

With a wooden arm, I reached up and felt my face. My jaw ached like crazy. I was aware of its new shape—more broad, more pronounced. I reached into my mouth and ran my fingertips over my teeth, causing my fangs to extend.

Normal wolves only had four fangs. I now had eight. No wonder the fools who challenged alphas rarely survived. Wolves already had crushing bites that injured and maimed. Two more sets of fangs ended lives, no question.

I slowly pushed myself up into a sitting position, swinging my long, stiff legs to the floor. I held my hands up in front of my face and willed my claws to come out.

Damn, I thought. I'd only seen claws like these in movies. They were so sharp, they could slice through flesh and bone like it was nothing. I retracted them, thinking that if I made one wrong move, I would be the one sliced up.

With some effort, I stood up for the first time on my new legs. I could tell I had grown but I couldn't be sure how much. As I stretched out, I groaned with relief because my body felt like it was tied up in knots. The bones in my shoulders and back ground together as they shifted around. It wasn't painful but it was a feeling neither me nor my bones were used to.

"Who the hell are you and what have you done with Xavier?" I looked up to see Remy standing in the doorway.

"Hey," I said. I froze because my voice was deep as hell, like two octaves deeper. Smiling, I accepted that as a good thing.

"So I'm thinking I need to talk to the king about loaning me some of his blood," Remy said. "Metamorphosis would change my life, boy."

"Do I really look that different?"

"Hell yeah. I'm actually kind of scared of you now."

"You should have been scared before, punk."

"But I wasn't though."

I laughed and moved to go stand in front of the mirror. What I saw surprised me. I still felt like me...but I didn't look like me. At least, not the me I remembered.

I'd been right. I was at least two inches taller than I had been before, putting me at a solid six foot five inches. My skin was darker, at least a couple of shades, though I still wasn't as dark as Nez.

"Damn, X," I muttered. I really was big as hell. I wasn't one of those oversized fools shooting steroids six times a day, but I was packing some serious girth now. And it was all solid muscle.

"You kind of look like Nez," a voice said from the doorway. It was Darien. He entered the room and stood by Remy.

I couldn't deny it. I did kind of look like the king, minus the dreadlocks.

"Hey, D," I said, turning away from the mirror.

"What up? Welcome back to reality." He sounded chill, but his expression said he was anything but. My appearance was as shocking to him as it was to Remy.

I turned back to my reflection. I studied it for a moment. "This didn't happen to Uncle Bart. I saw the pictures of him before his metamorphosis. He changed but he didn't look like Nez's father."

"Diallo blood does different things to different alphas," Darien said.

"I know, but still."

"Maybe a Wesley stepped out on their mate somewhere along the way and you're actually a Diallo," Remy said. "It's possible. The Diallos got those good genes. Nez's sisters could make me step out on a lot of things."

"Shut up, fool," Darien replied. "Didn't nobody step out on their mate. Just look at Kane. He can barely get out of bed because he misses Aspen so much, let alone summon the energy to cheat on her. Wolves mate for life."

"Unless they don't. I know that's what we've been told, but what if that only applies to non-shifters? What if we, because we are half-human after all, don't? I'm just saying, nothing is impossible. Look at us. Most people would think humans shifting into wolves is impossible."

The fool had a point, but I wasn't ready to dig into any of that mess just yet. "My mom here?"

"Yup," Darien said. "She never left your side the entire time."

"Until today, she wouldn't let anyone see you either," Remy said. "She caught me trying to peek in your window a few days back and I swear, my entire life flashed before my eyes. I don't think I've ever ran from anyone so fast before."

I laughed. "Yeah, my mama can be scary when she wants to be. But especially when it comes to her pups."

"All of our moms are crazy." I smiled.

"Are you ready to go outside?" Darien asked. "The rest of the pack is dying to see you."

"I know," I said. "But I need a shower first. I smell like a stray."

Remy held up his hands. "I wasn't going to say anything, but you really do."

I rolled my eyes. "Gather the pack in the dell in about an hour. I'll meet you there." My cousins nodded and turned to leave. "Oh, and tell everyone I'll be announcing the new beta then, too."

"You got it, boss," Darien said on his way out of the room. Remy only grinned and pointed at himself.

"Get the hell out of here," I laughed. He laughed too, then ran after Darien.

After my shower, I joined my mom in the kitchen. She had cooked enough to feed our entire pack even though it was just me and her. While we ate, we talked, but not about my metamorphosis. I could tell the whole thing had been hard for my mom to witness and honestly, I didn't want to hear the gritty details. I remembered the pain just fine, no reminders were necessary. So we used the time to laugh about Remy's many attempts to sneak into my cabin and watch me wolf out.

A little while later, the sound of howling let me know the pack had gathered in the dell and were calling me to join them. My mom, though reluctant, finally went home to her mate and pups, and I left my cabin for the first time in over a week.

All talking and howling stopped the moment I appeared in the dell. For a minute, everyone just stared at me. I couldn't help but feel a little self-conscious, even though I understood how they must have been feeling. I looked completely different and that wasn't something they would just get used to in an instant.

"Hey, X!"

"What's up, X?"

"How you feelin', X?"

I spoke to everyone who spoke to me, making sure to take a moment to shake hands with Kane. He didn't seem so bitter anymore, but I knew this thing with Aspen was far from over.

He gripped my hand, then pulled me into a one-armed hug. "Make our fathers proud, X," he said to me. "Be the alpha I wasn't able to be."

"I'm gonna try, cuz," I replied. I didn't know what had changed in Kane, but I hoped it was there to stay.

"Speech! Speech! Speech!" Remy started chanting after I'd hugged Foster. It took less than a second for the rest of the pack, which only consisted of a large group of the younger members and enforcers, to join in.

"Okay, okay," I said, moving to stand in the center of the dell. "To be honest, I really don't even know what to say right now. This is the first ascension for all of us. I know this...new look of mine is going to take some getting used to, but I'm still the same Xavier I was before all of this. My changes are only physical and now that the metamorphosis is over, we can move on. Uncle Bart left a great legacy behind, and it's going to be up to us, not just me, to keep that going." The pack sounded off their support with a chorus of howls.

"But first," I said, "I have to name the beta."

"Ooohhhh!" the pack goaded me. I just laughed at them.

"The person I've chosen is more than worthy of being beta," I said. "He's not only a cousin, but one of my closest friends. I trust him with my life and I trust him with all of yours as well." I pointed. "I have chosen my boy Darien as the beta of the Wesley pack." The pack erupted with howls and cheers because everyone liked Darien and I knew he was the right choice.

"Really?" he said, coming to stand beside me. He sounded about as shocked as Remy looked.

"Yeah, really," I said. "You deserve it. When it comes down to it, I know that I can leave our pack in your hands and not have to worry about a thing."

"Damn, X. I don't even know what to say."

"Just say yes, fool."

He grinned and stuck out his hand. "I got your back, cuz. I'm in."

"Better be," I laughed. We shook and then I held up my hands for silence. "I know everyone expected me to pick Remy," I said to the pack, "but I have a different job for him."

"Oh yeah?" Remy said. I watched his disappointment morph into curiosity.

"Yeah," I said. "I want you to be the pack general."

"What?" His expression let me know he hadn't seen that one coming at all. "You serious, X?" Pack general wasn't beta, but it wasn't too far from it.

"Why wouldn't I be serious? No one has hops like you. No one can fight like you. You're a natural warrior and I'll expect you to turn the rest of these mutts into warriors, too."

Remy laughed into his fist. "That's what's up!" He came over to dap me up. "Thanks, X."

I grinned. "It's nothing, cuz."

All the tension behind my reveal was gone now, and the pack was already getting comfortable with the changes. I let them spend some time saluting Darien and Remy's new positions while fielding questions myself. But after a while, Darien pulled Remy and I aside. The other wolves looked a little confused, but of course, they weren't going to ask what was going on.

"What's wrong, D?" I asked with a laugh. "You look scared." Remy smiled.

"I'm not scared, X. I'm concerned."

"About what?"

"About the kingdom," he said. "Is there going to be a war or something?"

I stiffened. "Why are you asking?"

"I don't know. I guess because Uncle Bart never saw the need to have a general. First official day on the job and you've already got Remy signed up. What's up with that?"

I didn't see the point in lying to them. "Look, at my ascension, Nez told me the supernatural realm is in danger. He didn't say why or what the danger was, but I believe him. Whatever it is, we need to be ready for it, that's all."

"Damn," Remy said. "Guess I better start getting their asses together now rather than later."

"I agree. Start next week, in fact. But don't tell anyone the real reason why you're going so hard. Tell them to just get used to it."

Remy laughed. "That won't be a problem."

"Good. Darien, you and I will meet first thing in the morning. A lot of ideas came to me during my metamorphosis and I wanna talk to you about them."

"You were able to think through all that pain?" he asked.

"Yeah, I know. Shocked me too. But it happened."

"Okay. I'll be there, boss man," he said with a smile. "But tonight, we celebrate. I've invited everyone to my den later. You coming through?"

I didn't really want to, but how could I say no? "You know I am. Wouldn't miss it."

"All right, see you then." Darien met up with a few of the other pack members and they vanished into the woods. I assumed it was either to go for a run or go on a hunt. Our human side preferred the grocery store, but our wolf side still enjoyed hunting fresh meat. As far as we were concerned, we had the best of both worlds.

"I'm headed to the library," Remy said.

"The library? Do you even know where it is?"

"Ha! You're such a comedian. Yes, I know where it is, asshole. I need to study up on battle strategy. That way, I'll know how to train the enforcers."

I didn't think all of that was necessary, but I wasn't about to deter Remy from taking initiative. "Sounds good," I said.

"I'll see you at the party tonight." He left and that was the rest of the pack's cue to swarm me. They loaded me up with more questions about everything from my metamorphosis to my plans to find an alpha female. I answered the questions the best I could, but my mind wasn't really there. There was just too much going on inside.

Now that I'd ascended, it was time to lead my pack. That meant all the hard decisions would now be mine to make. Anything went sideways, and I would be blamed for it. I answered directly to the king and Nez wasn't going to give me a break just because we were friends. In fact, he would probably be harder on me than any of the other alphas.

I couldn't help but think on what threat to the supernatural realm could have Nez so stressed out that he would bring it up during my ascension ceremony. I knew it had to be serious and I was already feeling the pressure of how I was going to protect my pack from it. Because if I didn't do it, who would?

Who would fight for us, if not me?

Who else would die for the pack, if it came down to it? I would, without hesitation.

I wasn't afraid. I was determined.

I was going to do whatever I had to do.

Danger could bring it.

And the Wesley werewolves would be waiting.

FOR YOU
(THE LETTERS #2)

Angela B. Chrysler

FIRST LETTER

Waking up has never been so cruel.

Too soon, the morning comes and rips you from my arms. The son we never had slips from my fingers. Another part of me screams in terror. I don't have the power to reach for you. Too soon, I'm awake. Again, I scream your name knowing you won't answer. Again, I'm all alone.

The alarm blares four AM at me. I open my eyes to the dark and remember. The memories flood back. The smell of you and our son. Your hard arms wrapped around me. Your kisses that swallowed my gasps. Then the cold cruel morning that reminds me there was no son…and you're gone. Alone, I curl into myself. I shiver, cry, and wish for my death. I lay there knowing I won't fall back asleep. Instead, I reach for the book on my desk.

Mara.

How that name sits with me and churns a vile taste in my mouth. Again, I read through every clue and every word, desperate for an answer to my curse. But your name, it haunts me. Too soon, I close the book and take up the pen and paper beside my bed. Again, I write to you, my dearest love. My sweet. Another night, another day without you. I've recorded every day of my life since our first, our last…our only… Every dream, every wish, every moment. If I can't have you, then I can talk to you at least in note. Here I safely tuck away every thought I have ever had since that night. Our private exchange of you and I. Here on these pages, we live.

A year ago, I didn't have any demons to fight. Now, they're everywhere and I can't keep my head above water.

SECOND LETTER

Your letter had been quite clear. If you see me, if you know me, you will watch me die all over again. Your memory of me in exchange for my life…that was the deal you made with Death. Usually I cast aside such nonsense, but the memory of that night and the scar on my chest where a bullet pierced my heart is a daily reminder that I had died that day and woke again, all on the whim of a death witch and the deal you made with her.

I can't stay away any longer. I'm back again tonight. The club smells like stale booze. It matches my mood, and makes me feel something. In the last year, it has become my favorite place to be. I never want to leave.

I order my usual with a wordless look that the waitress has learned to read. A moment later, she brings me a cold Guinness. A routine heavy tip guarantees the uninterrupted brooding I've been craving now since that night and secures the solitude I want. All drinks are returned to sender. Any attempted advances are quickly and quietly redirected. This is my domain. And you, my king, sit high on your throne center stage, oblivious to my existence. Exactly the way I like it. You take the stage and there it is: the ache, the pull. Just when I think I've gotten over you, I see your face and forget all else but you. One word, one sigh, and I'm yours all over again.

I nurse the drink in my usual place at the back. You can't see me behind the stage lights, but I have a clear view of you. Envy builds in me as I watch your fingers slide up and down the guitar's neck. Too well, I know what that feels like. The sleeves of your black shirt shift with your arms. I remember my dream and welcome the wave of pain that washes over me.

The band plays on, but I only see you as I turn the bottle of Guinness around in my hand. As your music sweeps through me, I replay the only night we had. The memories build in me and threaten to break my will right here. By the second song, I'm entertaining ideas of walking on stage and greeting you. Or you, by some miracle, see me and know me. Perhaps you buy me a drink. I've stolen your heart for the second time in this life, but this time you remember and keep me.

We'd end the evening mouth to mouth. Before my drink is done, the song is over. You're waving to the audience and packing up your guitar with the same affection in which you cradled our dream son.

The knot in my throat returns with the ball of ice in my stomach and I fight back another wave of hot hurt that will later turn to cold hate. Not toward you, my love, but for the death witch whose deal forged the life we now live.

I grab my purse and slip out the door, but tonight I have no doubt. You see me, I am certain. Maybe I'm off my game. Maybe the dream affected me more strongly than usual. No matter the reason, I ignore your gaze at the back of my head and vanish into the night before you can stop me.

THIRD LETTER

I lay on my bed, staring at the ceiling and waiting to feel whole again. For a moment, I feel you here with me. I think, foolishly, that I'll be alright. But the second ends with a heightened state that leaves me sensitive to pain. The bitter bite of absence moves in. I yearn for you. I turn to hold you, to fill the void, but you aren't there. The hole you left in me returns colder than I ever, and I break.

Shivering, I sob. I tuck my knees into my chest and I cry.

I fall asleep like this every night. You have no idea how much I love you. How much you are a part of me…and how much I miss you. I say your name and feed my fingers through my hair then dig at my scalp, wishing my death would return and take me away from this life as it once did. I sob just one more time until I run out of tears.

Forget the death witch and your vow. Forget loneliness and her bitter bite. Forget all of this life. I relax as my resolve settles the matter.

Whether I should or not, I'm going back.

FOURTH LETTER

No matter how many times I hurt, I can't stay away. You're playing again tonight. I have to go back again. Just one more time. Without you, I can not breathe. I know this. I've tried.

I smear the black eyeliner under my eyes to match the muted red lipstick. I don the usual faded jeans, the kind that rest on my hips while I slide on a tank that hugs my form. Guilt warms my gut and I want to throw up. A part of me is dressing up for you, in the off chance you see me and know me, and will want me. I know a part of me wants you to see me. And I know you can't. I shouldn't go. I'm taunting Death. It's you or I. Only one of us can watch from afar and remember. Me alive, alone in silence. Or you standing over my grave. I know I shouldn't, but I can't stay away. I can't…

I zip my boots that touch my thigh then grab my leather jacket, the one with a tint of purple buried in the black. The look is not mine, but where I'm going, it serves as camouflage. Nothing more. Dressed like this, I'm invisible despite not looking at all like myself. All the more to hide me from your eyes.

I step outside and the cold air hits me. I breathe deep the stale, thick wet in the air left by the recent rain. What little sky I can see, beyond the rows of buildings, is black. The pavement shines beneath the orange street lights like black gold. My leather boots grind the wet pavement as I walk toward the pub where you're playing tonight. There, I can breathe easy again. I hasten my step, eager to get to you once more.

I'm early tonight. An hour? Maybe two? It doesn't matter anymore. My life is on hold for you. The music beckons me and I go. Paying no mind to the tats, the piercings, and body mutilations, I descend the steps into a hole where a cloud of smoke engulfs me. I squeeze my way past a euphoric couple who reek of alcohol and cigarettes. I envy their happiness. It doesn't matter if it wasn't natural.

A band—not yours—is playing. Based on the time, they have maybe ten minutes left on stage. I find my seat and slide into the black steel chair pulled up to the little round red table. Here, I'm invisible. It's far enough from the stage that you can't see through the shadows, but at such an angle that I can see you no matter where you stand.

You.

I feel calm, complacent, and the anxiety melts away. I order my usual from the waitress and do as little as possible to draw attention. The club and bar scene has never been my thing. I much prefer my quiet gardens back home with a book. I don't belong here. I know that, but this is as close to you as I can get.

You're not here yet, but I expected that. I usually come late and slide in through the back just as you walk on stage. Only then can I guarantee your eyes won't find me. Even if you did, I doubt you would recognize me like this. When last we met, I looked like a fairy child stepped from the stories. Tonight, I look like a succubus freshly born of Hell. You'll never know me. I am certain. I hope.

Within the hour, you're on stage. I feel the breath return to me, but I can only take short gasps. *Speak to me, my love. Please come back to me.* My heart selfishly pleads. I wish this knowing it's wrong.

I watch the crowd respond to you and you to them. You eagerly fuel the symbiotic relationship between performer and fan. While you prefer the limelight, I bask in the shadows. As much as this world isn't mine, it clearly belongs to you. Often, I wonder how we could live if you were to remember me. The thought doesn't matter so I shove it aside, and I sit in silence, nursing my drink and loving you alone in the shadows.

Your fans squeal and scream their affections and I watch you smile at the attention, oblivious to my existence. Once more I watch you bid goodnight and, as always, I sit and wait. You'll pack up your things and slip out the back long before I abandon my table and emerge from the shadows.

The next band is already on stage. They're playing something slow and sensual. They're not half bad. I shift my thoughts to you and use the music to slip into our fantasy.

Kiss me, love. Open your mouth for me, I imagine you saying. I obey and you take what is yours.

"Hello, lass."

Lass.

The word cuts my legs out from under me and just like that, I feel again.

I raise my eyes and inhale so sharply it hurts. For the first time in a year, you look right through me. Tears burn my eyes and I force a false smile as my blood turns to ice. I can not move. I know I've gone white. I can't breathe. I can't move. I can't think. You see me and all I want to do is run to you and fall into you. Excitement and dread collide in my chest and I wait.

I drain the last of my drink, but before the bottle hits the table, a second black bottle drops in front of me.

Don't move. Don't breathe.

"What can I do you for?" I ask. My words are so out of place here.

Your presence mutes the music. It's now just a dull thing in the back. You pull out the empty chair across from me and sit. Leaning forward, you put your weight on the table and close the space between us.

"You come here often," you say.

You noticed. My heart soars with glee. *You still love me enough to notice.* It's all I can do not to cry.

"I do," I say.

"Why?" Your eyes dig hard into me.

"I like music," I say, digging back. You smirk with a gentle playfulness in your eyes.

"Just music?" you say.

"And Guinness," I add, purposely puckering my lips to the bottle's head.

"And Guinness," you repeat, not believing my lie.

I swear you purposely pause to let the heat build. You're enjoying our little game. I won't lie. I'm starved for it too and play back.

"Will you be here tomorrow night?" you ask.

"No," I say and watch your smile fall.

"Why not?" you ask.

"Tonight is my last night."

"Oh…" You look wounded. "Why?"

"I've decided I don't like music."

"Or Guinness?" you ask, seeing right through my lies.

"Or Guinness." I smile back and take another sip.

"Shame." Another heavy pause sits between us.

I can't have you here. You have no idea how much I want to jump on you and take you right here on the floor. You have no idea how much I want to tell you all of this and jog that memory of yours.

It isn't fair, I want to scream. You're mine. You just don't remember. I'm dangerously close to saying too much.

"You need to go," I mutter.

"I do," you say.

"Goodnight," I say.

You nod. "Goodnight." But you don't move. We sit instead and study the other. I swear my pain is mirrored in your eyes.

Oblivious to the demons I fight, you say, "If you're not doing anything tomorrow, would you care to grab something to eat?"

The pain, it encompasses me. The pain rips right through me. We're playing with Death. Any moment you could remember. Any moment I could fall dead. What would you do then, my love, sitting here, suddenly forced to hold my still body while a year's worth of memories floods back? You'd hate you. And you'd have to live with it all alone. Tears swell up. They burn my eyes. All I want to do is love you. Is that so bad?

"What do you want?" My voice is a whisper. I drop my guard and I look at you. I let you see my hurt. I know you see the torment in my eyes. I know I sound cold and cruel, but manners right now will only lead you on to false intentions. I can't explain what you should know, but I can show you. Maybe then, you'll understand.

"You," you say too simply.

Heat explodes within my breast and pours right down my front. You smile gently as if you already love me. I alone know you do.

"But I'll settle for your story instead," you say.

"My story?"

"Just your story." You kiss me with those words.

"I don't have a story," I whisper.

"Everyone has a story," you say. "What's yours?"

Oh, kiss me and be done with this. Kiss me, and remember…to hell with the consequence.

"Why do you want my story?"

"I like stories," you whisper. "Who are you?"

"Just a nobody," I say. "Loved and spoiled too much by her daddy, who tried to compensate for the mother who ran off and left her alone."

"The father?"

"Worked his health off to ensure his daughter had all the luxuries in life to make up for the one thing he couldn't bring back."

"The mother," you say conclusively.

"The mother," I agree.

"And the spoiled brat?" you ask.

"Emerges now and then from her gardens to mingle."

"You should emerge more often."

"I should," I say. "And you should be careful."

"Should I?" You grin oh so mischievously. You are trouble. But I already knew that.

"The night is growing late. And I need to go."

I collect my things and stand from the table. You stand with me.

"Do you have someone waiting at home?"

"I have to go," I whisper. Your mouth is inches from mine.

"I'm afraid," you say. If I rise up on tiptoe, your mouth would be on mine.

"Of what?" I ask.

"Never seeing you again."

I lock my knees to keep from falling.

"I get the distinct feeling that if you walk through that door tonight, I'll never see you again."

"Maybe you won't," I say. You shake your head at me.

"I'm not okay with that, lass."

Another spike of heat to my gut. I shake my head slightly to try in vain to clear it.

"Maybe you should be," I say.

You shrug.

"What can I say? I love danger. How do you feel about adventure?"

Before I can answer, someone grabs your shoulder, pulling your attention away from me and breaking me from your spell. Cursing my stupidity, I run for the door, rudely shoving my way through the crowd. I'm gone, down the alley before you even realize I'm gone.

FIFTH LETTER

With every step, I stab the wet pavement with the heel of my boots.

"Selfish," I mutter, cursing myself for being so stupid. I shake my head, forcing back the tears that threaten my cool composure. What was I doing? You'd see me, know me, and then what? I put you through the hell of watching me die all over again? And for what? All for the chance of seeing you again? Selfish. I was risking too much for my own interests. It's a mistake I wouldn't make again. I will not be going back to the club. I shove aside the wrenching scream that tears at my insides. I have to deal. Maybe I'll move to some remote plateau or curl up in my forest and die in a place where I can't hurt you ever again.

You call my name, and I stumble over my feet. Cold runs down my legs.

My name.

I never told you my name since your deal with Death. You would have no way of knowing, unless...

I gaze over my shoulder and into your eyes. In that moment, you own me. I'm yours, and again, as before, your words are the commands I'm eager to follow. My mouth is agape. It's as if I've stepped into one of my dreams. I see sadness in your eyes…the moon, the sun, the world all hang in your eyes. You look at me as if you know me. I want to ask, but fear takes me. What I want I can't begin to have, but if I don't start walking now, I never will.

"You shouldn't be here," I say. I don't know where I find the strength to speak. "Please…" I say. "Leave me be." I turn to leave.

You call my name and it pulls at my heart, but I keep walking.

"I remember!"

I stop and look back, my eyes wide with disbelief. Everything about you has changed. Your games are over. For a moment, I think you're angry with me. I can't name the look in your eye.

"What did you say?" I gasp, unable to breathe.

"I remember," you say again. "I remember everything."

I brace for Death's cold hand. I wait for the earth to open up and take me away from you. But none of that happens. I'm afraid to move. Perhaps with my first step, Death will see us and she'll know. I'm too afraid to move. The earth begins to shift.

"The forest. The hunters. The gun shot," you say.

That day comes back to me as you walk me through it—all of it. It's as if the last year never happened at all. This can't be real. The street is spinning, but you keep talking.

"The blood…and Mara."

Mara. Death's name leaves a vile sick in my throat.

"My deal with Death," you say. "All of it."

I hunt your eyes for truth and truth glares back at me. My blood turns to ice as my legs buckle. As if waiting for me to fall, you're on me, catching me just as my legs give out. I fall to my knees and I cry.

You take my face in your hands and you pull me into you. And just like that, my love, the world comes rushing back, and, for the first time since that night, I can breathe. I gasp between my sobs. I curl my fingers into you, too afraid to wrap my arms around you, should you be a wonderful dream I'll soon wake up from. Too afraid to let go should you be real. You hush me as you rock. But I feel you shaking. You're just as scared to lose me. If you let go…perhaps I'm not really here at all.

"How?" I ask.

"I never forgot, lass," you say.

"But the letter…" I gasp. I can smell you and your scent clouds my head. "Why…Why did you write…?"

"I wrote what she allowed…"

My heart is pounding as if beating the life back into me.

"I didn't lose my memory, lass. You did. That's why I wrote you the letter… because you didn't remember."

The world is spinning and I am teetering on panic.

"You didn't lose…" I gasp. "You didn't lose… I…?"

All the letters. All the dreams. All the nights spent clawing at my skin, wishing for death. I force my brain to focus. You were still holding me there. You next to me. Telling me I couldn't kiss you. I couldn't speak. I couldn't move. I couldn't think.

"What," I whisper. My head is spinning.

"I never lost my memory, lass," you say. "That was part of the deal."

I'm hyperventilating as I battle against the air to breathe. "Why are you telling me this?" I gasp. "For a year… A whole year… You knew? What I lived through? The hell I lived through?"

"I lived it too," you say gently.

"Why?" Tears streak my face, and you wipe them away with your thumbs. "Why are you telling me this now?"

"You were at the club. You were there every night. I thought it would be easier if you thought I couldn't remember… If you stayed away—"

I'm shaking my head, desperate to clear it…to think.

"I saw how you looked at me," you say. "It was killing you."

"Of course it's killing me… You're…"

I can't bring myself to say it.

"Why?" I whisper.

I think about it for a moment. I see you holding me right now, rocking me…

"If I saw you, knowing what you know now… Could you then see me and not have me? Could you let me go?"

I thought about the months that had followed that day. Of nights spent screaming. I hadn't eaten, hadn't slept. I lay in bed for months, writhing in pain. When I did finally moved, it was because I had moved to find the club where you played. I lived to see you, to know you, to hear you. Aching to speak to you, and touch you. And this now. You, so close, right there, sharing now in the hell and the agony, knowing what we both want but can't have. If we do…if we do… I don't know any more.

"Was this just a game to you?" I ask. "Is that what this is? Something you could play with, handle, have, toy with then just throw away?"

The question upsets you and at once I regret asking it.

"Not throw away," you say.

"What am I to you?" I ask. "Is this just a game? Was any of it real? What really happened that day?"

"I believed…if you thought I couldn't remember, it would be easier."

And it had. It did. I had to admit.

"Until I saw you," you say. "Not knowing, suffering this alone…it was clearly taking its toll on you. I knew you when you first came into the club. I watched you fall apart. This was eating you up inside. And you carried it all alone."

"So what now?" I ask. "We're to go back to what we were? Me hanging back, watching you from another life? Pretending none of this ever happened? That I don't love you? That we didn't—"

But you don't let me finish. Your mouth is on mine so fast, so hard, I suddenly don't care about any of it. You silence me with your kisses, and I rise up and respond.

I don't know how long we sat in the street, kissing under the lamplight. I don't know when or how we came to be in the manor in the wood where you live. I do remember thinking just as I fell asleep with you beside me how many questions I had with too few answers. I do remember having no care or concern for the death witch who we had just betrayed or the price we would soon pay.

SIXTH LETTER

For you, sweet lass, I would lasso the moon and pull it down for you… If only I could.

The moonlight spills across the bed. You sleep soundly. I could watch you sleep all night and for the rest of my life. I'm too restless to sleep or stay still, and my empty stomach urges me to hunt for food. Rising from the bed to not wake you, I silently step into the hall.

I don't know what the day will bring. I don't know what any of this means. What games Death plays. It was from an old story that I first heard her name and how, if you knew that name, she could be called upon for a favor. Little did I know how much it would cost us.

I follow the hallway down the stairs to the grand foyer. A moment later, I'm searching the kitchens for something on hand while I think about what I have in the fridge, but I can't steal my mind from Death.

Abandoning the fridge, I head to the library. I browse the books, gliding my finger across the spines, until I find the title I'm looking for.

"Mara," I read aloud. I pull the book from the shelf and open it to the page marked with a scrap of paper covered in my hurried handwriting. A moment later, I'm scanning the text for anything at all that stands out.

"Mara," I read. "Of death… Nightmares." The passage goes on to describe its roots in Hinduism, Buddism, Slavic, and Scandinavian cultures as well as Old English and Greek.

"Known in many cultures as being of and/or related to nightmares, death… In some cultures, she is the Succubus…the ancient Druids…Celts…"

"Fascinating, isn't it?"

I look up from the book, closing it quickly on the note, bookmarking the page I was on as I gaze into Death's cool, black eyes.

She's here, sweet lass. The light bathes her body like a fine cloth. She possesses me. I feel it. It's all I can do not to ravage her right there. I fight a primal ache that I know stems from her games and not my desires. That's when I realize she has the power to puppet me like a marionette on shackled chains if the wish becomes her.

"Your instructions were clear."

Her voice is like silk. "You knew what would happen if you spoke to her again."

I know I have no time to barter. On a whim, she could strike you dead.

"Anything," I say. "Anything at all."

"You said this once."

She turns her back to me and pretends to browse my collection of books.

"Anything, Mara," She glances over her shoulder at me. "Name it. It's yours," I say.

"You possess nothing that I want," she spits.

"Is it my memory you want?"

My words provoke her, and before I can blink, she is on me. Her cheek presses into mine. I breathe deep her intoxicating scent meant to torment the strongest of men. Her lips graze my ear. I drop the book.

"I want you writhing in pain," she says then pulls away. Her spell thickens and I try to shake it off. If she lacked her venomous poison, I'd be inclined to scrub her filth from me, the wretched bitch.

"Me," I say.

"You?"

"My life."

She scoffs.

"Your life is nothing to me."

"My servitude then."

I see the desire dilate her pupils at the thought of keeping me as her obedient plaything. I know I just found my bargaining chip.

"That's what you want," I say. "What you've always wanted. Me...bound to you for all eternity..." I let the words marinate as she rolls them over. "Name your command. I'll obey."

"Slavery..." Her lips rise in a smile that pours a chill down my back. "This is the price you'd pay?"

For you, my love. Anything.

"Yes," I say, knowing I'm binding my fate to Death's will. Hating that once again, I find myself bartering with Death.

"No letter this time," she says. "No goodbye. No answers. This time, you'll just go."

No answer. I imagine you living and never knowing what or where or why... Never knowing what happened to me. Would such a life be worse than death?

"Vanish. Gone...without an answer," she croons, spelling out the terms for me. "Only then will I let her live."

Live. With life, you'd have a chance to love another. With life, you'd have a chance to forget and go on. With life, there is such possibility. Whereas with death…

Just then the solution is clear. Possibility, this is what I was exchanging my freedom for. And just like that, I have no doubt. For you, my love, I'll do anything.

I gaze into Death's black eyes and speak the word that seal my fate.

"Done."

And just like that, I am no longer of this realm.

SEVENTH LETTER

Sweet, lass… Will you ever forgive me?

I watch from the other side as you scream and writhe in torment. I am here, always here, since the moment you woke. I am still here, watching as worry turns to fear then panic.

Those first few hours were the easiest. Once realization set in, the real hell began.

You stopped searching the house and calling my name. Now you just sit on my bed, breathing me in, rocking and screaming. I thought the first several hours were agonizing…then you started to scream. Part of me wished for Mara's orders, but they never came. I think she wallowed in watching my agony as your pain set in.

You passed the first day in bouts of panic and screams. The second day came and went in one endless scream. On day three, your screams were interrupted by long stretches of silence. By day four, there was only silence. I watched helpless as you lay staring off into nothing. Still, Mara didn't call. So I sat beside you and waited while you muttered my name.

How long has it been? Weeks? Months? The life in your eyes is gone now, replaced with a deadened stare. Today, you finally showered and dressed. You tried to eat, but threw everything up. Next day, you tried again. After a week, you finally kept it down. A month later, you left the house. I thought you would never return, but not you, sweet lass. You returned hours later with your barest of essentials. By the end of the day, you had made my vacant house your own as if perched in my nest, waiting for me to return.

Your work consumes you, but the spark and life in your eyes is gone. Nights always were the hardest. With no club to escape to, you spend your nights pouring over my books. You're still looking, sweet lass. Let me go. You talk in your sleep and I listen. You call for me less and less. Then you wake reaching for me and I watch helpless as another bout of weeping takes you.

Your love seems like ages ago. Mara now calls constantly and, as promised, I do her bidding. On occasion, I check in with you. Life seems to have resumed for you. While, for me, eternal imprisonment has just begun.

In silence, I gaze, forever watching only inches from you, but a world away. You'll never see me. Never hear me. But you'll live, sweet lass. Perhaps one day you'll find another. Live long and hard, find another. Forget me, lass. This I do for you.

###

Thank you for your support. – Angela B. Chrysler

Congratulations! You have unlocked "The Letters." Proceed to http://www. angelabchrysler.com/the-letters/ and enter the case-sensitive password "Raven" to access the bonus features, deleted scenes, and download the unrated version.

WHAT WE DO FOR LOVE
J. Kim McLean

Water poured from the showerhead, hitting Alex with enough pressure to be pleasurable without being painful. She rested her head on her forearm against the back wall of the shower. Every single stress of the day melted away with the pounding pressure. As she watched, she saw black streaks of mud trailing down her body. It had been a hard day, but then every day seemed hard for the young woman lately.

Slowly, almost reluctantly, Alex reached for the shampoo and began washing her hair. It was not unusual to see mud streaks pouring into the tub anymore. Working for an environmental firm in Louisiana wasn't what she thought it would be. Remediation was not what she had in mind when she studied environmental sciences, nor was walking through swampy lands trying to get water and soil samples to measure for contamination. One of the few perks of her job was the solitude. They had tried giving her a partner on more than one occasion, but they didn't last.

It was unnerving for people when Alex could tell them what they were thinking before they said anything. She had been called a freak, or worse, but no one could argue with her work ethic, or the quality of that work. Not many people wanted to put on hip-waders and walk through the marshes where snakes, alligators, and other not-so-friendly beasties lived, but Alex didn't mind.

The marshes and swamps of southeastern Louisiana were not hospitable unless you knew how to respect the land. Alex was a city girl, but in a short time, she had come to respect the wilds that made up her field area. The solitude her work afforded her gave her time to think...about past choices, past mistakes. Sometimes, though, getting too into your own head had its own issues.

The shrill tone of a cell phone pulled her from her silent contemplation just as she washed the last of conditioner and soap off her body. With a breathy curse, she turned the water off then stepped out, grabbing her towel and phone simultaneously. The caller ID made her frown as she hit *answer* and put it on speaker. "Alex here."

"Alex, it's Jesse. I'm in the neighborhood. Can I come up?"

Alex frowned as she started to dry off, and stared at the phone. "I don't know, Jesse. I've had a long, hard day in the field..." Being in the neighborhood meant Jesse had made an effort to stop by, given that Alex didn't live anywhere near the more populated parts of New Orleans. It wasn't that she was antisocial, she was just social on her own terms.

"As if being tired ever stopped you from having a beer with friends before," Jesse replied.

To this, Alex arched a brow and stared long and hard at the phone for several tense seconds. "Grab a six pack and come on over, then." Truth be told, when her and Jesse were together, she never said no to a beer after work. Even the hardest, hottest days in the field wouldn't keep her from enjoying a drink or two.

"Already got one. See you in five." Alex thought she could hear the smirk in Jesse's voice.

The line went dead. "Shit." Alex finished drying off and walked naked from the bath to her bedroom closet. So much for PJs. No way she was going to look like an absolute slug for her ex. Instead, she opted for jeans and a simple black t-shirt.

Fortunately, Alex was not much of a slob, and the small house was passably clean, aside from the odd dish or two in the sink that she hadn't gotten around to putting in the dishwasher. She poured herself a glass of water and downed it before Jess arrived, knowing she needed to hydrate after a day out in the marsh. As she finished refilling the water jug, she heard the knock at the door. About the same time as the knock, Alex felt the familiar presence of Jesse's hyperactive mind encroaching on her.

Alex had long ago discovered her ability to sense other people's thoughts and feelings. She struggled to find a way to keep others 'out' so she didn't lose herself, though it felt like a losing battle. There was a reason she preferred to work and live alone, with few other souls near by. Her home was her sanctuary, and it took a lot for her to trust someone enough to let them in. Jesse was one of the few.

Before opening the door, Alex took a centering breath. Jesse and Alex were often like oil and water. Their passion had burned bright when they first got together, but both could be stubborn and neither liked to lose an argument. It made communication hard, despite Alex's unique gift, and the pair had never quite figured out how to make it work. Alex still regretted that they hadn't found common ground, because a part of her still very much loved Jesse, and letting go had been...a challenge.

Not quite smiling when she opened the door, Alex turned her brown-eyed gaze to Jesse, not expecting those alluring blue eyes to still give her the same pause as when they met. Since separating, the two had tried to maintain a friendship, though, admittedly, Jesse tried harder. It didn't help that Jesse had since started seeing their mutual friend Jim. Alex did try to take some solace in the fact that Jim seemed to make her happy, happier than she'd ever been when she'd been with Alex.

Jim also kept reaching out to Alex, and she found it hard to turn her back on either of them, even though it stung a bit to see the pair together. She had a feeling that the two would eventually marry. While part of her was happy in that knowledge, another part of her felt...lonely. She did her best to smile at her ex, and stepped aside to let the woman in. "Do I dare ask why you were in the neighborhood? It's not like I'm a hop, skip, and a jump away from any part of the city."

Jesse just grinned goofily as she sat on the couch and slid the six pack closer to Alex. "Okay, so I went out of my way to stop by. Sue me! I needed to tell you, and this isn't news to share over the phone. I've been out looking at venues."

Sitting on the opposite end of the couch, Alex took one of the bottles and twisted the top off before taking a big pull of beer. She arched a brow as she looked back to Jesse. "Venues for what?" She did her best to keep from reading her ex, but in her soul, she knew what was coming.

Her ex's grin grew wider as she held out her left hand. Sitting on the ring finger was a massive sapphire surrounded by two smaller diamonds. "Jim proposed last week!"

Alex felt herself grin while she also felt her heart slam into her throat. Part of her was happy that her ex had found happiness with Jim, but deep down? It stung. The grin was partly real, and partly forced. Jesse had no idea how much of an effect she still had on Alex. She looked at the ring before meeting those blue eyes once again. "Congratulations, Jesse... Wait, did you say last week?"

"I did!" Jesse exclaimed. "We decided to keep it secret, only telling our parents. We also wanted to tell you the news in person before announcing it publicly. I figured it was the least we could do," she explained.

At least they had taken her feelings into account to some degree. The grin became a wry smile. "I appreciate it, but it wasn't necessary, Jesse. You know I'm happy for you two...happy that Jim brings you such joy." She also knew Jesse still cared for her, not just because she could sense it, but from what she said. She did her best to focus on the happy feelings, but it was easier said than done.

"I know, but... Look, Alex, I'm not stupid, you know? I know you still have feelings for me, okay? I still care about you, and love you...just not as a partner. I drove you nuts, right?" She smirked knowingly.

"Only as nuts as I drove you," Alex replied. Jesse didn't know the full extent of Alex's gift, but she knew her ex had an uncanny ability to know what she was thinking. She never did put two and two together. "So...if you are looking at venues, does that mean you're hoping to have the ceremony sooner rather than later?"

Jesse nodded. "Yeah. I think we're going to see about having it in Audubon Park, and the reception at night at the zoo. I was thinking about holding it in Jackson Square, but it's too...busy."

If it had been in Jackson Square, Alex would have politely been able to decline the invitation. Jesse knew she didn't like crowds, but with it in Audubon Park? There would be no easy way to refuse. "The park would be lovely, and the zoo at night... That's got to be expensive?" Alex asked. She knew neither of them were wealthy.

"Jim's parents are paying for the venue," Jesse replied. "The thing is... Alex, we want you to be a part of the ceremony."

Alex arched a brow and looked at her ex sidelong. "You want me to be... I don't know if that's a good idea, Jesse."

Jesse's infectious laugh filled the room, and Alex felt her heart skip a beat when she put her hand on Alex's knee. "You haven't even heard what we want. Look, you know I have no other family. I have no one to give me away. I'd like you to walk me down the aisle."

It had always struck Alex as odd when she could feel her heart break. Jesse had no idea what she was asking of her ex... How deep her feelings still ran. There was a time that she had hoped to marry Jesse. Jesse did want to walk down the aisle with her, just not as partners. What made it all so hard was picking up on the pure joy coming from Jesse. How could she say yes and live with the heartache it would bring? At the same time, how could she say no and live with the consequences of crushing someone she still cared so deeply about?

Alex managed a weak smile and gave a simple nod. "Fine... I'll do it, but only if I get to wear a tux."

"Deal," Jesse said as she took a beer and held it up to toast her friend. "To new beginnings."

"New beginnings," Alex mumbled, smiling but not feeling it in her soul. "So when is the ceremony?"

"Next month. August 28th," Jesse replied.

Alex almost fell for it, but she picked up on the humor coming from her ex. She smirked. "I know you aren't holdin' your weddin' on the aniversary of Katrina. Spill, Jesse."

"How do you always know?" Jesse laughed. "Fine... We're actually holding it on the tenth of September, so about two months from now. We don't want anything super fancy, though Jim's mom is hiring an event planner for the reception. She seems keen on planning it, and neither Jim and I are too bothered."

Alex offered a warm smile. "Seems like you win, then."

The two trailed off into light banter as they enjoyed their beer. Alex knew Jesse wouldn't stay for more than one, which gave her a deep sense of relief. She feigned disappointment, though, when her ex announced she had to be on her way. As the telepath closed the door behind her friend, she rested her forehead on it and opened herself to the joy Jesse felt, even though only a very small fraction of it was meant for her. She missed the jovial spirit Jesse had when they once shared the small house together, and Alex found herself wondering if she'd ever find someone to share such joy with again.

※

Two weeks after learning about Jesse and Jim's pending nuptials, Alex learned she'd once again been assigned a partner to help her in the field. She had learned not to argue with her supervisor, as the older woman thought she knew best, even though Alex got more work done when she worked solo than when she had a partner. She seriously considered arguing, though, when she found out who her partner was.

"So, Alex...the boss said you've been working at the agency for a while. Why are you still a field grunt?" the man asked.

For her part, Alex concentrated on the drive, but spared him a brief glance as she considered how to answer his question. She was also trying her best not to skim his thoughts, but he made it virtually impossible, as his thoughts almost drowned out his speaking voice for her attention.

Everyone says she's a freak. She ain't social, hasn't had a steady field partner in the five years she's been at the agency...and after five years is still in the field. She has enough experience to be the supervisor. She's a dike too... Look at the short hair, and the clothes.

The thoughts came one after another, and it was all Alex could do to ignore them and focus on what he actually said. Casting another sideways glance at him, she started, "It's Todd, right?"

"Yup." *Can't believe Jesse ended it with me and started seeing her. Can't see what Jesse saw in her. Not like she could do her better than me.*

"Well, Todd, I happen to prefer the field to a desk. If I were to take a supervisor role, the chances of me getting out to the field are virtually nonexistent," she explained. It was the simple truth, though she didn't think it prudent to mention *why* she preferred the field. It also took a great deal of her self-control to call him out on his errant thought about her clothes, and even more effort not to cold-cock him for his misogynistic and homophobic thoughts about her and Jesse. About the clothes alone, she was dressed for the field... How feminine did he think she could get? Pink steel-toed boots, a pink safety vest, and a pink hard hat? She almost rolled her eyes at the thought, but stopped herself. As far as his thoughts of her and Jesse's sex life, it seemed a typical and narrow-minded way of thinking.

Giving her a look of disbelief, Todd replied, "You don't want a promotion? It's better pay, and an extra week of vacation. Are you nuts?" *There's gotta be something more to the story, or she's bat-shit crazy. Field work is for grunts and noobs.*

Alex arched a brow and flashed a wry smile. "One person's definition of insanity is another person's definition of sanity, Todd. And yet here we are, you have been assigned to me as my partner. Tell me, how does it feel to have to learn from the freak of the agency."

"Wh...what?" he asked. His nervous laugh gave him away, along with the various unchecked thoughts running through his mind.

Laughing, the telepath shook her head. "Think I didn't know? People around the office talk. I'm not stupid, despite what some might think. No one who comes to the agency wants a field rotation longer than they absolutely must... except for the Freak of the Agency. It's not like I care what anyone thinks, either. I happen to like my job, and have no desire to babysit a bunch of field whelps who complain when they get bit by ants."

We do not need babysitting. Hell, I don't even need to be here with her. I could do this by myself. Probationary field tech, my ass.

When Todd didn't seem to have anything to add to the conversation, Alex opted for a little fun. She hadn't been told he was on probation, and she shouldn't be privy to something of that nature. "So, tell me... What did you do to get put on probation and sent to me?"

With a look of shock and dread, Todd replied with a high-pitched squeal.

"What? No one's supposed to know about that. What the hell, man? That bitch of a boss..."

"Boss didn't tell me shit, Todd. People aren't made my assistant because they want to glean from my experience. With the reputation of the Agency Freak, no one chooses to be my assistant. I just simply guessed," Alex lied.

Cocky dike think she's got one up on me. Whatever. I can still do the job better than her. I don't deserve this. I was supposed to be assisting the GIS tech and training under her. Damn but she's a sight hotter than this bitch.

Alex did her best not to smirk. "I bet I can guess something else about you, Todd. Up for a game?"

"You just tryin' to prove you earned your nickname? You don't know me, woman. Don't know anythin' about me. Guess away. You'll be wrong," he countered. If he'd been walking, he would have strutted like a peacock.

"Maybe. Though I suspect part of the reason you are so annoyed was you signed up to train under Emily, the GIS tech. Instead of her, you're stuck with the woman who not just slept with your ex, but had a relationship with her. You also get to enjoy the near ninety degree temperatures, near one hundred percent humidity, the mosquitoes, moccasins, and 'gators," Alex explained, not trying to hide her smirk as she watched his mouth drop open.

Todd didn't say anything for several seconds, before finally shaking his head. "Whatever, woman. Lucky guess. Can we just get going? Faster we get this done, faster I can get home."

"By all means," Alex replied as she pulled into what would be their parking spot for the day and put the truck into park. "You take the station south of here by about half a mile. I'll take the one a mile north of here. Come back to the truck and wait for me, then we'll go to the last station together." She climbed out and started getting her gear together before pulling her hip-waders up.

Every so often, Alex would look at him as he tried to get his gear together. It was clear he was struggling, so she went over and offered a few friendly tips. "Two things you need at your fingertips are your clipboard and the GPS." She showed him her clipboard that had a cover taped to it, and a pouch on the cover that held the GPS unit. "I modified my case to keep the paper dry so long as I don't drop it, and put the clear pouch on so I didn't have to keep fishing for my GPS unit. Feel free to copy the design when we get back to the agency.

"Other than that, keep your water handy. You need to drink more than you think you do. I tend to only snack at the truck, but that's because I've lost one too many granola bars to the swamps. Any questions?" Alex asked.

I have to go on my own? This is nuts.

When his reluctance to split up was also obvious in his expression, she offered, "If you're not sure about splitting up, we can go to each of the monitoring stations together. I read, you record. How's that sound?"

Thank god yes!

"Eh, whatever. That's cool," came Todd's verbal reply. He didn't understand why she kept looking at him as if she knew what he was thinking.

The rest of the afternoon passed without incident, though Todd still thought he didn't need her help. She went easier on him, though, knowing he was as stuck with her as she was with him.

❧

Two months passed rather quickly, and before Alex realized it, the rehearsal dinner was upon her. Jesse had a lot of friends, but not much family. None of her distant family was close enough to invite to the wedding. At the rehearsal dinner, it was just Alex, and Jesse's three bridesmaids. Danika, Linda, and Penny had all gone to university with Jesse, and all four belonged to the same sorority. The foursome had pledged the same year and become fast friends.

Alex knew the three bridesmaids, of course, having met them when she and Jesse had been together. All three were outwardly nice to Alex, though Danika was much more superficial than the other two. Linda and Penny were always welcoming in both what they said and the thoughts that skimmed through Alex's mind. Danika was another story.

If Alex had her choice, she'd rather not live with the 'gift' she had, especially when it came to 'hearing' what some people really thought of her. Danika would always think Jesse could do better. She was too polite to actually say anything, but Alex couldn't avoid the thoughts that came to her when she was near Danika.

Linda, Penny, and Danika were fawning over Jesse as everyone waited for the minister to finish addressing Jim and his groomsmen. Alex kept to herself off to one side, doing her best to keep to her own thoughts, but failing.

I can't believe she's here... She's the ex! What was Jesse thinking? She must feel sorry for Alex. It's not like she could manage to find someone as good as Jesse.

Danika was certain in her feelings, and that certainty gave strength to the thought, making it that much harder for Alex to ignore. She did her best, forcing one deep, slow breath after another as she went through the various checks she would do at any test station she monitored for work.

I can't believe I'm marrying Jim tomorrow! I can't believe how lucky I am! It never would have happened if it hadn't been for Alex. I can't wait to tell her I'm pregnant. I really hope she'll agree to be the godmother. Jim and I would be heartbroken if she said no.

Alex did a double-take as she looked up and found Jesse standing right next to her. She hadn't even realized her ex had approached. "Jesse," she started, unable to hide her surprise.

"Did I startle you? I'm sorry, Alex. You seemed in your own little world. The minister says he is ready to begin."

The rehearsal itself was a blur, as was the dinner that followed. With nearly twenty people in attendance, Alex found her senses overwhelmed during the meal, but did her best to participate in the conversation around her. She was sitting with Linda and Penny while Danika was off trying her best to flirt with one of the groomsmen. Alex thought to save the woman some embarrassment, as the man she was hitting on preferred the company of other men, but then...it wasn't really any of her business.

As things began to wind down, Alex decided it was time to leave. The strain of so many 'voices' was starting to make her head hurt. Jesse and Jim pulled her aside before she could make her exit. Her ex was radiant, and the joy both of them felt seemed to radiate off them. She couldn't explain why, but it warmed her own heart to know the happiness both her friend and Jesse brought one another.

"Before you leave, Alex," Jim began. "We, well...we have more news, and another question." He looked to his bride.

Beaming, Jesse took Alex's hands in her own. "I'm pregnant, Alex. And...Jim and I were hoping you would be the godmother to our child."

The warmth of Jesse's hands as they took hers caused her heart to skip a beat, and this helped her look surprised. "Pregnant?! You guys...you want me as the child's godmother? Are you sure about that?"

Jim answered in both words and thought. "We are one hundred percent certain, Alex. You have been so giving and supportive of us. We know it...it's likely not as easy as you seem to say it is, but we also know the kind of person you are. We know you and your heart, and we want our child to know how to love as you love."

Tears welled up in Alex's eyes as she struggled to find words. The tears spilled over when she weakly replied, "I... Jim, Jesse, I am speechless. I, honestly, I have no words. Congratulations to both of you, I could not be happier. I would be honored to be the godmother to your child."

Jesse and Jim pulled Alex into the biggest bear hug they could manage before letting a stunned Alex take herself home.

❧

Alex stood in front of the mirror as she worked her magic on the dark blue bow tie that matched the blue in the blue and black vest that was part of her tuxedo. Once she was happy the tie was done correctly, and straight, she grabbed the tails to complete the look. Alex could be considered pretty, sure, but she was more handsome than pretty. As she adjusted the sleeves of the tuxedo shirt, there was a knock at the door. "Come!" She already knew it was Linda.

"Well, don't you make the dashing figure," Linda said with a smile as she came to stand behind Alex. She casually wiped away imaginary dust from Alex's shoulders. "It's time to shine. Have you seen Jesse in her dress yet?"

Alex turned to face the bridesmaid. "Not yet. And as dapper as I might be, it doesn't compare to your radiant beauty in that dress, Linda." She couldn't help the smirk as she studied the woman who stood in front of her, admiring the dark blue strapless dress. She offered Linda her arm. "Shall we go collect the special woman of the hour?"

"Let's."

Danika was fussing over the train of Jesse's gown while Penny helped the bride with her veil. It was all Alex could do to remember to keep breathing as they entered the room. Linda, though, saw the expression on Alex's face. "Stunning, isn't she?"

Not trusting herself to actually form words, Alex simply nodded, and rewarded Jesse with a warm smile when the bride looked up to see her and Linda enter the room.

"Oh my, Alex... You make a tux look good," Jesse said before Alex could even compliment her on the gorgeous dress.

Yes, she does!

The errant thought came from Linda, and another one that followed nearly caused Alex to blush. She had no idea Linda thought of her that way, and wished she could bow out of the private thoughts.

A woman in a tux...not even a 'woman's' tux. Who does she think she is?

The more venomous thought came from Danika, who moved herself between Alex and the bride. "Let me just adjust..."

"Danika, stop fussing, and step aside. I was talking to Alex," Jesse countered, though her mood didn't waver. She offered Alex a warm smile. "Thank you again for agreeing to give me away. I know there are a few people who think it is insane, but aside from Jim, you know me better than anyone, Alex. We both want you to know we consider you very much a part of our family."

Once again, Alex found herself at a loss for words. "If you are not careful, you'll get me crying, which will get you crying, which will get these three crying. I don't think your makeup artist, or the photographer, would appreciate the smudged makeup." She flashed a smirk, hoping humor would deflect from her just a bit.

Before anything else could be said, it was time. One by one, Penny, Linda, and Danika left the room, leaving Alex and Jesse alone. Jesse smirked. "I think Linda likes you, Alex. She's single, you know."

Alex couldn't help the blush. "I was wondering...on both counts. Let's see where the evening takes us, hmm? Besides. Today is not about me, but about you and Jim. Let's get you hitched, eh?" The grin Jesse flashed warmed her heart.

On hearing the start of the bridal march, Alex offered Jesse her arm and the pair walked down the aisle just as they'd practiced the night before. The minister looked at the pair of them. "Who presents the bride?"

"I, Alex Randolph, present the bride to her future husband," Alex replied. The minister nodded and Alex released her ex's arm before approaching Jim. She offered him her hand, but he pulled her into a huge bear hug and whispered, "Thank you."

Alex wasn't one to cry at the drop of a hat, but she couldn't keep the tears from flowing freely through the rest of the ceremony. A small part of her might have been sad, but she felt joy for everything else.

The venue for the wedding reception was the Audubon Tea Room. It was a building Alex had often seen from the outside whenever she visited the zoo, but tonight was the first night she'd gotten to see inside. It was huge, but Jesse and Jim had invited far more people to the reception than to the ceremony. It was an elegant venue, and the catering had thus far been superb. Alex was doing her best to relax and mingle, but there were a lot of minds and a lot of random noise buzzing around her head. It made it hard to concentrate. It also made her head hurt.

The telepath was thinking of calling it a night soon when a random thought caught her attention and made her blush. Not a second later, a hand appeared on her shoulder as Linda leaned down and whispered, "Jesse told me this might be the time of night you think about making your exit. I hope, for both our sakes, that is not the case."

The bridesmaid was leaning over Alex and pulled back so she could look her in the eye. The smirk on Linda's face was enough to hint that she might want more than just a dance from Alex. The string of very personal thoughts confirmed what had become Linda's agenda for the evening.

Alex found herself smiling almost shyly as she looked at her lap. "Well, Jesse would normally be right, but perhaps you could convince me to stay." She didn't need convincing, but figured she'd play the game. The blush on her cheeks, though, was very real. She'd always liked Linda, and found her attractive, though she hadn't thought Jesse's friend was into women.

Without skipping a beat, Linda pulled Alex's chair out just enough so she could slide onto her lap and let one arm casually hang around Alex's neck. Her smirk didn't waver as she leaned down and placed a gentle, yet sensual, kiss on the other woman's lips. It was the briefest of kisses, but enough to get Alex's heart nearly pounding its way out of her chest. Linda pulled back, her smirk replaced with a warm smile. "Convincing enough, elusive one?"

The butterflies in Alex's stomach were doing flips, but she managed a warm smile of her own as her arms went around Linda's hips. "I'd say it's a good start." She gave the bridesmaid a cheeky grin, and was about to say something else when the DJ put on *Girls Just Want to Have Fun* by Cyndi Lauper.

Linda jumped off Alex's lap, took her hand, and exclaimed, "I love this song! It was my anthem when I was a teenager!" She didn't give Alex a chance to protest and dragged her onto the dance floor. They half-stumbled onto the parquet wood floor, both already laughing up a storm as Linda started dancing. Alex did her best, but she wasn't a big dancer, at least not to fast songs.

There was such joy and happiness throughout the room. Even though there were a ton of random thoughts that crossed Alex's mind, the convergence of so much happiness, combined with Linda's pure glee, was intoxicating. Alex found herself smiling bigger and laughing harder than she had in a long time, and it felt good.

As the song came to a close, Alex started to head back to her table. The lights on the dance floor went low and the DJ put on *Chasing Cars* by Snow Patrol. Alex got one, maybe two, steps in before Linda grabbed her hand and pulled her back.

When Alex turned to face Linda, the bridesmaid's green eyes met her brown-eyed gaze. There was something solemn in the way Linda looked at her, but what impacted her more than the look was the feeling coming from the other woman. There was a sense of longing, and it was one Alex felt as well. Linda slid her arms around Alex's neck, and Alex found herself embracing Linda as the two began to dance to the song, which Alex had never given much thought to until that moment.

Part of her was terrified at the feelings rushing towards her. The feelings she picked up from Linda, along with her own. They seemed to become so intertwined so quickly, it was hard to differentiate between who felt what. Halfway through the song, Linda pulled her head back, locking her gaze on Alex's once again, and then kissed her. This wasn't a brief kiss, though it was just as sensual as the first kiss shared moments ago.

When they broke the kiss, Alex took a shaky breath and felt herself blush. The song came to an end all too soon, and she hadn't yet recovered enough to have her wits about her. Fortunately, Linda wasn't quite so distracted, and escorted Alex back to their table. It was time for the bride and groom to cut the cake.

No one seemed surprised when Jim was polite and fed Jesse her piece of cake, nor was anyone surprised when Jesse took advantage of the moment and rammed the mostly icing covered slice all over Jim's face. After that, there was the usual delay in serving out pieces to the guests. Linda took advantage of the time to, in her mind, put Alex at ease. "Just so you know, I do like you, but I'm not expecting anything. If you might want to give me a call, perhaps go to dinner sometime, I would most likely say yes," she said, offering a warm smile.

"You would most likely say yes? I don't know. There's still a chance for rejection," Alex teased.

Poking the other woman, Linda laughed. "It's no fun if it's a sure bet, is it? We can keep it simple, if it puts you at ease, Alex."

Tilting her head slightly, she looked at Linda with an arched brow. "Why would I need to be put at ease?"

"Because you haven't dated since you and Jesse broke up, and that was ages ago. Because we haven't seen you at all since then, and Jesse said you haven't really been going out or being social. We are social creatures, Alex, even you. You should get out more. I'm offering to accompany you on a date," Linda replied, her smirk turning to a warm smile as she took Alex's hand in hers. "I meant what I said. I like you. I've always thought you were funny, attractive, but...not available."

Alex found herself without any witty comebacks, and simply squeezed Linda's hand. "Linda, you are being too kind to me. I would love to go on a date with you."

Linda's warm smile turned to a full on grin. "You would? You would! Excellent!"

Alex laughed softly as the bridesmaid squealed with delight. Underneath the joy Linda exuded, there was a hint of jealousy. Alex turned in time to see Danika approach and place wedding cake in front of both her and Linda. She looked flatly at Linda. "Thanks for helping with the cake."

Rolling her eyes, Linda replied, "Relax, Danika. There are a ton of people helping to hand out wedding cake. The only one who misses my presence over there is you, and that's because you want to try and hit on the groomsman again. I'm busy."

Danika rolled her eyes and walked off, causing both Linda and Alex to laugh. "I don't think she likes me very much, " Alex admitted,

"No, but then she doesn't like most people. Jesse, Penny, and I are stuck with her because we've known each other so damned long. We just call her on her crap. It's effective. You should try it sometime," Linda replied.

By the time the two finished their cake, it was time to see the groom and bride off. Linda and Alex walked outside to fall in line with everyone else. As she looked around, Alex realized the zoo was a busy place. She knew there were more events going on, but the parking lot near the Tea Room was full. There were a lot of people heading to other venues, and she started to pick up on some of the wayward thoughts from strangers who had nothing to do with Jim and Jesse's wedding. Most people seemed full of joy, but there was an undercurrent that tugged at Alex's nerves.

Looking around, the telepath tried to pinpoint what she was picking up on. The smile she'd worn since Linda first kissed her now waned, and she felt her pulse quicken. Something was not right. She scanned the crowds more frantically, looking beyond where the limo for Jesse and Jim was parked.

Anger. Hate. Confusion.

"What's wrong?" Linda asked, her brows furrowed in concern.

Alex shook her head slowly, but released Linda's hand as she turned around, still scanning the area. "I don't know. It might be nothing, but...something doesn't feel right."

"Feel right? What do you mean?"

Death walks here.

The thought came in clear now, and chilled Alex to her core. She heard cheers off to her left, and it registered that Jesse and Jim had walked out of the Tea Room. Everything seemed to slow down for the telepath. Someone was not happy, and that someone was close.

The joy coming from those cheering for Jim and Jesse interfered with Alex as she tried to spot where the more troubled thoughts were coming from. "Alex, what's wrong? You're starting to worry me," Linda asked.

Pausing for a moment, Alex looked at Linda. "There's... It's hard to explain, but someone nearby is angry. There's more to it than that, but I can't find them."

"What are you talking about?"

Giving Linda a small smile, she reached up and gently cupped her cheek. "I will do my best to explain later. I need to find this person." She gave her a quick peck and then walked behind the line of people, going in the direction of the black thoughts. Jesse and Jim had just passed Linda as everyone continued to cheer. They were almost to the car, and for Alex, the sooner they were in the car the better.

No one deserves love. Jesse... She should have been mine. They must die. Everyone must die!

Alex's eyes went wide as the thought slammed into her clear as a bell. She looked at the end of the procession line, opposite to where she'd been standing, and saw him. Todd. The man looked deranged. She knew him, but not like this. He had come across as a bigot and a sexist, but a killer? Looking to her left, she saw Jesse and Jim closing in on the car, and her blood drained from her face.

The bride and groom were his targets, and she just needed to act. Time seemed to slow to a standstill as the man stepped into the middle of the procession line and brandished a gun. He aimed for Jesse as he kept thinking, *Die, die, die!*

Alex cried out, "NOOO!" She barreled her way through the crowd, and unknowingly pushed Danika to the ground. There was no hesitation as she inserted herself between the gunman and her friends. There was no hesitation as the man pulled the trigger three times before he was tackled by two of the groomsmen as everyone else screamed.

At first, Alex thought he had missed. She looked down, and thought it odd he missed at such a close range. Somehow she ended up on her knees.

"ALEX!"

Jesse, Jim, and Linda all seemed to shout her name at the same time. Jesse was at her side a moment later. She looked up to her ex. "Did...did he miss?"

"Oh, Alex," Jesse said, her eyes welling up with tears as she gently laid her friend on the ground. One of the groomsmen knelt next to her and put pressure on her chest. It was then the pain hit her, and she found it hard to breath. She coughed and saw crimson droplets land on Jesse's dress.

"Oh, Jesse...your dress. I'm sorry," Alex said, turning her eyes to meet her ex's.

Jesse cupped her cheek. "Shush, Alex. Stay with me, okay? I don't care about the dress."

Alex tried to swallow, then coughed again as she started to shiver. "Why is it so cold, Jesse?"

"Don't talk, love."

Her eyes started to grow heavy, and Alex realized what was happening. He hadn't missed after all. She looked back at Jesse. "You...you and Jim be happy together, and raise that child right. I'm sorry... I'm sorry I won't be here to watch her grow up."

"Alex, shush, don't talk like that. The paramedics are on their way," Jesse said, tears pouring from her eyes. Jim stood behind her, crying with his wife. He knew Alex had likely saved his wife and his unborn child's lives. She'd given everything she could to make sure Jesse and Jim could have their happily ever after.

Smiling weakly, Alex shook her head. "Don't lie to me, Jesse...never works. Tell Linda I'm sorry we can't go on that date. I really like her." For the first time in as long as she could remember, there was silence in Alex's mind. She looked at Jesse. "You and Jim should know...I love y'all like family."

And the life went from Alex's eyes.

OUTREACH: PART ONE
(AN ORLOSIAN WARRIORS STORY)

Daniel Raye

Dedication

For my beautiful girls and boy who have passed on, Isis, Tauris, and Jackson – thank you for your love and loyalty. I really miss you. Beautiful baby boy, Jackson, thanks for reminding me that age doesn't mean you stop getting excited over the little things. Now, for my new baby girl, Brianna, you are a mischievous whirlwind. So glad I found you. Thanks to my Mother and my supportive Sweetheart for being there, my fabulous friends and supporters, Romance Ravers, and of course, the fabulous ladies of O2O. Special thanks to my supportive readers and author friends. Dreamkeeper, you are a precious jewel.

Special Note to Reader

Part One ends in a cliffhanger; however, to receive your FREE copy of part two, just send an e-mail to the address provided at the end of the story.

Gasping for air, Jaci threw off the cover with her hands, kicking the rest loose with her legs. Her feet hit the hardwood floor and she ran for the bathroom, propelled by instinct. Fire rushed through her chest, a hand tightening around her heart. She flipped the toilet seat up and leaned over it, balancing herself with her hands, and retched, the acid from her stomach abrading her throat. *Water. Nothing but water. Good thing I couldn't eat last night.*

She closed the lid, washed her hands in the sink next to it, and reluctantly looked at her image in the medicine cabinet mirror, noting the dark circles underneath her dark brown eyes and a slight redness surrounding her pupils. *I am entirely too young to look so old.* She rummaged through one of the caddys surrounding her sink and grabbed her toothbrush and toothpaste, then pulled her mouthwash from the linen closet behind her.

Frowning as she brushed her teeth and continued to look at herself in the mirror, she shoved her free hand into another caddy and felt for her facial cream, mentally sighing over her downward spiral in the housekeeping department. Jaci was so accustomed to the burning in her throat that she considered it commonplace. *Always the same. Always the same nightmare.*

"Well, one good thing about insomnia, the big boss loves me. I'm always early for work," she said aloud, talking to her bedroom as she turned the light off in the bathroom.

She grabbed the remote from her chest-of-drawers and turned on the surround sound in her apartment to hear the early morning news while she got ready for work. Stooping over one of her moving boxes along the wall, Jaci removed a pile of mail and other random papers from the top of it, dropping the mess on the floor, and opened the box. The once heavy cardboard flap was so worn from being used as a permanent storage place, it felt soft and flimsy to her hands.

This was at least the fifth time she had moved in the last three years, and she'd barely bothered to unpack. Other than waving at her neighbors on the rare occasions they crossed paths, Jaci made no effort to be friendly or approachable. She never remained in the same place long enough for it to matter, and she could count the people on one hand who knew where she lived at any given time.

She reached into the closet and pulled out a pantsuit. *Eenie meenie miney mo.* Blue for Monday. It really didn't matter which one. They were all the same, just different colors, all neutral, comfortable, and perfect for work. Best benefit of all, one less thing to have to think about.

After a quick shower, breakfast consisted of dark roasted espresso Romano, one of her few luxuries, and a slice of toast.

She shook her head from side to side to loosen her thick hair, then finger-combed the coils of her natural. She had spent hundreds of dollars trying a menagerie of "natural" hair products when she decided to return to her roots, but she had to admit that it paid off. In seconds, she was ready.

Jaci grabbed her briefcase from the bar, set the alarm, and checked the time on her car dashboard when she started the ignition. She had fought the incessant encroachment of electronic contact as long as she could, nearly ending up as one of the few people in the 21st Century without a cell phone, but duty called, and she eventually gave in. She still owned watches too, but somehow always managed to forget to wear any of them. Since the accident, time no longer seemed to matter, so she tried her best to forget about it.

❧

Taking her usual route to work, the scenic one, she arrived exactly twenty minutes later. The interstate would have easily shaved fifteen minutes from her commute, but she hadn't been able to handle going near the busy highways since her husband and two-year old daughter were killed.

Jaci parked her Nissan Rogue in her reserved spot, unlocked the steel door at the back of the three story building, turned off the alarm, and unlocked her mailbox in case the weekend skeleton crew had left something for her. Breathing in the elusive sound of complete silence, she took the stairs to the third floor and walked into her office at 5:43 a.m., nearly two hours early. As usual, the office was empty. No printers whirring, phones ringing, computers jingling, or whatever the many sounds computers made these days were called, and best of all, no people chattering or asking her inane questions. Just the way she liked it.

Despite wearing the title, Director of Social Services, Jaci had become quite antisocial over the past three years. Her office was directly next to the big boss, Director of Child and Family Services, or DCFS as most people called their little slice of state government.

She placed her three containers around her desk, "Urgent," "Important – File," and "Trash," then thumbed through her mail, making the most of her quiet time until she got to a large brown envelope with the return address, "Federal Department of Corrections Outreach Initiative."

A knee-jerk reaction took her by surprise. She leapt from her desk, covering her mouth with shaking hands. She had been waiting for a reply to her grant proposal for over six months, and the bureaucratic idiots had chosen to send it over the weekend.

It's probably a rejection. "Shut up," she told herself as she took a deep breath, reached for her chair, and sat down at the desk again. Placing her forearms squarely on the flat surface, she tried to compose herself. Until now, she hadn't realized how desperately she wanted this. Despite a master's degree in psychology and a doctorate in social work, she still wasn't at all sure why, but she knew that if this was a rejection, she would plummet even deeper into the dark abyss she had just started to crawl out of.

"Okay, Jaci. Open the thing. Just open it."

She took one more breath, pulled the small metal prongs apart, then removed her letter opener from her desk organizer, mumbling a series of nonsensical sounds under her breath the entire time she slid the letter opener under the top flap, breaking the seal. With the seal broken, she still had to sit a few moments longer before removing the contents of the envelope.

Dear Dr. Rothschild:

Your request for the Youthful Offender Parolee Outreach Program has been approved for a four-year term. Please review…

"Yesss!" Jaci pumped a fist straight into the air and ran around her desk doing a tribal-like happy dance, hopping and jumping with a sense of something she hadn't known she was missing until that moment: hope.

Now, if only she had someone to share it with. Her parents were gone, murdered while she was away in college. Since their deaths, she'd made a point to avoid her extended family as much as possible – something about them had never seemed "right" to her, and the two people she called "friend" were both night owls.

Jaci chuckled to herself, thinking about Diana and Renee as she glanced at her wall clock. If she called and woke either of them before 6:30 a.m., they might not be friends anymore. She satisfied her need to celebrate by making a copy of the entire packet and tacking the award letter to the corkboard beside her desk.

Summer meant vacation time for most of the DCFS employees, so as the official new project manager for the "Outreach" program, she would have to work fast to confirm sponsors for her new clients. She spent the next few minutes of quiet time pouring over the program specifics.

❧

Andreus stepped into the prison yard and looked around, always aware of every sound, every smell, and every movement. He took a moment to enjoy the warmth of the sun and watch the birds flying overhead. He envied their freedom, but his desire for autonomy warred with his fear of the unknown.

Despite not being allowed to set foot outside the prison during the fifteen years, nine months, and five days he'd been incarcerated, he noted the sounds of more cars passing since the opening of the casinos in the small town of Atmore and wondered how he would cope with other changes facing him once he was released on parole in seven days.

Well aware of the other men watching his every move, Andreus strode to the far end of the yard and sat on one of the corner benches, giving him a perfect vantage point. The others shot hoops and hung together in small groups, but even here, in this social castaway zone, he did not fit.

He slid his tongue across his pointed incisors. While the world changed outside, he had undergone a secret metamorphosis inside these walls, and searching for answers about who and what he was had turned up absolutely nothing.

Whatever the explanation, the sense of something lying in wait was always with him, ever present, and it had been a part of him as far back as he could remember. Everyone around him felt it, their fear of him instinctual. The reaction he received from most people reminded him of deer sensing the presence of a lion, but Helen, his adoptive mother, had been different. She had accepted him, even when she saw his skin instantly knit together seconds after being wounded.

Andreus closed the door on his memory of her again, putting it away safely until later when he needed her image to help him get some much needed sleep. Playbacks from his nightmares haunted his days as well, hounding him with swords clashing, molten rocks exploding, deep chasms filled with fire splitting the Earth, multi-timbre voices of war, and huge wings rushing toward him, claiming him. Even now, Helen's image held the power to offer him a measure of peace. She was the only one who had ever cared for him.

He walked over to one of the exercise bars on the prison yard, set his playlist to a classical mix of Chopin, Rachmaninoff, and Debussy, and inserted his earbuds. When he looked up, the group of inmates who'd been hanging around the bars just seconds ago had sauntered off, giving him a wide berth. He had no interest in getting to know them or sharing their company for that matter, but being left alone within these four walls with nothing but his own disturbing thoughts made the maintenance of sanity a challenge.

Like most of his possessions, he had purchased the electronic device with "gift" money he'd earned for keeping another inmate safe. Easy money. All Andreus had done was to allow the bullied prisoner to sit with him in the mess hall and hang with him in the yard for a few days. He maintained a calm demeanor, never advertising his services, but business always came his way, particularly since the casinos had opened.

Andreus heard footsteps approaching from behind as he contracted his muscles and continued his daily exercise routine. He already knew exactly who approached before turning around, so he didn't bother to stop what he was doing.

"Shannon, you too. The warden and the social worker want to see you."

As if he hadn't heard the guard, Andreus took his time finishing his last set of pull-ups, then leapt down from the bar. He snatched his t-shirt from the concrete bench and pulled it over his head. The moment he turned to face the guard and four other inmates, he saw and smelled their fear.

The putrid stench infiltrated his nostrils, and no matter how hard they tried to keep their expressions neutral—tough, even—he couldn't miss the signs. They blinked frequently, their eyes like cut glass, and he saw tiny beads of sweat over their lips and on their foreheads.

"Let's go." Four more guards joined the original one and led the prisoners back inside and down the hallway to the warden's office. With the exception of one of the guards, Andreus walked behind the others, who kept glancing back at him every minute or so until they reached their destination.

Once they arrived at his office, the warden led them to one of the classrooms and told them to be seated. He addressed them first, then turned the meeting over to the social worker, Gavin Sumner.

Gavin was a heavyset man, and stood almost as tall as Andreus. Despite his name, he was Italian through and through, often throwing in a word here and there when he really got into what he was doing. Wearing a plaid polo shirt and stonewashed jeans, his presence was a staunch contrast to the other prison officials in the room. He also taught anger management and facilitated the AA groups. Andreus had never needed either of the classes, but they were required for every inmate convicted of involuntary or voluntary manslaughter, and that included him.

The social worker sat on the desk at the front of the classroom and removed papers from a large envelope before he started talking to the five of them.

"Good afternoon." He waited for their response, as social skills were a large part of their rehabilitation.

"Good afternoon," they chimed in unison.

"As all of you know, you will be leaving here over the next few days and reintroduced to society at large. Several months ago, each of you signed up for this partnership program between the State Department of Corrections and the Department of Child and Family services."

After pausing for effect, he continued. "Now you know I'm not usually so formal, but this is a big deal, and you are our first guinea pigs. You need to make this work. It'll help you and a lot of men after you. Capire?"

They nodded.

"I'm gonna hand you the paperwork you filled out for the "Outreach" program and I want you to look it over so you know what information we already sent your sponsors about you."

After handing the paperwork to the other men, Gavin placed his hand on Andreus' shoulder. "Shannon, come with me for a minute."

Gavin led Andreus to a corner of the room away from the guards and the other inmates. "Hey, man. Just want to let you know the reason you'll be the last one released is because it might take more time to find a good sponsor for you. There's an addendum included with your bio with the complete account of what happened that night based on your adoptive mother's testimony, but the way you killed him will probably still make some people shy away. We've talked about why your case is different before, but I'll be here the rest of the week if you need to talk about it some more. Okay?"

Andreus stared into the social worker's eyes to ascertain whether or not the man was telling him everything. When Gavin looked away, Andreus blinked and attempted a more relaxed stance.

"Is that it?"

The social worker cleared his throat before responding to Andreus' question. "Yes. That's it. Un-unless you, uh, need to—"

"There's no hold-up with me getting out of here, is there?"

Gavin shook his head. "No. Absolutely not."

"Thank you." It wasn't his intention to intimidate the man. Gavin had been good to all of them. Andreus just needed to be sure he wasn't lying.

Andreus returned to the desk to review the information the facility had sent to the "Outreach" program coordinator. He completely understood why he would be the last prisoner to leave. The problem was that despite remembering every minute detail of Karl's abusive behavior toward Helen, his memory remained sketchy about what happened afterward. He only recalled scattered pieces of what took place after he walked in on Karl kicking her.

Whether he recalled doing it or not, Helen had recounted the details in court, making sure everyone knew that she was certain Andreus had saved her life from the abusive monster. The bruises from Karl's beatings could be seen on every part of her body visible to the naked eye, but Andreus saw even deeper, his stomach boiling with the need to avenge the broken woman inside, the woman who had taken him in when he had no one. Even Karl's death did not ease his rage.

The judge called Karl's abuse of Helen a mitigating circumstance, reducing Andreus' sentence from twenty years to fifteen. The bottom line was that Karl had ended up mutilated and very much dead, and Andreus had spent almost half of his life in a cage. One thing he remembered saying at his own trial was that faced with the same circumstances, he would do it again. He still felt the same.

❧

"See ya tomorrow, Frank." Jaci stuck her head in her supervisor's office.

Frank Avinger looked up from his computer. Most of the other employees were either on vacation or they were just there to catch up on some last minute business before the weekend.

"You leaving me too, Jaci?" He looked at the time on his computer screen. "It's not even eleven yet."

"Yeah, I wasn't able to find anybody else brave enough to sponsor one of the "Outreach" clients, so I'm going to pick him up now. He's getting out at noon. Oh, and he and I have the same birthday. Same date and year. What are the chances of that?"

"That *is* interesting. Was he born here too?"

"No, it didn't say where he was born. Just said he committed the crime here in Alabama."

Frank narrowed his eyes, and she knew he was about to say something she didn't want to hear.

"You sure you're up to managing the project *and* being one of the sponsors too?"

"Well, I don't have much choice. The Department of Corrections was so late sending me the award letter that all of the participants were about to be released when I got it."

"Thought you already had all the sponsors lined up."

"I did, but the last couple backed out when I sent them the bio and they saw how the victim was killed—not that I'd really call him a victim from what I read. Doesn't matter how somebody like that was killed as far as I'm concerned. It just means the child, and he *was* only a child at the time, was strong. Plus, he did it to protect someone he loved, and unlike some of the others, he has no priors.

I think he deserves credit for that. The bastard he killed beat the woman with a blunt object, then knocked her down and started kicking her, all because she cooked something he didn't like. Honestly, I think his killer deserves a medal."

Her boss frowned, concern in his eyes. "So who exactly was his victim, or not victim as you say, and how was he killed?"

"If you don't mind, I'll keep the details between me and my client for now. I don't want to betray his trust. It's bad enough the couple that backed out on him know. Let's just say he had to be extremely strong, extremely angry, or both, but he was only sixteen. He definitely deserves another chance, and right now it's either me or a halfway house, and I get the feeling he wouldn't do well there."

He just looked at her for a few moments before breaking the silence.

"Jaci, you sure you're not getting too involved? I mean, I agree with what you're saying and all, but you've gotta keep in mind that he's been in prison for fifteen years. He's a grown man now, and probably hardened from…"

Jaci stared at him, grateful when he trailed off and stopped trying to tell her how much to care about her clients. After a few more seconds, Frank threw up his hands, letting the topic go.

"Thanks for all your hard work getting that grant approved, by the way. Not many people even think about that sort of thing. You know Cynthia and I would sponsor another one, but with Chloe graduating this year, we're gonna have our hands full just keeping up with all of her last minute needs and sponsoring the one I picked up already."

Following another brief pause, he added, nearly whispering this time, "But, Jaci, please be careful. I know how much you want this to work, and I know you care what happens to this man, but if this gets to be too much for you, don't hesitate to—"

The mention of graduation was a painful trigger, as was his allusion to her not being able to handle things. She stared at the carpet, reminded of the fact that she would never see her Jathany graduate from high school. She didn't want to put a damper on Frank's excitement, and the last thing she wanted was to pull him into her personal hell, but she was not about to be told to play bureaucrat when a man's future was in her hands.

She kept her face averted. "Now, Frank, you know me. I'll make it work."

Before he could respond, she threw up her hand as she turned and headed toward the elevator. She couldn't let him see her crying.

Despite her recent antisocial behavior, she enjoyed learning about people and getting to know them better. That was the main reason she'd chosen social work as a career. She wasn't sure why, but she had always been interested in people who had been thrown away by society.

Jaci considered it her calling to be their crusader. In order to gain more experience and insight, she had completed her practicums and internships in prison settings, written her dissertation on felony offenses, sentencing, and rehabilitation, and worked in the system since college.

She decided against returning to her apartment, fearful that her cold feet would plant themselves in Mobile and she'd never make it to the prison in Atmore. Her car was parked just across from the elevators, so she filled two plastic bags with ice from the machine at the office, then opened the back door and dropped them in the traveling cooler she always kept with her during summer months.

Next, she hoisted the cooler onto the passenger seat for easy access to her chilled lemonade, her go-to drink since the ugly reports about drinking too much coffee making people nervous had started to get to her. Atmore was only a few miles from Mobile, so she drove the distance in silence, mulling over the information she had read in Andreus' file.

Instinctively, Jaci placed her hand over her heart, her mind vacillating between caution over the way Andreus had killed his adoptive mother's boyfriend, and admiration because he had done it to protect her. With the exception of a trained killer, Shannon's method of killing his adoptive mother's boyfriend would have given anyone pause.

He had force fed Karl Pugh the dinner the man had thrown in his adoptive mother's face, stuffed his nose with table napkins, then broke his back with his bare hands. The amount of force it took to break a man's back without the use of a weapon was substantial, and although Andreus' bio listed his height as 6'3" with a weight of 200 pounds, she still marveled over the fact that he had only been sixteen when the crime was committed.

On the other hand, Andreus Shannon was the only parolee out of her five initial outreach clients who had not been protecting or avenging himself. Instead, he had done it to protect his adoptive mother, who had testified on his behalf before later dying of a heart attack.

The closer she got to the prison, the more jangled her nerves became. Tears flooded her eyes, making tracks down her cheeks. She was back in the car on the interstate, trapped and helpless to save Jathany, James' inert body crumpled over the steering wheel and tilted at an impossible angle, blood flowing freely from his temple.

Jaci's hands started shaking so badly, tears flooding her eyes non-stop, that she had to pull over to the side of the road. *Suppose I really can't handle this. My life is such a mess right now. I'm such a mess. I can't take care of my own life, let alone help someone who's been in prison for fifteen years get* his *life together. I couldn't even take care of my own child. I can't do this.*

✒

Andreus stood leaning against the prison gate. His curly, blue-black hair and rich tan skin were offset by piercing emerald green eyes. He knew all too well what was behind him, so he looked straight ahead, glancing periodically down the road in hopes of seeing a car coming for him. All of his belongings were contained in a brown duffel bag at his side.

He had spent nearly half of his life behind these walls, and during that time, the darkness that gave him the strength to destroy his adoptive mother's boyfriend had grown inside him, taken root, and become a permanent part of him. He tried his best to hide it, but each day it grew stronger, as if he had left a part of him behind, or perhaps it had lain dormant. Now, he felt it stronger than ever. His pointed incisors and the restless flow of excess energy just beneath his skin served as constant reminders.

He had been waiting for over an hour. His sponsor, Dr. Rothschild, had given him her number, but with no cell phone, he had no way to call her, not that he would have. He refused to set foot inside the prison again, not even long enough to make a phone call, so he waited, placing his earbuds in his ears to pass the time and quiet his mind.

✒

Jaci dropped her briefcase on the bar and kicked off her shoes as soon as she made it home. Exchanging her suit for a kaftan, she sighed with the relief accompanying the removal of her bra, then padded back to the kitchen in her house shoes. Washing her hands three times first, she opened the refrigerator door and pulled out a small container of chicken salad and a take-out garden salad with a special order of extra blue cheese dressing.

Placing the salads on the bar, she sat down, then reached back in and added a few strawberries and grapes to her menu for the night, along with two bottles of water. The way she saw it, as long as she added vegetables and fruit, everything else was fair game. At least no one could say she had completely strayed from her diet.

The minute she took the first bite, her stomach lurched. *What am I doing? What gives me the right to...?*

She shoved the food back into the refrigerator and ran down the hallway to her bedroom. Donning a pair of jeans, she considered skipping the bra, but decided that might not be the impression she wanted to make. After adding a t-shirt, she grabbed her wallet and keys, setting the alarm before she dashed out to her mini-SUV.

Dialing Frank's number as soon as she pulled out of the parking lot to confirm, she raced toward the halfway house where she'd asked Frank to deliver Andreus.

"Hey, Frank. Did you take him to the one on Old Shell?"

"Yeah. What are you doing, Jaci?"

"I'm on my way to get him."

"Why don't you wait until—?"

"Don't they still lock the doors at seven?"

"Jaci, listen to me. I really think you should—"

"You know I'm not hearing that. Thanks for covering the gap, Frank. I'm gonna take tomorrow off. I'll check in with you later."

She turned into the driveway of the halfway house and hit the "end call" button on her cell. Glancing at the digital clock on her dashboard before turning off the ignition, she took note of the time, letting out a sigh of relief that she had made it before lockdown. Jaci took another deep breath, then stepped out of the SUV.

She had barely rang the bell when the door swung open, revealing a tall, thin blonde man with a familiar face. "Jaci?"

She smiled, genuinely happy to see him. He was one of the few men she knew who wouldn't give her a bunch of bull about whether or not she should be sponsoring a parolee who'd been convicted of voluntary manslaughter. He'd worked at the prison with her, and knew she could handle herself.

"Hey, Steve. I'm so glad you're working tonight. I had an emergency earlier today so Frank brought Andreus Shannon here for me. Where do I sign to pick him up?"

Steve whipped out the record book for Jaci to sign. "I showed him his room and he hasn't been back out yet, not even to go to the head. You know I watch 'em like an overprotective papa when they first get here. He declined dinner, so maybe he'll eat something once you get him settled. He's a cold one. You can see it in his eyes."

"Brrr." Steve shuddered, then laughed, his shoulders moving up and down as he thoroughly enjoyed his own joke.

Nothing quite like the sense of humor of a reformed ex-con, Jaci thought.

"Guess I might be a little cold myself if I'd been in prison since I was sixteen," Jaci said, offering him an accommodating smile.

"I know that's right. I was pretty cold myself when I first got out, but this is different. Something else going on with this one. I wouldn't say evil, but something… I don't know."

"Creepy?" Jaci offered.

Steve hunched his shoulders and lifted his hands, palms up. "You'll see what I mean. I'll go get him for you."

Still exhausted from crying all afternoon, Jaci leaned against the front desk and waited.

A few moments later, Steve returned with Andreus several feet behind him, a brown duffel bag slung over his right shoulder. The details of his crime etched in her mind, Jaci did a quick once-over, noticing his striking features, but once she looked into his stark green eyes, she could not look away. *Mesmerizing. This is gonna be interesting.*

Although she was not one to wax mystical or paranormal, the first phrase popping into Jaci's head was "dark force." If the man's presence hadn't been so intense, she would have laughed at herself for sounding like a sci-fi nerd, but Andreus' aura flooded the room, overtaking it like a flash tsunami. No one and nothing else could compete for her attention when their eyes met.

Andreus approached her, obviously being careful not to get too close.

Jaci extended her hand. "Hi. I'm Dr. Rothschild. Call me Jaci."

Andreus looked at her hand, and time seemed to slow to a crawl, the old wall clock ticking loudly.

Finally, he accepted it, covering her hand with his. "Andreus."

Unable to help herself, Jaci gasped. The very air seemed to spark, crackling around them with kinetic energy, and she was sure he felt it too because the spark was reflected in his eyes and he took a step back from her.

Jaci shook it off as a fluke

"I…apologize for not being there to pick you up. Thank God for Frank."

"Thank you for coming here now."

"You're very welcome, and on that note, we'd better get out of here before Steve locks us *both* in."

"Good to see you, Steve. Catch ya later."

She turned and headed for the door, Andreus on her heels. She was careful not to touch him again, but found that his deep, melodious voice left her wanting to hear more from him, to know more about him.

❧

Andreus followed Jaci to her car and held the door for her to slide into the driver seat before walking around to the passenger side. The night air felt good, but his back began to ache, his shoulder blades and spine suddenly throbbing. He knew it was not a result of his workout. In addition to the pain, a sense of foreboding grew more intense the longer they remained outside.

The moment he saw her, memories started to resurface from his dreams, Jaci's face front and center. They had never met before, but there was a strong connection between them in some way. When they touched, he had felt intense pain, hers, and he sensed that some entity or group of entities would take great measures to keep them apart.

"Thank you, Andreus. Nice to meet a rare gentleman these days."

He had no idea what to say to her. Starting conversations wasn't something he had ever been good at, so he simply watched the road, periodically surveying their surroundings.

"So Steve told me you didn't eat anything. Prison food is the worst, so I'm sure you have a craving for something. I'm not much of a cook, but we can stop and get whatever you want. Just say the word."

Jaci seemed oblivious to the ominous energy brewing around them as its intensity continued to grow, making it hard for him to concentrate on what she was saying.

"You're right. Prison food is crap, so I'm sure anything will be an improvement. I'd appreciate it if you just take me to one of your favorite places for takeout so we can get inside as soon as possible."

"Okay. You like seafood?"

"I'll eat just about anything." Andreus smiled, his pointed incisors scraping the inside of his upper lip.

"You're easy. There's a nice place close by with some variety, so if you have a taste for more than one thing, that's fine too."

When he didn't respond, Jaci glanced at him, her dark eyes narrowed. "You okay, Andreus?"

He didn't want to alarm her, but he knew she would have to deal with whatever dangers they were about to face, sooner than later. His ability to concentrate was now nonexistent. The pain in his shoulder blades had become unbearable, as if someone was tapping their way out with a sledgehammer. "No. We need to hurry and get off the—"

Sssss! Boom!

Andreus felt the air crackling around them just milliseconds before a single bolt of lightning came out of oblivion, striking the ground in front of them and knocking out two of the car windows. Sudden, inexplicable seismic activity shook the ground directly underneath.

The front of the car tipped up, and Jaci bumped her head on the door as the car tilted. Blood trickled from her wound. He pulled her to him, shielding her from the wreckage as well as he could, refusing to let her go even as shards from the windshield embedded in his back.

The hammering at his shoulder blades increased, ripping his back open with such force, he levitated against the car ceiling, breaking through the fiberglass as if tearing tissue paper. Andreus heard the back window crashing just as the car tumbled over and landed upside down.

That's when he saw the wings: his. Heavy black and green feathers shot out from his back, each one appearing to be as long as he was tall. He realized the wings had propelled him from the car, allowing him to hover over the SUV with Jaci in his arms.

Her eyes were like saucers as she looked up at him. Her entire body shook, a thin line of blood continuing to trickle from her forehead.

Andreus placed his palm over the wound, and her pain rushed through him again, images of a man and child lying next to her following an accident—a car accident much like this one. Immediately, as if the knowledge had always been there, he knew they were Jaci's husband and child. Images from his nightmares flashed before him like movie clips on a screen, swords clashing, loud voices, high-pitched and deep at once, a cacophony of sounds, destruction, and wings rushing toward him, toward them.

Another laser-like beam headed in their direction, and three winged beings, men, as far as he could tell, zipped through the night sky. The lasers seemed to emanate from their hands, and one of them fought the other two. The realization that they were in the open and still in danger struck him like a boulder.

He moved away from the road, dropping to his feet several times before successfully managing to carry Jaci to the line of trees. The newness of his wings seemed more of a hindrance than a benefit as he did not know how to use them to shield Jaci, and lasers continued to shoot through the sky, a few of them landing on the ground not far from their makeshift shelter.

Suddenly, everything was silent.

"You can come out now." Startled, Andreus turned to find the winged man who had been fighting the other two standing directly behind him.

He stumbled back, shocked that someone had been able to get so close to him undetected.

"Rehobeth." The man extended his hand and smiled, revealing pointed incisors exactly like the ones Andreus had spent a large part of his life hiding.

Realizing the danger had passed, he set Jaci on her feet, but kept her close as she glanced nervously from one of them to the other, her lips slightly parted.

"Your things." Rehobeth had obviously retrieved their belongings from the decimated vehicle. He glanced at Jaci, smiled warmly, and handed them to Andreus.

"Are the other two dead?"

Rehobeth nodded. "I'm sorry I arrived so late, but I didn't know about you until very recently."

Jaci's breaths were shallow and short, and Andreus knew that not only was she experiencing shock from their immediate situation, but she was reliving the accident that killed her family.

She glanced at Rehobeth again, then whispered to Andreus, "You look like him."

Rehobeth's smile turned into a grin, and Andreus had to admit that there was a strong resemblance between them. The resemblance extended to the same kind of energy or life force he had always sensed within himself. Rehobeth's wings were no longer visible, but Andreus recognized him as kindred, and immediately trusted him. Considering that he had never trusted anyone besides Helen and now Jaci, that was saying a great deal.

"Now that I've located you, we can discuss that later. For now, we'd better get you two some place safe. Those things I just killed are called minions, and not the funny cartoon kind. They were sent to kill both of you, and I'm sure there will be more of them soon. I have a truck just down the road."

Andreus turned to Jaci and she swallowed, her nails digging into his side as she clutched him. Her free hand shook as she brushed it across her forehead.

"Can you walk that far, or do you need me to carry you?"

Jaci nodded, her movements jerky. "I-I can walk, I think. Yeah. I need to walk."

Rehobeth led them to his truck and Andreus helped Jaci onto the seat. Her wound had healed as if it had never happened, but he felt her body still trembling. He admired her calm resolve. She seemed to be handling things well, despite everything she had been through.

Bracing himself, he felt the painful retraction of his wings as they receded into his back, no longer needed. They folded and joined with the muscles and nerve endings along his spine. When the pain finally subsided, he was able to breathe again.

Rehobeth waited patiently behind the steering wheel, a satisfied gleam in his eyes. "It only hurts like that the first time. Eventually it will be like lifting your arms and putting them down."

Andreus climbed in beside Jaci, watching her carefully as she slid as close to him as possible. The poor woman had to be in shock. Despite remaining questions, the feeling of shock was oddly absent for him. Instead, he acknowledged a sense of coming home, and anticipated finally learning more about who and what he really was, whatever the answers turned out to be. One thing had already been made clear to him: his instinctive need to protect Jaci from whatever dangers she was about to face.

One step at a time, Andreus thought. One mystery at a time.

To Be Continued

After three attempts at writing different urban fantasies with complete endings, the main characters in "Outreach" insisted on being a part of this urban fantasy anthology. I hope you've enjoyed their story so far.

For your FREE copy of Part Two, send an e-mail to: darielsdreamkeeper(at) gmail(dot)com. Please include "Good Things Anthology: Outreach" in the subject line.

PERSONAL RESPONSIBILITY
(A BLOOD RIGHTS STORY)

K. B. Thorne

I sat in the chair on the other side of my boss's desk, watching her read over the report I had just placed in front of her. Crossing my legs, I leaned back in my seat and crossed my arms over my chest to keep from chewing my already-devastated fingernails. I could see her eyebrows keep lifting like she wanted to look at me but was stopping herself, and my foot started swinging in the air entirely of its own accord.

"Torres," she finally said, closing the folder and setting it just to her left. She said my name but then nothing else, just took a deep breath and rested her elbows on the desk. She folded her hands, leaning her chin against them. I was just about to tell her that she had in fact gotten my name right, anything to prompt her, when she continued. "I can't do anything."

"Oh, come on," I all but whined. Uncrossing my legs, I planted my feet on the FBI regulation carpet and leaned towards her. "Nobody died." It seemed I put more weight on the zero-count death tally than anyone else.

"You discharged your preternatural abilities on a suspect," she stated, sounding exasperated.

I held up my hands with a shrug. "I didn't shoot anyone!"

She didn't look impressed. "Frankly, it would have been less paperwork for me if you had. Do you know the current agency regulations and filing for a

DPA?"

DPA equaled Discharge of Preternatural Abilities. It was a brave (insane) new world.

My name is Serafina Torres, and I'm an agent with the Federal Bureau of Investigations, stationed in the preternatural satellite office in Boston, Massachusetts. In the years since Cameron's Law, making all preternatural beings legal citizens of the United States, the country had changed—had to change—a great deal. Now there were things like the preternatural satellite office of the FBI. As an electrokinetic—which meant I could create and/or control electrical currents—I was assigned there.

Basically, I'm a human taser.

In the case before us, that was all I did. I used my abilities to stop a suspect who was running. He didn't die, although he did end up in the hospital for a few days. Just like when any force is exercised on a suspect, you file a report. I was sitting in front of my boss, hoping that there wouldn't be too much trouble rolling down the mountain about it. I didn't feel like riding a desk.

I didn't reply to her question, because I didn't think anything that would come out of my mouth would actually help. She sighed, either frustrated with me or relieved that I didn't speak.

"You're not going to be shelved," she assured me and I blew out a breath. "However, you're not going to like what you'll do instead."

"I hate it when you do that." I narrowed my eyes at her, and waited.

"Protective detail."

"Babysitting?!" I sounded like a teenager asked to babysit their toddler sibling, but I didn't bother trying to correct myself. I'd been working under this woman for long enough that she knew me for who I was.

She looked thoroughly unimpressed with my annoyance. That was how it usually was, so I wasn't bothered. I knew that nothing I said could change her mind.

Dropping my head, I sighed.

"Who?" I asked, defeated.

I saw the edge of a file folder enter my vision. Without looking at her, I took it and opened it. Inside, there was a picture clipped to the top left. The name was Ben Collins, and from a quick look at the image, I would guess he had some Pacific Islands in there. Maybe he was from Hawaii. Although why anyone would leave islands like that to come to chilly New England, I couldn't guess. Reviewing the stats, I saw that he was a vampire, but a young one. It had only been a few years since he Turned.

"He's a witness for the murder trial of Cameron St John," my boss said before I got to that part. That automatically made my eyes widen as I looked up.

It was widespread knowledge by now that a top level member of LOHAV—the League of Humans Against Vampires—had been arrested for the murder of Cameron St John, the werewolf who introduced the Preternatural Rights Act in the first place, back in 2010. He and his girlfriend Sadie Stanton had been attacked. Cameron was killed, and Sadie nearly.

But it had been years, and there had never been enough information to make an arrest. I now knew what had changed, but they'd been keeping word of a witness pretty tightly locked.

"As you can imagine," she continued, "we are highly concerned for his safety. Members of the LOHAV organization have been known to attack and kill preternatural citizens on the street for less reason than being a star witness for the prosecution of one of their elite."

Suddenly, this job looked much bigger.

"So far, we have no reason to believe that his identity has been leaked; we don't even think his existence has been leaked, but we're taking no chances. He's a vampire and completely vulnerable in daylight, so a guard during those hours is going to be the most important. I plan to have an agent on him at all times. We have to swap out the daytime agent, and you'll be taking his place. Only one more week until he testifies."

"So you're not really punishing me for the DPA?" I asked with a small half-smile.

"Not really," she agreed with a mirror expression. "Still, this will get you out of everyone's line of sight for a while."

I nodded. "When do I start?"

It took a whopping two whole days before my "quiet" daylight assignment went from standard to 'shit got real.'

Contrary to popular belief, vampires don't sleep in coffins in mansions better suited to Miss Havishim. Ben Collins lived in a modest first floor apparent, with one bedroom that was sealed off with heavy, oversized blackout curtains. As a young vamp, he was going down halfway through dawn and not waking until full dark. The night agent showed up before that happened and I arrived after dawn, so I never even spoke to him. He kept to his dark room in that coma vamps go to during daylight hours. I played on my laptop, caught up on paperwork, and started reading a new book.

This all changed on my third day.

It started with the smell of something burning. Instinct made me jump up and rush to the oven in his small, stuffed-in-a-corner kitchen. I happen to hold the world record for burned cookies and muffins, so the smell of burning anything made me jump and think I'd done it again. It took until I had a grip on the oven door's handle before I remembered that I wasn't cooking anything.

That's when the smoke detectors went off.

My human brain just shrieked: fire, panic! My FBI brain told me that someone had found out about our witness and where he lived. They were going to burn him alive while he was temporarily dead to the world. It might not have been the case, but I suspected. Whatever the source of the fire, however, one thing was before me: I had to get Collins out.

During daylight hours, vampires are asleep. It's a coma-like state that no amount of effort can wake them from. Only the sun can do that, and only by setting. Otherwise, the sun isn't exactly healthy for them. A little can burn, a lot can destroy.

It didn't pass my notice that this could be a ploy to get Collins out of the building; him like a dead man, and me compromised by dealing with his body. I checked the door and found the hall clear and traces of fire licking the end of it through the open door of another apartment. I rushed back in and called for back up and emergency services as I ran to the bedroom. The space was so short that I had only just gotten a person on the line as I opened the door.

I was explaining the situation very hurriedly as I looked into the pitch black room. Even though I couldn't afford the time, I was momentarily disoriented. In the age of electronics, and my chronic curtain shortfall, I had never seen a truly dark room. Only the light from the open door I stood in fell on anything, but it was enough to guide me to his body.

I almost tried to wake him, just out of habit, but caught myself. I finished with the phone and stuffed it into my pocket as I hurried to the side he laid on.

By quick estimation, I guessed Collins was 5'9" or thereabouts and happily not a big man. However, I'm only 5'5" and unlike shifters in human form, human psychics don't have super strength. At least I kept up with my physical fitness as a fed. I knelt down and pulled his dead weight to the edge of the bed and over my shoulders in a sort of firemen's carry. Grunting with the effort, I stood and staggered awkwardly out of the room. Both the smell of smoke and the smoke itself was getting stronger.

Not bothering to hide my noises of exertion, I made my way across the small apartment and to the door. I fumbled to get it open, finding the handle was already growing hot. I knew that was a bad sign. Entering the hallway, panicked people ran past me to get to the door. I followed a half-clad man down the smoky passage and to the exit.

Sunlight poured through the door as a stark reminder of the guy on my back and what his species was. I held him with one arm as I struggled to pull my gun, just in case this was a trap.

As I emerged, I didn't see any obvious threats. The overhang above the door kept the sun off us for the moment, but I could feel the heat behind me. Sirens were in the distance, but I had the bigger issue of the vampire now. He grew heavier by the moment and I needed to put him *somewhere*.

I looked up and down the street and my eyes fell on my car. I was parked at the curb not very far away.

Unfortunately, I had to holster my gun to get my keys. I staggered along the sidewalk and was more aware of the sun than I had ever been in my life. All I needed was to get my thumb on my key fob. I unlocked the doors twice, locked them, and set off the alarm as I jammed blindly at buttons before finally popping the trunk. I thought I heard sizzling behind me, but couldn't be sure if I was imagining it as I threw him—not very gently, really—into my trunk. I slammed the door, cutting off all light and providing some safety as I turned back to the building.

Above all the noise, I heard someone calling for help. With my eyes already on the building, I saw someone carrying a child out. I guessed the little one couldn't be more than two and the woman was wailing. "My father is still in there! He can't walk very well and I couldn't get them both!" She sobbed around the words.

Again, my brain wondered if this was a trap...but could I live with myself if it wasn't?

"What apartment?" I demanded of her.

She had that panicked deer look for a moment, like she couldn't get past the screaming of her child and the smell of the smoke to comprehend my words. I shook her and asked again before she stammered the number.

Still on the first floor.

I ran into the building.

The smoke was clogging the hall now and the heat hurt like hell. I crouched low and covered my mouth with my sleeve as I hurried forward, looking at door numbers.

1D. I hurried in and through the haze, I could see an elderly man with an obviously stiff leg trying to walk with his hands on the walls. I ducked under one of his arms. "Come on, sir," I said. "I'm a cop."

"Did Lisa get out?" He coughed before he finished the question.

"Yes," I replied, walking forward as quickly as the scenario would allow. "She and the kid are outside."

"Thank God." He sounded like he was crying, and I couldn't help feeling choked up. It was just the smoke, of course.

It was sensory overload and deprivation at once. I can't really recount how I made it out, but we did. Falling to the cement, I kind of dropped the guy but hey, we were out of the burning building. I hacked up a lung, but managed to look up and see that my car was still there and with no signs of an open trunk.

If this had been a trick, it was the most detailed and yet least successful.

Leaving the woman, Lisa, to her father and child, I pushed myself weakly to my feet and hurried to my car. I opened the trunk long enough to assure myself that the origami vampire was still there. He was, so I slammed the top shut and then sagged back to just breathe. My eyes stung, so I didn't bother looking at the source of the sirens drawing nearer.

A pair of agents came to take Collins—and my car with him—away to another, safer location. Meanwhile, I was down the street, sitting on the back of an open ambulance being offered oxygen that I swatted away, though I accepted the blanket because by now—with the adrenaline waning and fire further away—I was beginning to feel the late winter chill, even if it was abnormally warm for late February. I watched my boss walk up.

"Are you okay, Torres?" she asked, folding her arms across her chest and eyeing me up and down like she could see the state of my lungs with just her eyes.

"Yes, sir," I replied simply. "Have they put the fire out?"

She nodded. "For the most part." Pausing, she glanced back at the building beyond the line of fire trucks. "They can't get in to investigate yet, but I'll bet anything that it was arson."

I sighed, and resisted the urge to cough. "I would agree."

Her x-ray eyes returned to me. "Go home and get some rest," she said, turning and starting to walk away. She paused and looked back over her shoulder. "Good work, Torres."

"All I have to do to get a compliment is nearly burn to death," I said to myself and started chuckling, which made me start coughing, and the medic gave me the oxygen mask again.

My "go home and rest" only lasted a few hours.

I got a call, which told me to wait for a car. The car came and took me to some nondescript building that I could barely make out in the dark. The agent who drove me, who I didn't know very well and didn't bother to try and fix that, walked me up to the door.

At the door, after some hoodoo I wasn't witness to, it opened to reveal my boss. She led me inside while the other agent left.

"He's asked to see you personally," she told me by way of greeting. And there was only one "he" this could be, given the day and the setting.

Ben Collins looked *almost* exactly like his picture. With a human, that would of course be expected. Vampires, however, don't change physically. I knew the image in his file had been after he was Turned, so seeing that he had a scar at his hairline—pronounced with a small stripe of missing hair going back a couple of inches—was a surprise.

He stood up from the couch as I walked in, smiling as he held his hand out. I took it and shook.

"I am told that I have you to thank for the continuation of my un-life," he said with humor. "I never imagined I'd be so grateful for the trunk of a car."

His humor surprised me, and I laughed. "Yes, well. We work with what we have. I'm just glad it worked."

Collins inclined his head to me. "As am I, I assure you."

"Mr. Collins has asked that you be shifted to head up his protective detail from now on," my boss said. "That would put you on the night shift, starting tonight."

"If you're up to it, of course," he interjected. "I know that you took in some of that smoke."

Even if I hadn't been up to it, I never would have told them that. First off, because I didn't like admitting any kind of weakness in front of anyone. Secondly, this was a boon to my career, leading a detail and at the request of a star witness. I wasn't stupid enough to turn that down. I nodded instead. "I'm fine," I assured them.

"Good." My boss patted me on the shoulder, and then left.

"Well," Collins began a moment after we heard the door shut. "At least you will only have to put up with me for three nights, and then I testify." He gestured to the couch and we sat. "I hope to be better company living than dead, so to speak."

"I'm sure you're fine." I didn't settle in too much. Although we were now in a "safe house," I remained on edge. After what happened to the last place, who could blame me? I had never been on a protective detail like this before. What did one talk about?

The protracted, awkward silence proved I wasn't the only one. He got up and went to the other room, and I took out my phone.

And that was how the rest of the night went.

I wasn't looking forward to work the next night.

After an exhausting day and the night shift, I had gone home and collapsed. I slept straight through the day and woke up only once the alarm went off.

Although I was happy that I had gotten recognition, as with most things, it wasn't all it was cracked up to be. It had been boring. Now I got to do it for another two nights before making sure he made it into the courtroom for his star testimony. I would say for a man living under the shadow of assassination, he looked pretty collected.

I relieved the agent on shift after I arrived and proved I was who I said I was—a process that was far more complicated in an age of shapeshifters. I settled in for another boring night, but Collins had other plans.

"May I call you Serafina?" he asked as we sat on the couch. The television was on some reality show, but the sound was low.

"If you like," I said. "Friends call me Sera."

He smiled, resting his arm on the back of the couch. "I don't know I know you that well, but then again, you shoved me in a car trunk. That suggests we must be on friendly terms." He paused when I couldn't help but chuckle. "You're more than welcome to call me Ben."

It was hard to miss that he was, indeed, a good looking man but he also had a disarming way about him. I wasn't sure that was a good thing when you were required to be all FBI around a person, but still, it put me at ease that this night would be less boring than the one before.

"All right, Ben," I said, wondering if this was improper behavior. I didn't really need another mark against me with the DPA still over my head.

I'd read his deposition once I'd officially been made lead on the case. I knew that he'd been leaving a friend's home when he'd heard the commotion and seen the tail end of the beating that killed Cameron St John—humans with "brass" knuckles made out of silver. As preternatural beings, like vampires and werewolves, are allergic to silver, it can damage them bad enough that a human could beat them to death.

Which was what happened. Ben saw it and witnessed those who ran away. They'd shot him with a silver bullet when they saw him and before he could get away. He "went to ground" right away, which (I had recently learned) was when a vampire could sink into the ground into a coma far deeper than what happened to them during the day. It allowed their body to heal better, like a vampire's medical coma.

That explained the scar.

We chatted on and off through the evening. Around midnight found him standing and looking at the window. The shades were down, for protective reasons, but he looked like he wanted to see outside. I didn't blame him.

"Do you know why I was there that night?" He didn't specify what night, because we both knew I knew.

"Your deposition says you were visiting a friend," I replied, curious where this was leading.

He turned to me with a rueful smile. "A suicidal friend. I was talking him off the ledge, so to speak. I was trying to save a life, and then what happens? I'm too late to save another and nearly lose my own."

That surprised me. I couldn't reply for a moment then asked, "Would you do it again?"

"What's that?" His expression was curious.

"If you knew what would happen, would you still help your friend?" It might have seemed like a stupid question to most, but there were too many people out there that might say they wouldn't if they knew they would nearly be killed.

"Of course," he replied without hesitation. "It's why I'm here. No one knew I existed except the killers, and they wouldn't tell anyone. When I finally healed enough to rise, there was a cop car right at the end of the street. I went straight for him to tell him what'd happened, and find out how long it had been. I didn't know until I rose."

He had the bullet. His blood and brain tissue was still on it, proving it was in his head, and the rifling matched a gun that had been registered to the defendant. It explained why they didn't shoot Cameron, but why had she brought it at all was the question. At the time, she had been a lowly member of the burgeoning LOHAV group but had risen quickly in the years to follow.

"Don't you believe that if you can act, you have a responsibility to do so?" he asked. "You joined the FBI, so you must feel some sense of responsibility for others."

"You've got me there," I said with a smile. "I was a cop first."

"Why did you join the force?" He returned to the sofa and sat down, turning his body to face me.

I narrowed my eyes at him, but not with actual rancor. "I'm the cop. Aren't I supposed to be asking the questions?"

He smiled. It was full of teeth, but his fangs were "at rest." He said nothing, but the expression was just as disarming.

"I guess it's what you said, I felt a responsibility. There's shit everywhere, bad things happening to people. I guess I thought I could...do something. And my grades weren't good enough to be a doctor." I chuckled, shaking my head. "I guess that doesn't make me particularly unique. Shouldn't I be telling some dramatic story about what led me to this job?"

"Life isn't always dramatic."

My brows lifted. "Says the vampire star witness against the nation's biggest anti-preternatural organization?"

That made him laugh. "Well, my life wasn't so dramatic before that."

"You were Turned into a vampire," I pointed out. "Wasn't that dramatic?"

"Remarkably? Not really. It wasn't violent or a surprise. It was a mutual agreement." He shrugged casually, leaning into the back of the couch and resting his head on the fist.

I smiled. "I guess that makes us a couple of boring people."

The next night saw us playing poker. Never play poker with a vampire.

He had just raised the bet when there was a knock at the door. We both tensed and I pulled my gun, starting for it. Someone called the password, though, and I relaxed. I didn't put my gun away however, not until I was absolutely sure.

I kept the burglar chain on as I opened the door to check through it.

I was greeted with the business end of a can of mace straight to the eyes. I shrieked and stumbled back a step. "Saferoom!" I shouted, pawing at my eyes as I heard someone start banging against the door to break the chain. I kept my gun tight but down while I couldn't see and instead lifted my free hand, loosing a random shot of my electrokinesis. Someone let out a strangled sound.

Forcing my eyes open, I could see blurry images. Someone was on the ground in front of the door but I thought I saw a second. I released another stream, but they dodged back. I stepped back and dug my phone out of my pocket, calling the office for help. There was supposed to be an agent outside the building as well. What had happened to him?

As I staggered past the table where the poker chips and deck of cards remained, I saw that Ben wasn't there so he must have taken my command.

My vision was slowly coming back as I hurried to find Ben, who was in the small room hidden off the closet. I entered and nearly got my throat torn out before he recognized me. I stared at him in the dim light for a moment.

"I wonder why you need protection," I whispered, gesturing for him to follow me.

This hidden room connected to stairwell that led to the basement and then an exit. It was an old building with many odd quirks, which made it ideal as a safe house. I could feel my magic lingering just under my skin, unlike the pits of my mind where I usually stuffed it. It was like static electricity to normal people, that feeling that no matter what you do, you'll spark when you touch something.

I kept my gun out and held up, even if holding it and my magic so close together was painful.

This stairwell was narrow and dark. I knew he could see in the dark, but I wasn't feeling so great about it. However, knowing it was a straight shot, I knew I wouldn't get lost. I was more worried about someone following, but so far so good.

We reached the basement and some moonlight came through the high windows. I scouted everything and then went to the door. It was a non-descript wood creation at the very back of the building, overlooked by most unless they were looking for it. I checked to make sure that Ben was still with me and then I opened the door, using my aching eyes to peer out.

I saw a muzzle flash in the darkness and just barely slammed the door before a bullet drove itself into the door frame. My heart tried to crawl out of my mouth but instead a stream of curses that would make a sailor brush came free.

Right as they started banging on the door there, I heard them back at the metal door that led from the stairwell.

"Get down!" I shouted and then dropped my gun, putting my hands out to either side—one toward the wooden door and one toward the metal. I rarely had reason to stretch my powers this much, but desperate times... Electricity shot like lightning from both hands, striking bolts into the cement of one side and the metal frame of the other.

The end result was a blocked wooden door, and a melted metal frame.

I passed out.

When I woke, it took me a moment to remember where I was...and then I sat up like a shot. It was so fast that my head immediately swam and I fell back, only to realize that my head had been on his legs. Blinking up at him, I sat up again—this time more slowly—and looked around. We were still in the basement, and the doors were still blocked.

"You weren't out for long," he answered the question I hadn't asked. "If they're still trying to get in, it's been quietly. I haven't heard anything for a while now."

I rubbed my eyes, which still hurt, and then dug my phone out of my pocket. I realized it hadn't broken when I fell. Unfortunately, there was no signal down here either. I knew I had gotten my call out, but where were they?

"I can't tell if this means I'm good at my job or really bad," I quipped with a half-smirk, rubbing my neck. I looked around at the small basement. There were two windows, less than twelve inches high, toward the very top. I wondered why they hadn't tried breaking them in, but then I remembered how many plants were growing around the foundation. Maybe they couldn't see them.

"I'm not dead," he replied. "Or at least not in a more permanent state of death. That's something."

I chuckled. It was something.

I heard the sirens about fifteen minutes later, right about the time I began doubting I'd actually talked to anyone in the first place. I heard some shouting, then someone tried to open the door, and then someone banged on the windows. I grabbed my gun, just in case, but heard my boss's voice shouting through a few minutes later and let out a breath of relief.

"How well can a vampire move a pile of fractured cement?" I asked him with a tired smirk.

Despite their best attempts, Ben Collins made it to court and gave his testimony. The defense attorney tried to trip him up, but they really do give you a Cool, Calm and Collected spell when you become a vampire. He tripped over nothing and just glided through, totally together. I still didn't know him that well, but I couldn't help but feel a little proud.

Ben would remain under guard until the trial ended, but we were betting that LOHAV wouldn't try as hard now that he had testified. Revenge was an issue, but a little less of one. We moved him to a new safe house, and there was an investigation—separate to my protective detail—to find out how they'd learned the two addresses. We suspected a leak, but that was my boss's problem...until they showed up at our door again.

While Ben sat at the corner of the couch reading a book, I sat at the small dining table with my boss.

"So, do I get that DPA wiped off my record for a job well done?" I asked with a half-smile as I nodded back at Ben. I glanced over and saw him lift his eyes, smiling over the edge of the open novel.

"Yes," my boss replied, to my surprise. "Only to add two more."

"Oh, come on!" I exclaimed. She gave me The Look. I sighed and then smiled weakly. "At least I didn't shoot anyone?"

PSYCHED
(A LEGENDARY CONSULTANTS STORY)

Abigail Owen

CHAPTER 1

How had she gotten herself in yet another rough situation? Maybe she was a jinx? Or an all-things-evil magnet? *Try to be a good person, help out my fellow man, keep my nose clean, and all that. And what do I get for it? A bucket full of trouble everywhere I go.*

Quinn's mind spun on a continuous loop as she sat in the high-traffic coffee shop across the street from where she worked, waiting to meet her rescuers. Outside the large windows, New York City bustled by, all intent on getting where they were going for the workday. Many were sweating in the summer heat. Inside, she tuned out all the conversations, both spoken and mental, with practiced ease.

What had her on edge wasn't the noise in her head, but the conversation she'd overheard at work yesterday. People—ones like her—needed help. Fast. And then she needed to disappear, or risk ending up like them. She checked the door again and glanced at her watch. Where were the people she was meeting? They should've been here by now.

She tried not to shift as she sat in the green pleather seat, although her back was killing her. After spending the night in the cheapest, most out-of-the-way hotel she could find, with a granite boulder masquerading as a mattress, she'd concluded sleeping in an alleyway would probably have been more comfortable and about as safe. She'd try that out tonight. Maybe an alley by a clothes store, because she was already sick of the black pencil skirt and red blouse she'd been wearing for two days now.

"Quinn Ridley."

She glanced up at the deeply masculine voice and sucked in a sharp breath. She'd been sent his picture, of course, so she would be able to identify him today. While her phone had shown her a man not remotely her type—dark hair longer than she preferred, beard hiding what she suspected was a highly masculine face with hard planes and jaw, and a deadly serious demeanor—the image hadn't quite captured how tall he was, or the breadth of his shoulders and leanness of his body. Or, for that matter, the air of utter confidence and danger radiating from him, or the piercing blue eyes which seemed to see into her soul.

Daniel Cain.

Even his name instilled a strange combination of trepidation and confidence.

Quinn crossed her legs as a kick of unexpected attraction ricocheted through her. *Damned inconvenient timing.*

"Excuse me?"

She blinked up at the frowning man. Had she spoken that last bit out loud? She cleared her throat. "Yes. I'm Quinn Ridley."

"May we join you?" He indicated the other seats at her table.

Oh! He had brought friends. How had she missed them? Shock bounced around inside her, joining the slow burn of attraction. Usually she was more observant.

When she'd called Delilah—the woman who'd placed her in her current job—for help, Delilah had mentioned Cain would arrive with a team. His friends were equally large, muscled, and intimidating. And equally hot, except her body wasn't interested in them. All three men were dressed in pants and button-down shirts rather than the tactical gear they'd sported in the picture provided. Delilah always had the most interesting contacts.

Cain raised his eyebrows. She was sitting like an idiot, just staring at them. She gave a jerky wave to the seats. "Of course."

"She's nervous, boss," one of the two men said to Cain as they took their seats. How the tiny wooden chairs with their green padded seats held the three large men was a total mystery.

Deliberately, Quinn glanced between them with wide eyes, then took a sip of her coffee, barely noticing the rich flavor on her tongue as she pretended not to understand the language he'd used. *Russian. Perfect accent. Interesting.* Hadn't Delilah explained to them about Quinn's job, let alone her abilities?

"That's to be expected," Cain replied in equally perfect Russian.

She wasn't nervous of them. She was pissed at what she'd overheard yesterday, at what people could do to each other, and was determined to find a solution. But if these men wanted to make stupid assumptions about what she might understand or not, she wasn't about to correct them. Instead, she'd listen politely, then ask Delilah for a different team. She needed serious people to solve this problem.

Her glance strayed to Daniel Cain, who studied her closely. Did he suspect she'd understood? Maybe not so stupid after all. His air of utter confidence settled her in a weird way. What was with her anyway? She never responded to anyone like this.

Cain sat directly across from her, his blue eyes pulling her gaze like gravity. "I'm Daniel Cain."

Duh. She nodded an acknowledgment, though she didn't offer to shake his hand. Touch was complicated for someone like her.

"And this is Sawyer and Shaw."

Two dark blonde heads nodded in turn.

"Brothers?" she asked.

One—Shaw, she thought—grinned. "Twins."

That explained why the two men had the same general appearance—similar eyes, nose, builds, and so forth. "I see." She turned back to Cain. "And your other associate?" The picture had showed four men.

He didn't even blink at her knowledge of a fourth man on the team. "Max is outside in the car."

Her shoulders dropped a fraction. Everything matched Delilah's descriptions. "What do we do now?"

He eyed her speculatively with…what? Respect? Why? Because she was jumping straight to the point, perhaps? Did he expect her to be a frightened little rabbit?

"First, you're going to tell us everything. After that depends on you," he said.

"Me?"

He searched her expression, for what she had no idea. She stared back, giving nothing away. "Depending on what you have to say, we'll give you options."

Options sounded promising. Getting the hell out of here sounded better, as long as she knew the bad guys would be stopped first. Quinn stood up, her chair scraping across the stained concrete flooring in protest. All three men tensed. Not visibly, more a tightening around their eyes as they regarded her with careful interest.

"Going somewhere?" Cain asked.

"What I have to say shouldn't be discussed in a public coffee shop."

He narrowed his eyes. "You'd leave with four strange men? On their word?"

"Easy, boss," Sawyer murmured. Russian again.

Quinn put her hands on the table and leaned in, refusing to be intimidated. "I was provided pictures, descriptions, and names. You match up." She stood back up. "Do you want to waste more time on lectures? Or do you want to get started?"

Shaw choked back a laugh. "Feisty one, isn't she." Again with the Russian. Delilah's idea of funny could tend to the warped on occasion. Not telling these guys about Quinn's ability to understand all languages had to be her idea of a joke. In this case, even Quinn's funny bone was tickled. Always interesting to know what people were thinking when they thought you didn't understand.

Cain rose to his feet. Trying to intimidate her with his greater size now? "People can disguise themselves."

"Not from me. There's truth in words." Besides, she wasn't the helpless little girl she'd once been.

Cain's gaze sharpened as he absorbed her retort, as if he could delve into her mind. "You're a Psy." His words were a statement, not a question.

"No shit!" Shaw exclaimed, sitting up straight in his seat.

Sawyer elbowed him. "Shut up."

Quinn flicked a quick glance toward them. They'd used words she hadn't heard before. Did the twins have their own made-up language?

"Yes," Quinn confirmed, returning her gaze to Cain. Each of these men was also a Psy, though Delilah hadn't shared their specific psychic abilities.

Giving a grunt Quinn interpreted as satisfaction with her answers, Cain turned to the door. "Let's go."

Quinn grabbed her purse off the back of her chair and her laptop bag off the floor and followed him out of the shop, with Shaw and Sawyer bringing up the rear. Outside, a generic black sedan pulled up and Cain held the door for her. She ended up in the back seat with the Thor-look-a-likes on either side. Cain sat in the front, and Max was in the driver's seat.

He turned and gave her a once-over. "I'm Max."

"Quinn."

He faced forward and put the car in gear. "Where to, boss?"

"Our hotel."

CHAPTER 2

They made the trip in silence. Before she knew it, she was in a hotel suite—generic with the usual two queen beds, desk, TV, mini-fridge, and a view of the fire escape and the brick building next door. At least it smelled better than her room last night. Not much, but still. The air conditioner propped in the window made a high-pitched whine. The thing had to be on its last leg.

She turned from her quick sweep of the room to find four large men all staring her down. "How do you decide who sleeps together? Draw straws?"

Shaw sniggered, but a glance at Cain's rock-hard jaw showed her humor was lost on him. Rather than comment, he pulled out the desk chair and placed it facing the end of one of the beds, then sat and indicated she should sit on the bed facing. "Tell us everything you know."

She lowered herself to the mattress, her feet barely touching the floor, and tried to ignore his proximity and mouth-watering scent—evergreen and something darker. "What did Delilah tell you?"

"Not enough, apparently." His tone was even, but she'd bet money Daniel Cain was not happy with Delilah. "I'd rather hear it directly from you, anyway."

"Right." She settled her purse and laptop bag on the floor. "As we established earlier, I'm a Psy. My specialty is communication."

Cain leaned forward, elbows on his knees and gaze intense. Way too close, but she refused to back up or give an inch. Was that a flicker of awareness in his gaze? Quinn gave herself a mental shake. Of course not.

"In what way?" he asked.

"I understand every language and communication. All human languages, of course, but also animals, computers. Anything that can communicate."

"So you understood our Russian earlier?" Sawyer asked.

She flicked him a glance. "Da. Ya ponyal."

"And our twin-speak?" Shaw asked.

She quirked a smile.

"Damn."

Quinn's lips twitched at his disgruntled expression, but she returned her gaze to Cain and continued. "About five years ago, Delilah got me a job as an interpreter for the major world-wide political body which is headquartered across the street from the coffee shop where we met."

"What languages?" Max asked. She glanced at the man who stood in the corner of the room behind her. Broader than the other three, he had dark hair cropped military-short and fathomless dark eyes. Hard to get a read on him.

"English, French, and Spanish primarily. I also interpret Russian when the other Russian interpreters aren't available."

"But you speak everything?" Cain's question pulled her gaze back to him.

"Yes."

"Then why not interpret the other languages?"

"Delilah's suggestion—most people don't speak everything. Limiting the list looked more normal and helped me blend."

"Something happened at work?"

She considered the man in front of her. Daniel Cain caught more than most. Maybe because he paid such close attention. She could feel his gaze on her like a caress. "I overheard a conversation I shouldn't have."

"When?"

"Yesterday during the General Assembly, a delegate's aides were discussing the trafficking of supernaturally gifted people. From what I caught, they are slavers for people like us. I don't think the delegate knows."

Even now, fury and terror gripped her simultaneously. Trafficking and slavery in any form was horrendous. That they targeted her kind had Quinn on edge. She couldn't go through that again. Hence the goon squad to the rescue.

Cain raised a single eyebrow. "They discussed it openly?"

She didn't blame Cain for his skepticism. With translators of six languages listening, you'd think they'd be more careful. But…

"They were speaking Sumerian."

The men exchanged baffled glances. Only Cain remained focused on her, waiting.

"Is that unusual?" Max asked.

"Sumerian is an ancient language."

"So they assumed anyone listening wouldn't understand." Cain caught on quickly.

"Exactly. I only know two races who still speak ancient languages. Angels…" Terror again zinged through her and she couldn't quite hide her shiver. "And demons."

Silence hung over the room, thick and heavy.

"You're telling us we're dealing with demons?" Max rumbled from his spot in the corner.

Cain said nothing, though she could see his mind ticking over.

Unnerved by his penetrating gaze and what it did to her body—highly inappropriate given the current situation—she focused on Max. "Most likely. Angels wouldn't do the things they were talking about. Vampires are another possibility, given how ancient some are, but these didn't look like vampires."

"What? No pale skin or pointy teeth?" Shaw asked.

"Not exactly." In fact, the demons appeared as rather plain humans. Smart. Too ugly and they stood out. Too beautiful and they stood out. Better not to draw any attention. In their true form, supposedly, demons were astonishingly beautiful. Even more so than angels. Quinn wondered if that was true.

"What delegation?" Cain asked.

"Mauritolla."

"Damn." Cain muttered the word under his breath, but she caught it, though the others might not have.

Quinn's thoughts exactly. The Mauritolla archipelago, one of the world's most beautiful island destinations in the Caribbean, visited almost exclusively by the world's wealthiest people, also had several uninhabited islands, perfect for hiding captured supernaturals and using shipping lines to send them around the world. Also, a fair distance away from where they sat in New York City.

"Did they know you overheard?" Cain asked.

"I don't think they realized I could understand. Both of us interpreting French that day heard. Sarah, the other girl with me, wondered what language they spoke. I said I didn't recognize it."

"Then why the call to Delilah?"

She raised a single eyebrow. "I wanted to check off my good deed for the day."

Four sets of eyes stared back at her—three confused. Cain was...amused? No, that couldn't be right.

Quinn stood and put her hands on her hips. "Do I really have to spell it out? They are hunting our kind. Not only does that put me in danger if they discover me under their noses. But people like us—" She waved at the men in the room. "—are being held captive and slaved out for their powers. I couldn't let it go."

Before she got the hell out of Dodge.

"Okay." Cain held up his hands. "I had to know."

Comprehension dawned and she glared. "You were testing me?"

"Sorry." He didn't even have the grace to grimace.

"No you're not."

Sawyer, or maybe Shaw, coughed to cover a laugh, and Cain shot him a glare over her shoulder.

Quinn resumed her seat and glared at the man in front of her. "You said I have options."

Cain leveled a calculating stare her way. Was that a spark of respect in his eyes? Why did a warm glow ignite in the region of her heart at the thought? This man was nothing to her after he got her out of here.

"Yes, options… Two."

She waited for him to continue. When he didn't, she crossed her legs, prepared to outwait whatever test he ran on her now.

His lips quirked. Barely. "Option one: we relocate you somewhere safer."

Sounded good, but what about the demons? "And option two?"

"You help us investigate the demons and put a stop to it."

CHAPTER 3

To give her credit, Quinn didn't appear nervous as they made their way through security. In fact, he'd been impressed with how calm she'd been, given the situation. A trafficking ring was bad enough, but one which would be interested in her should've had her terrified. While he detected nerves, he could see that she focused only on what was to be done.

Cain's new employee badge had been overnighted, and he sailed through without a hitch.

"How did Delilah get you access so quickly?" Quinn whispered as she led the way to the elevators. "The process usually takes a while."

Cain flicked her a glance. "I don't ask how when it's Delilah."

She hummed a response he interpreted as agreement.

They rode to the third floor in silence, her soft floral scent teasing him, though he was determined to ignore the kick of attraction which had started the moment she'd looked up at him in the coffee shop yesterday. Along with a strange sense of familiarity. But he'd never met Quinn before. He didn't think he'd forget her heart-shaped face, or those soft eyes which seemed to take in everything.

He waved her ahead when they reached their floor, and they exited the elevator into a long, generic hallway lit by fluorescents above, which buzzed quietly in the background. Fewer people in this area than downstairs.

"Hey, Quinn!"

His companion waved at the two ladies passing in the hall.

"Thanks again for bringing my favorite muffin yesterday. Made my day," one said.

Quinn's answering smile was pleased. "Of course, sweetie." She didn't stop to chat, though, pulling him along in her wake as she kept walking.

As they passed him, both women stared at Cain as though he were a chilled bottle of wine and they wanted a drink. Focused on the job he had to do and the woman at his side, for his part, Cain nodded politely but otherwise kept moving.

Hard not to focus on Quinn Ridley. The woman was a dynamo in tiny packaging. He doubted she was more than five feet on a good day and slender with it. Her hair was a thousand colors which, if pressured, he'd call brunette, but golden brown with streaks of blonde was more accurate. She wore it to her shoulders in long layers she tucked behind her ears, adding to the pixie-like impression.

Usually he preferred platinum blondes, so why he was attracted to this particular pixie was a damn mystery. Yesterday, he'd walked into the coffee shop and taken a sucker punch to the gut when she glanced up, defiant and wary, and lust had slammed through his system. A strange reaction he intended to leave an unsolved mystery. His job was dealing with the demons she'd uncovered.

"Interpreters dress better than I expected for people who are heard but rarely seen." The comment popped out of his mouth.

She gave him a glance that clearly said she found the comment odd, but shrugged. "Sorry you had to bother wearing a suit. We're professionals. Plus, on occasion, we are asked to perform individual interpretation, which requires being seen."

He rumbled an unintelligible reply. The suit didn't bug him. In his line of work, disguises were often necessary, so he wore suits with practiced ease. That wasn't why he'd said it. He knew exactly where the thought originated. From the way her skirt hugged her curves and how her heels made her legs incredibly sexy. But saying it out loud? What on earth was wrong with him today?

"In here." She turned the handle on one of a series of doors spaced across one wall and led the way into the French interpreter's booth. The space was glass-fronted, impersonal, and well lit, about the size of a jail cell. In the cramped area, Quinn's light scent, flowery and sweet, stole around him. Through the one-way glass, the desks of the delegate hall spread out in a semi-circle, sloping, stadium-style, to the podium center stage below. The delegate hall was currently about half-full, occupied mostly by men in suits.

Quinn took one of the two seats and pulled her computer out of her bag, setting it on the desk. "Sarah will be in any second, which means, unfortunately, you'll have to stand."

Disregarding her, he took the other seat. "No, she won't."

She swung her gaze away from her computer screen to stare at him. "What do you mean?"

"Sarah's on paid vacation. I take it she won an all-expenses paid trip to Paris. I'm your partner for the foreseeable future."

Crossed arms and narrowed eyes greeted his statement. "I assumed you were here for protection."

"Too conspicuous. Better if I'm here in a professional capacity."

"Fan-frickin-tastic," she muttered.

"Excuse me?"

She flicked a wide-eyed glance, full of surprise, his way. Then her expression blanked and she went all professional on him. "What languages do you speak?"

Unaccustomed amusement tickled at him. He got the impression she hadn't meant to say her first comment out loud. "English."

She waited for him to continue. "And…?"

"That's all."

Quinn's lips flattened. "So how will you be translating, exactly?"

"I'm going to borrow your power."

She straightened in her seat. "How?"

"My ability is psychometry. Among other things, I have Ability Learning and Knowledge Replication. As long as I'm touching you, I can mimic your abilities, including anything you've learned through experience."

She sat back in her seat, mollified. "I see. Handy trick."

"It has its uses." Why wasn't she more impressed? In the Psy world, psychometry was a rare and coveted skill.

"As long as you don't—" Quinn broke off with a barely audible gasp. If he'd been an empath, he'd bet anger would be sparking off her now.

Cain turned to follow the direction of her gaze to find a group of men entering the delegation hall. "Is that them?"

"Yes." The word came out like an expletive.

Despite himself, Cain was impressed. Most would cower and hide in the face of that kind of danger. Not Quinn Ridley. Instead she was fuming. As fast as she'd jumped at the opportunity to help take the demons down, he got the impression this was a personal vendetta for her.

At the same time, he had to wonder if her sense of self-preservation was off. Not only was she willing to go after demons, but she showed zero trepidation around him. Most of the time, people avoided him, gave him a wide birth. Not that he deliberately pushed them away. Max said he had *one of those faces*. However, Quinn didn't act intimidated or nervous of him. Annoyed—yes. Intimidated— no.

She pulled her glare away from the Mauritollan delegation and raised her hands to the keyboard. Hands which trembled uncontrollably. So Quinn *was* afraid. The strangest urge to protect her thrummed through Cain, and a bitter tang hit his tongue. If he didn't know better, he'd say he tasted fear, but that couldn't be right. Granted, his original job was to get Quinn out of the situation safely, but he never got personally involved. Never.

"Don't worry. I'm here." The words were out before he consciously thought them. Another odd reaction, all these thoughts coming out as words. Did she have another power he wasn't aware of yet?

Cain almost laughed out loud at the incredulous glare she slowly turned his way, those grey-blue eyes disbelieving.

"Lucky me."

He couldn't miss the sarcasm. Strangely, instead of finding her sass annoying, he fought another urge to chuckle. Damn, he must finally be losing it. Psys had a higher rate of mental illness than most. Still, the fear that had her shaking needed to be addressed. She needed to know he had her back.

He held her gaze with his steady one until her shoulders dropped slightly. After a deep breath, she nodded, and the acceptance of his offer of protection hit him like an arrow to the heart. He *would* protect her from harm, he silently vowed, at the same time perplexed about his unusual reaction to her. While he helped a lot of people in his line of work, emotional attachment wasn't his thing.

"Time to get to work," she murmured, businesslike demeanor firmly in place, and she tuned him out as she turned back to her computer and flipped on her microphone.

Almost immediately she began translating, taking notes here or there, he guessed to help her remember what the delegate had said. Cain watched and listened in fascination as, real-time, she took what was being said in English and repeated it in French with hardly a pause and no ums or uhs or other verbal fillers. Making it more difficult in this instance, the delegate from China was speaking. Consequently, the Chinese interpreter would first interpret any spoken Chinese into English, and Quinn would translate into French. Not that she needed the assist, but still.

After twenty minutes, she indicated he should switch on his own microphone. Before he did, he took her hand—warm and delicate under his grasp. Momentarily, he was distracted by an odd sense of peace that washed through him at her touch, but shook it off and closed his eyes, concentrating. A sensation like ice slithered up his fingertips, through his nerves, up his spine and, like shards splintering through him, into his brain. Gaining someone else's knowledge, even temporarily, was never pleasant. Agony might be a better term.

Suddenly, a cacophony of noise fractured through his mind as her ability to understand all communications kicked in. Holy crap. She hadn't been kidding. What she hadn't mentioned, however, was she received everything, like every radio station playing at the same time. Even phone calls, the computer thinking through its programming. Everything. The urge to slap his hands over his ears and make it stop was overwhelming. How had she not gone crazy listening to all the noise?

His Knowledge Replication took over next. That part usually took longer to sink in. Gradually, he found he could tune out the noises, focusing only on what he wished. He wondered how long it had taken her to master the skill? How long had she lived with the voices and chaos inside her head?

As the pain of his ability faded to prickling, he had everything he needed. After what constituted ages to him, but probably only a minute to her, he opened his eyes to find Quinn watching with avid curiosity. Like a seasoned vet, he switched on his microphone and started interpreting the words being said in the delegation hall on the other side of the glass.

None of the Mauritolla delegation turned or acted surprised in any way to hear a man's voice. Good.

CHAPTER 4

Quinn watched the streets of New York blur by as the taxi took her and Cain away from the headquarters after they'd finished work for the day. "Explain to me again why we're going back to my apartment, rather than the hotel?"

The hotel with all the other members of his team. Wasn't there supposed to be safety in numbers?

"We want to act as normally as possible."

"Normal doesn't include having a man in my apartment," she muttered at the window.

"Oh?"

Quinn scrunched up her face. Shoot. She'd said that out loud. Again. What was it about Cain that had her blurting out her thoughts like this? If she didn't know better, she'd think interest had sparked in his deep voice, but she refused to turn his way. Resigned to the next few hours, she remained quiet the rest of the ride home.

George, the super for her building, stood outside working on a window. "Hey, Quinn!" he greeted when she stepped onto the sidewalk. "Thanks again for those Broadway tickets. Sally loved it."

She grinned. "I'm glad."

He glanced at Cain with avid curiosity, but she kept going inside.

"Tickets?" Cain asked as they hiked up four flights of stairs.

"I did a personal interpreting job at a party for the French delegates, and they gave them to me as thanks. Sally had mentioned wanting to see that show. No biggie."

Cain's grunt told her he wasn't so sure, but she wasn't in the mood to argue with the man.

She unlocked and opened the door to her apartment cautiously, semi-expecting her place to be ransacked, like in the movies. But her apartment was exactly as she'd left it. Relief surged through her in a wave. The mere thought of strangers going through her things gave her the heebie-jeebies.

She put down her laptop bag and purse by the door, kicked off her shoes, and moved further inside, flipping on lights as she went. Wrung out didn't begin to cover her current state of being. "So this is what? Friendly dinner with the new colleague?"

It didn't escape her that Cain filled her small one-bedroom apartment more than was comfortable, taking up her breathing space.

He didn't comment. Instead he searched the place thoroughly, not that it took him long. Even after five years here, she still kept it pretty basic. Bed and dresser and night stand in the bedroom. Couch, coffee table, and TV in the living area, and a small kitchen table in the kitchenette. Even the décor was still the generic stuff Delilah's team had furnished the place with at the time—reds and tans. She liked it well enough, so she didn't bother to change it. Cain took off his jacket and draped it on the back of a kitchen chair before he dropped casually onto her couch and loosened up his tie.

She ignored the pitter-patter of heart at the sexy image he presented and lifted an eyebrow. "Make yourself at home."

He ignored her sarcasm. "Nice place."

"Thanks."

"Not a lot of pictures."

Especially of family. Damn observant man. "I'm camera shy." She'd rather not hear his psychoanalysis of her life. "Can I get you a drink? Water? Iced tea? Beer?"

He let her change the subject. "Beer sounds good. Thanks."

Quinn spun on her heel, headed into the kitchen, and pulled a bottle of her favorite beer and a pitcher of iced tea out of the fridge, then got down a glass.

"I assume you'll get a taxi back to the hotel?" she called.

"I'm not leaving."

She paused pouring the tea into a glass.

"Why not?"

"As your new fiancé who moved here from Paris and got a job with you to be closer, it would look odd if I went and stayed with a bunch of men. Don't you think?"

Quinn snorted and opened a canister of sugar which sat on her countertop. "Good one."

Silence greeted her. She stopped spooning sugar into her glass and glanced over the counter to find him watching her with patient expectance.

She scowled. "Hell, no."

"I'm afraid so. We need to appear normal. You need protection. There's no chance I'm leaving you alone."

"Has it escaped your notice there's not enough room here?" She waved at the apartment. "Where do you think you'll sleep?"

"In your bed."

Her heart kicked it up a notch and her body screamed yes, but her mind balked. "You really don't value your life. Do you?"

Was that a smile tilting the corners of his mouth? *Nope. Not sexy. Do not think of him as sexy.* She chanted the mantra in her head, refusing to acknowledge how she was failing miserably to adhere to her own instructions. The man was sex appeal wrapped up in a fabulous package. Instead she narrowed her eyes. "What? You think I'm funny?"

"I think you're fighting the inevitable."

"I think you're delusional. It's sofa city for you, sweetheart."

Cain broke out in a full-bellied laugh. His smile transformed his face from broodingly handsome to drop dead gorgeous, and heat pooled low as fierce attraction swept through her in response.

"I don't think anyone's ever called me sweetheart before."

She didn't doubt it. She pointed her spoon at him. "I'm serious. You're not sleeping in my bed."

"Your fiancé would."

She spread her arms wide. "No one is here to know the difference."

"Honey, we're dealing with demons."

His calm logic only infuriated her more. If rumors were to be believed, demons could see through walls. Quinn gritted her teeth. "Fine," she spat. "But I sleep on the left. Touch me and I'll cut off your hand. And you'd better not snore."

He held up both hands. "I make no promises."

"Grrrr." Quinn growled her frustration and refused to acknowledge the panic tingeing the emotion. What if she did something really stupid? Like jump Cain in her sleep?

She moved around the counter, shoved Cain's beer at him, then yanked her cellphone out of her purse. She'd had a crappy couple of days. She needed pizza. Her favorite place picked up on the second ring. "Hi, Tony. It's Quinn. Yeah, I'll need the usual, please."

She glanced at Cain, who listened with raised eyebrows. "Make that a double order. Thanks."

❧

Quinn bolted upright in bed, gasping for air. Her nightmare, the one she had every night, dissipated as consciousness returned. But fear of a different sort seized her in the dark of the middle of the night—someone was in her room, in her bed. Without zero hesitation, she whipped out the knife hidden between her mattress and box spring and was on top of her intruder, knife at his throat, in a flash.

She froze as recognition slammed into her. Daniel Cain lay under her as she straddled him, his hands held up in a surrender-like gesture. Only the blaze of his pale blue eyes told her he hadn't surrendered. The sound of her panting breaths was the only noise in the room.

"Quinn?"

"Oh, god, I'm so sorry!" she mumbled.

As fast as she'd jumped him, Quinn rolled away, careful not to nick him with the knife. She sat with her back to him, legs dangling off the side of the bed, and stuffed her weapon back into its hiding place before dropping her head into her hands.

"If you didn't like my beard, all you had to do was say so. No need to shave it off for me."

His unexpected teasing pulled a huff of a laugh from her. "Normally, I don't like beards on men."

"But you like mine." An interesting tone of satisfaction layered his words. The rustle of sheets told her he sat up.

In fact, she found his beard, neatly trimmed to a point and sporting streaks of grey that gave him a distinguished air, sexy as all get out. "Maybe. Not very comfortable for kissing though." *Dammit. Did I just say that out loud?* This was becoming a bad habit.

"Were you planning on kissing me?"

She scrunched up her face. She had said it out loud. Time to screech this conversation to a halt before she said something that got her in real trouble. "Sorry about the knife."

His grunt told her he'd caught the change of subject. "Was it your nightmare or having a stranger in your bed that set you off?"

"Both." She lifted her head from her hands and scooted around to face him, crossing her legs. That she was comfortable with him as she sat there in a t-shirt and pajama shorts, and he in nothing but his boxers, struck her as odd. Though she didn't mind the eye candy his bare chest provided.

"Tell me."

Surprisingly, she didn't take the softly couched words as a command, more an invitation.

"I'm guessing Delilah didn't share much with you about me?"

His lips quirked. "Remind me to thank her for that, by the way."

She gave him a half-smile. "Like most telepaths, I came into my powers when I was seventeen."

"Did your family have any history of Psys?"

She shook her head. "Not that they knew of. I had a great-aunt who'd been institutionalized at the same age for schizophrenia. One day, she just stopped talking."

Cain nodded. In families who didn't already know the signs, blaming mental illness was common.

"I was taken to a series of doctors because of the voices in my head."

Another nod.

"One of those doctors turned out to be a Psy. With my parents' permission, he had me taken to what they were told was a hospital to treat my illness."

"But it wasn't?"

Quinn swallowed. "No. It was a...cult, for lack of a better word. Not unlike being slaved out. I was taken to a facility in the middle of the wilderness, impossible to escape. I was used for my powers." For two long years. She shuddered.

"How did you get out?"

As usual, the black hole where that memory existed sneered at her. "I don't remember. I woke up in a hospital. Delilah was there. She said her team got me out. After I recovered, she got me my job here and this apartment."

"When was that?"

"Six years ago."

A flicker of emotion passed over his face, too quick for her to catch. "Where were you held? Do you know?"

"Somewhere in Alaska."

He was silent so long she wondered what was going on in his head, but his expression was carefully neutral.

"What's your nightmare?"

She blinked at his sudden question, then inhaled before speaking. "I'm still there. Trapped. Used. Terrified. I promised myself I'd never be vulnerable again. Delilah helped by having me trained to fight."

Again that flicker behind a mask of blankness. What was running through his head?

"I might be able to see more about your escape. Do you want to know?"

She'd bet her life the offer was a rare one for him to make. "So Retrocognition is another one of your skills?"

A hum of affirmation.

"Why?"

He seemed to understand what she was asking—why was he helping? "Maybe knowing will help your nightmares go away."

Doubtful. They came to her every night. Still…maybe finding out was worth the try. She licked her dry lips. "Okay."

He gazed deeply into her eyes, as if searching for any shred of doubt, but she gazed back steadily. Finally, he nodded. "I have to touch you."

Quinn grimaced. "Okay." Physical touch could be weird for Psys—a constant bombardment of their senses making it difficult for them to form relationships. For her, the connection could make the voices in her head, the ones she'd learned to block out, louder. Although come to think of it, today at work, when he'd touched her to gain her abilities to translate, nothing had happened. Weird.

Cain reached out and placed both hands on either side of her face. Again, no amplification of the voices. If anything, an unusual peace settled over her. Was he using his power on her? But no, a psychometric couldn't soothe. Maybe being near another Psy helped?

He closed his eyes and inhaled deep and slow. "I see caves? Cells?"

"Where we lived. An abandoned mine system."

"You're locked in a room." His lips tightened. She knew what he was seeing. How pitiful her living accommodations were. The room where she'd been held had sported a bed and small table. Overhead lights swung from the rock ceiling, but she hadn't controlled when they were on or off. At least she'd been well fed and had books supplied.

"I wasn't kept in there all the time. Mostly at night. They needed my... services...too often."

"You're asleep."

His brows drew down. "Loud noises. An explosion."

Why couldn't she remember?

"Gunfire now."

Total black hole for her.

"It's gone quiet." He continued to concentrate. "Someone's coming down the hall. You can hear footsteps. The door is opening—"

He was quiet for a long moment.

"What's happening?" she whispered.

"A man opened the door. He's holding a samurai sword. You asked him if he was there to kill you." The way he said kill made her shiver. A bottomless depth of fury laced the word. Why? For her? At her captors?

"What'd he say?"

"He said he was there to get you out. That you'd be okay now."

Cain opened his eyes, a blaze of heat lashed at her from his gaze—anger, desire, triumph, something darker that she couldn't identify. A confusing cocktail of information. He didn't need to say the words for her to hear the emotions.

She licked her lips. "What did I say?"

He didn't speak. She wasn't even sure he caught the question, too intently focused on her. Her lungs squeezed tightly, making it difficult to breathe. Carefully, she placed her hands over his. "Cain?"

He jerked slightly under her touch. "You kissed him." The words were dragged from him—rough and tortured. His gaze dropped to her lips, and need pulsed through every nerve in her body. What was going on?

"Daniel?"

With a low groan, he pulled her to him, his lips covering hers in a kiss both possessive and demanding. Sensation blew through her, the heady scent of his skin, the rasp of his beard against her face, the taste of his tongue as he claimed her mouth. Needing more, she practically climbed into his lap when, suddenly, the tenor changed. Gentle hands pulled her away as he broke the kiss.

"Not a good idea."

He set her away from him, on her side of the bed, then got up and left the room.

CHAPTER 5

Ten days later, Cain followed Quinn into her apartment. After putting her purse and laptop bag down, she stood there with her hands on her hips.

Concerned, he put a hand to her shoulder, her tension screaming at him through the stiffness of her shoulders. "Hey. You okay?" She'd been unusually quiet at work today.

"We're not getting anywhere, Cain." Frustration filled every syllable.

Quinn Ridley truly cared about the people the Mauritollans had taken and were selling to the highest bidder. After learning about her history, he understood why she cared so much. That she hadn't run away in terror, to protect herself, impressed him. That he shared her frustration connected him to her in a way he didn't understand and was reluctant to explore.

He still hadn't told her that he was the man who rescued her in Alaska. As soon as she'd described that night, he'd known. Maybe he'd known on some level anyway, having the strangest sense of already knowing her since meeting her in that coffee shop. But he didn't want her distracted by the past. He needed her focus on this situation. Hell, he needed his own focus on this situation. He shouldn't be thinking about that kiss—one that hadn't ever quite left him in all these years.

He squeezed her shoulder. "We'll get there. These things take patience."

She turned her grey-eyed gaze—which seemed to reach into his soul—in his direction. "Why do you do this?"

"What? Hang out with a gorgeous woman? I'd think that self-evident."

She rolled her eyes. "No. Why do you use your abilities to help others? You're in just as much danger as I am from these people. So why?"

He considered her earnest expression. Unable to resist, he reached out and tucked a silky strand of hair behind her ear. Beyond a soft flush on her cheeks, she didn't react or stop waiting for an answer.

Making a snap decision, he whipped out his phone and texted Max his plans. Then he bent down and grabbed Quinn's purse, holding it out to her. "Come on."

She regarded him with raised eyebrows. "Where are we going?"

"I need coffee—good coffee—if I'm going to talk about why I do what I do."

Quinn took a sip of her coffee and cocked her head at Cain, who sat across the table from her in the cozy, boho-style shop, a look of pure bliss on his face as he gulped down scalding coffee. Black.

"I don't get it," she said.

He gave a hum of enjoyment as he lowered his cup. "Don't get what?"

"I like coffee as much as the next girl, but, while this is good, I don't taste much difference from the coffee shop on the corner by my house."

"Then you're not a true coffee lover." Cain grinned, and the impact struck her in the solar plexus. He didn't smile often, and now she was kind of grateful for that fact. Over the last ten days, her awareness of Cain had blossomed into full-blown attraction.

Despite the fact that he was a battle-hardened Special Ops leader, Cain had a chivalrous streak a mile wide. Small thing like holding doors. Bigger things like taking her out for coffee to try to get her mind off the people they weren't saving.

Fact was, she liked him—as a person. She wasn't quite sure what to do with that.

Cain leaned back and propped his foot on his knee. "You asked why I do this?"

She took another sip of her coffee. "Yes."

"I went into the navy as soon as I graduated from high school. With my… special abilities, which include ability learning, enhanced marksmanship, and weapons proficiency, I did well. Eventually, I became a S.E.A.L. and spent several years putting my skills to use for my country. I'd like to think I saved lives."

That explained the dangerous edge she could sense in him. And the way he moved. The way he entered a room and took in every detail. Despite the humbleness, truth rang in his words, and she could sense what he wasn't saying. He definitely saved lives.

"Why'd you quit?"

"I got a call from my parents. My sister was missing. Like me, she had inherited their telepathic abilities, hers manifesting in a true psychic ability to see the future."

Darkness infiltrated his voice now, and Quinn wasn't sure she wanted to hear what came next.

"Max was her fiancé. She'd met him through mutual friends like us. Together, we managed to track her down."

Quinn closed her eyes. "It was too late, wasn't it?"

Cain twisted his cup in his hands, gaze far away, trapped in memories which made his mouth flatten in a grim line. "Yeah." He took a swig of coffee.

"Like you, she'd been taken to be used for her skills. When she deliberately started feeding them false futures, losing them millions, they killed her. Two days before we found her."

Unable to help herself, Quinn leaned forward and put her hand on his arm. He tensed under her touch, not in a psy-to-psy kind of way, more like he hadn't been expecting it, but she refused to pull away. "I'm sorry."

He stared into her eyes for a long moment, and somehow she knew that he'd taken comfort, even a small amount, from her words and her touch.

"Yeah," he muttered.

"Delilah was involved in our finding Casey, my sister, in the first place. She offered me and Max a job, hooked us up with the Thor look-a-likes, and the rest is history."

Quinn's lips twitched at his description of the twins. That was how she thought of them. But she wasn't letting him just skip over the important part. "You couldn't save her, so you save others now."

Again, that steady gaze reached inside her. "Is that what your powers tell you?"

She shook her head. "I don't need to be a Psy to see that." She placed a hand on the side of his face, his beard tickling her palm. "You're a good man, Daniel Cain. You would have saved your sister if you could. Your sister would have seen that. She knew you loved her."

If she hadn't been touching him, she would've missed how much her words shook him up. He tensed under her hand, and desolation—bleak and dark—filled those blue eyes. "I know," he muttered.

She lowered her hand but jerked when he suddenly grabbed hers before she could sit back. "You remind me of her sometimes," he murmured, soft and low. "Same feisty streak. Same determination to help others. Same caring heart."

Her turn to be shaken now—he seemed to see her. The real her. If she wasn't careful, she could fall for Daniel Cain. Every doubt associated with that thought made her panic and pull back. Time to do something to cut through the thick intimacy which surrounded them.

She squeezed his hand. "I like her already."

He smiled and let her go. "Same way of not letting anyone get too close."

Her eyes widened as she caught the teasing twinkle in his. Did he want to get close?

Part of her wanted an answer to that, and part of her didn't. She definitely needed some distance, and they had more important things to deal with right now. "We need to get these guys, Cain. Before they ruin another life."

"We will."

CHAPTER 6

Cain sat, his butt numb, in the uncomfortable seat in their interpretation room and listened as Quinn translated with amazing ease while the delegates on the other side of the glass did their thing. Even though he could do the same when he touched her, the skill never ceased to impress him. Yes, her gift gave her an advantage, but still, her job demanded cognitive prowess to both listen and speak almost simultaneously while jumping through additional linguistic hoops such as syntax, humor, and colloquialisms.

Plus, he could listen to the husky rasp of her voice all day and never tire of the sound. Lately, he'd taken to fantasizing about hearing her voice as they made love. A fantasy not helped by the soft flowery scent of her skin, which filled the small space and surrounded him. The same thing happened at night when they slept. Or she slept, and he lay there wide awake.

Cain gave himself a mental shake and focused on the Mauritolla delegation. His attention needed to be on Max at this instant, not on the woman in the booth beside him. After the first week of getting nowhere, Cain ordered Max to employ his Illusion Manipulation, disguising himself as one of the Bahamian delegate's entourage, who sat beside the Mauritollans, in an attempt to get someone closer. That had been two weeks ago.

With a weary sigh, Quinn flipped off her microphone and pushed back from the desk, her chair rolling silently across the carpeted floor. "Should be it for the day."

A quick check told him the U.S. delegate was speaking now, giving him and Quinn a break for a while, as they had no need to translate to English.

Today she'd worn a black swishy skirt paired with a white camisole hidden under a black suit jacket. She crossed her legs, and the silky material of the skirt slid back. Even her knees were sexy. And definitely her feet in those bright red heels, though the shoes currently lay in a pile under the desk. Amusement tickled at him. Quinn never kept her shoes on long.

Get your flipping head in the game, Cain, he harshly commanded himself.

"Max okay?" she asked.

He flicked a glance at both their mics, but the lights were off, so no one else could hear them. "Fine."

"He hasn't learned anything new. Has he?"

Cain kept his expression neutral as he turned back to the delegation hall beyond, where Max sat. "He's making progress."

"Liar."

He whipped his head toward her to find her laughing at him.

"Thought that would get your attention." She grinned, unrepentant.

He grumbled his irritation.

The smile fell from her lips as she sobered. "I know you're trying to protect me, or save me worry, or some such thing. I'm a big girl."

He'd noticed.

"Have we learned anything?"

"No."

"Too bad we don't have a true telepath on the team."

"Yeah." Cain often wished for that skill. The twins were telekinetic with different focuses. Usually, the combination of the four of men on the team was more than enough. However, when their primary duty was surveillance, like now, a telepath sure would come in handy.

"Time for a different tack, don't you think?"

Cain frowned at the resolution behind her words. Only three weeks with Quinn and he could read her like a book. He refused to acknowledge the suspected reason for that. Now wasn't the time. Yet. "What do you mean?"

"They're trafficking supernaturals."

He crossed his arms, already not liking where she was going with this. "So?"

"So it's time to offer up bait."

"You?" He tried to keep his gut reaction out of his voice but must've failed.

She cocked her head. "Why not?"

"I've seen what you went through last time you were slaved out." Even now he had to control the rage which boiled through him at the knowledge. That he had been the one to save her, the man she'd kissed that night, the man who'd assassinated those who'd held her captive—a fact he'd yet to share with Quinn— made little difference. He despised himself for keeping her in harm's way now. She was too…important…to him in a way he wasn't ready to label yet. But no chance in hell was he allowing her to get close to those men.

She narrowed her eyes. "I'm stronger now. Smarter. I'm not a seventeen-year-old girl anymore."

That was for sure. "No."

Like a rattlesnake striking, she spun to the desk and flipped on her microphone. She spoke softly in a tongue he'd never come across. She only got out a sentence or two before he managed to turn off the machine.

"What did you say?"

She tipped her chin defiantly. "That I know who they are and what they're doing."

He stood, both hands planted on the desktop and tried to reign in a mounting anger, a rock of pure fear weighing heavy in his gut. A glance showed the Mauritollan contingency not looking, but stiff in their seats. A couple of other delegations turned to stare up at the glass wall at the top of the room which hid the interpreters' booths, probably confused by the odd language suddenly spoken in their headsets. Only Max, in his seat with the Bahamians, appeared relaxed. No doubt they'd heard her. "What have you done, Quinn?"

"Too late now." She sat calmly, staring at him boldly despite the anger he was sure reflected in the scowl he turned her way. "You might want to stay at the hotel with the guys tonight."

"Like hell."

He spoke softly, but she still flinched. So she wasn't oblivious to how furious he was with her.

"Once they have me, I'll call and relay my location as we go."

He clenched his hands at his sides. "And how will you do that when they take your cell phone?"

The woman smirked. "My ability includes cell phones. I don't need to have one physically on me. I can hook into the cellular and wireless signals flying around."

She grimaced, but he already knew because he'd experienced for himself… all those signals made the noises in her head, the ones she blocked out constantly, worse. His cell phone vibrated, and he pulled it out of his pocket to discover a text from her.

I can reach you from anywhere and send you GPS coordinates. I'll be fine.

A hiss of breath escaped him as he put his phone back in his pocket. "Why couldn't you just listen into their calls?"

"I've been doing that. Nothing turned up. It's been weeks, Cain. We need to move faster."

Cain crouched in front of her, not that his suit gave much room to do so easily. He placed his hands on her knees—the heat of her skin through the thin silk of her skirt warming his palms—and the same odd calming effect which happened every time he touched her settled him, if only a tiny bit, and despite the fact that he wasn't using his power on her. "If anything happens to you because of me—"

"It won't be because of you, but because of me. I chose to turn these goons in to Delilah. I chose to help your team out. I am choosing to be the bait. If I can keep what happened to me from happening to any other person out there, I will."

He could see the resolve in the soft grey eyes that gazed steadily at him. Jaw tense, he rocked back on his heels and stood. "Do-gooder."

"Who me?" She pointed at her chest, all wide-eyed innocence blended with pure mischief. A combination he found irresistible.

Cain huffed a laugh. Behind the tough, often sarcastic, exterior she presented to the world lay the heart of someone truly decent, as evidenced by the fact that every person who came into contact with her loved her. Quinn's goodness manifested as small acts of kindness every day. Only this morning she'd snuck out of the apartment to get him the coffee he liked. Of course, he'd come down on her hard. What if she'd been taken? What if he couldn't find her? Even now, panic spiked, despite what she'd just revealed about her ability to get in touch with him.

He leaned back against the desk, trying to put distance between them and gain perspective on the situation, and crossed his arms. "If they take you, no heroics. Use your powers to contact me and wait. Agreed?"

"You're no fun," she pouted.

Why did he want to laugh? "That's not funny."

She winked. "It's a little funny."

"Promise me."

She scooted her chair over to her computer and shut it down, then stuffed it in her laptop bag. Standing, she scooped up the bag as well as her purse. "Ready?"

He remained where he stood and waited.

She shook her head at him. "Are you this overprotective with all the women you rescue?"

Just one. The one he'd rescued once already. The kiss that had haunted his dreams for six years. How he hadn't recognized her when they first met, he'd never know. His only excuse being how dark the cave cell had been, and she'd been whisked away before he got a good look at her. Besides, six years and a happier life could change a person's appearance.

"Fine," she huffed when he didn't budge. "No heroics. I promise."

CHAPTER 7

Cain laid down another hand and glanced at his phone, which sat, disturbingly silent, on the end of the desk. The hotel room only had the one piece of furniture they could use as a poker table, so they'd dragged the desk to the center of the room. Sawyer and Shaw sat on the end of the bed, using one long side. He and Max had grabbed the chair and stool and took the two short sides.

They dressed like they were off duty—jeans and t-shirts—which bugged him in a weird way. Quinn was out there, and he wasn't even dressed to react quickly.

"She'll be fine." Max rubbed at the scar on his wrist hidden under the leather band he always wore. Clearly, he didn't believe that any more than Cain did.

Cain grunted and waited for the guys to finish out the hand. He ignored the trickle of sweat running down his back. The air-conditioner was a piece of junk even Shaw couldn't fix without new parts. The heat and humidity of the summer night blew in through the open window, along with the noises of the city. The breeze did little to alleviate the smell of sweat and humanity permeating the room.

Didn't take long before Max scooped up the pot. Sawyer shuffled the cards and dealt. Cain checked his. Trash. He waited for the flop. Still trash. Sure he could bluff it out, in fact, he'd usually try that, but instead he folded. And checked his phone again.

"I've never seen you like this, man." Sawyer's gaze remained on his cards.

Tipping his chair back, Cain ran his hand over his beard and didn't comment.

"You like her." Sawyer's uncanny powers of observation had nothing to do with his telepathy, but Cain often thought it might as well have.

Cain sat forward, the legs of his chair hitting the carpeted floor with a muffled thud. "She's got guts. I'll say that for her." No way was he going to voice his real opinion. His team needed him to lead, not turn into a sappy, distracted ass.

Max glanced up from his cards and pinned Cain with a dark, unwavering gaze. "This is different."

Max was right. The level of his interest in Quinn scared the hell out of Cain. "Remember our first mission?"

Shaw laid down the turn card. "In Alaska? That cave system holding all the sups?"

"Yeah."

Sawyer frowned over the cards in his hand. "You think this is them? We took care of them."

"All of them," Max added, a hard light in his eyes.

"No. This is not them. But she was there."

All three of his men jerked their heads up to stare at him.

"No way," Sawyer said.

"Quinn was one of the sups they held prisoner?" Shaw asked.

Cain nodded an affirmative. Not the youngest being held, but close. Cain glanced down and shock pinged through him at the sight of his own clenched his fists. With a shake, he forced his hands to relax under the table where the others couldn't see.

"How'd you find out?" Max asked.

"She had a nightmare. I touched her, saw everything."

Max leaned back, studying Cain's expression. "Is she the one?"

"Yeah." After everything had settled in Alaska, Cain had tried to find her, needing to know she was okay. Max had helped, but Delilah had several teams there that day, and another group had taken Quinn to safety.

Max's eyebrows shot up. "I'll be damned."

Exactly.

"So let me get this straight..." Sawyer leaned his elbows on his knees. "She set herself up to be taken into the same situation we rescued her from?"

"Yes."

"Guts doesn't begin to cover it," Sawyer muttered.

Also right.

"How'd you let her go, man?" Shaw asked, only to be cuffed over the head by his brother. "Ow! What was that for?" He threw his cards at his brother.

"You're about as sensitive as a knife to the gut." Sawyer tipped his chin at Cain.

Shaw's scowl cleared. "Oh. You have a thing for Quinn. I get it."

Before Sawyer could whack his brother in the head again, Cain's phone signaled a message.

—*They've picked me up. I'm unharmed.* —

A sensation akin to panic twisted up his insides. *—Send coordinates.—*

—Don't be mad.—

Not good. *—Send coordinates.—*

—Not yet. I overheard something. They'll take me to the islands soon.—

—When?—

—A day or two. I might not be able to get in touch. Something about a ship, which could limit communication options. But once I'm there, I'll contact you, and you can come get me.—

"Damn," he muttered. This woman was going to put him into an early grave from stress alone. Or put more grey in his beard at the very least.

"What?" Max asked. All three men had dropped their cards, their focus fully on him.

He shook his head and kept typing on his phone. *—You promised. No heroics.—*

—I'm not being a hero. I'm getting more info so we can stop more than the deal going down here.—

—No. What if you don't wake up in time or can't contact me from the islands. Too many risks.—

—I know you, Cain. If I give you my coordinates now, you'll come get me before they put me on the ship. I'll keep in touch as much as possible, so you know I'm okay. —

—No. Tell me where you are. Now.—

He waited, phone gripped tightly, but she didn't respond. He never should have left her side. He should have let them take him too. Cain paused. As often happened, his mind cleared as a plan formed. He raised his gaze to his second-in-command. "Max?"

Max's arms flexed as he crossed them. "You about to do something stupid?"

"I need your help. We need to get the demons to take me too."

"Bad idea, boss," Shaw mumbled. Sawyer said nothing, but his agreement with Shaw was stamped across the closed expression on his face.

Max studied him through narrowed eyes. "You say never separate the team."

"She can keep us connected."

"What if they take you to a different location. She won't know."

"Then you'll have to come find me. I can't leave her."

Max's jaw hardened, but he nodded. "Okay."

Cain blew out a breath. "We need more help." He dialed a number he'd memorized long ago. "Delilah?"

CHAPTER 8

Quinn stared out of the bars to her cell, down a long dark hallway with naked light bulbs hanging from a wire every ten feet, casting a dim light throughout the chamber. Her cell was one of three, each about the size of a closet, situated at the end, which meant she could see every new capture brought in. At least, those who posed no risk of escape. From what she could tell, another block of cells which neutralized physical abilities in various ways was located down a different hall.

Good thing they hadn't stuck her in one of those, or she'd have no access to Cain and be up a creek without a paddle.

The accommodations here weren't nearly as good as those in her previous hellhole in Alaska. There, at least, she'd had a bed and covers. Even some books. Here was just the cell. She sat or lay on the hard cement floor. They did feed her, but no utensils were provided, so she ate with her hands. Worst of all, she peed in a bucket in the corner. Thankfully, the building was air conditioned, keeping the summer heat at bay.

Now she sat on the floor with her back against the wall. With a deep breath, she closed her eyes and leaned her head back against the concrete wall. Loneliness and fear made her want to reach out to Cain just to talk, but she didn't want to drive him nuts with idle chatter.

You talk a good game, Ridley, but inside you're a coward.

She plucked at one of the wireless signals floating through the air. While she couldn't see them, she could sense them there, and, more importantly, hear them. Tapping into them had taken a ton of practice. She used the signal now to check the time. Almost seven at night, just a few more minutes and she'd check in with Cain. She'd been here two days, every second eternal, but she'd caught a conversation on a walkie-talkie which led her to believe tonight or tomorrow they'd take her to a boat to be shipped to their longer-term holding facility in the islands.

Anticipation stirred as she mentally composed her text, using her Telecommunication ability to convert it into the digital signal which would travel a cellular signal she'd hooked into—a signal which she couldn't see or touch, but she could hear it and speak to it. The noises that came out of her reminded her of the clicks dolphins made to communicate. Cameras throughout the area caught her making the noises, but no one would understand her. However, she tried not to do it too often. Better to not draw extra attention.

—Checking in. I believe they'll take me and several others to the islands in the next day or so.—

She waited for Cain's reply. "Bet five bucks he asks for my location," she muttered, smiling to herself.

—*This is Max. Keep an eye out for Cain.*—

With a jerk, Quinn sat forward abruptly. —*What do you mean?*—

—*He's joining you. They took him an hour ago.*—

Quinn forced herself to relax back against the wall, acutely aware of the cameras, when what she wanted to do was pace. *Of all the stupid, idiotic... Don't be a hero, he told her. What about him? She should've made him promise the same darn thing.*

—*What if they don't bring him here? Or put him in a different cell and I don't know where he is?*—

—*His call, Quinn.*—

Which told her Max wasn't any happier about it than she was. He didn't tell her that Cain wouldn't be in this situation if she would've just shared her location. But she was thinking it. A frantic sensation clawed at her insides. She had to find him.

—*Transmitting my coordinates now.*—

—*Received.*—

And now she waited. Not passively, though. Quinn methodically started checking every transmission and digital communication out of the area where she was held, listening for any sign of Cain.

Nine hours later, exhaustion dragged at her eyelids, but she forced herself to stay alert, searching for the man whom she trusted above all others. A few weeks of constant contact and she found she craved his presence, his voice, the odd sense of calm his rare touches brought her. Her nightmares, a nightly occurrence for six years, had ceased completely with him in her bed. She hadn't wanted to examine why too closely before, but now she had nothing but time and her thoughts. And the knowledge that she was falling for Daniel Cain. Hard.

The clank of the metal door at the end of the chamber dragged her from her telepathic stupor. She gave a slow blink as footsteps echoed down the hallway, preceding the figure of a man too lean to be Cain or any of the others on his team. She straightened as she recognized the man who brought her food and a fresh piss bucket every day. Only he carried neither.

Key in hand, he stared at her through the bars with a blank expression and the eerily beautiful pale blue eyes of a demon. "Stand up, turn around, hands on the wall." He spoke in broken English.

"Where are you taking me?" Quinn used Sumerian, the language she'd overheard the islanders speaking weeks ago. She didn't need to fake the fear which lent a wobble to her voice.

His eyes widened, but he didn't answer, merely repeated his instructions in perfect Sumerian. Yup. Demon.

She did as he asked as quickly as muscles weakened from two days of minimal food and water and limited movement would allow. That she couldn't control the shaking of her body irritated her.

He unlocked the cell door with a metallic click, then took her hands and bound them behind her with industrial zip ties. A blindfold came next. That part didn't worry Quinn too much. Immediately, she sent a signal to Cain's cell phone, confident Max would receive it. Using a tracking app, she allowed him to watch on a map as she was led out of the cell, down the hall, and out the heavy metal door. After that, she would've lost track of the twists and turns through the building if not for her own signal.

A blast of humid air, followed by the sound of water lapping against a shore, and she was outside the building. Were they at a dock?

Her footing changed, and they were walking uphill. A gangplank? Had to be. She was grateful she'd worn running shoes when the demons took her because the stilettos she sported at work would've been crap at negotiating the slatted metal flooring she was walked along once inside what she assumed was a large boat. Finally, they stopped and a door was opened with a rusty creak. She winced as the demon cut her zip ties off, nicking her skin with his knife. Her blindfold was whipped off, and she stumbled as he shoved her roughly inside before he slammed the door closed.

Wherever he'd put her had no window and no light. Quinn felt her way through the pitch dark, glad her previous experience hadn't resulted in claustrophobia or a fear of the dark. Otherwise, she'd be wigging about now. Encountering smooth metal walls, she explored the space by touch alone.

"Ow! Son of a—" She bit off the expletive and rubbed her shin before bending down to feel for what she'd walked into. Pleasant surprise washed through her when she discovered a bed with a mattress in the corner. Even better, more exploration and a couple more bruises revealed a toilet and sink as well. Better than her little cell in what must've been a dock-side warehouse.

With a resigned sigh, she plunked down on the bed. Max had her location. He'd be coming. She just hoped he found Cain, too. Her own searching had turned up nothing. How long would it take before Max came anyway?

Despite the fact that she strained her ears for any sound of a fight, of rescue, she had zero warning when her door jerked open. A broad-shouldered man stood silhouetted in the doorway and memory slammed through her. In a split second, she mentally transported back to the prison in Alaska when her rescuer had opened her door.

Quinn gasped, but before she could do more, the man in her doorway was shoved roughly inside, and the door slammed closed behind him. The lock turned with a thunk.

"Quinn?"

One syllable, but she'd know his voice anywhere.

"Daniel," she choked as she threw herself in his general direction.

The dark hampered them both, and she managed to slam into a wall of muscled man and bump his chin with her forehead. His strong arms closed around her, and calm descended over her body. She was safe as long as he was near.

Without thinking it through, she went up on her tiptoes and pulled him down to place her lips over his. The kiss was sweet and hot, zinging through her nerves in a delightful way. After a shocked second of hesitation, he pulled her closer and took over, claiming her lips with his and stoking the fires inside her.

With a low groan, he pulled back, their panting filling the room.

"Why'd they put you in here?" she asked, voice raspy.

"I managed to touch one of the humans involved. He was easily manipulated to get orders to hold us together. Touching any of the demons would've been useless, so I got lucky."

She pulled back and punched him in the shoulder. Hard.

He didn't even give her the satisfaction of an 'oomf,' nor did he let go of her. "What was that for?"

"Next time you promise *me* not to be a hero," she grumbled.

A low chuckle reached her ears. "I should have been with you in the first place."

"Oh!" Realization struck. "Max has the coordinates and is on his way. I should stop him."

"Why?"

"Now that we're together, I'm taking these jerks down. No one should be held against their will. Ever."

CHAPTER 9

Consciousness returned slowly in the pitch black room. Quinn's body told her morning had arrived, but she'd only know for sure when the lights came on in the room. They had zero control over the lights. Still, their captors could've left them in the dark the entire trip, so she wasn't complaining.

The heartbeat under her ear thumped slow and steady, a comforting sound she'd come to crave over the last nine days. A little voice in her head said she didn't need anyone—not anymore. But this was different. Not pathetic like she was when she'd been taken the first time. There could be strength in needing another person. She became her best self in Cain's presence.

Weakness, however, came in the form of the other small voice in her head wishing they'd never reach their destination, because she'd have to give him up. They were forced to sleep like this because of the tiny single bed in the room. Otherwise, Cain hadn't touched her again since that kiss. Every so often, she'd catch him watching her with a strangely intent expression. Did he remember? That he was the one who saved her from her captors? She hadn't mentioned it, and neither had he.

"We docked last night." The deep rumble of his voice vibrated under her cheek.

"I heard the anchor drop." Hard to miss the heavy battery of metal on metal as each massive link of the chain attached to the anchor unreeled. After three days of using the boat's system to communicate, she'd finally been able to tap into a cellular signal. "I've alerted Max. They'll be waiting."

A soft buzz preceded the lights blinking to life, and she squeezed her eyes closed at the sudden brightness. With a reluctant shove, drawing a grunt from Cain, she sat up. "When all this is over—"

"You're going to take a shower and put on clean clothes."

Quinn chuckled because she'd been saying that every day. She'd washed herself at the sink as best she could, washed her undies too. However, that didn't help much. They were both rank, and her hair was a greasy mop pulled back in a ponytail. No wonder Cain hadn't wanted to touch her.

"No. I'd like to—"

The lock to their door clicked, and she let her words fall away. Rather than breakfast being slid in on the floor, however, the door was opened wide and four men stood in the corridor, each with a pistol trained on her and Cain.

The shortest of the bunch waved his gun at them, indicating the far wall. In

Sumerian, he said, "Hands on the wall."

She caught Cain's glance as she turned. "He said to put our hands on the wall."

Like before, when they were put on the boat, they had their wrists strapped behind their backs and blindfolds roughly tied over their eyes.

As they clomped through the inside corridors of the boat, Max's message came through. —*In position now.*—

—*Being led off the boat.*—

A distraction for their captors might not be a bad idea. "Is where you're taking us going to have a bath? We stink." She used Sumerian to speak with the demons who held them.

"Humans always stink," one of them spat.

"Right, because smelling of rotten egg is so much better."

And angry hiss sounded from behind her.

"Might not be a good idea to piss them off." Cain's rebuke was conversational. Not that he'd understood a single word, but the hiss was a decent hint.

"Demons always smell of sulfur to me. Don't they to you?" she asked in English now.

"The few I've run across smell like rotting meat to me. Putrid."

Finally, they made it outside. A humid breeze feathered across her face, and sunlight penetrated the rag tied over her eyes. The hushed murmur of surf rose in the distance.

"An island?" She pretended to not know where they were. The ground tilted under her feet as they led her down what she assumed was the same gangplank she'd used to board.

—*Get down.*—

"Cain. Drop!" she yelled as she allowed her body to go limp, doing a great imitation of a potato sack as she rolled to the ground.

The whistle and burst of bullets was drowned out almost instantly by the thunder of an explosion. Heat kissed her back. Then running feet, and someone cut her hands loose. Quinn yanked away her blindfold to see their four escorts on the ground with bullet wounds to each head, the only way to kill one. A series of low buildings were on fire along the docks. Cain, now on his feet, held out a hand to help her up. She stood and threw her arms around Max.

"Hey, we helped too! I'm the one who blew shit up," Shaw complained.

Sawyer slapped him on the back of the head, but she laughed and hugged the brothers too. "Thanks for coming to our rescue."

Cain accepted a Beretta from Max. No samurai sword for this rescue, as when he'd saved her, she guessed. He glanced her way. "You stay here with Sawyer."

"The hell you say!"

He crowded her. "I can't protect you and lead my team at the same time."

She narrowed her eyes. "Who says I need protection?" She looked at Max with raised eyebrows, glad she'd already asked him to bring her a weapon. Reluctance pulled at his mouth, but he pulled out a .357 Magnum.

"We don't have time for this." Anger and another emotion—fear maybe?—gave Cain's words a dark edge. She refused to back down though.

The sounds of screaming pierced the air above the roar of the flames. "Max?" Cain demanded.

Max shook his head. "Radios are down, boss."

"I can hear them," Quinn said. "They've split up. Two of ours are engaged with four demons at the far side of the complex in some sort of lab. The others are across the island dealing with a larger group."

She implored Cain with her eyes. "Let me come. I may come in handy."

He nodded at Max, who placed the gun, grip first, into her outstretched hand. Without hesitation, she checked the chamber, then unloaded four shots into the bodies on the ground with absolute accuracy.

Cain's jaw could've been hewn from granite. "Fine." He pulled off the tactical vest Max had handed him and passed it over to her. The man had a hero complex, but he was letting her come, so she wouldn't argue. With efficient motions, she strapped it on over her t-shirt and yoga pants, once again glad the demons had taken her during a workout. She also accepted several mags from Max, tucking them into the vest.

Cain tipped her chin up. "You stay close to me."

As a unit they moved, silent and swift with weapons at the ready, past the row of burning buildings and into the complex beyond. They entered through a side door, careful to check the corners. "Clear," each murmured in a low voice.

Moving quickly, they navigated a series of hallways—generic, with cream colored tile, white walls, and white doors every ten feet—when suddenly, Quinn pulled up short. "Wait."

The network of computers here wasn't as secure as it could've been. The demons had become arrogant and lazy on their own island. She talked to the array of servers, sifting through data. "This way."

Cain grabbed her arm. "I lead."

"Do you know where you're going? Can you see with the security cameras?" If those blue eyes had been lasers, she'd be dead about now. "Because I can."

He didn't take long to debate the point. "Go."

Using the information at her fingertips, Quinn led the team through the buildings. Mostly dark, the only light coming from small windows close to the ceiling—someone must've cut the power—the buildings were strangely office like. Or maybe the best comparison was a hospital, with its long corridors shooting off from a hub at the center. "Two around the corner," she said, as they neared one of the hubs.

Shaw and Sawyer stepped forward, as Max guarded their rear. Cain stayed beside her. "Where?" Shaw whispered.

"Either side of the door, crouched low."

"Got it." Sawyer's face contorted with concentration until, suddenly, the two creatures on the other side of the double doors howled in pain. With speed and precision, Sawyer and Shaw burst through and took out their opponents with two quick pops.

Cain waved her ahead, and she moved around the corner and through the swinging double doors. She glanced down at the demons as she passed and couldn't help but notice the blackened burn marks both bore on their hands. A demon's primary weapon was an energy ball they could form at will, then throw at their enemy.

"What happened to their energy balls?"

"Sawyer's telekinetic. His specialty is energy manipulation."

Ah. He must've fried them with their own energy. "Cool."

Sawyer grinned.

Quinn checked the cameras in the building again. "This way. We're close. Be ready."

A few more halls and turns later, and the reek of antiseptic hit her nose. The fight must've opened up some of the containers in the lab.

"There are eight demons now, instead of four. One of our guys is down. The other is pinned behind the large table to the right."

"Where are the demons?" Cain asked.

"Scattered across the other side of the room. Go in blazing."

Shaw pulled out an odd device, which he attached to the door. "Always do. Sawyer manipulates energy, but I got mechanical manipulation." He turned to his brother. "Sawyer?"

Cain grabbed her arm and pulled her around the corner. After a second, howls of agony echoed through the room. "Cover your ears," Cain warned.

She did just before an explosion blasted around them, shaking the wall she leaned against as a wave of heat blew past her down the hallway. Without hesitation, she followed her men through the smoke and damage. Gunshots echoed in the room as the team opened fire. The demons hunkered down across the large room filled with lab tables, the walls of bottles already a mess of broken glass and dripping chemicals.

While the demons were unarmed, so to speak, after Sawyer's manipulations, they wouldn't stay that way long. Quinn stooped behind a tall piece of equipment and used her abilities to check the cameras. Difficult to see through the smoke, but she could make out where most everyone was. She stayed in position as Cain and the team spread out. The first blue blast came from the right, like a miniature lightning bolt. The air sizzled as the energy ball passed her to explode against the wall above Cain.

Demons were powerful but often stupid. They were lucky none of the spilled chemicals had gone up in flames yet. Chaos erupted around her as they exchanged fire.

Quinn stayed in position and saved her ammo, until, finally, an opening presented itself. As subtly as possible, she popped out from behind her shield just enough to see her target, aimed, and squeezed the trigger. Clean shot to the head. One down.

She dropped back behind her cabinet, as a barrage of bullets slammed into the machine. She checked the cameras and waited again.

Cain managed to take down another demon, and Max got two. Sawyer put out as many energy balls as he could, but with this many demons, he couldn't douse them all. As he concentrated, he worked his way around it to where the downed man lay and dragged his body back behind a barricade of tables. A movement caught her attention across the room.

"Throw it to the back right corner," she yelled to Shaw.

"Fire in the hole," he yelled. The grenade in his hand went sailing, and Quinn braced for the explosion which ripped through her ears. The floor under her feet shuddered with the impact. A high-pitched ringing in her head brought tears to her eyes. All sound ceased to exist for her. She shook her head, trying to clear the pressure in her ears, but she couldn't hear a damn thing—not Cain who was yelling at her across the room, not the computers. Nothing.

A flash of fear froze Cain's features just before an arm snaked around her neck from behind and jerked her upright. Her hair stood on end in reaction to the blue energy coming from the ball of light held near her temple as her captor dragged her out from behind the cabinet.

He was yelling, she could tell by how the sound reverberated off her back, but the ringing hadn't subsided and she couldn't hear. The demon let her go, backing away slightly, and pressed the energy ball close to the back of her head, if the stench of singed hair was anything to go by.

Cain, Max, Sawyer, and Shaw all put their weapons on the ground. She might not be able to hear, but the message was clear. Surrender or she'd die. On the other hand, the demons were as likely to kill her men either way.

Quinn took a calming breath and concentrated on her self-defense training, compliments of Delilah. Six years of hard work better payoff, dammit.

In a rapid series of moves, she turned, bringing her arm down, which aimed his hand upward. Holding his wrist for leverage she brought her leg up and kicked him in the neck, crushing his windpipe. The demon dropped to the ground and she followed, bending the arm she held and slamming the energy ball still sizzling in his palm into his chest. Then she dove back behind the cabinet.

The demon screamed, his beautiful face contorting in agony and his body thrashing as the condensed source of energy devoured him from the inside out. In seconds, he went limp. Dead.

Cain and the others picked up their guns and resumed the fight. Quinn, who no longer had her hearing or her gun—she must've dropped it when he grabbed her—waited it out from her shelter. About the time the firefight wound down, the ringing in her ears had lessened.

Finally, Cain stood, and the others followed, telling her the battle was over and they'd won. After a cursory check of the room, he moved to where she still sat on the floor and crouched down.

"You okay?"

She caught the words in blips, pieced together with the movement of his mouth.

"My hearing is shot, but it's coming back."

His quick smile told her she'd shouted the words. "That's all right. Shaw got the radios back up, and the fighting is over."

"What about the prisoners?"

"Still looking."

The memory of the map of the facility she'd pulled from the computers flashed through her mind. "I know where they are."

CHAPTER 10

Quinn sat on the tail of a pickup truck outside the compound and submitted to being examined by Sawyer, who was apparently also a medic. The others were nowhere to be seen.

After checking her eyes, her balance, her reflexes, and checking for other signs of concussion, Sawyer stuck an otoscope down her ears. "Looks like your ear drums are still intact."

"I told you. My hearing's almost all the way back," she grumbled.

He held up both hands with a grin. "Don't shoot the messenger. Cain said to check you out, and that's exactly what I'm doing."

She rolled her eyes, but let Sawyer get on with it.

"How is she?" Cain's deep voice skittered down her spine, and she turned to find him leaning against the side of the truck.

"Fit for duty, sir." She gave him a sassy salute.

He ignored her, gaze on Sawyer.

"She'll be fine. No permanent damage."

"She's right here." Quinn waved her arms.

Cain ignored her and gave Sawyer a curt nod, then jerked his head. Sawyer gathered up his gear and left them alone, giving Quinn a wink as he left.

Cain moved around the truck to stand in front of her.

"So…" She raised her eyebrows. "What now?"

"Delilah's other teams will handle things from here. But we got them."

Relief and a heady sensation from the knowledge she'd helped save a lot of people swept through her, and Quinn smiled.

Her breathing hitched at Cain's answering grin. "You did good today."

She sobered. Now the bad guys were history, she had to face facts— knowledge sunk like a lead weight to the pit of her stomach. *This might be the last time I ever see Daniel Cain.*

"It doesn't have to be."

What? Oh, holy crap, she'd done it again. Spoken her thoughts out loud. Then his response finally penetrated her mortification at that particular flub. "What do you mean?"

He moved closer, hands on either side of her hips, taking up all her space. She inhaled the spicy scent of him.

"I wanted to talk to you about something."

After only a few weeks in Daniel Cain's constant presence, Quinn sensed his hesitation. Though how, when his expression gave nothing away, she didn't know. If she had to put money on it, she'd bet Cain was nervous. Why?

"We'd like to offer you a position on the team."

Quinn sucked in a breath. She hadn't seen that one coming. Everything in her screamed yes, but she had one tiny problem. "I'm flattered, but I don't think that will work out."

"Why not?"

She sighed, but held his gaze with her own, heart thundering away. "I'm falling in love with you."

There, she'd said it. Now he could shut down and walk away.

His lips flattened. He stepped back, out of her space and away from her body, and her heart cracked at the obvious signs of rejection. "You remembered, didn't you? That I'm the one who got you out of the hellhole in Alaska?"

Confusion joined her heartache. What did that have to do with it? She nodded slowly. "The night they put you in my cell on the boat."

He ran a hand over his beard, his blue eyes flinty. "I see."

Confusion swirled through her. What did he see exactly? "I'm not harboring a hero crush if that's what you're thinking. Didn't I prove I could take care of myself?"

A hint of a smile made his mustache twitch. "You certainly did that."

"But you don't believe I'm in love with you." This had to be the strangest conversation she'd ever had. She'd expected him to be cold or spooked. She certainly hadn't expected to have to argue about the true state of her feelings with the man.

"I believe you think you are." The heaviness in his eyes sparked a glimmer of hope inside her. Did he want her to be in love with him?

She hopped off the tailgate and stepped up to him, right in his space, though she had to tip her chin to look up at him. "Kiss me."

Shock widened his eyes. "What?"

"Put those amazing psychometric powers to use. Kiss me and see exactly what my emotions are."

He stared at her a long moment, and she could see the debate in his eyes. So she took the decision out of his hands. Quinn went up on her toes and wrapped her arms around his neck, pulling his head down to hers. Tenderly, she lay her lips over his in the sweetest of kisses. Desire flamed within her, but she banked her need. Desire could come later. This was about connection. She allowed her emotions to flow freely and hoped like hell his gift would kick in. He needed to know.

The second his unyielding lips softened, she pulled back. His blue eyes blazed at her, almost sizzling her with the heat of desire within.

"Do you believe me now?"

"Quinn—" He groaned the word.

"No?" She grabbed his hand and dragged him back into the building.

"Where are we going?" She ignored the amusement in his voice.

Finally, she found the rest of the team still in the cells where the demons had held their prisoners before sale. Purpose in every step, she marched up to the brawny man who was Cain's second-in-command. "Max, I need you to kiss me."

Cain stopped cold and jerked her around, yanking her into his arms. "Like hell." He took her lips in a possessive kiss that left no one in the room, least of all Quinn, in doubt. Daniel Cain claimed her for his own.

A wolf whistle sounded somewhere in the background of her pleasure. Probably Shaw. She ignored it, ignored everything and everyone, in favor of the pleasure this man could bring with such a simple touch.

Only the need for oxygen stopped them. He pulled back to lean his forehead against hers, both of their chests heaving as they gasped for air. "I think I've loved you since the first time you kissed me."

"Oh? Maybe I trigger a savior complex in you," she teased. How she could go from having no clue as to his feelings to trusting in his love in the span of moments, she had no idea. But the glow of contentment, and safety, and pure joy told her, in no uncertain terms, she could trust him, trust them together.

He chuckled. "I couldn't get you out of my head for six years. No other woman stood a chance."

Satisfaction swelled inside her. "Good."

"So about joining the team…"

Quinn grinned. "I could use a job anyway. I'm sure I've been fired from my current one."

KAMRY'S HOPE
Crystal G. Smith

Kamry stood and gasped for air as her body came down from the high she always got from working out. God, she was definitely out of shape and had no idea what she was doing, but one way or another, she was going to make sure that no man would ever be able to get the best of her the way Steven had.

She hated him. She had only been married to him for a little over a year, but had been with him for four. She hated that the minute 'I do' was said, everything changed.

In his eyes, she never did anything right. They would argue and scream. He would throw insults just as quickly as the last one registered in her brain. He would make her feel completely worthless. Then she had decided that when he wanted to yell and scream, she would ignore him and move on.

Then one day, it happened. He was screaming and telling her what a complete loser she was. She took a deep breath and kept cutting the carrots she was preparing for supper. Wrong move.

Before she knew what happened, she was on the floor. She remembered her head and the floor connecting, and then she was waking up. Of course, Steven was standing over her, asking her if she was okay and telling her how sorry he was. She fell for it.

The next time, he didn't shove her. He straight up close-fisted her face. It escalated until he was no longer even apologizing for it. She couldn't take it. She packed up and left while he was at work, never looking back. With help of her family, she filed for divorce.

Two months ago, she was lying in bed when she realized that she would never really be able to defend herself against a man if it happened again. She began watching YouTube videos of self-defense training and now, she was sitting on a bench after kicking and punching the heavy bag in front of her.

Everyone watched her, but she didn't care. She really didn't care that she had no clue what she was doing. What she did know was that she was not going to take it again. If the bag did nothing more than help her build strength, she would at least be able to kick and punch.

"You know, I've seen you coming in here and I have to say, you got some heart, kid."

Kamry turned and stared at a young Hispanic man.

"Thanks," she said, wondering why he was still standing there. She looked him over and knew she hadn't seen him in the gym before, but he looked familiar. She just wasn't able to place him. Maybe it was... Hell, she didn't know. The man was covered in tattoos from his wrists, up his arms, then down his chiseled chest and back. He looked maybe mid-twenties or so, with short cropped hair and big brown eyes that reeked of mystery.

When her eyes returned to his, she realized she was busted. She hadn't really been checking him out, well, she had, but not for the reasons she was afraid he thought.

"Heart is attractive and heart can get you a trainer. What are your goals?"

"I'm sorry, what?"

He chuckled, sitting next to her. "Why are you here?"

"I want to be able to fight," she answered, not willing to tell the truth of it to a complete stranger.

"How long have you been split from him?"

"How do you know this has to do with Steven?"

He smiled. "I didn't until you answered that way. I've been coming here for years and I only see women fight like you do when they either have something to prove, or someone they need to protect themselves from."

"I see." She wiped the sweat from her eyes. "Well, then I guess you have me figured out."

"Look, I don't mean to bother you. I just thought I would offer you some advice. It's not much, but I can help you out if I'm here when you are. I can give you ten, maybe fifteen minutes if I see you here."

"What, are you saying watching YouTube isn't going to help me?" She was only half-serious.

He laughed. "I like your sense of humor just as much as that oversized heart. I'll see you around, kid."

Kid? He looked around her age, and she had just turned twenty-six. He didn't look nearly old enough to be calling her a kid. She was far from it.

She watched him walk away, still chuckling at her lack of knowledge or skill, depending on how a person wanted to look at it.

She grabbed her bag and tossed her towel over her shoulders. She would take a shower when she got home. Normally, she took one before leaving, but today she would just wait until later.

The walk home was great. Living in NYC was as far away from him as she could get. Well, technically she could have gone a lot further, but she figured the larger the city, the better off she was.

Her apartment wasn't anything to brag over. It was nothing more than a studio apartment with a bathroom that had walls. She didn't mind, though. It was large enough to split the bedroom area and the living area. She didn't have a kitchen table because she didn't need one. She never invited anyone over. In fact, the only person to see the inside of her apartment was her neighbor Jess.

Jess and Kamry had hit it off from the start. Jess was also twenty-six, a small town girl who was also running from her past. They spent their evenings when Jess wasn't working talking and having popcorn slash scary movie festivals in one of their apartments.

Jess worked two jobs as a waitress, so they only met up about once a week, twice if they were lucky. Thankfully, Kamry was an occupational therapist and found it rather easy to find all the work she needed. Sure, she could afford a larger apartment in a better neighborhood, with all the bells and whistles, but she didn't want that because she knew if Steven ever came looking for her, he would look in nice areas. The only thing that scared her about work was him finding her address, if he wanted to dig enough.

She couldn't go on living her life without working, though. She had for a while, but after six months of NYC prices, her savings were about out and she missed working anyways. It was a risk she didn't have a choice but to take.

After her shower, she flopped on the couch. She stared at the ceiling for a minute then reached for the remote. She didn't have many favorite shows, but she enjoyed house hunting, remodeling, and cooking.

She flipped through the channels and when she found a show she was interested in, she grabbed a pillow and cuddled it as they began stripping out the bungalow the couple had just purchased.

At some point, she fell asleep. It wasn't until she heard a loud crash and shattering glass that she was startled awake.

For a moment, she froze. Unable to move. Barely able to breathe. Her heart raced and the fear was almost crippling.

Without moving her body, her eyes searched what they could see. With a sigh of relief, she sat up.

"Damn it." She ran her fingers through her hair and then went in search of the broom and dustpan. She had left her water glass on the coffee table and must have knocked it over.

She swept up the mess and headed back to her original spot. The rest of the day was going to be straight up lazy and then back to work tomorrow.

🕸

Kamry looked over her schedule for the day. She worked mainly in long term care, but because she required a full work load, she worked for a company that would send her to three different locations to get her hours in.

She smiled. She would be visiting Brook Haven today and that was one of her favorite places to go. She loved Ms. Maybelle.

Ms. Maybelle was an eighty-seven-year young lovely lady who could light up Kamry's day with just a smile. Her blue eyes were always twinkling and she was never in a foul mood. She told stories of how she had been an actress back in her day, and Kamry would soak it all up. The woman had a knack for telling stories. Whether they were true or not, Kamry didn't care. She loved her and that was all that mattered.

She really loved the stories about how Ms. Maybelle met her husband. He preceded her in death, and it had been seven years, but she loved him just as much today as she did the day he had gone to Heaven.

The minute Kamry walked into Brook Haven and around the corner to the therapy department, she saw her and smiled.

"Good morning, Ms. Maybelle."

"There's my favorite young lady. How are you today?"

"I'm fantastic. How are you today?"

"Didn't sleep well last night. I keep getting these headaches that just won't go away."

"Did you tell the nurses?" Kamry asked, raising an eyebrow because she knew Ms. Maybelle hadn't said a word.

"No. They are so busy. Them girls run and run and run some more. I feel sorry for them, actually."

"Ms. Maybelle, we have had this discussion before. That's their job, and obviously they love doing it because it's the field they have chosen to work in."

"Just because you work here doesn't mean you love it."

"I love it and I work here."

"But you, my young friend, are a special breed of woman."

"Thank you," Kamry said, patting her hand before grabbing the back of the wheelchair and pushing her into the department.

Forty-five minutes and a lot of hard work on Ms. Maybelle's part later, her session was over. It always seemed like the time flew by during their sessions, because of the stories. She pushed Ms. Maybelle to the dining room where bingo was about to begin. After getting her situated, Kamry went to the nurse's station and reported the complaint about headaches. They both frowned.

"Its starting," Suzy, one of the LPNs there, said.

"What's starting?" Kamry asked.

"She has an aneurysm that is inoperable."

"Oh, no." Kamry turned, looking to where Ms. Maybelle now played with the four cards she had chosen.

"She doesn't know. She has pain medication that she can ask for, but it's obvious she isn't going to, so I will call and get them scheduled."

"Thank you."

Kamry turned, walking back to Ms. Maybelle and kissing her head before going on to the next resident of the day.

Kamry arrived at the gym shortly after six. She changed into her workout clothing and stepped up to the bag. The place was unusually empty, but she didn't mind. She preferred it this way, because there were less people staring at her.

She stretched her legs and then her arms. She didn't know a lot about working out and learning to fight, but stretching was right up her alley.

"Hey, you came back."

Kamry jumped at the deep voice behind her. She quickly turned to see the same man that had approached her before. "Um, yeah."

"So I was thinking, show me how you handle the bag and then I can help you with the technique. Then I thought maybe you would want to do some self defense on the floor. I've never had a need to learn to fight for the same reason as you, but I do know that when I am in the ring with my back flat against the mat, ju ju comes in handy."

"Ju ju?"

He smiled. "Jujitsu."

"Oh. Thanks, I think. I'm Kamry." She held out her hand.

"Jose, nice to meet you," he replied, shaking her hand.

That explained why he looked so tough then. She assumed when he said ring, he meant MMA. His body was definitely in shape, at least six foot one, maybe two or three. He was rather large, for sure. Probably weighing in at one-ninety or so. She didn't know much about MMA, only what she had heard the guys in the gym talking about.

He walked to the back of the bag and gripped it. "Well, shall we?"

"Don't laugh at me and don't make fun of me. I appreciate your help or any advice you can give me, but I won't be laughed at."

She watched his face turn serious as he let go of the bag and stood in front of her. He brushed a strand of hair from her face and locked eyes with her. "Everyone was a white belt at one point or another. I would never laugh at you."

She nodded.

He walked back to the bag and she began alternating kicks and punches. When she was finished, she waited for him to begin criticizing her every move.

"That was pretty good. My only thing is this..." He come to stand behind her, and then his breath was in her ear. "Don't knock me out." He placed his hands on her hips, pivoting them slightly. "When you kick, rotate just a bit like this. Go with the flow." He reached out and gripped her hands. "Make a fist." She did. He gripped her wrist, pointing to the ring finger and pinky. "These knuckles here, you can fracture them easily."

"Yes, a boxer's fracture."

"Exactly, so you want to make sure you are hitting with these two digits."

"Gotcha." She knew about boxer fractures. She just never really thought about the possibility of punching wrong and so had never paid attention to it.

"Okay, let's hit the floor mats."

She followed him to a set of mats.

"Lay on your back."

"What?"

He smiled and then lay down in the position he wanted her in. "Like this." Then he stood and waited for her. He had laid flat on his back, knees bent and feet flat on the mat.

She took a deep breath and then as she started to lay down, her body began to grow nervous, trembling. Tears began to pour from her eyes. Sweat broke from her skin to a point that it was like a water hose on a slow drip, just drizzling down her body. The feeling of pins and needles came across her body briefly before she felt numb, almost paralytic.

The room began spinning and then the earth around her followed.

She could feel the weight of Steven laying on top of her. All the control she felt she had in her life now was rapidly disappearing. Suddenly, all she could feel was the overwhelming need to get away. She needed to escape and run for her life.

The next thing she knew, Jose was sitting next to her with the palm resting in his as he used the thumb of his other hand to massage it.

She locked eyes with him and in that moment that she stared into his…it was as if she had just stared into his soul. There was something inside her telling her to breathe with him. She watched his shoulders move up and down in an exaggerated way. He was breathing slowly and deeply just so she could see his pattern and catch on to the rhythm.

Slowly, the nervousness began to fade. The trembling was no longer noticeable. The tears dried from her eyes. The sweat was a glisten on her skin instead a fountain. Her feet seemed to be okay with sitting still instead of running. She began feeling her limbs come back to her and with that, the control as well.

She knew that she should have felt embarrassed for the reasonless panic attack, but then, most people who suffer from them seldom know the trigger for their attacks. They come on so sudden that most just deal with it the best way they can and move on.

Before long, she could feel herself wanting to smile and she did. "Thank you. I don't know how you knew or how you managed to help without even saying a word, but I sincerely can't thank you enough."

"My mother used to suffer from panic attacks. It's no big deal. I learned early on to give the person who is in the middle of losing their minds, or so they feel, every ounce of control I can and mainly something to focus on other than what is running through their bodies."

"It's a nice trick. One that I should remember."

"Do you have them often?"

"No."

"Can you share with me what you think might have triggered it? You don't have to; I would just like to avoid that if I can."

She took a deep breath and went to move her hand from his, but his grip tightened and he slowly and very calmly shook his head as he continued to massage her.

"Steven used to do most of the damage when he had me pinned to the floor."

"I see. Shall we work on that?"

"I don't know if I can."

"Sure you can. You just have to make a choice, right here, right now. Do you want to be a survivor or a victim? The choice is yours."

"I'm a survivor."

"Not yet, but you can be."

She didn't have to ask him what he meant by that. She knew. If she was a survivor, she needed to overcome her fears and put every single ounce of effort into moving on and forgetting him all together.

Jose smiled as she returned to her position on the mat and moved to lay down next to her. "I just want you to look up at the ceiling for a moment. When you are ready, close your eyes and take a deep breath several times."

"Okay," she replied, concentrating on one single stain on the ceiling where it was apparent there was a leak. When she was ready, she closed her eyes.

"Keep breathing, relaxing, and keep telling yourself that I am here to help you. I will not hurt you. I am going to show you how to kick a man's ass so you never have to fear abuse again."

After several minutes, she was ready to go. She opened her eyes and turned to look at him. He was staring up to the ceiling, patiently giving her the time she needed.

"I'm ready." She smiled.

"Good." He moved slowly and explained every last thing before he even touched her. The few minutes he was supposed to spend with her had turned into an hour before it was over. He continued to attempt to control her from the top and with his instruction that she followed so well, she was able to break away from him with ease before he smiled and collapsed to the mat beside her.

"You did excellent today. I have some work to do, but I'll be here next time you're here."

"How do you know when I will be here?"

"I don't. I pretty much live here, though."

"Oh." She stood and walked to the bench where her belongings were. She grabbed her towel and patted her head a few times before turning back and seeing he was gone. She felt a bit of disappointment because she hadn't got to thank him. She would tell him tomorrow, though. If it was the last thing she did every day before going home, she was coming back to get all the help she could. For the first time since leaving Steven, she felt like she could actually partially hold her own.

It had been three months since she met Jose and began training with him. In that short time, she had transformed to a woman that wasn't so jumpy around men. A woman that was in the best shape of her life. A woman that wasn't in total fear of walking down the street and being found. She rarely thought of Steven anymore. The only time she needed to remember what he had put her through was when she was ready to quit training for the day and Jose would use him to give her the push she needed to finish.

Over the last three months, she had found another friend. She had developed a bond with Jose that couldn't be described. She trusted him with every ounce of woman she was, and loved him like a brother. He had been her angel in the dark when she needed someone the most.

"Jose, I need to tell you something. Something that I haven't told anyone."

He smiled, wiping his forehead. "Okay." He sat on the bench next to her.

"When I left Steven, I decided that if I couldn't get over it, I would end it myself. I didn't want to live in fear of him finding me and I surely didn't want him to find me and actually go back to what I had worked so hard to leave behind." She took a deep breath and wiped a tear that was trailing down her cheek. "I had this bottle of hydrocodone. It was the last bottle that I had filled before I left him and the divorce was final. I had kept it and my plans were to take the entire bottle if I couldn't cope. If he found me. I was going to end my life because I didn't want him to have any more control and I wasn't willing to give him the power to take anything more from me. I have stared at that bottle every night since then. But last night, I pulled the bottle from my nightstand like I always do and for the first time, I started laughing. I realized there was no way in hell I was going to take that bottle and do what his ultimate goal was. I found a new pep in my step as I went to the toilet and flushed them. I want to thank you. You really have no idea how you have saved my life."

She watched as his eyes glistened and his chin twitched. "No, it is you saved me. I am so glad that I found you. I have a confession to make now. Days were passing when I was searching for someone like you. Someone that needed me to help them. I was beginning to lose faith that I would ever find you. Then I looked across the gym and saw this woman who…well, since we are being completely honest with each other now, had no clue what she was doing and I knew right then, I had finally found you. My life hasn't been the greatest either. I lost my way there for a long time and I found my way back in helping you. It's you that I owe many thanks to."

"Wait, what? You're not mad about my admission? About the pills?"

"No. You never would have taken them. You're too strong for that. You may have thought you would, but you are not a quitter."

He reached for her and pulled her into his chest. "If I had only met you sooner," he whispered, kissing her cheek and then walking away.

She wanted to chase after him, but her cell began ringing and she knew that it could only be work-related.

"Hello."

"Hey, Kamry. This is Suzy. I wanted to tell you that Ms. Maybelle has taken a turn for the worse and we have called in hospice. Her grandson is here with her now and he wanted you to be called. Ms. Maybelle had been talking with him about you."

"How bad is she?" Kamry asked.

"She won't be with us by tomorrow, we're afraid."

"I'm on my way." Kamry ended the call and began a steady jog home. She showered, changed, and headed to Ms. Maybelle.

The minute she walked into her room, she saw how bad she was. Suzy was there and she had the familiar bottle of MSIR—morphine sulfate instant release. She knew they usually only used that particular medication when the end was near, because just a few drops of medication under the tongue and it would get into the system. It was used when the person was unable to swallow anymore or when the pain was too severe, because it would get into their system faster than swallowing medication.

"Hey, Kamry," Suzy whispered.

The man sitting in a chair with his back to the door stood, turned, and smiled. Damn, if the circumstances were different. He was tall. Six foot, athletic build. Short, dark hair that looked like he had just gotten straight out of bed and ran his fingers through it. Dark brown eyes that were lit with attraction, with a tan complexion and long legs. He was wearing a white t-shirt that had some kind of black shape on the front and dark embellished jeans. He was a walking, talking GQ model and there was something very familiar about him. He was definitely Hispanic. That had to be it, Kamry decided. Jose was Hispanic, so maybe she was relating the two of them because of that.

He walked towards her, still smiling. He held his hand out. "I'm Garret, it is so nice to finally meet you. Grammy has talked about you every day for the last four months. She really loved you. I believe her words were, 'you have to meet her, Garret, she is the tea to my cup and she could make your cup runneth over too'." He smiled. "You know Gram. She's always looking for the happily ever after. It was never her fault, though. A hopeless romantic to the bone."

Kamry laughed. "Yes, she is. Nice to meet you as well." She shook his hand, feeling a bit of a shock as their hands touched. It was something she had only read about, but had never felt anything like it before. It was like electricity tickling her hand and moving up through her arm then down her entire body. One word was all she could think of: amazing.

She took a deep breath and then let go, walking towards Ms. Maybelle. It took her a moment to gather her wits before she could say a word or even ask a question that made any kind of sense. "Has she been awake today at all?"

"No. Unfortunately, she hasn't," Garret answered, sitting back down and taking Ms. Maybelle's hand in his. "She has been like this all day. I came as soon as I could. They called me last night and I was here in, like, thirty minutes or so. I was hoping that it was just a spell or maybe another mini stroke. Since her big stroke, she has had several of those. It's not though. Is it?"

Kamry wasn't a nurse or doctor, but she could tell Ms. Maybelle was going to be visiting Heaven soon. Kamry gently checked her eyes, noticing they were glazed over, and her color was pale. She gently raised the blanket's footing, noticing that Ms. Maybelle's heels were purplish. Not a good sign at all. "No, I'm sorry."

He nodded.

Suzy knocked quietly on the door before coming in with another chair. "I thought you might need this. The kitchen is preparing a tray with coffee and stuff, you know the routine. If you need anything else, just let me know."

"Thanks, Suzy."

"Yes, thank you." Garret didn't take his eyes from his grandmother's hand.

They sat quietly for a few moments before Garret spoke. "So, I know this is kind of weird, but all this silence is killing me. Can we talk about something, maybe take my mind off of what I am soon to see?"

"Sure. What would you like to talk about?"

"Well, tell me about yourself. Are you married? Kids?"

Kamry stiffened, taking a breath and beginning to rub her hands on her knees. "Um, no and no." She silently thanked God for no children. Not that she didn't want children, she just didn't want any children with Steven. "How about you?"

"No and no." He chuckled. "I work a lot and my life, well, it's kind of crazy and a lot of women are just in it for money or bragging rights."

Her curiosity shot through the roof, but at the same time, he hadn't actually said what it was he did for a living, so maybe he didn't want her to know exactly what it was. "That's too bad."

"Yeah. So, I can tell by your accent you aren't from NYC."

This time it was Kamry that chuckled. "Nope. I'm a SEMO girl."

"A what?"

She smiled. "Southeast Missouri."

"That's it. That midwestern/southern accent combined. But it's nice. It's different. I like different." He looked up and they locked eyes. For an inkling of a second, the world stood still. Then Ms. Maybelle's SPO2 monitor beeped and brought Kamry back to reality. Both Kamry and Garret started. Ms. Maybelle's heart rate was dropping. Kamry stood and silenced the machine.

"Do you want to keep this on? I can shut it off and let the nurses know."

"Yes, please. It's bad enough watching, but I think hearing it will be worse." Garret reached up and wiped a single tear from his cheek.

Kamry sat with Garret for several hours before Ms. Maybelle took her last breath. For the first time in a long time, she wrapped a man in her arms and held him while he let the tears fall.

When the funeral home arrived and left with Ms. Maybelle, Garret walked Kamry to her car. "Can I have your number? I would like to let you know about the arrangements."

"Absolutely." She reached into her car and grabbed a business card, scribbling her personal cell on it. "Call me any time, even if you just need to talk."

"Thank you."

She watched him walk away. She didn't know where his parents were because Ms. Maybelle had never talked about her children. Kamry assumed it was something along the lines of hard feelings or maybe they had already gone to Heaven, because Garret hadn't called anyone from when Ms. Maybelle had passed.

Kamry finished her day at work with a sadness in her heart. She had known that Ms. Maybelle was going down because she had been growing tired with therapy, but had insisted on continuing. It wasn't going to be the same without her there, though.

She turned into the gym parking lot. After entering and changing her clothes, she did her warm up. Usually Jose didn't show up until after she was finished working the bags over, but today, he didn't show at all. She worked through the routine they had been working on. She was proud of herself for being able to do the things she was doing now and she owed it all to Jose.

She owed a lot to him. She would have to invite him to dinner or something to thank him. She knew it wasn't much, but something told her that Jose enjoyed the smaller things in life and that no amount of money would mean as much as a good dinner.

When she was finished, she started worrying about him, but grabbed her bags and went to leave. A poster that she hadn't really paid attention before, which hung next to the exit, caught her attention for reasons unknown to her.

She smiled, raising her brows. It was Jose, Jose Cortez, and apparently he had just won middleweight champion belt in MMA. He looked completely overcome with joy. Next to the poster was an article about him. She began reading it, and noticed words like had, was, and past, and wondered why the article was written in the past tense. Maybe it was because he was no longer fighting, she thought. She read through his entire career and then reached a sentence that stunned her.

"Jose 'Hope' Cortez was at the top of the MMA world before his life was taken tragically in a head-on collision."

"What?" That couldn't be right. Something was wrong with the article. Panic began to fill her when she realized he wasn't there today and she looked at the date of the article, which was five years old.

Her hand clamped over her mouth. "No way."

She kept reading and then learned that he had a brother that continued to fight and was also making his way up to the top: Garret Maybelle.

Her blood seemed to drain from her body. That explained why he looked so familiar, as reading that put all the puzzle pieces together. He did favor Jose. How was this possible? How was Jose training her?

How?

How?

How?

Kamry didn't return to the gym for the next few days. She did go to Ms. Maybelle's funeral after receiving several phone calls she didn't answer. Garret had left a voicemail with the details. She paid her condolences at the service, but nothing more. He had asked her out for coffee after, but she turned him down, using the excuse that she had work to get back to.

Really, she just wanted to get back to her apartment and try to wrap her mind around what was happening. It didn't make any sense to her. For the past few days, she still couldn't figure it out. How could he be dead? Why was he training her? How had she met him, Ms. Maybelle, and then Garret?

If she ever wanted to tell someone, to see if their brain could make sense out of it, they would assume she had lost it and needed a straitjacket. Nope, that wasn't an option either, but calling Garret back and taking him up on his coffee offer was.

She reached for her cell and quickly dialed his number. Three rings later, he answered.

"I was afraid I would never hear from you again."

"I'm sorry about that. There's been a lot going on. Do you want to meet up, maybe have that coffee today?"

"That's a nice surprise. Absolutely. Do you have a place in mind?"

"Do you know where Jay's is?"

"Do I ever. They have the best cinnamon rolls in NYC. Meet you there in an hour?"

"An hour it is."

She hung up and quickly changed her clothes. She opted for casual and comfortable: embellished Silver jeans with an AC/DC black t-shirt and her ever-faithful, black flip flops. She may have lived in NYC now, but country was forever in her blood.

She reached the cafe about fifteen minutes early. She found a table and ordered her favorite cup of coffee, black. She would have ordered his, but she really didn't know what he would take in his coffee. She knew he would order a cinnamon roll, but assumed he would want it warm.

The minute she heard the bell of the door, her body began to tingle. The hair on her arms began moving with the beat of something… She didn't know what the beat belonged to, but she did know they were in perfect rhythm with something. She looked up and sure enough, he was walking towards her table. He smiled that smile that would make any woman stop and stare at him. The man was walking perfection when it came to looks.

But what she liked the most was his eyes. They were full of mystery and sexy and yet so warm and inviting. Knowing what she knew now, she had seen those eyes long before she met Garret. They were Jose's eyes.

Garret sat at the table and used his hand to gesture for the waitress. "I'm glad you called. I seriously thought I had seen the last of you. I was a bit disappointed."

Kamry smiled. "I'm sorry. Things are…complicated. I lead a very private life and there are things in my past that I don't want to exactly talk about in detail and to this day, I run from. I didn't kill anyone or harm anyone or break any law. It's just…complicated."

"I like complicated as well. It's a puzzle. I enjoy them too."

This time, Kamry smiled. She didn't know why, or what for, but she had this soothing feeling coming over her like a warm blanket on a chilled night. She liked it.

"So…I'm so terribly bad at this. I don't even know what to say."

Garret laughed. "That makes two of us then."

They both laughed. "How about something that piqued my curiosity?"

He raised his eyebrows, giving her a devilish grin. "I do enjoy piqued curiosity almost as much as I enjoy puzzles and complications. Tell me, what has yours piqued?"

She looked into his eyes, seeing the humor and hidden meaning behind his words. They normally would have bothered her, but there was just something about him that made it easy to let the guard down that she had built up and made permanent with every bit of cement she could find.

"You're pretty easygoing, aren't you?" she asked.

"Kamry, is that what has your mind asking questions over and over again or is that something that just popped in the wonderful brain of yours? And, yes, I am really easygoing. I'm laid back. I'm not one for drama or stirring a pot that doesn't need stirring. I don't like arguments and I haven't even raised my voice in…well, outside my work, in a very long time."

"Um…no. That wasn't the question I wanted to ask. You fight, don't you?"

She watched his shoulders square a bit. She could tell he wasn't upset for her knowing, but something else. "I do."

"Does it bother you that I know?"

"No. Of course not. How did you find out?"

"It's the funniest story, really. I work out at this gym and there was a poster of Jose there. I read the story about him and then saw your name."

"You work out at a gym that specializes in MMA style fighting?"

"Yes. It's close to where I live and I was pretty much left alone until…well…" She laughed. "That's even a funnier story and you probably wouldn't believe me."

"He came to you, didn't he?"

Kamry's eyes grew wide. "How did you know?"

He let out a sigh. "I still see him and talk to him and train with him. It's amazing. I don't know how it happens or why it happens, but I can't wait for him to come back to me each time he leaves."

"Oh my God! I seriously thought I was going crazy for a bit."

"Wait. Is that why you called me? Because you found out I fight in MMA and that Jose fought and please tell me you're not like the others."

"Of course not. I met your grandmother long before meeting you. I began training long before meeting you. I met him only because I didn't know what the hell I was doing with the bag I was trying to kick but was really kicking me back harder than I was delivering. I'm not like them. I saw the poster, and that's why I was so standoffish at the funeral and didn't answer your calls. I was freaked out. That's all." She really hoped he believed her, because it was the truth and she liked how easy it was explaining things to him. Had it been Steven, she would have been laid out on the floor by now.

"Kamry, I believe you. You just can't imagine how many are only after that."

"Oh, I do actually. Wait, no. I mean, I can imagine. I watched *Rocky*, like, a billion times and I can see how everyone acts. Not Adrian of course, she was awesome. But you know, the fans."

"I love that movie. They are all my favorites. Actually, anything with Stallone in it is on my favorite list."

"Mine too. I love him. I even loved it when him and Dolly were singing together."

"That's funny. I have every single one of his movies."

"Wow. I have a few, but not all of them. Maybe one day."

"Would you like to come to my place sometime? Have a Stallone marathon and eat extra butter popcorn with cheese sprinkled on top?"

"Well, I could watch all of his movies at home because I could just order them on demand, but since you added the popcorn and cheese, count me in."

They both began laughing and for the next several hours, they sat there, getting to know each other and planning when their movie marathon was going to happen. When the streets began lighting up with something besides the sun, Kamry sighed. It was definitely time to be getting home.

They both said their goodbyes, after Kamry refused to allow him to walk her home several times. She watched him get into a cab and then she waved. She hadn't felt this good in a long time. She was finally comfortable with a man close to her again. Well, a man that she liked and was attracted to, anyways.

Kamry lay in bed thinking about Garret and how they had so much in common. It had been two hours since she had watched him get into that cab and she was still thinking about him. There was just so much about him, but what she loved most was how easy she felt sitting there and talking, laughing and sharing stories. It had been great.

She had learned that Garret had a masters degree in English lit. That he had once wanted to go into publishing because he enjoyed reading so many books. She had asked his favorite genre and he just smiled and said he didn't have one. He loved them all. He even admitted to reading romances as well.

His favorite movies were of course action stories, but again, he would watch anything that had a good story to it.

His favorite color was blue, same as hers. He loved all music but enjoyed opera most, which surprised her. Just thinking about him made the hair on body come to life again, while the little butterflies in her stomach began to wake up. She smiled remembering the first time they had touched. It had been innocent, but the pull and electrical vibe she had felt was the most wonderful thing she had ever experienced.

Kamry heard someone knocking quietly on the door. She ran her fingers through her hair and walked to the door with Garret still on her mind. When she opened it, the air in her lungs was sucked from her. The smile and look in Steven's eyes were filled with dangerous intent.

Stupid, Kamry, she thought. She should have looked through the peep hole. She had been so caught up thinking about her date…coffee meeting with Garret that she didn't even think about it.

She quickly tried to close the door, but he used his large frame to stop it. With one hand, he gripped her throat, shutting off her airway and smiling the entire time. He threw her backwards once inside, shutting the door slowly and locking it.

"You are one tough bitch to track down," he said.

Kamry picked herself up. "Yeah, and you are one son of a bitch who shouldn't be here either. You're breaking the restraining order. You shouldn't be here. Please leave."

She reached into her pocket, grabbing her phone to call 911. He was on her before she could hit talk. He smashed the phone into pieces before giving her one good blow to the face. The last thing she remembered was hearing him laugh.

When Kamry woke, she was in his vehicle driving down the highway. She tried to move but before she could get anywhere, he elbowed her in the face and knocked her out again.

The next time she came to, she was laying against a wall. He was sitting on the side of the bed, drinking whiskey like it was water.

"Steven, where are we?"

He looked over at her, smiled and began laughing. "Somewhere you can scream all you want and they will never hear you."

"Why are you doing this?"

"Because you owe me."

She watched him walk around the room. Pacing back and forth slowly. He looked like he hadn't showered recently and he definitely hadn't shaved in a few days. He reeked of sweat and booze.

Her head was pounding and her ribs hurt each time she took a breath.

"Why are you just sitting there? I taught you better than that."

She looked up and Jose was standing there, looking down at her.

"You know who I am now. More importantly, you know who you are as well. Get up and fight!"

"I can't," she whispered.

"You can't fucking what!" Steven yelled, but Kamry didn't look at him. She kept looking at Jose.

"I'll help you," he said, reaching down and grabbing her arm to help her up. "There you go. Stay on your feet and if he gets you down, you fight!"

Damn, she didn't know who to be more afraid of: him or Steven.

Steven started laughing when Kamry raised her fists in the position that Jose had taught her. "What do you think you are going to do?"

"I'm going to leave here," she said, her words trembling.

"Don't you show him you're scared," Jose coached. "Show him that you are a strong woman. Show him he can't victimize you any longer."

She took a step towards Steven as Jose kept guiding her.

"Feed off of all that anger he has made you feel. All that fear you have felt. You are a survivor, Kamry."

Steven swung and Kamry ducked, coming back up with a fist to the bottom of his chin, knocking him backwards.

"Stay on him, Kamry. Don't let him get a chance to come back at you. You keep on him." Kamry took a deep breath, heading towards him. She was going to show Steven he could not hurt her anymore. He could not scare her anymore. That he was nothing.

She swung again, pounding her fists into his face, his ribs, giving him liver shot after liver shot.

He kicked his leg out, knocking her down and making her land on the side where her ribs hurt, taking the air from her.

He mounted her, using both his hands around her neck. She couldn't breathe.

"Use your hips, Kamry."

She swung to the side, laying on her right hip. With her left leg, she managed to place her foot on his hip and push him back. She brought her left elbow down over his arms, breaking his hold on her.

"Don't worry about gasping now. Stay calm. This isn't over yet, Kamry. Use your other foot."

She pulled her right foot up, kicking him in the chest with everything she had and knocking him completely off her.

"Get up!" Jose yelled.

Kamry stood, walking to Steven, and began kicking him in the ribs. The rage poured from her body with every last kick. She watched his face become wrinkled almost, his eyes squinting with each kick. She loved it.

She kept going but then she realized she was not going to kick him to death. She was going to do to him what he had done to her so many times. She reached down, rolling him onto his back and mounting him. She placed both hands around his neck and began choking him. No matter what he did, she held on. She watched his color go from red, to purple, to blue. He was weakening and she was loving the power she had over him. His arms dropped to the side and that's when it hit her. She wasn't going to be the one to kill him. She let go, and stood.

He gasped for air, grabbing his throat and coughing.

"Yeah, that's right. I'm not weak anymore. You will never be able to hurt me again."

"He will never be able to hurt any other woman or child again. I have some people that can't wait to get their hands on him," Jose said.

"What do you mean?" Kamry asked, but Jose didn't have to answer. She heard a growling mixed with a low roar. "What is that?" she whispered.

"It's his end," Jose answered.

She watched as black shadows rose from the floor around him. He began screaming. "No, don't take me. Kamry, help me!"

She smiled. "There is no help for you." And then they took him. It happened quickly, and he was gone.

The room began to blur then. She didn't know what was happening and she didn't really care. He had gotten everything he deserved.

"Where did they take him?" She asked, hoping for the answer she received.

"Hell."

What happened next, she wasn't sure of. She remembered hearing a loud crash and then arms were around her waist, pulling her into the body they belonged to. The room began to spin and everything went dark.

"You did a good job, Kamry. Just rest," Jose whispered.

A steady beep was in the background. Otherwise, silence filled the area. There was a clean smell to the air. She was waking up, and could feel her body being touched. Her hand, her cheek were being rubbed.

"Time to wake up, sleepyhead."

"Jose?" Kamry looked around the room, finding his familiar eyes on her and then someone else in the chair next to her.

"Jose, where am I?"

"The hospital. You've been asleep for a bit longer than we had anticipated. Steven thought a good swift kick to your head while you were out would add to the multiple injuries you had."

"Oh." She was never happier than that day to see Jose. Had it not been for him, she never would have been able to get free.

Jose gripped her hand. "It's time for me to go now, Kamry."

There was both sadness and happiness in Jose's eyes. "But, why?"

"Because I did what I stayed behind for."

"Jose, what are you talking about?" Tears filled Kamry's eyes.

"Kamry, I know that you know I'm a ghost. I had unfinished business and you helped me finish it."

"I didn't help you with anything, Jose. Whatever business you had is something you still have."

"No. You were my unfinished business. And him." Jose nodded to the man asleep in the chair. His head was facing the opposite direction, but she knew who it was. Garret.

"How did he find me?" Kamry asked.

"I may have dialed his number on your cell phone so he would hear you and track you down."

"How did he find me, though?"

"I'm not sure. That's a question for him." Jose smiled. "Before I left here, I wanted to do two things. One, help someone that needed me. I thought that you needed me, but in all reality, I needed you. You reminded me that there are still many things out there worth fighting for. You were always a survivor, you just needed a push in the right direction."

"I don't understand what you are saying."

"I had been watching you for weeks, pounding away at that bag. You showed so much heart and determination that I knew without a doubt, you were never going to stop. That's very admirable. I've only seen that much determination two other times before. Once in myself and then once in Garret. I never thought I would see it again until you came along."

"You're not making any sense to me," Kamry cried.

Jose chuckled. "It don't have to make sense to you. It was my business to finish."

"What was the second thing that you had to do?"

"I not only watched you at the gym, but I saw you with Grandma. You took care of her like she was royalty. You cared for her. You made her laugh. You were there for her when I couldn't be."

"Ms. Maybelle," she whispered.

"Yes. Garret is my younger brother and he was my second thing I needed to do. You see, when Grandma died, she was the last one in our family. I didn't want Garret to be alone. And then I saw the chemistry between you two and knew that you were perfect for each other. Cupid in the making, I am." He smiled.

Kamry turned her head towards Garret. She had felt a chemistry between them, but was she ready for a relationship again?

"Don't over-think it. A ghost is standing here telling you to let go and follow your instincts. Allow your heart to lead you."

"I know," she whispered.

"Well, I hear them calling me."

"Who?" Kamry asked.

"Grandma, Grandpa, my mother and father. They are waiting for me."

"I don't want you to go."

Jose smiled. "You're not alone. He's a really great man. He deserves you just as much as you deserve him. I won't be far. I'll keep tabs on the two of you. They are very impatient. Take care of him for me, Kamry. I know he will take wonderful care of you."

"Wait!" she hollered, watching him walk away. "Can I ask you something really quick?"

"Better hurry." He smiled.

She could see his body becoming almost translucent. "Why did they call you hope?"

He laughed. "Because there is an old saying: where there is life, there is hope. Well, I lived by that motto in the ring. My first fight, I was the underdog. I was losing but I wouldn't give up. I kept going until he was worn down. After I won, they were asking me questions and a reporter asked me what gave me the drive to keep going. I said, hope. It stuck."

"Thank you." She smiled, watching him wink at her then turn, take a few steps, and disappear.

Kamry laid there staring at Garret and then she smiled. Ms. Maybelle had rubbed off on her grandsons, and she suspected that Garret would be a cupid as well. She laughed, watching him sleep, and was thankful for meeting Jose, who would forever be known to her as Kamry's Hope.

AN ACT OF LOVE
Kat Jameson

The first thing Jesse was aware of was something in her eyes. She didn't remember going to sleep, or even going to bed, so she had no idea what was on her face.

Right away, she could feel that it was hot, and wet. She tried to lift her hand to touch it, but found that something was around her hand. In fact, she felt entirely trapped in place. Her brain was moving out of unconsciousness slowly, and couldn't reconcile the facts. In fact, she was having trouble understanding what the facts were.

"Don't move," a man's voice said from beside her.

She didn't recognize the voice and that jolted her closer to being awake. Now she tried to open her eyes properly, and found that she couldn't. There was something on them, almost gluing her eyelashes. Panic began to set in and she started moving.

"Don't move," the voice repeated. She felt a squeeze and realized that someone was holding her hand, but she knew that it wasn't Tom.

"Who are you?" she asked, hearing her own voice and how small it sounded. There was a strange, tinny echo to it. "Why can't I open my eyes? Where's Tom?" She started to struggle again, but remained trapped and when she moved too much, it hurt.

"You were in a car accident," the voice said. Jesse kept trying to open her eyes. It hurt her eyelids but felt like with each attempt, she was able to achieve more. The voice continued, "Tom, I'm assuming he was driving. He's right beside you, but he's unconscious. I've called the paramedics, sweetheart, you just stay still. I don't know what injuries you have." She felt the squeeze on her hand again. "Help is on the way."

Why couldn't she remember a car accident? She felt tears well up in her eyes, but it actually helped. It loosened whatever was sticking her eyelashes together so she was able to peel them open, and she instantly found the truth of the stranger's statement. Before her was the shattered windshield. Turning her head slightly, she was able to see him.

Jesse didn't know this man kneeling beside her open car door. She was sure that she had never seen him before in her life, but he on the ground with her feeble hand clasped in his. "Help is on the way, I promise," he reassured her. His voice was kind and he looked at her like he was earnestly concerned, even though they were strangers. She felt tears choking her throat again, but they hurt and she swallowed them back down.

Weakly, she tried to turn her head the other way. She saw Tom. He was slumped back in his seat and she saw blood covering his face. The tears returned and she couldn't stop them. "Tom?" she asked in that weak little voice again, choking back emotion. "Tom? Wake up, honey, please. Tom? Tom?"

"Wait till the ambulance gets here," the stranger said again. "They'll be able to help him."

Jesse tried to remember what had happened, but everything was so hazy. The effort made her feel like she was going to be sick and she let her head fall back against the headrest as she tried to take a deep breath around the nausea.

She closed her eyes again. "What's your name?" she whispered.

He once more squeezed her hand gently. "Anthony."

Jesse forced her breath in and out, slow and steady. "I'm Jesse." She bit down on her lip, swallowing hard against the pain. She wanted to crawl into the seat beside her and hold her husband until he woke, but she knew she couldn't. Her seatbelt had her pinned and she didn't feel like she had the strength to unfasten it. What else might be broken was a deep concern to her mind, and she didn't want to move too much and make it worse.

Sirens echoed in the distance, but she couldn't tell from which direction. She listened as they grew closer and louder, overwhelming her aching head. Tears rolled down her cheeks as she heard the sound of rolling tires coming to a stop, doors opening and shutting as she opened her eyes again to try to look out. Everything beyond that broken windshield was a blur, but she saw those dark figures drawing near.

"Tom," she told them weakly. "Help Tom."

"Excuse us," a paramedic said as he came around to the passenger side.

"Help Tom," she whispered.

"We are, ma'am," he said. "We are. We're also going to take care of you." As he began working on her, she tried to look beyond him to find Anthony, but there was no sign of him.

Sniffing, she felt her throat tighten again. "Thank you," she whispered to someone who was no longer there as she listened to the sounds of their rescue.

Comparatively, Jesse wasn't as bad off. She was covered in bruises and lacerations, and had a sprained ankle from where it had been resting when the car hit that tree, but the driver's side had taken more damage. Tom had taken the hit for her, like he always did—or always tried to. Jesse was up and about in just a few hours, limping around and feeling like she'd been beaten.

Her husband was another matter.

She sat by his bedside. He was still unconscious. No, he wasn't just unconscious, he was in a coma. The doctors had used words like "intracranial pressure" and "bleeding." All she knew was that it was bad, and they didn't know what was going to happen. They were doing things like "monitoring the situation" and "preparing for contingencies."

As he lay there, she wrapped one hand around his, the other gripping her Tree of Life pendant, and pressed her forehead against the bed beside him. The possibilities rolled out before her in stark terror as her mind tried to suggest she consider a life without him. Those thoughts were shut down as hard as they came, because she couldn't do it.

Tom and Jesse had met in high school, had become inseparable almost instantly and had stayed that way ever since. Married just after they turned twenty, they were coming up on their tenth anniversary. They had been planning to...

They had been planning.

"Tom," she whispered at the floor, unable to lift her head. She had known this man for over half of her life, and she couldn't imagine the rest of it without him. The doctors might be planning for all contingencies, but she couldn't. He would be okay, because he just had to be. She squeezed his hand, but knew he couldn't recognize it for what it was.

She was still in that position, half-dazed with the surrealism of it all, when the door to this small Intensive Care Unit room opened. It might have been a visitor for the other patient, so she didn't bother looking up. Even when the footsteps approached her, she didn't look up. Jesse felt a heavy hand on her shoulder.

"I'm sorry," the owner of the hand said. She recognized the voice of Tom's boss down at the autobody shop where he had worked for the past five years. Marcus was a good man and had even become a friend. She murmured a "thank you" but couldn't summon the power to do much more. The hand left her shoulder and she heard a chair scrape closer. "What do we know?"

"Not much," she said. It was an effort to draw in a deep breath, but she managed to do so and relayed what had happened and what little she knew of what the doctors said. Marcus, not being a man of many words, just offered the appropriate grunts of sympathy or frustration.

"If there's anything I can do," he said, patting her shoulder with his bear paw of a hand one more time. After she mumbled another word of gratitude, he left.

This was roughly how it went for the next two days.

She moved occasionally, strongly encouraged by the nurses to take care of herself. It never equated to eating much, but they managed to keep her fairly hydrated with cups of ginger ale and ice water. Others visited—Tom's coworkers and friends with the volunteer fire department, and her sister came by as well, a pair of friends stopping by later. There were choked up phone calls with Tom's parents.

In Tom himself, there had been no change. He wasn't any worse, and that was something, but he wasn't any better either. There was no sign of his waking any time soon.

Squeezing his hand often, she talked to him. It was the most energetic thing she had managed to do since they ended up in this terrible place. She felt like she nearly had roots stretching into the ground, to be uprooted when they came to move him to another room for longer-term care than ICU could provide.

Jesse didn't like when that happened. "Long term" were words that poked holes in her brain and her heart, letting her hope leak out and run off down the hallway. The fog around her thickened and she followed the wheeled hospital bed with the orderlies through the hospital until they reached the new room.

This one had four people in it, all curtained off. Not all of them were in a coma, but they were all "long term" care.

Long term...

Sitting beside his old bed in its new location, she traced the lines on his hand over and over again. She'd lived with these hands for over ten years now, but had never spent as much time contemplating them as she had these past three days. The door opened, but now there was only a one-quarter chance it was for her. She didn't bother looking up, but the clicking of a pair of professional pumps on the tile floor drew near her.

"Mrs. Dixon?" the voice belonging to the heels asked. As expected, the voice was female.

Jesse forced herself to look up and received an overly sympathetic smile. She introduced herself as Ella Ari, and she was a social worker at the hospital. She came to talk over...'things' with the patient's wife.

It had taken only the length of a breath for Jesse to decide she hated the woman. She stared at her like steel doors were shutting around all the open ports in her mind. She blocked away her hatred, but stared silently and blankly. The social worker just droned on, and everything she said sounded like a grief counselor come to console Jesse.

"He's not dead yet, you know," Jesse murmured.

"What was that?" the other woman asked, still with her funereal air.

"I said..." Jesse replied, forcing her voice louder as she lifted her dead gaze to Ms. Ari. "I said, he's not dead yet. Stop talking to me like you're here to help me mourn." She spoke each of these words with enunciation, hints of her emotions slipping into it.

Ari blinked. "I... I didn't meant to imply otherwise, Mrs. Dixon. But we must face the possibilities—"

Jesse cut her off harshly. "No, I mustn't!" Pressing her lips together, she forced herself to reel it back in. There was nothing this social worker could do to her or Tom, except bother her deeply. She ground her back teeth together for a moment. "My husband is not dead and until they come in and tell me otherwise, that's the only possibility I plan to focus on."

To her credit, Ari recovered quickly and nodded. She put a card down on the small table beside Tom's bed. "If you need anything," she said and hastily made her exit.

When the door shut, Jesse shuddered with her entire body. Once again, she gripped Tom's hand tightly in hers and then pressed her forehead against their fingers. Squeezing her eyes shut, she tried to stem the flow of tears as they welled up in her eyes but there was no stopping them and they spilled over their joined hands.

She cried for what seemed like forever before finally lifting her eyes to look over Tom's face. It just looked like he was sleeping, nothing like he was hovering on the verge between this world and the next. What would it take to pull him off that point and into this existence again?

Rising, she stroked his cheek and then pressed her lips to his ear. "If I have to crawl into the hall of the gods and strangle the All-Father myself to bring you back, I will." She pressed her lips to his cheek and then left his room.

Jesse knew she could do nothing for him just sitting and crying at his bedside.

Their studio apartment felt bereft the moment she walked into it. The emptiness and darkness was so total that she almost turned around and left again. She stopped herself from doing so and walked in.

She turned on all the lights, whether she needed them or not, and she turned on the television to a show Tom liked and let it run. It didn't matter if she liked it, just that its noise filled the space. Jesse even turned the heat up to where Tom liked it, and where she was constantly turning it down from in their Thermostat War.

Some part of her knew that she should eat something, but instead she went right to her laptop. Setting it up on the bed, since she didn't have a desk for it, she let the background noise start to soothe the gaping pit in her soul—which she could feel like a physical pain just below her breastbone—while she pulled up the internet.

Jesse accessed the saved links she had for her pagan studies. Although not wholly Asatru—those who were devoted to the Norse gods and reforging their ways—her pantheon was full of the deities of the Northmen. She knew others that she could call and ask questions of, but she didn't want to.

There was an idea blossoming in her mind, but she didn't want to share it. She knew they would think she was crazy, but she had always believed that the gods were all around them. If you looked hard enough, you could find them. She was more literal than a great many of her fellow pagans, but that was okay in their world.

Just searching the internet for the old tales from the North about how people used to gain the attention of the gods was overwhelming, and she knew there was a task ahead of her to sort through them all and find the ones that might be useful. She knew that simple prayers, even over her altar, would not call them down. If it did, then there would be a lot more chats over beer with Thor and Freyr.

Time ceased to have any meaning. At one point, she forced herself to get a glass of water.

She found a notebook on the dining room table and flipped past pages of shopping lists and things to do until she found blank pages. Setting it on the bed beside the laptop, she began taking notes. Some of them were direct from the pages she saw, and others were about eddas and sagas that she needed to find and research. She knew that she had some in books that she already owned.

Names and years and places began to swim before her vision and started to make less and less sense. When she had to re-read the same word four times and it still didn't make sense, she began to wonder if maybe the lack of sleep and food was telling on her.

Closing the laptop, she put it on the nightstand and then laid down on the bed just as she was. She had taken off her shoes earlier, but left her clothing on.

She didn't sleep.

Every time her eyes opened, she saw the empty side of the bed. When she flipped over, her bruised arm hurt and she saw Tom's winter coat as it hung by the door until the season when it was needed again. She tried lying on her back, but just wasn't comfortable. It felt unnatural to try to sleep that way.

Getting up, she grabbed her pillow and then Tom's and carried them to the couch. With her own under her head and his in her arms, she resisted the pain from her bruises to keep that pillow clutched to her chest as she closed her eyes and tried to go to sleep.

Eventually, her exhausted body and mind forced both to shut down into a state of restless, dreamless sleep.

In the morning, she went back to the hospital. There had been no change in Tom's condition, and she hadn't really expected there to have been. This time, she laid down on the bed beside him. These beds really weren't made for two, but for a few moments, she would make it work. Closing her eyes, she laid next to his unmoving form and choked her heart back down from her throat to where it was meant to be.

Her boss called while she was driving home.

"Jesse... How're you doing?" She could tell that he was trying to sound sympathetic, but it had never been his strong suit.

"I'm holding up," she replied. It was as honest as she intended to be.

He didn't reply right away, like he was trying to figure out how to say whatever he wanted to say next. Either it would be some awkward question about Tom's condition, or...

"Do you know when you'll be coming back to work?" He took a straightforward approach, which suited him better. He simply was not a man prone to empathy or subtlety, but neither were traits that helped one succeed in the business world.

"I just need a few more days," she sighed. "Isn't Nancy managing alright?"

He grunted softly. "She's fine, but you're better at the job."

That was only because she was the only secretary there who knew how to organize things in the way her boss preferred, and he didn't like having to deal with people who didn't know all of his systems and idiosyncrasies.

Work just wasn't a priority for her right then, and she couldn't force it to be. She had something more important to take care of. "I just need a few more days. I promise, I'll be back to work soon."

He grudgingly agreed and hung up without saying much more.

Jesse shook her head as she parked on the street outside the public library. She pulled the folded piece of paper out of her purse and went in, using the computer to pull up where all of the books she needed were. She took them down one at a time, bringing them to one of the long wooden tables in the center.

Open books and more handwritten notes. Once they were all put away, she had her paper scribbled over on both sides with notes being written in every direction. She emerged from the library with a single reoccurring theme, but she couldn't know if it was the answer.

Could it really be that easy?

On her notebook were the words "blood oath" and they were underlined several times because she had found it come up in several different sources. When mortals wished to gain the attention of their deity, they took an oath marked in blood. The gods of the north took such things very seriously.

She also knew that they would not be kind if they didn't feel she had summoned with good purpose.

When she got home, she found the apartment hotter than she liked. The heat made her choke up as she crossed the room and returned to her computer. Opening it up, she spent all of her time until dark researching blood oaths. Being that it was the internet, she had to spend a fair amount of that time avoiding websites about "vampires." Searching for the word "blood" was apparently very risky.

Once it was dark, she closed the computer and moved to the window. She looked out over the cement jungle she lived in, and knew that this wouldn't do. Seeing the lights across the city, she took a moment to ask herself what she was thinking. Did she really believe that she could *summon a god*? She believed that the gods existed and that a believer could call upon them, but she had never known anyone to gain a response. At least, not a response in as much as she needed.

However, this was 2016. It was not the days of battle and blood, not like it used to be when the gods walked the Earth at their strongest. Did anyone truly make proper blood oaths when they called upon their gods? Did they understand what it took?

Jesse hoped she did. Her life depended on it, because if she lost Tom, she lost everything.

She had to drive outside of the city just to find a small tract of forest. Her purpose was so intent that the shudder she'd felt when climbing into a car didn't touch her now as she pulled onto the side of the road along the trees. She was pretty sure that, technically, it was private property, but not anything that anyone would come out to in the middle of the night. Not believing anyone would go in looking for her, she felt the most she risked was having her car towed and she was willing to risk that.

Shutting the doors and locking them, she stuffed her keys in her pocket. Everything else had been left at the apartment, because she wanted to be as little burdened as possible.

Jesse walked resolutely into the midst of the little forest until she was out of sight of both the road and the city's skyline. It was dark and that amplified the faint chill in the air, making her pull her jacket closer. When she felt she was secluded enough, she pulled out the pocket knife that was the only other thing she carried with her.

She unfolded the blade. This wasn't exactly something she was good at. In her adolescence, she hadn't been a cutter. In fact, getting injured was something she generally worked hard to avoid. She knew that this, however, was her first test. It didn't matter what she wanted or what she was good at, it was what she had to do.

As she pressed the tip of the blade to her palm, she winced. Finally, she just had to shut her eyes and let the blade slide down her skin, hoping she didn't cut anything important. The blood ran hot and free, sliding down the wrist of her upheld arm. The strange, thin pain made her feel slightly lightheaded but she opened her eyes.

She squeezed her hand into a fist and let her blood drop onto the Earth. "I call upon Odin the All-Father, the god of wisdom and poetry and warriors. I call upon him with my blood to pledge myself to him in exchange for a boon of life and death. Please, hear my call."

The blood tapered off until it stopped, and nothing happened. Jesse let out a long breath and dropped her hand. What really had she been expecting, she chastised herself. Of course Odin wasn't going to show up just because she called. He was king of the gods, not a taxi driver.

Turning around, she shrieked and fell back on her ass.

Somehow, she had stopped being alone in the trees and she had never heard a thing. She looked up at the figure of a large man who had been standing a breath away from her, and she'd *never heard a thing*. Her eyes roamed from his boots up to his head, taking in quickly that he had to be well over six feet tall, almost as broad through the shoulders, with long blond hair tied back low, a blonde beard, and...

...a patch over one eye.

Jesse felt all of the air sucked out of her lungs.

"All-Father," she breathed the word, feeling her heart skip every other beat.

"You sound surprised." His voice was low, rumbling like mountains shifting against each other, but also amused as one brow rose. Swallowing hard, she saw that he was wearing...a suit, a dark suit with the shirt open. "Did you not call me in blood?"

"Y-yes, I did," she said, swallowing her heart back down into her chest as she forced herself to get back up. Her gods did not ask for groveling but for strength, and she had already shown more weakness than she should have. Once on her feet, she pulled herself up straight and tossed her hair back over her shoulder. "Yes. I did." She forced herself to be calm, even as her throat began to seize up for what she wanted to ask. "My husband hangs on the verge of death, in a coma. His brain is swollen and bleeding. I can't lose him.

"They can't do anything. I see that in their eyes, even if they won't admit his. His life is..." She paused, realizing just how true her statement was. "His life is in the hands of the gods, and I want to weight the scales. I've called for your help."

"You all do," he replied, not angrily but resignedly. "You humans always call on us most when you are in need of something." Locking his hands behind his back, he began to walk around her in a slow circle. He was so intimidating that she had to fight to keep her knees from audibly shaking. It wasn't just his size, although that was considerable, but the aura he radiated that tried to push her to her knees. She wouldn't let it. She didn't turn to follow him with her gaze, because to her, that would show fear.

She was terrified, but she'd be damned—and maybe literally—if she showed it.

"What do you offer in return for this?" he asked while still behind her.

"What do you want?"

His laugh sounded more like a bark and it made her think of wolves. In the trees, large birds flapped their wings and she felt a chill. "That is not the point. I am Odin. I want for nothing. You are the one who wants. What are you willing to sacrifice to get it?"

Jesse didn't reply at first. She would have died for Tom, but yet, she loved him too much to put the weight of her death on him. Not like this. And this was not like the devil of the Christians, who traveled around trying to buy souls. "I don't know," she whispered, already feeling like she had failed. "I would give my life if you demanded it, but couldn't have him know I died for him and let him live out his own life with that. It would break him."

"Hmm." The king of the gods made a noncommittal noise. "So you are willing to give all for him." His footsteps continued until his hulking form came before her again. His gaze was like steel as it stabbed into her. "You beings live in such a faithless age now. Your modern world is full of oathbreakers and those who do not value the blood they are given, or that they give. I cannot believe you will hold to your oath—"

"I will!" Jesse exclaimed, galling herself by *interrupting* Odin. She swallowed hard, almost wincing as she waited for rebuke, but didn't stop. "I don't break my promises."

"I require your proof," he said simply, unimpressed with her. "I will bring you to my realm, to the land of the gods, but you must find your way to my mead hall. Only when you do will I consider granting you this favor." He held up his hand before her face just as a pair of large black birds—ravens—flew down and landed on his shoulders. She had just looked into the eyes of one of the great birds when the world went black.

When she lifted her face, she was no longer where she had been. She had no idea where she was at first and felt panic suffusing her, until she remembered Odin and what he had said about sending her to the realm of the gods. Once she remembered that, she panicked even worse.

"What have I done..." she whispered as she scrambled onto her feet, dusting off her clothing without even thinking about it. Then she thought about Tom lying on the hospital bed, needles piercing his skin, monitors stuck on, and tubes hanging around him. When she thought of him, she remembered and she squeezed her eyes shut to control the panic.

There was no chance of getting rid of it, so the best she could hope for was to control it rather than let it control her. She wiped her sweaty palms on her thighs and looked ahead to see what was before it.

The sight didn't inspire confidence.

Stretching on towards the horizon was a grey wasteland. The land looked dead and covered in a haze, dried and broken trees jutting from the ground in random angles and the land itself parched and cracked. As she followed along the line, she saw a forest at the other side and the forest lived at the base of a mountain. At the top of that mountain sat a long wooden building that somehow managed to convey both rustic and stately.

Odin's Hall.

Once that sunk in, it sunk to her feet as her eyes moved back to the dead ground. The only way to get there was through. She felt the call of the trees on the other side like a longing, but everything between her and it sent a chill of terror. She couldn't imagine walking over such a land, to feel nothing beneath her. Even the concrete of the city still had the song of the Earth under it, but this, she just knew instinctively would not feel like that.

"Tom," she whispered as she lifted a sneaker and set it on the grey, cracked dirt.

As she had suspected, it felt of nothing. She suppressed a shudder as she made each foot move one step at a time. It had to be harder than simply crossing unpleasant scenery, so she was waiting every moment for some beast of old to leap out at her or a giant to come running down that hill.

The first hint of something was far more subtle than that. A faint whisper came past her ear, like a voice on the breeze. She spun and looked, but there was nothing. She forced herself to keep walking forward. The whisper came past her other ear and she spun in a full one-eighty, but there was still nothing. Her heart felt like it had started skipping its beats while her breath shuddered in and out. Turning, she moved forward again.

Then, all at once, the sound assaulted her. A maelstrom of whispers and shrieks and groans came at her like a tornado. She could just pick out words as she clutched her ears to either side of her head, trying to block them out as the pain in her ears drove her to her knees. She was crying before the ground rose up to meet her.

"...you're going to lose him..."

"...he'll die and you'll be left alone..."

"...you can't live without him, but you will have to..."

"...going to be taken from you..."

"...be left alone..."

"...will die..."

"...gone..."

"*Stop!*" she shrieked against the wind, but it did not listen. The words kept assaulting her and she felt physically battered.

That's when she realized that it wouldn't stop. It wouldn't stop until she was on the other side, so the only way to get there was through. Even though she felt like her ears were bleeding, she forced herself to push back onto her feet. She started walking, then began running. Her face was wet and she could even feel her tears in her hair, but she kept running. She tried to ignore the voices, but they wouldn't stop. Like being hit with metal rods, they drove hard into her.

She tripped more than once, but every time she did, she kept running. She wouldn't stop, because she couldn't stop. If she stopped, she would die.

With each moment, the trees grew closer. As she neared the edge of the wasteland, the voices became louder and their words harsher. So thick and so fast, she began to feel like she was pushing through a tangible cloud. The air itself was thick and her breathing became labored, like choking on sobs that weren't coming.

Her eyes remained hard on the trees, knowing somehow instinctively that if she could just reach the trees, the voices would stop.

Putting her head down, she pushed ahead. She started screaming back at the voices to shut up, and she screamed so much that her voice became hoarse and incoherent to her own ears until the trees came to meet her. She ran so hard that she almost drove herself head long into one and fell to the ground just to stop, crashing in the wet grass.

As she had known, the voices stopped as she fell on the forest floor.

She stared up at the canopy, panting and gasping. There was a stitch in her side that made her want to cry again, but she had nothing left.

It seemed like forever that she laid there, but Odin's Hall was not here. It was on that mountain, and that's where she had to go. To prove to him that she was willing to do whatever it took, she had to climb that mountain. To find the key to saving her husband's life, she had to get through this forest. To save the key to her life and sanity, she had to get up.

And so she did. She took one last rasping breath, she pushed herself up to her feet and started trudging through the trees. Her legs felt like lead. Jesse was a fairly athletic woman, but even she couldn't have done all she did without feeling like she was about to die.

She would not die. She would not stop.

The forest felt so much better than the wasteland. She could feel the song of the living here, rather than the silence of the dead. She did not trust it, of course, for she knew that her test was not over. She still had more to do until she got what she wanted.

Yet she continued to walk and nothing happened. She heard nothing and saw nothing, and it just made her anxiety and paranoia rise higher with each step. It was like watching a horror movie when you knew The Scare was coming, but you didn't know what or how or when. You just knew that it was coming, and grew preemptively scared.

Then she saw that she was coming upon a clearing. It looked almost like the one that Odin had come to her in, and she wondered what would be in it.

She didn't have to wonder long before she crested the edge and entered the clearing, where she saw another giant of a man sitting beside a giant of a wolf. The man wore jeans and a black t-shirt with bare feet, leaning back against the base of a tree with those long legs stretched out before him. She took in his long hair and goatee, as well as the giant grey wolf that lay beside him like a big dog. His arm rested over the wolf's back, and when she saw the stump instead of a hand, she knew.

"Tyr," she said slowly, coming to a stop at the edge of the clearing. If he was Tyr, that meant the wolf was... "Fenrir." She greeted the wolf son of Loki with respect as well, for he was a magnificent creature.

"You are Jesse Dixon." The god smiled, although she couldn't find that it was the happiest or most welcoming of expressions. "You are here because you need something, and the gods are tired of granting favors that have not been earned."

"I'm here to earn it," she stated brazenly. She knew that Tyr, god of things like justice and battle, only respected strength.

"That has yet to be seen," he replied. "You know my friend here." He nodded toward the wolf, who was easily the size of a horse and who twitched his ear lazily. "You knew enough to summon the king of the gods, so you must know how I lost my hand."

She nodded. "I do," she said. There was a sinking feeling in her stomach. "It makes your friendship here a surprise."

That actually drew a short laugh from him. "We live in strange times now, don't we?"

"That's hard to dispute." Jesse inhaled deeply and held his gaze. "So, what would you have of me to prove myself?"

"Do you have courage?"

"I'm here, aren't I?"

He laughed again, the same short, near-bark sound. "That might as well prove that you're a fool."

She felt herself bristle inwardly. God or not, he stood between her and her best chance to save her husband's life. She would not be laughed at, nor would she be delayed. However, she knew she had no chance if she fought him. "I suppose time alone will tell."

Was that a look of approval in his eye? She didn't risk hope. "I suppose it will." Again, he nodded to the wolf. "Prove it."

Jesse lost her annoyance when she didn't understand what he meant. It wasn't until the giant wolf opened his mouth that she understood, and her stomach dropped into her feet. This was the wolf that had bitten off the hand of a god... What could it do to a mere human? If she felt like she had breathed shallowly before, she was sure that she stopped entirely now.

She could live without a hand, right?

Even as her brain made that resolution, her feet didn't seem to agree. They were filled with concrete as she forced herself to take those steps closer to the creature. He remained as still as a statue, just waiting for her. Just as her hand was close enough to slide between those giant, terrifying jaws, she put her slender hand between those giant jaws. She winced, but refused to let her eyes shut.

He hadn't said for how long, so she simply stood there and trembled from head to toe.

Jesse stared at the face of the wolf. It stared back at her. As her hand trembled, he made no move at all.

It was just as she was going to ask how long he expected her to wait when she saw the first twitch from the wolf. Suddenly, those jaws were shutting. It all moved in slow motion as she watched them begin to close, but some force she didn't understand kept her from trying to tear her hand away. She knew that she would fail if she did, so she held firm and let out a small shriek.

Just as the jaws closed, the non-corporeal teeth passed through her and the wolf vanished.

She gasped and shook, unable to pull her hand back as she looked at Tyr. He was smiling, and this time, the expression was less dark. "Fenrir and I are not friends," he said, his voice low like he was sharing a conspiracy. "Perhaps you do have courage. Climb the mountain, girl. Odin awaits."

With that, he stood from his indolent position and left the clearing.

It took her a moment before she was able to swallow her heart and force her trembling body to move forward again.

As she cleared the edge of the forest and came to the base of the mountain, she felt like she was breathing again. Barely. Putting her hands on her hips, she waited until she stopped feeling lightheaded. Lead bars were still in her legs and she knew her hands were still shaking, she could feel it on the inside.

At the top of this hill was where she needed to be. She was almost there and she could almost feel him up there. His power radiated like a storm cloud and she felt it pull her. The metal in her legs and the shallow breaths in her chest could not stop her. She started walking.

It was easy at first with the shallow incline at the base, but it soon became harder. The mountain rapidly became steep. The ground was dry and dusty, with rocks that came loose of their spaces too easily to use them as grips. It came to the point where she had to dig her hands directly into the dirt.

Grit pricked underneath her fingernails. She coughed as the dust climbed down her throat, coming up in puffs as she panted from her exertion and couldn't avoid inhaling it. She felt the strain in her muscles rapidly moving from sore and fatigued to painful. It felt as though her bones were going to break with each step.

The mountainside was just shy of being impossible to climb without gear.

It felt like the further she got, the further the top was. She began to despair of ever reaching it. How could she have thought she could do this? The gods themselves had literally set out these challenges, so she couldn't imagine how she thought she'd be able to do this... It was too hard...

She stopped right where she was, clinging to the side of the mountain. These thoughts got her nowhere, and she began to feel like she had when she heard the whispers and when she moved nearer to the image of Fenrir. This was another test. She had to get through. The only way to get there was through.

Inhaling deeply, she looked up again. Suddenly, the hall seemed a lot closer.

If she hadn't been so exhausted, she would have smiled. Instead, she just started climbing again with renewed determination. The rocks still tumbled away from her grasp, tumbling down the mountain behind her. She stopped looking at the top and just focused on moving forward, hand after hand and foot after foot, until suddenly, she crested the top.

There before her stood the Hall of Odin.

After having collapsed for several long minutes just to find her breath and heart beat again, she pushed herself up and strode into the hall of the gods.

When she opened the heavy doors, she had expected the revelry and drinking that one might hear about in a tale of the Norse. Yet it was perfectly silent. The sound of the door slamming behind her made her jump as she strode between the long, empty wooden tables. The tankards remained in their places, some overturned and some upright, plates scattered, all as though they had left suddenly.

At the far end of the hall was a large but otherwise plain wooden chair, with a one-eyed man in a dark suit waiting for her.

He rose as she approached.

"I have made it to your hall, All-Father," she announced. She was out of breath and wanted to collapse, and just weep, at any moment, but she would not fall just before the finish line. It was there before her, standing with an unreadable expression. He stepped down the short dais as she neared him.

"Yes, you have," he agreed. "You have earned the right to ask your favor."

Something inside her was suddenly suspicious. She had earned the right to ask, but he did not say he would grant it. "You know what I want," she returned, her throat thick with her exhaustion and emotion. "I have passed your tests. Will you grant this?" Desperation seemed to flood her limbs, because she had nothing left to give. She might fall to her knees right at that moment, or die herself if he said no.

He didn't reply. Instead he stepped until he nearly pushed her back by his presence alone, but she did not relent.

In a flash of movement she barely even saw, his hand was at her throat. She gasped in shock, grappling at his thick wrist but he did not relent. With just enough room to breathe, she still could feel her head growing light. Tears sprung up at the corners of her eyes. She simply had no strength to fight him as he practically slammed her back against one of the empty tables, knocking over mugs and pressing a plate into her back.

"You would do anything," he demanded, his voice still low yet now flooded with intensity bordering on anger. "Anything at all would you give for this man you say you love."

"That I *do* love," she corrected, practically spitting in his fate. "I would have let the wolf bite off my hand to get here." Tears flooding her throat made her breath even less, but she would not let go of the fire in her gaze as she stared at this god holding her by the throat. "I swore anything, and I will! Name it! If you say no, I will call upon you again. I'll call upon Thor and Baldr and Freyr and all of your house until someone grants me this. I will not stop."

"You would call on Loki?" he said, the intensity suddenly gone.

She didn't reply right away. "No," she finally said. "That silver tongue is not to be trusted and I would just as easily end up in Tom's body and he in mine before I was granted the favor I have wished."

The stern countenance broke into a knowing smile, slight but real. "I like you, mortal. I will grant you what you ask and will return your man to you, hale and whole."

Her heart suddenly felt like it might burst, and she practically forgot he held her.

"However—" he continued and she froze inside. "—there can be nothing granted without something given. Your heart is mighty, and it is what will truly grant the favor. From this day forward, the Norns shall weave your thread together will his, and a great deal of any luck they would have favored with you shall be used here. No road taken onward shall ever be easy, and there will be little more than existence for either of you without the other. You must be sure in your answer, for you will be nothing without each other and thus will forever be bound in more ways than your mortal mind could ever conceive."

She swallowed painfully, fighting against his still iron grip. Staring up into his single, pale-colored eye, she forced herself to not answer right away. She forced herself to envision a hard life with him compared to an easy life without. They were still young and marriages changed, ended, every day. They would wither away without each other, but might wither away with each other...

No. Deep down in the very center of every cell of her body, every corner of her spirit, she knew that wasn't so. She would be nothing without him, regardless of what the Norns wove.

"I accept," she whispered. "I want him back and I will live with nothing so long as I have him. Please, grant me the favor I have asked and I will pay that price."

"I hope you do not regret your choice," he rumbled.

"I won't." She spoke with confidence and her gaze remained unwavering on his.

He smiled, and the world went black. As she fell under, she thought she heard the sound of wooden needles clicking together.

Jesse woke up in the forest where she started.

She found herself on her back and as soon as consciousness entered her body, she sat up hard and fast, gripping her throat and hacking for air. When she finally felt like her throat and lungs were no longer burning, she looked around. It was still night. In fact, it looked like no time at all had passed. She began to doubt herself that it had been anything other than a dream, but her eyes fell on a black feather by her hand.

As she lifted it and examined it, her phone rang.

She answered it, both in a rush and in a daze. She recognized the number of Tom's boss and she choked up instantly as she answered.

"Where are you?!" he shouted. He seemed to realize that he was being too loud and his next words were quieter, more level. "I've been trying to reach you for an hour, but your phone kept going to voicemail."

"W-what's wrong? Is i-it Tom?" she stammered.

"Yes," he replied. "He's awake!"

She stared ahead in shock for several long moments before she started sobbing. If her hand hadn't been frozen around her phone, she would've dropped it.

"Do you need a ride? Maybe you shouldn't drive," Marcus said, although he didn't sound sure of himself.

Jesse started to say no, but then she thought he might be right. She didn't care about her car, she could come back for it. She told him where she was. He paused and asked what she was doing out there.

"It's a long story," she said, her voice still thick as she pushed herself to her feet.

They hung up and she walked to the street.

Her car was missing. It had been towed.

It took every ounce of self-control that her poor, exhausted body had left in it to keep from sprinting through the reception area. She had to check in and get her visitor's pass, Marcus right on her heels. She walked, very fast, through the halls to Tom's room, just barely keeping from knocking people down. She just didn't care.

She reached his room and stopped in the doorway, trembling again as she found herself fearing it was a mistake. Tom wasn't awake. It wasn't okay. Nothing had changed, or worse, it had taken a downward turn.

Swallowing hard and forcing a breath, she once more fought her wooden legs and pushed herself into the room. When she reached his bedside, she found him sitting up. He was alert and awake, talking with a nurse. The nurse turned to Jesse as she gripped the plastic railing at the foot of the bed just to keep from falling down.

"The doctors can't explain it," the nurse said before either Tom or Jesse even had the chance to speak. Jesse could only stare at her husband, and he looked back. "The swelling and bleeding have just gone away, and all of his vitals are...

normal. He's a very lucky man." The young woman paused, like she was waiting for something.

"Thank you," was all Jesse said.

The nurse seemed to take the hint and left. Jesse moved around to the side of the bed and crawled up beside him. It didn't occur to her to wonder where Marcus was, but a good guess would've been he was giving them privacy. Tom didn't say anything as he pulled her into his embrace and she burrowed against his chest. The fabric of the gown they'd put him in was coarse against her face, but she didn't care. She cried. She sobbed.

"I love you. I love you. I love you," she whispered over and over again, her fingers gripping fabric as if to hold herself to him, like she was afraid to let him go.

"It's okay," he murmured into her hair. "You heard the nurse. I'm alright."

"I know, I know," she said around a hiccup.

"Everything's going to be alright now."

She nodded and sniffed. "I know," she whispered. "It's you and me, and everything will be fine. I'm with you until the wheels fall off."

Somewhere outside the window, she heard the sound of flapping wings, and thanked the gods.

WINDSONG
Christi Rigby

Jemine Windsong stood under the green and gold striped awning of the used bookstore she had just exited, watching as the lights went off behind her. The woman in the shop had made her tea, and let her sit in one of the reading areas all afternoon. Jemine had not eaten the cookies the woman had set out, even when her stomach rumbled, because she knew she could barely pay for dinner, let alone one of the books the woman sold, and it felt like she was taking advantage. She offered to help the woman stock books, or to sweep the floors, but the woman had said that it had been slow lately and she didn't need any help.

Wasn't that the story of her young life so far? A willingness to do, but the world's lack of acceptance and an unstable path behind her, now made worse with her last choice to try and return home. It felt like it was the right choice, but making her way had not been easy.

She pulled her sweatshirt hood over her head. Colorado summer days were warm, but the evenings cooled, especially when the huge thunderstorms rolled in, lighting the clouds with spectacular shows in black and white, just like Great-Aunt Winterhawk's ancient TV. Another wet evening, and the need to find a place to stay dry. The Waffle House down by the freeway had let her in a few times, but then the manager told her more than a cup of coffee was needed as booth rental, leaving her in a position of trying to pin down which car was his so she could see if the nicer waitstaff would let her stay when he wasn't there.

A sound next to the building caught her attention, and she moved around the corner into the dark of the small town street and looked into the parking lot. There the woman from the bookshop was locking the door as she talked on the phone. The pale blue of the phone's light built shadows into the older woman's face as Jemine had seen in the fires of the reservation cast upon dancers and storytellers. As they always did, the thoughts of her home brought a lump to her throat, but foster care had dried away the tears. The woman turned and her purse caught on the door handle, sending her phone sliding across the dark pavement, almost to Jemine's feet, as the other woman cursed into the night. "Fuck."

Picking up the phone and offering it to the woman, Jemine smiled shyly, then turned to go once it was taken. As she moved, the woman waved a hand at her, then held up one finger, asking for Jemi to wait. Blue eyes looked appraisingly at Jemine and she began to squirm under the scrutiny, tugging nervously at her long, black braid. The woman was a few inches taller than her, and understandably more well fed, considering Jemi's homeless state. As the other woman had let her stay and read earlier, Jemi decided to see what she wanted to say.

The phone conversation from this end was mostly, "Yeah I'm fine," then listening, "Yes, I will get that and see you soon." Jemine listened, but unlike the loud conversations her mother used to have over the phone, she could not even determine if the other speaker was male or female.

The bookstore woman hung up and continued to look at Jemine. "Thank you, I appreciate it," she said and gestured with her phone. "Have you eaten dinner yet?"

Jemine shook her head, eyes narrowing slightly.

"Good. I am Gabby and I have to go pick up some things for a meeting, I could use help carrying them. In exchange, you can eat with us," Gabby spoke with a gentle smile, and Jemine could almost feel the tension she was holding, ready to bolt at any sign of danger, melt from the woman's kind demeanor. Gabby turned to her car, then looked back at Jemi. "Come on. You don't expect me to leave my phone's rescuer unfed, do you?"

Returning the woman's look with a guarded one of her own, Jemi shook her head and followed, getting into the passenger seat of an older car. The interior was neatly kept, just like the bookstore, except a bag in the back and a few books on the back floorboard. She stayed quiet as Gabby got in and started the engine.

"Afraid dinner is likely to be a mishmash of whatever everyone brings. It's my chance to be in charge of the meat, do you like chicken?" Gabby asked, not looking at her as the woman carefully pulled out of the lot, signaling as she turned right towards the main area of town.

"Eat about anything," Jemi said softly.

Gabby chuckled. "Me too, as is obvious," she said, then turned up the music. It was the same as had been on in the bookstore, piano and soulful singing, some horns, but nothing like Jemi had ever heard. "You like jazz?" Gabby asked.

"That the music?" Jemi asked, then when the other woman nodded, "Seems okay."

"Find it gets me through my Mondays, no matter what day they fall on," Gabby stated with a chuckle as if she had made a joke.

Jemi just stayed quiet, looking around. She hadn't ventured far from the freeway in her time in town. She needed to find a ride north but the last ride had been with a foul-smelling trucker and she felt she had just gotten away in time before something bad happened. Great-Aunt Winterhawk was her grandmother's sister and she had always told Jemi to follow the spirit wind, as it would tell her what she needed. But while in foster care, she felt like almost all the spirits of her people had left her. Maybe it was because of the Christianity most of the homes offered. The church her grandmother had attended was one of tolerance, acceptance and peace, but in the foster homes, religion felt forced. One of the other girls had told her that foster parents were judged by the social workers and if the social workers felt they were not Christian enough, they might get less children.

In her young life, so much had changed. Jemi's mother was a white girl. She'd been sixteen, the age Jemi was now, when she got pregnant. Her father, a Lakota from the reservation, took her in with his family and did the only thing he could do at eighteen to support a woman and child: joined the military. They never married so when he came home in a flag-covered coffin two years later, the uneasy truce between Jemi's mother and grandmother ended, and her mother left, only to appear every once in a while asking for money and then threatening to take Jemi away. Grandmother said her mother was getting money from the government that should have been Jemi's because of her father's death, but there was no way to try and get custody unless her mother signed her rights away, which she always promised but never did.

That was why when her grandmother's spirit went to fly with the ancestors, Child Protective Services came onto the reservation and took her. She had no family left but her mother and her great-aunt, who was gone on a spirit walk when they came. Not that the spirits would have stopped them, nothing ever did once the county took interest in a child of the tribe.

Gabby had been speaking, but Jemi had been lost in her thoughts. "Sorry, wasn't listening."

The older woman looked at her. "I asked if you liked that book you had been reading in the store."

Jemine shrugged. She loved reading, but she didn't understand quite yet what was happening and it wouldn't do to trust this woman. "S'a'right."

They pulled into the small local market and Gabby grabbed her purse. "Come on," she said, that easy smile still in place. "The others will start to eat all the sweets and leave none for us if we don't appease them with meat." Getting out of the car, leaving it unlocked, she didn't even look to see if Jemi was following.

Curious, and hungry, Jemi got out and followed her. Once inside, Gabby was waving to the workers and chatting easily as she grabbed a cart. Filling it with a few items, she didn't address the small shadow behind her, just accepted her presence. Soon they were back in the car and headed north. Just as the last streetlights of the town left the edges to the shadows, she pulled over and said, "Here we are." The house was two stories. In the dark it was hard to tell, but the paint looked to be some pale color, maybe a yellow, or white. The house looked almost like a cookie house one of the foster homes had over Christmas, with colored shutters over wide open windows spilling light out into a slightly overgrown front yard with different flowers in bloom.

Continuing the pattern of trailing behind Gabby, Jemi picked up a bag and followed her into the house. All the lights were on, and once inside, she could see many candles lit. It looked like one of the groups she had read about in books, the ones that honored gods from the past, like her people, the gods before Christianity took hold. Seeing no places where it looked like they were about to cut her heart out, like in movies, she chuckled to herself and just accepted the comfort she felt when entering the place. There were five other people there, all calling out and asking what had taken so long with the food. Gabby answered them good-naturedly and led them all back to a dining room, which was easily as large as half of Grans' house.

"Everyone calm down, we have food," Gabby said, then began introducing the people before turning back on Jem. "I am sorry, I forgot to even ask your name."

Jemine's head was spinning with the whirlwind of acceptance she felt there, and she looked down. "Jemine."

The others welcomed her, then swarmed Gabby as she laughed and continued to empty the bags. The older woman grabbed two plates and handed one to Jem, gesturing toward the food. "Meetings are no fun without food," Gabby said, then started piling food on her plate. Watching to see that Jemi did the same, she then led them to the front room. "The house belongs to Wheaton and Marcy." A woman next to the fireplace filled with candles raised her hand and a older man with long grey hair and a long beard in a chair near the window did the same. "We meet here every week to talk, discuss books, the world, and life in general." Taking a seat in a high-backed chair, Gabby kicked off her shoes and tucked her feet under her.

Night, and the storm that rode with it, passed as everyone talked. The evening's topic seemed to be books, though they eventually moved on to things happening in their lives and in town, but all were respectful of Jem's choice to stay quiet. Some people left, and only Gabby, Wheaton, Marcy and one other woman, Jemi thought was Sheila, were left. Gabby looked at Jemi then, "Do you have a place to stay?"

Blinking quickly, Jemi shook her head. "Been staying where I can find a dry spot, but I can find somewhere."

"Nonsense," Marcy said. "We have three rooms, and with my children gone for a few weeks, you can stay if needed."

Sheila grinned. "Stayed here once or twice myself when the wine was opened too late in the night."

"I live just down the street," Gabby said. "You are welcome to come with me, but you might end up pushing dogs and books off the spare bed. I am not heading out yet, we have some work to do tonight, but you are welcome to stay, or go, just know you don't have to sleep outside if you don't wish." The way she said 'work' had Jemi curious, it held a weight to it, like it was something special.

Plates were cleared and the food was put away, then the others headed out into the backyard. Jemine followed. The smell of the rain that had passed was heavy in the night, and she was curious as they lit a small fire between a tree and a small pond. Sitting back on the porch, she watched and listened as they talked softly, calling to outdwellers and ancestors and then spoke the spirits of the land. This was more recognizable to the religions she had thought of earlier, but she had built trust in these people over the night and they seemed like truly good people, if there were any in this world. She was curious as to what they were doing, but gave them space. She was sure she was not in danger, but her great-aunt was a shaman and had raised her to know the spirits and the knowledge of their power.

As they worked, a blanket of comfort settled over her. Listening to them chant, talking quietly to each other and the spirits, helped her feel safe, protected, as if she was home again. While they worked, she began to notice things at the edge of the yard. At first, she thought they were just lights and shadows, but soon she could see the forms of animals and other things she had seen in her youth. She knew all about spirits. Her life had been filled with them until her grandmother died. She had never *seen* them before, except in dreams, but she knew that was what they were. The magic the people were doing was unfamiliar but the spirits of the land were not, and if they responded this well to these people, she knew deep inside that she was safe with them.

Watching with her outsider's eyes, the hazel of her mother, she followed the spirits they had welcomed. She saw her own people's, curious and welcomed as she was, and tears came to her as they neared, sensing that she saw them. Her great-aunt had taught her some of the White Buffalo Calf Woman's language, but had told her it was not a child's path. It was that of an adult and as she was not full-breed, she would have a struggle to learn all of their ways, but the spirits protected her the same.

The people in the circle spoke of their nine virtues: wisdom, piety, vision, courage, integrity, perseverance, moderation, and fertility. It reminded her of the seven Lakota virtues she had heard spoken of: praying, respect, caring and compassion, honesty and truth, generosity and caring, humility, and wisdom. All these things interlaced within Jemi's mind and built a connection with these people that took time to honor the land and the spirits as did her people.

Sitting calmly, she waited. The spirits' curiosity about her waned. Some danced around the fire, small human shapes, while the animals stayed further back, just watching. They circled as well, but she could tell the magic was an intrigue, not their calling. One circle of the flames, and Wolf padded slowly near her. The wolf was Winterhawk's spirit animal, protector of them all, and just seeing it made tears come to her again. Wolf came to her, laid its head on its paws, and watched the magic with her, curious but unafraid, much as Jemi was herself. When the people began thanking the spirits for their company and their inspiration, Wolf stood, looked at her and in her head, like a bell, she heard, "The seeker needs a guide home."

Turning its back on her, Wolf walked through the center of the circle and passed through their sacred fire before disappearing. Jemi was certain the others did not even feel the presence of Wolf, but then she saw Gabby's body tremble slightly, as if chilled. Gabby turned and the spirits of the land around them stilled, fading to shadows until she turned back to the fire.

Jemine thought she understood Wolf's message. She sought her home and in these people Wolf trusted. So, in her mind she made a decision, to share her story and seek guidance from those that welcomed her. Even if their religion was not the same, they honored hers and the spirits recognized them as safe.

Accepting Gabby's offer, Jemine went to her home to have a roof over her head for the first time in weeks. It was not until morning, with three dogs laying around the women's feet, that Jemi opened up. She did not share all of her past, but explained a shortened version of her life so far, and asked Gabby if she knew of a way to help her earn enough money to go home. Gabby was a good listener, taking in all she could, then she offered even more. She offered that once they went to her store, they would start searching the internet to see if they could find help. Grateful and with a full stomach, something she was not sure she had felt in months, Jemi and Gabby began a quest. This one wasn't guided by the spirits as if she had been on a vision, but one of technology and research.

It was a few days before they felt they had reached a cold trail. There was no information on her great-aunt, at least no mention of her after Jemi's grandmother's obituary. Gabby rubbed her temples. It was about an hour before closing. "I am closed tomorrow and Tuesday, my weekend if you will. What do you say we drive out to your tribal lands and see what we can find?"

Jemi sighed and twisted her hair. "I do not know if I am welcome now," Jemi said softly, curled up in one of the comfy reading chairs with the novel she had started the first day. She had never been outgoing, and not belonging anywhere for years had made it worse. To be in this place, with Gabby and a trove of books, was almost perfect for her.

They hadn't talked about Jemi's vision. Gabby had just accepted her trust once it was offered. Jemi had learned much about the woman. Her husband had been killed five years prior in an accident, and since then, Gabby had run the store and surrounded herself with the people of her home town. High school sweethearts, now separated by the veil, was what led Gabby to seek out the others in her town that were outside the boundaries of the Christian faith. She said they had nothing against Christians, but the One God did not speak to her the way the Many did. Jemi asked if they were witches and Gabby laughed, saying they were druids and being a witch would limit the definition of what they tried to accomplish in this world.

"We do not need to go to the reservation where you were raised if you do not wish. We can go to some of the other towns nearby, they might have better records than I can find," Gabby offered. "If nothing else, your great-aunt was a shaman and others who have power might know."

In Gabby's home, Jemi had read and studied some of the books Gabby collected, so many books on gods and goddesses, nature and the spirit realm. She even had books on Native American Shamanism, and when Jemi read one, she saw a few rituals her great-aunt had done, making her even more homesick. Thinking of Wolf, and her great-aunt, she said softly, "It cannot hurt to try, right?"

In a rare show of affection from Gabby to the shy girl, Gabby took her hands and held them tight. "All we can do is try and as we try, hope for the best. The energy we share with this world has a potent power, so it is good when we give our best effort."

When Monday came, they woke early and had a breakfast, then Gabby packed food into the car and a small bag for herself, as Jemi had her own things already. Before most businesses opened, they were on the road north and east.

Jemi laid her head on the window and watched the plains go by, green now, lush from the late spring/early summer rains. The circles made by farmers' pivots stood out in the landscape, perfect markings of deeper green, well fed by the large watering systems. Listening to the soft jazz Gabby had on, she tried to relax, though true relaxation with where she knew they were headed was impossible.

They stopped for lunch at a small cafe in Nebraska. Gabby made certain Jemi ate, and then they continued on towards the Black Hills and the Pine Ridge Indian Reservation. Unable to stay silent in her nervousness, Jemi said, "Our reservation was once part of the Great Sioux Reservation, but the elders made their own place in 1889."

"Really? I do not know much of the tribal areas around here. I probably should make a point of it as we try to honor the First People and their spirit kin in what we do. We know this is not the sacred place of our people, but we make an effort to pay attention to the spirits of this land, not the ones on European soil where our faith is based." Gabby spoke easily. They had discussed spirits and her religion enough that she was completely comfortable in speaking to Jemi of it.

"The land there is sad, depressed, but it is ours. Actions of our ancestors at Stronghold Table led in part to the destruction at Wounded Knee," she kept talking, growing more nervous the closer they got.

It felt like Gabby knew how she felt when she spoke next. "I am sure they wish you back, Jemi. They will be pleased at how you have grown and that you wish to be with them."

For the first time in a long time, full tears came. She wiped them away on the back of her hand. "I never wanted to leave. I never wanted to be anywhere but with them."

Seeing a rest stop, Gabby pulled in to it. "Your past was not your fault, not your decisions. You were taken. You didn't leave on your own, honey." Turning off the car and opening her door, she said, "Let's take a walk."

Jemi got out, still rubbing the tears, which refused to be held back, from her face. The heat of the southern wind teased her hair to allow pieces to fly free of her long black braids. The smell of the land was so close to what she remembered growing up, the scent of the prairie grasses calmed her a little.

Gabby began to speak again, "Our past shapes us, whether it is in the DNA passed to us from our ancestors who we honor, to the lessons, the joy, the hardships we encounter. Our future is something we can dream about, but we cannot see it yet. Our present is where we shape the future." She led them to a shaded picnic table then sat cross-legged on it. "As a child, you had little control over what happened to you. You are a young woman now, though younger than most would credit womanhood to. Your ancestors and mine were betrothed and had children at your age. To me, you have lived enough to know what you seek. This journey feels right to me, and I read the runes last night and they favored this. I want to see you home with your people so you can continue to shape the future you want, not one some court official tells you that you have to have."

Taking a seat next to the older woman, she thought on her words. The courts said she had to be eighteen to make her own decisions, but Gabby was right, she had already chosen her path. "I am just worried. I have been gone so long, what if no one wants me?"

A small prairie falcon floated overhead, its spotted belly and striped wings lifting on the same warm wind that danced around the women. "Know this, if there is no place for you with your people, there is a place for you with me. We will work together to figure out how, but I know the people of our town and county and I will make it happen."

Jemi turned her gaze from the falcon to Gabby. "For reals?"

"Yes, Jemine. I think you are a special young woman and I would be honored to be your friend and help you find your future." Gabby spoke quietly, "My friends say since losing my husband, I have been too alone. Having you with me has been a blessing. We will work together to find your people, your place."

Looking again up to the sky, the thermal had carried the bird high enough that his markings could no longer be seen. "Maybe going to the reservation won't be so bad." Jemi's words were as quiet as Gabby's had been. Knowing she had a place to go if this didn't go well made the fear of getting there ease.

Leaning back on the table, Gabby smiled and just let the quiet of the rest stop fall over them. That was until a big truck pulled in, rumbling and groaning as it found its way to a stop on the hot pavement. "Shall we move on? Maybe stop for gas and tea up ahead?"

"Only if the tea is cold," Jemine said. She could not yet get used to the fact that Gabby drank hot tea even when it was ninety degrees outside.

"It's a deal," Gabby said, then slid off the table, offering her hand to the young woman at her side.

Looking at the sign of peace and connection offered before looking into the blue of Gabby's eyes, Jemine took the hand with a smile and nod.

For the rest of the trip, the silence became filled with soft chatter, about the road, about nature, and more about Jemi's people and the towns ahead. A weight had lifted from her in a way, having someone she trusted to share all these things with and allow relaxation to just settle in.

The terrain gradually changed, gullies and wild lands on the sides became more farmland. "Whiteclay is ahead," Jemi said softly. "We may not want to stop there, a lot of people come there just to drink."

"Wherever you wish to stay, Jemi. We can go up to Oglala or even up to Rapid City, though the information we find will be better locally," Gabby spoke gently. Jemi felt her guidance, but was thankful it was not insistence. "If we have to stay the night, we can go to the casino."

"We go through Pine Ridge and Oglala before reaching the casino, maybe drive through and decide what to do?" Jemi replied after a few moments of thought, her fingers drumming nervously on the door's armrest.

She looked out the window as the town came into view. Weeds and small green trees gave way to a white building with red awnings that said "Divided...... We Fall" on the side with a mural painted in blues and browns of the first people and the bluffs. A wooden cross high the front the early afternoon sun cast its shadow on the crumbled concrete. At the corner, the sign of her people in this community, were bodies sleeping, or passed out, in the shade. Jemi turned her head away, almost embarrassed for Gabby to see this.

The buildings were in disrepair, and there was trash in the streets. A reddish building marked with Lakota Arts & Crafts on the outside had more people sitting in front of the store, taking advantage of the shade it provided. It was no more than a blink of a town, and none of it was attractive.

After they were through, Jemi tried to release the tension in her shoulders. Looking back at the town in the side mirror, she saw a shadow at the edge of her vision. Turning, she could not see anything, but no matter where she looked, she sensed something moving with them.

Looking at Gabby to see if she felt anything, she saw the older woman keep checking the rearview mirror. "You feel it too? Or see it? What is it?"

Gabby's heavier frame shuddered. "One, I think we just crossed a border, a defined space that we cannot see but has been long established. Two, since we stopped to talk, I have been feeling the presence of something working with us, guiding us forward. I didn't want to say anything if you didn't feel it, though. Some people are more sensitive to different energies than others."

"Like the energies you called when you were working at the fire? The spirits of my people liked the calling," Jemi said. It was the first time she had admitted this to the other woman.

"Yes... Wait, they did?" Gabby said, looking at her.

Jemi nodded slowly. "Yes, you called them outdwellers and then thanked the land there and they were curious and watched you all."

Gabby looked surprised. Her mouth opened then closed before she spoke, "It is what we hope. We know our religion is not that of your people, but we hope to honor the spirits that were here before us and give them and the land thanks for hosting us. We do not want them forgotten." She focused back on the road. "You saw them?"

Admitting these things among most whites would have had her ostracized or in child services again, but she trusted Gabby. "Since meeting you, I have seen spirits. Wolf came to me at your fire, that is why I decided to stay close. Anog Ite comes to me in dreams, even in foster care. She tries to teach me the ways of the women of my people, but I am not with them."

"Anog Ite?" Gabby asked.

"She is the double-faced woman, one face beautiful and one ugly. She teaches the young women in their dreams. Wolf, though, usually guides a hunt or war," Jemi explained. The memories of the stories she had been told as a child came forth.

"Wolf might be guiding your hunt for your family?" The older woman's question was gentle. "I can sense energy but I have never seen the spirits except in my dreams and mind's eye. I kind of envy you."

"Most people think those that can see are crazy, even among our some of our people," Jemi said with a shake of her head. "Grandmother used to say that Great-Aunt Winterhawk said I sensed the spirits even when my mother was pregnant with me. Every time she came over, I would kick my mother and she would complain."

"What a gift," the driver said, shaking her auburn hair. "No wonder you feel at such a loss away from your lands. If that border we crossed means anything to me, I think it means you will feel more at home soon."

Jemi grew quiet, wondering if Gabby would be right. She was so nervous about this trip that she thought she would not really feel comfortable until, or if, they found her great-aunt.

It only took a few minutes before Pine Ridge appeared ahead of them. A small group of houses to the east, then a sandwich shop and gas station. Pine Ridge was much better kept than Whiteclay had been, it was almost night and day in the differences on the main road. Up ahead, a white church gleamed in the afternoon light. "Do you remember where your grandmother lived?"

Jemi nodded. "Go right at the light then past the Pizza Hut and a left at the next light."

Gabby followed her directions, Jemi taking in the slightly more rundown area on the edge of town. There was graffiti on the walls of some buildings, less pride taken there than with the main road towards the casino. "The first left, then past the stop sign, the house on the right after it."

Soon they reached the house, trees and a fence surrounding it. Gabby pulled over and looked at Jemi. "Here?"

Tears were in the young woman's eyes again as she remembered being taken from here by her neighbors after she found her grandmother dead in bed. Watching from the window across the street as the emergency vehicle lights illuminated the house in the night. Then the tribal police came. They knew she had no one left but Winterhawk, and asked the neighbors if they would watch her until they could get ahold of the elder woman, which they said they would. It was the next day when one of her teachers had come with a white woman in a grey suit. The woman was from the county and without proper custody ever being taken for Jemi, the woman had taken her off the reservation. Jemi couldn't respond to Gabby's question as she just looked at her home.

They looked around the sides as they heard a sound. When they turned back, there was a coyote on the hood of the car. "What the f…" Gabby said then paused, because beyond the coyote was a tall man in a tribal police uniform.

It was hard to see his face, as the cowboy hat he wore shaded it, but with a sharp word, the coyote jumped down and sat at his side. It looked more dog than coyote now that it was sitting in the dirt, panting up at the man as if saying, "Look what I found for you."

He tipped back his hat, as if to peer better into the car. Jemi sunk back in her seat, trying to hide. "It is okay, Jemi. We will handle this," Gabby said softly, then rolled down her window. "Hello, can you help us?" she asked, smiling brightly at the officer.

"That is my job, ma'am," the man responded with a smile that broke the shadows of his face with gleaming white. "I am sorry if Mica startled you. We were at home and the next thing I knew, he was off down the road." He stepped around to the driver's side. "I would joke that you are not from around here but the Colorado plates give that away. If you are looking for the casino, it is further down the road."

Jemi shrunk back further in her seat as he leaned over to look in the car, "Shit, you are Slade's girl, aren't you? You are who Taku Skanskan told us to watch for. Come on, both of you, follow me. My house is just up the block. The old woman is going to be very happy to see you."

Without waiting for them to say anything, he just turned on the heel of his cowboy boot. "Do you know him?" Gabby asked, looking at Jemi.

"No," the girl responded. She had been so afraid of any authority on her trip home, but now it seemed she had no choice.

"Slade is your father, right?" the older woman asked as she turned the car to follow him slowly up the road, though his long stride was sure and she didn't have to follow for long.

Jemi swallowed. "Yeah, my dad, but Gran and Auntie always called him Twohorn."

Gabby took a slow breath. "We needed someone with answers and he seems to have them, but we can leave if you want."

"No," Jemi said, then paused. "He knows the name of my father, and he called his dog Mica, coyote spirit. Maybe he knows Winterhawk." It was hard to trust anyone but Gabby, but she knew Gabby would take her and leave if necessary.

He led them up north to where the road turned into a four-wheel drive path, then to a house that sat at the edge of town. A tribal police car was parked there and in the shade was a table with a plate of half-eaten food and a pitcher of water, catching the late afternoon sun in the condensation on its side. Waving them in to park next to a white truck, he nodded and picked up the plate before walking inside.

The women got out of the car and Jemi looked around. This home once belonged to Jerimiah Two Wind. He had been a friend of her grandmother and great-aunt, and had sat next to Jemi when Child Protective Services had brought her to the church for the funeral. Mica walked over to them both, sniffing Gabby but circling Jemi and shoving his head under her hand.

That deep male voice interrupted, "He was who told me you were there. I was enjoying my dinner break and then he was off down the road like he was chasing a rabbit."

Jemi looked up at the tall man. "Did you know my dad?"

"I did. My little brother and him went to high school together. I am sorry you lost him and Mary. My dad told me about you when I came home to help him," he said, and Jemi could see a sadness in his eyes as he spoke. "I am Tobias Two Wind."

As she petted the dog, she asked, "Jerimiah was your father?"

"He was, miss," Tobias said gently. "I was practicing law in New York when he began to have some health troubles, so I came home. It was shortly after your grandmother died and he and your great-aunt were trying to locate you, but you had already been placed and they sealed the records."

"A lawyer in New York to tribal police?" Gabby asked as she looked into his dark eyes. "Seems a pretty big change. I am Gabby Williams, Jemi is a friend of mine." Gabby offered her hand and he took it. Jemi watched as the two sized each other up, then Gabby drew her hand back with a smile.

"A big change, but I was working with some tribal law advocates in the city, so not too big of a shift to come home and see what I had been working for all my life, in the flesh, so to speak," he said, then gestured to the table. "I would ask you in but the breeze is starting and it will cool the afternoon."

He looked up into the sun as it was lowering, then he and Gabby spoke at once, "It will be a full moon tonight." The two looked at each other and laughed, then Gabby blushed slightly and looked to Jemi. "Want to sit? If Mica lets you, of course." Another small laugh escaped her as the dog pressed into Jemi's hand again.

She nodded with a smile. Touching the dog calmed her, but she was curious now. Jemi followed behind Tobias and Gabby, then sat at Gabby's side. "Do you know where Winterhawk is?" she asked as Mica put his head in her lap.

Tobias smiled at Jemi, then at Gabby. "She has been out on a walk for a week. She has been staying at Mary's home, hoping one day you would come back." He stopped and his eyes narrowed as he took off his hat. "No, she *knew* you would be back. She told me a little while ago to keep my eyes out as the spirit of the wind was blowing someone home, but she didn't know it would be you or she would have said."

"Is that why you said Taku Skanskan told you to watch?" Jemi asked, then turned to Gabby. "Taku Skanskan is the master of the winds, and Wolf is one of his creatures."

Gabby nodded, but turned to Tobias as he spoke, "Yes. In our last sweat lodge, he guided me that I would be welcoming a leaf upon the wind. It was pretty vague to be honest, but then the spirits usually are."

Gabby laughed, and Jemi felt she should explain Gabby to him for some reason. She looked to the older woman, who seemed to know what she was asking and nodded. "Gabby is a druid. She honors other spirits than ours, but holds the ones of the land here sacred as well, just has never talked with them. I was with her one night watching her when Wolf came to me, and since then, Gabby has been helping me find my way back."

The almost cocky grin the lawman had turned into a warm smile, dimples creasing his cheeks. "Then our people are in your debt, druid."

Blushing softly, Gabby smiled. "Jemi is my friend, no one owes me a thing."

He looked back at Jemi and asked, "You are what? Sixteen?"

Her comfort shrunk as he spoke. The legality of her being there was a problem and she knew it. "Yes, I couldn't stay with the home I was in though." She wouldn't talk of the abuse she had taken there, but she was sure the pain and shame was in her eyes as she dropped them.

She had never told anyone, not even Gabby. The other woman placed an arm around her shoulder and hugged her gently. "She needed to find her family, and I will work with the courts to become her guardian, if necessary, to ensure she has what she needs."

The woman's words were fierce and protective and exactly the support Jemi needed, but in case it wasn't enough, Mica pressed up on the bench and licked her face. "Is he really a coyote?"

Tobias' eyes were on them, Jemi felt it and saw the thoughts flash through them. She wondered what they might be, then he spoke, "He is, found him out in the prairie. His mother had been poisoned and he was sick from her milk, so I took him in."

As if knowing he was being talked about, the coyote looked across at the man, then sat and pressed his side into Jemi's legs as his tongue lolled out of his mouth in a wolfish grin. "He is very well behaved," Gabby said. "You have trained him well."

"More he trained me, these are his visitor manners. He is much more a spirit of hospitality than I am, and Jemi there seems to have a way with him," Tobias said. "I was going to put in a couple extra hours tonight, but with the full moon and all, should be a good night to try and find Winterhawk, don't you all think?"

Jemi's eyes lit up and her head bobbed. "You can do that? You know where she is?"

He shook his head slightly. "No one can find old wolf when she is alone but the spirits, and you, I think, as they are with you. But I am more than happy to help you on your way along with Gabby, if you will let me."

Jemi looked up at Gabby, who hugged her gently once more then let her go. "It is your journey, Jemi. I am only here to support you."

Looking back at Tobias, she said, "Please, I need to find her."

The man stood. "Let me get you the spare key for her house. You can put your things there and change if you like. I will put together dinner and some things we will need to be out tonight. Come back when you are ready for dinner."

"We appreciate your help," Gabby said, then stood. "Come on, Jemi. If we are going out tonight, I certainly need to change out of my skirt."

Tobias grinned, almost mirroring Mica's look. "That is a shame, it is lovely on you."

Jemi watched and laughed softly as Gabby blushed. "Thank you. We will be back later," the older woman said, then looked at Jemi. "Shall we?"

They took the key and parked Gabby's car at Jemi's home. Nothing had changed from when Jemi left except for her grandmother's room, which was clearly now Winterhawk's. Jemi teased Gabby about Tobias, Gabby blushed as they spoke and readied themselves for the hike, denying any interest. It made Jemi relax and tease her even more. She was sixteen, not a baby, and she could see Gabby liked him. They both changed clothes, though Jemi did not have too many clothes to change into. Locking the house up again, they returned to Tobias' home.

As they approached, they saw smoke and heard chanting. Walking around to the back of the house, they found him there, walking around a fire pit with a sage bundle. He raised and lowered it, making patterns in the evening breeze. His deep voice chanted to the spirits, and Jemi could see patterns and forms in the smoke. Gabby shuddered slightly next to her, then kneeled down to place a hand on the warm dirt. Mica came from within one of the plumes of smoke that carried from the fire out onto the prairie, stalking forward, slightly lowered to the ground, then lay at Jemi's feet.

Jemi didn't understand the words Tobias sang, but she felt them deep within her. As the spirits formed in the smoke, she saw them, the spirits of her dreams and of the stories Auntie Winterhawk told her, as they danced in the grey and the wind. Rising in height, then spilling out over the prairie, the last one, Wolf, curled around Jemi, then moved out after the others and made a path along the land that Jemi could see.

Stepping towards the path as Tobias' song ended, Jemi watched and began to follow the spirits. "Dinner first," Tobias said softly, stepping up next to her. "I will call again after we eat. That was the first call for them to bless our path, next call will be the one for guidance."

Tipping her head to look up at him, she asked, "Can you see them too?"

"I am not a seer, but I can call them and feel them," he said. "Around here, only your great-aunt can see them anywhere but dreams, and now you, it seems." Flashing her a warm smile, he said. "Steak and salad for dinner all right? I didn't know what either of you liked."

Gabby spoke up, her voice a little quieter than normal. "I didn't get to look this way avoiding meat. That sounds wonderful."

Jemi nodded and watched as Tobias looked back at Gabby with a smirk. "I am glad, never could understand a person that didn't like steak."

Tipping his head toward the house, he allowed Jemi to walk before him. When they reached Gabby, he held a hand out to help her up. "You can feel them too, can't you?" he asked.

Gabby looked up into his eyes. "Feel, yes, as you said, but I cannot see them. What you called is so different than what I normally work with, the wildness and depth of feeling they shared was almost overwhelming."

He smiled warmly. "Come and be welcome to our lands, Gabby Williams. The spirits welcomed you, now it is my place to." Jemi could see him squeeze Gabby's hand then let go, leading them all in to eat.

After the meal, they went out and Tobias chanted again with Jemi standing where Wolf had walked from her earlier. This time, the smoke and the spirits she saw danced around her, moving to the song Tobias called. At the end of the song, Wolf appeared again to Jemi and began to walk out along the trail that led from the house. Jemi stepped forward and this time, Tobias and Gabby stepped behind her.

The light of the moon was bright enough to light the path, but Jemi didn't really need it. Wolf led her along a rise in the dirt, guiding her over a path along which Jemi would sense, then see the other spirits step up and fade away.

They walked for hours, but to Jemi, it felt like only a few minutes in a dream. Along the edge of a ravine, Wolf began to quicken her pace and Jemi moved in time. Tobias and Gabby used their lanterns to help mark the edge of the path. A small creek ran through the ravine, then into some of the famous Black Hills before them. Rising high overhead, the aged rocks stood. Upon the cliffs, Jemi could see the shadows of the warriors of her people, watching over them. A little further into the canyon, a small hide tent appeared. No fire stood before it, but the moon's glow illuminated it in the dark of the night.

Slowly the flap opened and a small, older woman stepped out in a white deerskin dress ornately decorated with feathers, beads, and bone. Opening her arms, she cried as she saw Jemi walking to her. "Welcome home, daughter of Slade. Welcome home, spirit seer. Welcome home, my blood. Welcome home, earth's daughter."

Jemi ran into her great-aunt's arms and from behind them, Mica began to yip and howl. The world around them came alive with other calls of the night animals, all joining in to welcome Jemi home.

From the Author: The plight of the First People's children being taken from the reservations and placed in Caucasian homes has been a secret for a long time. The tribal lawyers fight, to keep their children, but it is an uphill battle. I would like to thank the Lakota Law Project for offering me answers to the questions I had about the issue, and for supporting me in my decision to bring this story to light. For more information on the Lakota Law Project, please visit http://lakotalaw.org/

I would also like to thank Reverend Melissa Burchfield and Reverend William E. Ashton for guiding me through all my diversity and spiritual questions of the past year and being the inspiration for the group of people I use for Gabby's religious group.

THE WILL OF NYX
Viola Dawn

(Five Years Previous to Main Events)

In Afghanistan, it was a great mercy when night fell. This war-ravaged country with its ancient hills and age old customs had the most beautiful sunsets. Yet it was the blanket of night that allowed for the most artistry.

The stunning moon let the mountains cast shadows over wavy fields of grass. Any precious water in the region could be kindled into twinkling, ethereal ripples. Old villages with collections of square mud buildings straight out of some long lost text were quiet and watchful.

Hoping to avoid destruction.

Scott was there to kill people. Specifically, the people there who wanted to kill him. To weed out the ones with the hateful eyes and murderous intentions. Remove their ability to control the region and be a threat.

There was no point sugarcoating a salty-sweat drenched, dust-caked quest for blood. He'd already experienced being face down with a dry throat, surrounded by clouds of smoke and showers of metal.

He'd grown accustomed to the pops and cracks that signaled incoming danger. The noises that meant a very possible, very real death. He'd fired his weapon along with his platoon, contributing to the racket of war. Eventually, the doom-laden vibrations would go away.

Scott, so far, had lived.

His patrol brought him past a poppy field. Here was the source of heroine and morphine: the opiate that could infect cities with crime and ruin, or provide hospitals with a means of pain relief. There was the occasional addict laying in waste as they patrolled compounds.

The very profitable drug trade, however you look at it.

Not like he hadn't seen a heroine addict before in his own country. Nights out in town were filled with strung-out lost souls, wasting away in the shadows. Outside of the cozy pubs and stylish wine bars. On the cold, wet streets of a relatively wealthy country.

England.

Don't give them any money. They will only spend it on more drugs. That's what everybody says.

One night, near Piccadilly station in Manchester, Scott leaned over a homeless man and gave him a bottle of water, a cup of coffee, and a cheese and onion pasty. He dropped a couple of pound coins into the bloke's little plastic cup.

Least he could have something to eat. A hot drink. He's not all alone.

The scrawny lad stirred and his dirty fingers grasped the crinkly white paper around the pasty.

"There you go, mate, look after yourself. You're too young to be wasting away like this."

Scott smiled and carried on to the train station. It broke his heart. He'd always had a soft spot for troubled kids.

The young men and boys trying to kill me are deeply disturbed, easily manipulated, troubled kids.

Now, walking past an opium field, he thought of that scraggly teenager and hoped he'd eaten the pasty. Drank the coffee. Pocketed the water, and realised how much more precious it was than the drugs. How the world should value things like water and love above profit and power.

But that wasn't something he could dwell on once the sounds of impending doom arrived. For now, things were quiet.

His boots trod the dirt path, his gaze scanning for any sign of IEDs. Perspiration dripped down his face and stung his eyes. Scott thought of the morphine auto-injector he carried in his pocket. He squinted, unable to escape the intensity of the air around him.

While his shock-proof glasses shielded his eyes and his helmet technically provided shade, his head still cooked inside it. It was like the burning sun had ways of slipping into every nook and cranny.

He couldn't wait for sunset, and night's descent. Freedom from the scorching sun. Scott was beginning to understand the simple pleasure of sitting in the shade.

He'd begun to crave it.

This would be his last tour. His dad had died a couple of years ago, and Mum long before that. He'd decided to go into teaching at a local school.

When his folks were alive, he would have lunch with them, sitting on a bench in St. Ann's Square. He remembered walking past St. Ann's Church, with its reddish brown stone structure and the stained glass windows. How different the ground was there in town. Scattered rain puddles would collect in the random depressions of the grey slates.

In front of the church, there were a couple of curved wood and metal benches where it was possible to sit and have a sandwich.

"I will meet my future wife here. This is it where I'll meet her." The romantic fantasy of a little boy.

And just before he passed, his dad had patted his hand and said, *"You go on, lad. You go to St. Ann's Square and meet your lady. I know you will... I know you will..."*

At the time, it was too painful to consider. Scott just wanted to escape into his call to be a warrior. To prove to himself he had what it took. To make the spirits of his parents proud. He'd almost forgotten his romantic side in the pain of his unbearable loss.

The day he'd walked away from the hospital after his father died, he'd felt some foreign touch on his arm. Like someone had firmly stroked him with the tip of their finger. *Written* on him. Yet Scott was too distracted by grief to pay attention or remember.

His platoon was nearly finished with their patrol. As they set about heading in the other direction, all Scott could think of was how those benches in front of St. Ann's church seemed like heaven.

He absently rubbed the top of his arm and looked to the side, bemused by the sensation. It felt like powdery dust had been smeared on his flesh.

Something he hadn't noticed before. *What the hell is that?* he thought, still trying to rub the side of his arm.

Then a shrill noise made him look at the sky. The pitch of it struck him like a blow. It was more of a *living* shriek.

Like an animal.

Then there was a pounding sound. The ferocity of his heartbeat competed with the pulsating noise.

A *helicopter?*

But it was wings.

Some sort of eagle, owl or falcon? he thought.

The mad scream hit the air again and he started looking around.

"Did you hear that?"

Scott couldn't catch his breath. The other members of his platoon didn't appear to be reacting. They continued in their quiet progress while he was captured by a menace only he could sense. Scott was being singled out.

Trapped.

Scott feared he was going to be one of those who cracked. One who lost it under all the pressure and heat, crumbled under the weight of fear. That he was now a liability to the others.

I'll get through this. I'll get through. I'll make it through to another night. I'll get to St. Ann's Square, clear-headed and intact. I will. I. Will.

The wings made a deep whooshing sound followed by the barbaric wail. The plumes of smoke got far too close. *Then* everyone else reacted. They threw themselves to the ground.

Someone or *something* was pulling him. It was like he was being split. *Something* was trying to rip him from himself. An agonizing tearing savaged his core.

The demon clawed at him. Scott screamed and roared back.

He didn't manage to get to his morphine injector.

He hated the sound of the helicopter blades. It was too similar to the beating wings, those awful expanses of doom.

Dozing in and out, the cooking heat turned to air conditioning. Air conditioning turned to cool, outdoor air. He couldn't move, couldn't speak. Could neither see nor feel his limbs.

There was the *beep-beep-beep* of medical machines.

The white and grey air in front of him had hazy moving shapes. There was pressure in his veins. Morphine? The world before him kept flickering. Scott wasn't sure what part of it he was in.

The light from whatever window beside him was getting dimmer.

It's nighttime. Finally. I've got to get to St. Ann's Square...if I can just get in front of the church.

And then, he could see it. The rain-wet stones, moon-cast shadows, street lights…

And the great night sky above the church in the very centre of the city.

❧

Five Years On

It was getting closer and closer to Summer Solstice, and the evening's late sunsets were bewitching. Like the darkest, most dangerous night masquerading with the innocence of day.

The dingy corners and alleys in Manchester never bothered Amanda. Her heart held an unwavering faith in the power of love. Kindness and love always took precedence inside her. Wherever she went, even in the rougher parts of town, Amanda could envision love taking place there.

But romantic love was her favorite.

Romance, kisses, binding ceremonies that signified a gateway to a life of loving someone. Knowing them.

There was something *wrong* with her. A sense of *loss* that had stunned her five years ago, and had stuck with her since. And there was no precise reason why.

Hence why she was on her back in her therapist's office, trying to explain it *again*. The voice of her counselor came through, questioning her.

"Amanda, do you ever feel you are placing too much importance on your notions and fantasies that there is no one out there for you to love in the way you feel that you *need* to? You work with couples, help them arrange their perfect weddings. Do you think you place romantic love up on a pedestal? Don't you feel that the fact that you never knew your mother and that your father was a war hero who died in the service is what troubles you? Or do you feel it's something else?'

Amanda shifted on the couch, closing her eyes. There were birds as well as traffic outside the window. "I love what I do. I've become good enough at it that I can choose who I work with. I don't accept couples who would marry out of convenience or money. My dad's sister did the very best she could with me. I've always had a romantic nature. I was always…*anxious* to love someone. But I am happy with me. This isn't some thing where I don't love myself enough. I mean…"

She sighed. The therapist crossed his legs and coughed.

"Amanda… These sessions have to work for you. And I must tell you." He cleared his throat. "You are a very beautiful, very successful woman. You would have no troubles finding a relationship. Tell me how you feel about love."

Amanda opened her eyes and rocked her head from side to side. The skylight in the office made her feel exposed. She wished it was night. Sighing through her nose and splaying her fingers on the furniture's cloth, she began again,

"I feel that love is taken for granted. That it deserves almost…worship in its own right. I mean, all the evil and all the violence in the world is a result of people who begin to value violence and bloodshed, who value money and power over the sheer, satisfying beauty of mutual love. I think it is a sin not to love."

Her therapist was quiet for a moment. Then he said, "Do you think that you sin? Or are blasphemous for not loving?"

"I…devote myself to making the days of others special. But I can't get past the fact that I can't…I haven't managed to *love* anyone. Not the way I should. Not the way I was meant to. But I can't force myself to accept the offers of someone just because. But at the same time…"

This was the worst moment. The awful moment when the tears burned her eyes and she fought for coherent thought.

I am a weak woman full of fantasies and notions that don't fit in the real world. And I can't handle it. I'm a dippy, needy cow. I want to be professional and strong. Not like…not like this. Not broken in a way I can't describe.

But no therapist could get those words out of her.

She swallowed her tears and said in a trembling voice, "Look, for five years I just haven't been right. I wish I'd known my mother. I wish my dad was still around. I want a husband and a family, but that just isn't going to happen. Because I won't accept just anyone. But I know I've got to move past it and accept that it might happen on its own. If I stop *feeling* like this."

But it won't. I know it won't. Something is wrong. Something went wrong. But I don't know what or who or where or why. And I can't say that. It's crazy.

"Amanda, I think our time is up now. I'll see you next week."

"Right."

The ticking clock that had been in the background, unnoticed beside the birds and cars, had stopped.

Later, arriving back at Oxford Road Station where she could walk to her flat, she looked up at the still light sky, despite the fact that it was nine in the evening. The light irritated her. She longed for the oblivion of night.

With a cup of tea in hand, Amanda sat down and went through her meetings for next week. The things she would have to arrange for her clients. She'd have to visit St. Ann's in town again.

Satisfied that all was in order, she took a sip of her hot drink.

I shouldn't do this really. It's like torture. But I can't not think of him.

Amanda had a habit of cataloguing the specific details of her lover, even though there was never a full picture in her mind. Just flashes and sensations.

The *exact* way he would hold her hand. The pressure of his fingertips. The texture of his palm. The spot where his shoulder met his neck.

Their wedding day. Not a grand affair, but a simple one. Intimate and binding. That would have been her choice.

There were handsome men who pursued her. Men clever enough to see past her exterior. To see that she was a committing type. They pushed her. But no amount of looks or cleverness lured her beyond a certain point.

The feeling wasn't there. They didn't have *his* face. Their skin wasn't the right temperature. The tenor of their voice wasn't right. The rhythm of their breath was all wrong.

It was in this stream of thought that Amanda began to prepare for bed. By the time she got there, the sun had finally set.

"Thank goodness…" she said, slipping into her sheets and placing her hand over her mouth.

Amanda had begun to perspire in her sheets, turning her body in an attempt to get comfortable. She'd finally settled on her back, when a noise quickened her pulse.

There was the sound of fabric rustling. A smell of smoky incense. It made her think of exotic, older places. Hot earth and inky skies. For a moment, her bed was the warmest summery ground.

It was reminiscent of a summer holiday in Greece, where her auntie had taken her one year.

The warmth on her back was soothing. Drifting off, the sights and sounds outside and within her head began to blur.

Amanda turned her head and groaned. The heat of the ground materialized into a cloak. In her mind's eye, blue-black cloth slid around her and held her still. Amanda opened her eyes.

Standing over her was a woman. The lady's ebony hair blended with the midnight cloak that surrounded her.

"Well, well, well. No wonder I could feel *your* appreciation. It isn't exactly worship, but I felt your admiration. Strong it was too. Sleep, dear one. And may the sweetest dreams comfort you."

Then Amanda, immobile, watched the woman's aquiline nose turn away. Her olive skin glowed, haloed by the moonlight outside the window. The lady addressed someone not in Amanda's line of sight.

"Morpheus, leader of the Oneiroi, come. See what you can do here."

A man appeared at the lady's side. Young, with the swarthy handsome features of an Italian or Greek. The type popular with sunshine-starved British girls. Yet inside, Amanda began to panic. He looked down at her with interest.

What are they going to do to me? What's this?

Fear welled up inside her, crowding her chest with paralyzing heaviness.

The midnight cloaked lady disappeared. Morpheus' brows lowered over the black opal eyes continuing to study her. Waves of sedation washed over her. Her veins felt as though they were humming, buzzing with a substance other than blood. She was able see him, watch him.

I don't know if I'm asleep or awake.

At this, the one called Morpheus' mouth curved up like he'd heard her thought. His voice came through. Focused on her. Like a practiced hypnotist. Some sort of master of meditation.

Something way beyond any therapist she'd ever spoken to.

"You are, for the moment, awake. What a beauty you are. And you've lived here all your life. I wonder…*where* is your mother?"

The Oneiroi leader was in her head, gathering every scrap of emotion and thought, scrutinizing every memory. For a moment, it made her feel uncomfortably vulnerable. He spoke again.

"Ah, I see. Don't worry. I can't touch you, and I fear the repercussions if I play too much. But I can certainly show you things. Do you want to see?"

Amanda wasn't sure if she did. At any rate, she could neither speak nor move.

"Of course you do. Watch me."

And he began to change. His olive features shifted to a paler complexion. His hair was no longer black but a very short-cropped light brown. Yet even in the dark, she could see his natural colors were burned by a harsh sun. He was straight-backed, strong.

A soldier's stance.

Only her eyes could move. In the moonlight, she saw where his shoulder met his neck. Her gaze looked to his palms. She knew their texture. The precise pressure of his touch. The scent of his skin. She knew those things, yet now could not sense them.

It's him! Oh my goodness, it's him…

Morpheus' voice even changed when he spoke again.

"It's me, darlin'. I wish we could have met. You're so gorgeous." His words were full of wonder. He sounded local. What got her the most, however, was that his voice was the correct tone.

She ached to have him closer. When he sat down, still staring at her, Amanda's heart rate and breathing stayed the same. Unable to move, it was like being barred from any excitement.

Yet he held her in his spell. Everything was falling into place. There was nothing unnatural about him being here in her bedroom.

He ate her with his eyes. Then he lifted one hand up and reached back to the side of his neck. *He's touching where his neck meets his shoulder.*

Soon as his hand touched his own skin, his eyes appeared to shine. As though he wanted to weep. As though he'd just been struck or pushed away. Denied something.

He removed his hand and faced his palms towards her. Anticipating his touch, powerless to react, Amanda watched his hands move closer and closer to her face.

The details of his skin and the lines crossing his fingers were so familiar. His gaze looked to her and then looked to the top of his arm. There, she could make out a faded gold smear. Some strange mark. He smiled at her.

If this is a dream, I'll take it. Anything to be united with him. I can see him, I can finally see him!

Then his hands stopped millimeters away from her face. His fingertips lingered over her forehead. Her vision was obscured by the top of his palms. Breathing was slow, she wanted to inhale deeply and acquaint herself with his smell.

Yet only the chilled air of her room, already known to her senses, met her nostrils.

His hands moved. There was no feeling, no fragrance. Only the tormented sight of him. His brows furrowed and lids closed. He turned as though she'd spurned him.

How can I react to you? I can't bloody move.

Then the expression shifted, and the corners of his mouth curved up. His eyes, in their ceaseless intensity, confounded her. Amanda wasn't sure whether he was being playful or dangerous.

Now, the lighting began to toy with his skin tone. It marred the way he looked. He didn't appear tangible. Natural sunburned flesh gave way to a gauzy grey. His features dulled.

Now her heart ached with his absence, even though he was still before her eyes.

He gazed in her direction, but it was like he couldn't see her. Like he was trapped behind a veil.

And she was trapped on the other side.

Then Amanda sat up. Control over her own breath and blood flow returned. She looked around the room, finding nothing and no one there.

Unease remained with her. Like she wasn't alone. It appeared that both her house and heart were haunted.

It was times like these Amanda wished she had her mother. Someone who understood her nature and who could reveal the secrets behind her dreams.

Nyx stalked through the city. Ever ready for specific attention, ever seeking worship. She'd felt the pull of the woman's attention. It was heady and focused.

No ordinary woman, but a demigoddess. Yet completely unaware who she belonged to. THAT Goddess's daughter? Lonely?

But then, powerful Nyx knew too well love and desire's fickle nature. She knew of loneliness. The one *she'd* desired did not return her affections with the necessary intensity. He wouldn't bow to her.

Great Poseidon.

The bastard.

She moved further to the city centre, taking a mortal form, and moved into the area known as St. Ann's Square.

Her opaque eyes spotted the church in the distance. The sound of her fingernails scraping on the stone of an old shop met the murky air.

This was a shade. The ghost of a fallen mortal. He sat upon a wooden bench, staring at the church. Nyx approached slowly. So transfixed was the shade in his prayer, he did not notice her.

Will you speak with me?

She moved closer. Approaching the courtyard where the benches were, Nyx stepped off of the cobbled road and onto the pavement surrounding the church. Her boots clicked on the old stone slates.

Two trees rustled in front of the church, though there was no midsummer breeze. They were acknowledging the presence of an ancient deity.

The shade's grey face turned in her direction. Despite the curved wooden back of the bench, the shade sat straight up. The ghost faced the church. His hands folded in prayer, willing the powers that be to make his life what it once was. So that it could be more.

Mental connections tethered him to this earthly place like a stubborn piece of thread. But the Fates had cut his life's thread some time ago.

Nyx addressed the shade aloud, "You were young, when you departed. Injured in a battle far from here."

His voice sounded like an echo when he responded.

"I want to be here. She'll come. It will all be fine. You can't make me go anywhere."

Nyx reached out and laid a hand on his arm. His eyes became the deep blue they once were in life, and they widened as the shade felt touch for the first time in years.

"Who are you?" he asked, his body jerking back, unaccustomed to being solid. The novelty of his own voice in his ears made him gasp.

Nyx paused, looking behind her at the old church with a raised eyebrow. She turned back to him.

"Let's just say, you likely did not come here to speak with me. But how lucky you are that I found you."

The man furrowed his brows. His mouth began to form a smile, yet the sensation was so strange, so foreign. It was as though the muscles of his face couldn't recall the procedure.

Nyx crossed her arms and scanned him with her black gaze. His eyes were familiar. In life, they had turned up to her in gratitude. Then, just on the side of his arm, she saw something glowing behind his clothing. A golden smear. Not a tattoo but something gifted to him without his knowledge.

He'd been marked by another goddess.

In life, he was marked by the mother of comely Amanda, who now lays in the arms of Morpheus.

The Night Goddess turned and grinned at him.

Nyx reached out and touched his face. Eyes, mourning the future denied him, looked back at her. She unveiled his name and began assessing him.

"You are a handsome man, Scott. Perhaps I could make things happen for you?"

He would be a beautiful devotee. A servant for me. Ever indebted. And his soul is strong.

The shade shifted beneath the stare of Nyx. He broke through the silence.

"I guess some girls thought so, but they never wanted to wait or commit. I…never had a lot of money. I became a soldier. My dad had been a soldier…"

"War brings Death on swift wings to many mortals," she said.

"I could hear them."

"Hear who?" Her voice did not betray any knowledge.

"When we were ambushed, I could hear these…shrieks. It was like something between a bird of prey and hysterical women. There were wings. It was like the pits of Hell were calling for me. Nobody else heard it. I thought I was going crazy."

Nyx knew the memory of his terror. Penetrating, sickening fear rolling in his stomach at the war cry of the Keres. The adrenaline galloping through his body to battle for life.

His own screams wailing in his ears.

Nyx also knew *their* bloodlust. That of the Keres. She knew of ruthless slaughter and how one could develop a taste for it. The Keres could be summoned to satisfy the grimmest needs. The unexpected pleasure of killing in those with a debased heart. Nyx understood the Underworld and all its demons.

"You heard the Keres."

"Aren't they death demons or something?" he asked.

They are my mad daughters.

But Nyx merely replied, "Something like that."

She reached out again and placed her hand on the side of his face, then moved it down to the side of his neck. Stopping to place her hand where it met his shoulder, her grip tightened slightly.

I could mold him. Loyalty is his strongest suit. If he were to believe I am his "one," he could be mine forever. He is certainly handsome enough. He could learn to be happy with me.

His eyes were wide again and Nyx sensed his fear. Removing her hand from his shoulder, she folded her hands in her lap. Scott looked down at her dusky fingers, entwined on the black folds of her skirt.

Nyx said nothing for a few moments more. It was apparent to her that he was trying to assess *what* she was. When Scott appeared to have calmed, she spoke.

"You should not stay here. Go to the home that will welcome you. You were a good man. No doubt your faith will see you through the necessary gates."

Nyx's eyes darted to his hands. They had begun to tremble. Goddess and soldier were alone in front of the church in the dark hours of the morning.

Scott struggled with his newfound breath. He swallowed and nervous words stumbled out. "No... No, I will not. My life was unjustly taken. Those.... *things* hurt me. It wasn't even like the gunfire or an explosion. It was *them*. I was supposed to meet someone here. I don't know what you are, but...you're not human. You are...like them, somehow."

His voice overcame the fear that attacked with a tremor in his speech.

Then, he watched Nyx's eyes change. She stood, and appeared taller than before.

"My nature is not *wholly* consumed by lust or murder, though I know the Death Demons and all their ways. You have not deduced at all who I am."

The goddess's voice had gone deeper. The air around them murkier. Scott moved his head back and forth, trying to reassure himself of his surroundings, but the buildings and the flagged stone paths were smothered by shadows.

He could just make out the fragrance of rain. Wheels going over a wet street in the distance. Scott winced as the sounds and smells became fainter. Like he was drifting farther away.

I'm in Manchester, I'm in St. Ann's Square, and this is all going to be a bad dream.

Scott...

The woman's voice threaded through his brain.

He turned to the source of her voice, unable to get his bearings at all. His vision was clouded.

Nyx paused for a moment and clenched her fists, digging her nails into her palms, when she thought of encounters with Poseidon. When she imagined that he would ask to accompany her, that he would desire her on a satisfying level.

After a shaking breath, Nyx continued, "It is worship and devotion I seek. For me and for those like me, it is a need. Like what water is to living men." The mention of water again brought the Sea God to her mind. The cooling, gravity-altering power of his vast oceans.

It was Nyx's turn to tremble inside, but it was rage that caused it. Taking silent, deep breaths, Nyx did her best to remain in mortal form.

A mirthless laugh escaped her throat. "And how dreary for me that you find me to be some sort of devil. Do you appreciate nightfall, Scott? Do you find it welcome? After a trying day that has done its best to relieve you of your soul? Try to think of me that way…"

And Scott recalled that in fact, he had always appreciated the evening. He'd welcomed night's still, quiet hours. Its gentleness in comparison to day's demands. His heart slowed and his eyes ceased darting around.

Night could be a haven for unknown danger. As well as a sanctuary from it. A sanctuary, like an embrace or a blanket.…

Then, the humming lips of Nyx were at his ear, a profound vibration the source of which he forgot. It went through his entire being and he lost all sense of what or where he was.

Nyx drew back. Scott found himself a living, breathing man again.

On a summer night in the city of his birth. Shadows everywhere accompanied by shades of blue, black and grey. Stars and moonlight glittered above.

She was still there, probing his thoughts and looking at him.

Loyalty. Sincerity. Kindness. A deep desire to stamp out the evil in this world. To make it safe for his family. Safe for the family he has yet to have.

Mothering instincts warred with her darker needs. The desires of a lover battled with the whims of a goddess.

Nyx began to pace in front of Scott. Chewing her mortal fingers then tapping them on her thighs.

Her mind drifted back to the woman she'd left in the arms of Morpheus. The woman, prone in the care of the Oneiroi leader and ignorant of whose daughter she was.

"Tell me then. Who this angel is you wait for, *Scott?*"

He sat back up, groaning at the rather mortal sensations of a sore back. Things he hadn't felt for so long.

"I never met her. But I knew. I *knew* I would somehow come to her here. I never had a lot of money, but I had been a good soldier. And I was going to be a teacher. Until I died..."

Relief was reflected in his face when her physical glamour turned yet more natural. She was to his eyes, a pretty Mediterranean girl with inky hair and large brown irises. Almost mortal.

She ceased pacing and sat down beside him.

"Do you know, I could be an angel for you? Do you not think that perhaps it was no ordinary girl you were destined to wed? But someone like me? Someone with sort of...divine qualities?"

And her lips parted in a smile that was wholesome. Deceivingly so.

He sucked in a breath. Then, after a gasp, Scott realized. "I really am... *breathing.*" A laugh escaped his parted lips. "You...you did this. But *you*...you are..." He fumbled with his voice. His *living* voice. His pumping blood. His solid skin and his...*breath.*

"For now, let's just say that you are reborn of the night. Shall we?"

Scott pressed his lips together and looked at her. His chest rose and fell in short, shaky breaths.

One corner of Nyx's mouth went up. One of her cloaked shoulders went up in a shrug. She continued explaining at his perplexed look.

"If you believe I serve some red, horned man surrounded by flames, you would be sorely mistaken. No bearded masculine entity holds sway over me. Though I do find beards terribly attractive when properly trimmed."

And dripping wet with seawater, she thought, clenching her fists.

"Miss?" The former shade, Scott, coughed and broke into the reminiscing goddess's thoughts.

She turned to him with a flash of pretty white teeth set against her plum lips and dusky olive skin.

"Would you like to be mine? I am sure that I could find a way to make you happy. To give you...some sort of joy in belonging to me. There are abilities I could give you."

His eyes remained far away and Scott looked down, unsure of what to say.

But he knew, *supernatural* abilities could be handy.

Imagine what I could do. Scott placed his palms on his legs and pressed down. He was still reveling in being alive. It was a miracle itself.

"I'm sorry. You are...beautiful. And obviously powerful. Really, I just want a simple life. I don't see you settling down in a semi-detached house with a couple of kids. You don't seem like the type to take an interest in gardening or camping trips." He laughed nervously, seeing her upturned eyebrow.

"How strong you are in your convictions." She sat back and crossed her legs, tilting her head as possibilities played themselves out in her mind. After her pause, Nyx addressed him again.

"Let's play a little game. I will let you wander this earth for a certain amount of time, you will see if you can get your destined lady to come to you here. On this very bench you chose in your other life." Nyx patted the stone rectangle they sat on. "If after the time has passed, you cannot find her, you will be mine. It won't be a bad existence. You will grow to enjoy worshipping me."

She stroked the side of his face again, watching his eyes widen. Then he turned to her.

"Is this the payment? For you...restoring my life?" he blurted out.

Nyx removed her hand.

"I don't require any payment. But I do wish to have you make a choice. You cannot stay here forever. *Someone* eventually would have moved you."

Scott shook his head.

"You'll interfere, somehow. I know. Somehow..." And his light brown brows drew together then came apart as he tilted his face back in her direction.

"I promise not to impede your progress." She laid one hand over her heart.

"Right," he said the word slowly. Then another sort of recognition crossed his face as he said,

"Won't...people be confused if they see me?"

Nyx put his mind at ease with the calmest of words.

"You died five years ago to this day. And you underestimate me. You can and will carry on as you wished to before. The memory of your death has been removed from this world. The last five years will have no impact on you. Only you know of your demise. And the time that passed. Go home. And after tomorrow, seek her, your great love and the one who will give you a reason to live this mortal life again."

"And where will you be?"

"You will find I am around most nights." A coy grin drew the corners of her mouth up.

"And what should I call you?" he queried further.

She turned towards the brightening sky, lids softening over her midnight eyes.

"You can call me, N…" Her name interrupted by a very human yawn, she said, "Nina."

"Nina…" He looked down.

Her name and other words fumbled out of his thoughts. His mind came alive with recollections of Greek Mythology. *You will find I am around most nights…*

"Nina… Nyx. Nyx!" As recognition dawned, he looked to the Night Goddess, who now was nowhere to be seen.

The church in front of him slowly lit up with the rising sun. He stood and began the journey to the last place he knew as home. The city new yet strange to him. People saw him. Some nodded.

Panicking suddenly, he dug in his pocket when he realised he would have no money. But there was his wallet. He swallowed at the date on his license. And at the collection of twenty pound notes there. Valid credit and debit cards.

He boarded a bus that took him to Piccadilly. Then boarded a train that got him to the last place he knew as home.

❧
(The Next Day)

Scott turned the key and opened the brand new, white door. All his belongings remained in the same place they were when he had left to go abroad. There was no sound inside the house, only the tweeting of birds outside.

Memories flashed through his brain of fitting the wooden floor. His dad had done the tiles in the kitchen.

When his father was diagnosed with a condition he knew would one day claim his life, the man had worked tirelessly to help purchase a home for his son. He'd insisted on helping with the work that needed doing until he grew too poorly.

Scott sat down on a cushioned armchair with rounded sides. It was so foreign. This comfort. And the smell of paint and new flooring. He stared into the doorway that led to the kitchen.

"Is this a dream?" he asked the freshly painted white walls. In the grey daylight, it felt barren. There was no television, no pictures on the walls.

He stood and went to the kitchen. He stopped in the doorway and looked to his right at a steep, carpeted staircase that led to the two bedrooms and bathroom. Scott ascended.

Weariness assaulted his eyelids. A heaviness that made him crave his bed. The very human experience of falling asleep. An escape. The time he'd spent as a ghost in front of St. Ann's church began to fade from his memory. He tried to recall the imitation of life he'd tried to do. His desperate conjuring to bring back his existence.

In the end, it brought Nyx to me. A bloody Greek goddess. A primordial one, no less.

Slowly, his memories turned to the cold in winter. The rain and wind. He remembered eating fast food and walking past St. Ann's. He remembered stumbling through the square after a few too many beers.

Getting lost in a fantasy of having a beautiful, hazel-eyed woman look at him with some sort of *recognition*.

He recalled coming back home from his last tour. Having an interview at a school he wished to teach at. Visiting his parent's graves. Telling them that he was back and that he was going to the house. Thanking his dad for helping with the floors. Trying not to weep on his way home.

When did I do that? Did that happen this morning? Yeah...it did.

Scott reached the top of the stairs and turned to the left where the bathroom was. He looked at the clear shower guard and saw his favorite "man wash." A blue beach-themed shower gel.

Another memory, of going to the store and buying new toiletries yesterday. Of seeing people he knew in the car park.

His wonder-filled voice came out, "These memories, she... She did them. She made them."

Nyx.

Scott placed his hands on either side of the oval white sink and looked at himself in the mirror. He still bore the results of an endless sunburn. A few new freckles had cropped up around his nose. His eyes were a little red from fatigue. But they were his original blue color. His previously cropped hair had begun to grow out, the strands still short but becoming shaggy.

He needed a shower.

He licked his lips and swallowed, then opened his mouth, taking note of every breath. "I'm knackered. Why am I so…" He paused, trying to digest all the things whirring in his mind.

Scott closed his eyes then opened them again. He placed one hand on the side of his neck, squeezing. The moment he did that, he found himself lightheaded. The light behind the frosted privacy window beside his white bath/shower flickered. As though something large and dark flew past.

A familiar voice hit his head. *Her.*

"You walked all around town last night, unable to find rest. But now…you will find it. Worry not."

One of the horses from the field behind his back garden whinnied. He was brought back to the moment.

Scott showered, enjoying every moment of hot water and cleanliness.

It's like I haven't experienced a shower in ages, but…it's just all that time in Afghanistan. When normal hygiene was a major luxury. When the stinking heat infiltrated every bastard pore. It's not like it's been years…

Leaning his head back and rinsing the last of the shampoo from his hair, he closed his eyes. Remembering all the months of fighting the sweat endlessly dripping into his eyes. At the same time fighting to remain alive.

Toweling off, Scott went into his room. The walls were a deep blue. The blackout curtains had been drawn. The duvet was black, inviting him to crawl into an oblivion-filled, restorative slumber. Scott decided to turn on a lamp on the bedside. He paused to stare at his unpacked things, then went into one of the boxes to find a plain white t-shirt, clean boxers and sweats.

He wanted…nightfall. Like a blanket.

Nyx. He swallowed.

It felt lonely without the goddess's presence.

I can give you abilities. Make things happen for you. You would grow to enjoy worshiping me.

She'd been like a comfort in the darkness. He was suddenly sensitive to the temperature, despite it being midsummer.

Scott switched off the lamp and climbed into bed. He'd never been a person to kip during the day, but this fatigue was overwhelming and the sheets beckoned him like a siren.

He slid his body beneath the duvet and found himself at sleep's mercy.

Unbidden dreams brought a reality he could smell. He felt it in the very soles of his feet.

He found himself standing on a vast expanse of soil. Not one blade of green grass sprouted from the earth. The moist dirt was warm. Overhead, the blue-black sky rumbled, and flashes of lightning provided lingering illumination.

He looked up at the sky. The top of what could be some sort of netherworld. That was when he heard it.

The demonic wail. Beating wings. Scott locked his feet to the ground and braced himself.

I can make you capable of god-like feats. You need not know fear or vulnerability.

Scott swallowed, squinting at the sky. The winged demons were there. They would come for him. The tearing and pulling would begin. His soul would be thrown to Hades.

They would make him into nothing.

Standing his ground, he began to tremble. He looked down at the hot soil flashing in the ethereal glares of lighting. It confused him. He felt he had seen these creatures, *heard* them before.

No...I remember the pops and cracks of enemy fire. I remember the helicopter blades. That's it... That's it. Right?

In that moment, Scott knew that if he surrendered himself to Nyx, devoted himself to her, she would free him. She would put him in a position where he could dominate the mortal world around him if he so chose.

Beautiful women would flock to you. Women with hazel eyes. You could pick and choose amongst them. For your own comfort. For your own joy. The beauties with enticing lips and smooth bare shoulders, ever ready to reveal more. A collection of willing, personalized favorites.

Temptation was there. A hook that pulled him from the base of his simplest desires, and fear of being so human and exposed before unconquerable powers. Before people who saw no value in love. Before people who saw kindness as a joke.

The lure threatened to tear him from himself. To make him something else.

It could be amazing. I could have heaven on earth. Maybe she doesn't even exist, my St. Ann's wife.

Scott took a deep breath, understanding that this was some sort of test. Grasping what was on offer.

He looked to the rolling darkness above him and pressed his feet into the soft ground.

"I accept that you might take away whatever it is you've given me, Mighty Nyx. But I want to live my life as a man. I want to go to St. Ann's. I don't want to be anything...*unnatural*."

The expanse above him rolled into dancing mists. The cries of the Keres dimmed until he could hear nothing. He couldn't feel the soil beneath him. The temperature meant nothing. And soon, he could see nothing.

Scott woke to find it was night.

His blackout curtains had been pulled open just a little. The moonlight shone onto the carpet. Worried someone had broken in, he sat up and turned on the light. The sudden glare made him reach to adjust it. He wound up knocking a magazine off the bedside table.

It was a popular film magazine he bought from time to time. Trying to keep up with what was in cinemas. The magazine was open to an interview with a stunning actress.

Her skin was flushed with an ethereally golden tone. Her tawny glittering eyes revealed a hot-blooded goddess. She shone with every imaginable power of desire and love.

Like she was a bit of an authority on such things.

Scott's heart began to hammer in his chest. Focusing on her eyes, it was like she was looking at him. It was a look of *approval.*

Scott leaned back in bed for a moment. "Well, I'm glad *you* approve of me."

He went downstairs to the kitchen and checked the answering machine.

"Hiya. This is Scott. Leave a message I'll get back to you. Cheers."

First was an offer of a job by the very school he'd wished to teach at. The second was an army mate, someone he had been in Afghanistan with, who wanted to know how he was. Scott stretched his arms overhead, staring at the landline on the tiled floor.

There was a fragrance in his house, the aroma of burning incense lingering in the air.

Scott moved towards the circular armchair before the window of his front room.

He stopped when he saw the crown of her ebony tresses, shining. Her eyes met his. She spoke to him.

"I've given birth to many terrible things, Scott. Death, the Keres, many entities of the Underworld fall under my domaine. But you, I am proud of. I can't lay claim to creating you…" She stopped.

He heard the rustling of fabric. Nyx adjusted her mortal form.

The goddess was thinking before she continued speaking.

Then she said, "But it is an honor to give you back to this world. Much good may you do here. And I would desire greatly that more men had hearts like yours. Good night…Scott."

And Nyx was gone.

Scott spent the night researching the Goddess Nyx.

One website said that Homer called her a *"subduer of gods and men…Zeus himself stood in awe of her."* And that the Keres were just some of her many children.

❧
(The Night Before)

Amanda was trembling with her knees drawn to her chin. Every shadow was a threat. A lurking man of Greek appearance was in one corner. The ghost of her would-be love was in another.

She pushed herself off the bed and went to her kitchen to fix some tea. Though every space seemed a potential harbor of spirits, she willed herself to make a brew.

Morpheus's haunting continued. He could use the voice of her love.

"You're so beautiful. God, you're beautiful. I can't believe you are going to be mine…"

The whispered words hurt. Morpheus was cruel. Before her love could even say hello, before their lips could even meet, then why show him to her?

"Leave me… Leave me… Leave me," Amanda said through her teeth.

The whispering stopped.

A fragrance hit her nose. Floral but not too sweet. Enticing fruit. It made her think of the word *ambrosia*.

A slight tingling happened under her skin. Even through this, Amber continued to remove the tea bag and pour in the milk. As though someone shouted for her, she went back into her bedroom. She placed the hot drink on the sideboard and lay down.

There were fingers threading through her hair, nails running down her scalp. It wasn't like the heavy sedation that had attacked her before once the night lady left.

"Daughter, I didn't think I'd ever be able to see you. But now it appears you have attracted a primordial one."

Mother?

Amanda had always dreamed of her mother being gorgeous, but this was beyond anything she could have imagined. The warm colors lit up her shadowy room. The lady was all soft textures and comfort. Tawny, golden, and ruby-hued.

"I love what you do, by the way. Weddings." Aphrodite's hazel eyes glowed with pride, then her supposed mother's voice changed when she looked to the corners of Amanda's room.

"*You*. Show yourself, Oneiroi leader."

The one called Morpheus emerged.

"Stunning Aphrodite. Whatever can I do for you?" Morpheus spoke in playful tones.

"I would know why you play a cruel trick on my daughter. Is it not enough that she suffers? That jealous Hephaestos marked and called the Keres to murder her father as well the male she was destined to love?"

Morpheus gave Aphrodite a closed mouth smile.

The Oneiroi leader remained silent.

So she spoke again.

"How goes never being able to feel touch, Morpheus? How goes your loneliness? Do you know I could make beautiful women worship you, *love* you with an intensity that would rival that of the greatest known *physical* encounters? The greatest pleasures begin in the mind. Do they not? I've always valued you, Morpheus. But I must demand to know what you are doing here, what part you are playing."

Morpheus spoke, "Beautiful Aphrodite, you flatter me. Hephaestos, though he can come up with the greatest instruments of destruction, summoned the Keres to murder one of your lovers, the father of *this* child. And in a continuation of his wrathful jealousy, rivaling even Hera, he cursed the potential loves of your daughter. To choke the happiness out of those in your line. So much like great Ares was her father, the Fire God's envy extended into a summoning not of weaponry or tricks, but of the violent death spirits themselves."

Amanda lay listening, all the while the goddess Aphrodite's hand lay protectively on her back.

"Aren't you and Ares..." Amanda began, questioning Aphrodite's, her *mother's*, history.

And the Love Goddess's voice came out, "Ares is who I would have chosen once upon a time. That all happened long before you were born. Hephaestos sought to best Ares with cleverness. Existence is cruel to us as well."

Then Amanda said, "And the one who you picked for me to love is dead." She knew it. Morpheus had played the part of the ghost of her would-be love.

Aphrodite stood and began to pace. She flung her hands in the air, wringing her delicate fingers together. Her legs revealed themselves between the floating slits of her long red gown. Her flesh was shining and glorious.

Despair rang out in her voice.

"I *tried* not to mark him in any noticeably way. And any god or goddess would be able to see it. But I liked him. I couldn't have just any person for you. You will bear my descendants! I would have this world overrun with true love. Never mind Ares and all his bloody battles! I tried not to reveal any intention to gift the man to you, but he had the call of Ares to War. And Hephaestos had to do little but call the Keres upon recognizing him. There is much machinery and metal work now in war. I..." The goddess's eyes shone with tears as she addressed Amanda. "I *loved* your father, as much as a Goddess can, but I could not protect him."

Aphrodite released a weary sigh and sat down. "I would spare my children such pain, if I could. But I haven't the power to prevent Hades from collecting his souls, once a life's thread has been cut. Only a truly ancient primordial could have such sway. To erase the grave and rebuild living futures. Tell me, Morpheus, is Nyx capable of this?"

The God of Dreams' whisper carried through Amanda's flat. "Dawn approaches. You underestimate powerful Nyx. Hades, Ares, Hephaestos, and Zeus combined could not deter the dark daughter of Khaos. He lives life anew, your dearest love. His name I will give you in a dream. Forgive my trickery, dear Amanda."

Then, Morpheus' voice raised slightly, to a polite, more business-like tone, when he addressed Aphrodite.

"Love and desire are common place in the minds of mortals, dearest Aphrodite. I have made use of such things as I lay out the dreams of sleeping mortals. I mean no harm...not really."

Again his mouth curved upwards. He bowed and disappeared.

Amanda turned to her mother. "I can't tell if he is good or bad."

Aphrodite smiled and reached out to touch the side of Amanda's face. "He flows in and out of many a mortal's subconscious. He knows the deepest origins of your thoughts and desires. He has to *perform* for the purposes of good as well as evil. Simply because both exist within all of us."

Amanda's mother adjusted herself. The bangles on Aphrodite's wrists and ankles made a tinkling sound, like tiny sweet bells. "I don't think you need to worry now. I will speak to dark Nyx. For now, you are free to sleep. Sleep, my daughter."

Amanda closed her eyes. The tinkling noise was just beginning to fade as her mother's soft lips rested themselves on her forehead.

Perhaps all this has been a dream, Amanda thought, beginning to drift off. The bells infused into her blood, bringing tingles just behind her scalp.

Before her eyes was a man with cropped light brown hair that was still wet. His body rested on ebony cotton sheets. She could hear the fabric rustling as he adjusted himself. She could hear his heartbeat.

It's him. It's really him.

Amanda smiled in her sleep, turned over, and whispered a name.

"Scott..."

ᴪ

(Sunset, Two Evenings Later)

Scott had woken late and gone for a run. His feet hit the canal path near his house in the old mill town. The calm brown waters were to his left, a tall moss coated wall to his right. Dirt and greenery scents mingled with cooking smells coming from one of the pubs he passed. After passing under the arch of a bridge, he went home.

After showering, he made his way to the train station to go into Manchester. The familiar walk would never be the same. Tipsy giggles and drunken chuckles accompanied the clack-clack-clack of heels and dress shoes on paved streets. He noticed a wedding party or two gathered in large glass and brick structures.

Places that once were factories.

Wine glasses, satin ribbons, and silver cutlery adorned the tables and chairs inside. Objects handled absently in the libation-swilling guests. Pretty, flushed mums in frocks and high shoes held champagne glasses and cooed at their new babies. Couples lounged together, entwining fingers and leaning coifed heads on their lover's shoulders.

June. A season for weddings.

It was a far cry from the baked earth interspersed with ancient mountains, irrigated fields of wheat, vegetables or opium. A hideous yet beautiful place. War-torn ground, once soaked by his own blood. A place of poverty and greed. And monsters.

Instinct took him to St. Ann's Square.

There will probably be another bloody wedding there.

How many times will I have to come here? Will Nyx just come and take me? Will I even have a choice?

It was late, yet sunset's last heated layers lingered in the summer sky. He sat down on a familiar bench. It wasn't long before the moon and stars dominated the heavens above. He looked up at the full milky shining circle.

People continued to titter and stroll around him. Then, wisps of cloud floated past the moon. Like ebony smoke. It swirled, threatening the bright orb of the moon.

Scott swallowed and looked down. He searched the vicinity for the raven-haired goddess in her mortal form.

Then there was a sound of a lone pair of high heels. A lush, fruity fragrance filled the air. Sweet and edible. It tantalized, but didn't infiltrate his senses. Not like the smokey, heady assault of Nyx.

He turned in the direction of it. There, wearing a red pencil skirt accompanied by a floaty white blouse with a v-neck, was...*her.*

She had the look of the woman in the magazine, yet Scott was aware that it wasn't exactly her.

Despite it being night, he could gather the blush in her cheeks and the ruby tint of her open lips. Large hazel eyes trained on him in astonishment. She came and sat down beside him. He could smell the difference between her perfume and whatever divine product she washed her hair with. Her gaze darted between his hands and the place where his shoulder met his neck.

"Hiya," he said, stupidly.

"Hello." She smiled then swallowed and he could hear her breath. Scott's stomach summersaulted. The air became hot. Even in summer, heat waves like this didn't happen often. Nobody *needed* AC in Northwest England.

"What's your name then?"

"Amanda."

"Are you out tonight?"

"I'm working… Are you alright? You seem a bit…pale. Can I do anything for you?" she replied. To his ears, her words sounded like an enticement. The way he was feeling, *anything* she said would sound like an enticement. Like she sought to lure him somewhere rather private. *Oh god… Oh dear. She's not a…*

Scott frantically sought some query he could make that was neither insulting nor condescending.

He was met with a friendly laugh.

"Weddings. I plan weddings," she said, covering her mouth and trying not to giggle.

"Oh. Right. Right. Got ya."

"What's your name then?" she asked.

"Scott. I'm called Scott."

"Scott…" The blush left her cheeks.

"Are you alright, Amanda? Now *you've* gone pale. You…you look like you've seen a ghost."

"Have I? I mean… Do I?" The blush returned to her cheeks.

"Not anymore," he said and reached for her hand.

Amanda's mouth opened in recognition of his palm's texture. Words deserted her in awareness of the pressure of his fingers.

The city's night life kicked into full effect around them.

❧

Nyx lay on her back in the sand. The cold sea lapped near her but didn't touch her bare toes. Her hands were beside her ears. Her fingers moved, making lazy paths in the sand. Meanwhile above her, tendrils of inky smoke curved in front of the pure, full moon.

The sea rolled against the jagged rocks on either side of the smooth beach.

Beside her, the crimson-adorned Aphrodite lounged, parallel to the surf. She lay on her side, the silky curve of her hip a beacon of womanhood on the otherwise murky beach. Pitch-cloaked Nyx was near invisible, save for her dusky feet and hands.

"You could have had him, you know. Forced his hand. I've no doubt you could have bent him to your will," Aphrodite said to Nyx, her smooth elbow pressing in the sand. Nyx's shadows caressed the shining, moonlit flesh exposed above Aphrodite's red gown.

"That would make me no better than the stupidest of men. Those false mortals who bully and devise plans to achieve one-sided, unnatural happiness," Nyx replied.

Aphrodite was silent for a few moments, lost in thought. No longer able to keep them to herself she said, "I know what you would ask of me, Nyx, but I cannot make the Sea God love you in the way you want. What you ask is obsession. It borders too close to violence. I can make men and gods love and I can summon the lustiest of urges, but I cannot enforce madness. If you want a cult again, I'm sure you could encourage some group of mortals. You can do what you want, Nyx. But I cannot create this...this mad devotion dressed as love you want."

"I know," Nyx whispered, still twirling her fingers in the sand, toying with light's access, and making shadows in the sky.

"Then why did you bother? Such a great deed. How do I repay you? You did not have to. You did not have to care. You could have even dragged him to Hades, finished the work of your insane daughters."

"You forget how old I am, dear beauty. But you obviously see the depths of my needs. It pains me to admit you are correct. Perhaps love is...not possible for me." There was a pause. Silence interspersed with waves.

Then, the Night Goddess finally said, "But kindness is. That I can do."

And with that, Nyx disappeared into her realm, dragging the inky sky behind her to meet the dawn, Hemera, in an ancient, friendly greeting.

From the Author: Some of the mythological details and information used here were found on the following website: www.theoi.com; http://www.theoi.com/Daimon/Oneiroi.html

ABOUT THE CHARITY

As stated in the Foreword, all of the money that would go to the authors will be given to the Random Acts Organization. This charity holds a mission that is close to our hearts, and we hope that it will be close to yours as well once you know more. With the blessing of their fundraising department, we have presented you with these ten stories that we hope you enjoyed.

Below is information taken from their website (www.randomacts.org) so you can know more about the.

What is the Random Acts Organization?

Random Acts is a non-profit organization that is aiming to conquer the world, one random act of kindness at a time. We're dedicated to funding and inspiring acts of kindness around the world.

Look around; there are simple ways to demonstrate kindness on a daily basis. A stranger needs help carrying their groceries. A homebound neighbor could use some cheering up. These opportunities crop up every day and most of us are so busy that we miss them. All you have to do is pay attention and offer kindness whenever, wherever you can.

How did it begin?

On December 3, 2009, Misha Collins, the angel Castiel on The CW's *Supernatural*, used Twitter to ask his followers (affectionately known as his "minions") to come up with ideas for a "minion stimulus" project. The goal was to obtain US government stimulus money (funding to aid endeavors to stop an economic recession) for non-profit initiatives.

The pursuit of government funding was soon abandoned in favor of morphing into a privately organized charity, formerly known as MinionStimulus. After visiting the fledgling website, Misha appointed Lisa Walker as the Director of Charitable Affairs and provided her with some initial direction. Together, Misha and Lisa began marshaling the forces of good at their disposal.

Since that auspicious beginning, our organization has gone through several changes, including our name. We've come a long way and now have non-profit status through our parent organization, The Art Department, Inc. In late 2011, Lisa stepped down, and we welcomed Cinde Monsam as our new Director.

With Misha and Cinde's direction and leadership, and the daily attention of an extraordinary administrative team, we have an organization poised to conquer the world, one random act of kindness at a time.

What is their mission?

At Random Acts, it's our mission to conquer the world one random act of kindness at a time. We are here to inspire acts of kindness around the world both big and small. We provide a vast network of caring people with the encouragement and support they need to change lives for the better.

Every individual can be a catalyst for positive change in the world and in their own life.

Everyone deserves to be treated with respect.

Each person can make a positive impact within their social network and community.

Kindness breeds kindness.

Being kind is fun!

ABOUT THE AUTHORS

A. STAR (DIANTHA JONES)

Diantha Jones loves writing fantasy books filled with adventure, romance, and magic. She's the author of the Oracle of Delphi series, the Mythos series, and the Djinn Order series (as A. Star). When she isn't writing or working, she is reading or being hypnotized by Netflix. She is a serious night-owl and while everyone else is grinning in the warmth and sunlight, she's hoping for gloominess and rain. Yeah, she's weird like that.

You can find her at her website (www.diantha-jones.com) and on Facebook, Twitter, Goodreads, and Pinterest.

ANGELA B. CHRYSLER

Angela B. Chrysler is a writer, logician, philosopher, and die-hard nerd who studies theology, historical linguistics, music composition, and medieval European history in New York with a dry sense of humor and an unusual sense of sarcasm. She lives in a garden with her family and cats.

In 2014, Ms. Chrysler founded Brain to Books: the marketing promotional engine and online Encyclopedia for authors. A passionate gardener and incurable cat lover, Ms. Chrysler spends her days drinking coffee and writing beside a volume of Edgar Allan Poe who strongly influences her style to this day. When Ms. Chrysler is not writing, she enables her addictions to all things nerdy, and reads everything she can get her hands on no matter the genre. Occasionally, she finds time to mother her three children and debate with her life-long friend who she eventually married. Her writing is often compared to Tad Williams. Her influences are Edgar Allan Poe, The Phantom of the Opera, and Frankenstein.

You can find her at her website (www.angelabchrysler.com/) and on Goodreads and Twitter.

J. KIM MCLEAN

Kim's love of reading came after her mother introduced her to Tolkien and the

Hobbit, followed by Lord of the Rings. She also lovingly blames her mother for her love of Science Fiction and Fantasy, thanks to being raised on Star Trek. Kim has always had a vivid imagination, but it wasn't until she finished with graduate school (where she earned a Master's of Science in Geology) that she found she could focus her imagination into creating her own characters and stories. Much of her writing has been for various play by email or forum role play universes, though Kim does hope this will be the first of many more stories she writes for publication.

When not writing, Kim can be found snowboarding, hiking, or doting on her furry beasts.

DARIEL RAYE

Dariel Raye is an award-winning author of powerful IR/MC (Interracial/ Multi-cultural) paranormal romance and dark urban fantasy with alpha male heroes to die for and strong heroines with hearts worth winning. Her stories tell of shifters, vamps, angels, demons, and fey (the Vodouin variety). Dariel is currently writing three series: "Dark Sentinels" (wolf shifters), "Orlosian Warriors" (Vampire-like Nephilim), and "Gateway" (a crossover erotic paranormal suspense with romantic elements).

For more about Dariel, follow her blog or visit her website. She also publishes a new release newsletter. If you enjoyed this book, please post a review on review sites. You can also follow her and contact her on Twitter, Facebook, or Pinterest.

You can find her at her website (http://darkparanormalromanceseries.com), and on Twitter, Facebook, Goodreads, Google+ and Tumblr.

K. B. THORNE

K. B. Thorne is the author formerly known as Mia Darien, who has evolved like any creature. While Sadie is off writing all the romance, K. B. writes the sci-fi, fantasy, and urban fantasy stuff. She lives in the snowy lands of New England with her menagerie, which includes a husband and a child.

You can find her at her website (www.authorkbthorne.com) and on Facebook.

ABIGAIL OWEN

Award-winning paranormal and contemporary romance author, Abigail Owen was born in Greeley, Colorado, and resides in Austin, Texas, with her husband and two adorable children who are the center of her universe.

Abigail grew up consuming books and exploring the world through her writing. A fourth generation graduate of Texas A&M University, she attempted to find a practical career related to her favorite pastime by earning a degree in English Rhetoric (Technical Writing). However, she swiftly discovered that writing without imagination is not nearly as fun as writing with it.

You can find her at her website (www.abigailowen.com) and on Facebook, Twitter, and Pinterest.

CRYSTAL G. SMITH

Born a small town Missourian, Crystal grew up in a time where reading was used for her escape from the everyday worries of a young girl. She then began developing ideas of how she would write a book and what she would do with her characters. Soon, idea came to typewriter and then thankfully computers.

Her love of reading is not centered on one specific genre, but with her writing, she has a tendency to stay with the romance genre. Whether it be modern day romance or paranormal romance, and a lot of steamy, she enjoys writing a story where characters find love in one another no matter how twisted their lives.

She has written several stories for charity to date and continues to write novellas and novels. She is an indie author with a large imagination and even larger heart. She is married with four children, (even though two of them have four legs). She works full-time as a pediatric nurse and when she isn't acting goofy with family, you can find her reading or writing.

You can find her at her website (crystalr022.wix.com/sisterauthors) and on Twitter.

KAT JAMESON

Kat Jameson has been having just plain wicked thoughts for about as long as she's been writing, so it seemed like a very natural progression that the two would end up together. She is a woman who seems perfectly average on the outside, but believes in a great capacity for the power of love and the joy of sex and thinks constraints should be put on neither so long as everyone involved is happy. So that's what she writes about.

CHRISTI RIGBY

Christi Rigby lives in Colorado with her husband and her two teen boys, rounding out the group is a bernese mountain dog and an old orange cat that can't seem to sleep in the morning past the need for some kibble at 5 am, then returns to the bed after it has been vacated by the owners. She has written a number of short stories for publication and is working on her first book to be published. When she is not writing at a keyboard she is always writing in her mind, so to say writing is her real life over the job she holds would be a fair representation. An avid guide along the path to geekdom for her children and friends, she is a fan of comic books, any number of Science Fiction/Fantasy television shows and movies, computer and console gaming, and just about anything Scandinavian or British Isles in nature. One day she hopes that her choice to make writing her life will lead to a visit to the Isle of Man.

You can find her on Facebook and Twitter.

VIOLA DAWN

Viola Dawn is obsessed with ghosts, vampires & history. She loves love and prefers to write deep, meaningful encounters or explore the torments of unrequited desire. She's also a poet who loves to read historical romance, erotic romance, paranormal romance, ghost stories, and some light horror. She writes the sort of thing she would enjoy reading. Originally from Illinois, USA, she's been an expat for many years and now lives in the UK with her husband, children and dog.

You can find her at her website (violadawn.wordpress.com/) and on Twitter.

Made in the USA
Columbia, SC
05 January 2022